DAYTIME
DRAMA

DAYTIME DRAMA

Dave Benbow

KENSINGTON BOOKS
http://www.kensingtonbooks.com

KENSINGTON BOOKS are published by

Kensington Publishing Corp.
850 Third Avenue
New York, NY 10022

All Kensington titles, imprints and distributed lines are available at special quantity discounts for bulk purchases for sales promotion, premiums, fund-raising, educational or institutional use.

Special book excerpts or customized printings can also be created to fit specific needs. For details, write or phone the office of the Kensington Special Sales Manager: Kensington Publishing Corp., 850 Third Avenue, New York, NY 10022, Attn. Special Sales Department. Phone: 1-800-221-2647.

Kensington and the K logo Reg. U.S. Pat. & TM Off.

Library of Congress Card Catalogue Number: 2002117374
ISBN 0-7582-0386-1

First Printing: June 2003
10 9 8 7 6 5 4 3 2 1

Printed in the United States of America

For Bruce
(He knows why)

Acknowledgments

There are two people I must thank first and foremost: One is my beloved friend, personal hero and cherished mentor, Bruce Vilanch, who encouraged me enthusiastically and challenged me to "put up or shut up."

The other is my amazing, handsome editor, John Scognamiglio, who took quite a chance on a poorly spelled manuscript and who couldn't have been more patient in responding to all my stupid questions.

I also have to give props to my fiercely energetic agent, Sally Wofford-Girand, who always manages to make me look good.

On the professional side, Louis Malcangi (who designed a terrific and sexy cover), Libba Bray (whose clever cover copy makes *me* want to read this book, and I already know how it turns out!) and Michael Carr (who had the daunting task of checking my punctuation) at Kensington—all did brilliant work on my behalf. Thank you so much!

And on the personal side, I'm glad to be able to publicly thank Cindy Blass and clan for adopting me into your wonderful, loving family. Michelle Jackino, Moises Bertran and David Pumo, Edward Blanchard, Dru Samet and Don Connally have always been there for me, and I couldn't be more grateful.

And finally, lame as it may seem, many thanks to my old dog Emmett, who's shown me the true meaning of the words unconditional love.

1

The midnight blue car idled at the side of a sandy road, its headlights blazing straight ahead into the night. A steady breeze coming off the ocean caused gentle ripples in the sea grass that bordered the road, while down in the dunes, crickets chirped their mating call. The moon, full and ripe, hung overhead like a sentinel, guarding all under its domain.

Inside the luxury sedan sat two people. A man, dark of hair, with the square jaw and full lips of a magazine cover model, occasionally glanced into the rearview mirror to make sure his hair was exactly in place. The woman, as blond as a Nordic princess, with striking features and perfect white teeth, could see the man checking out his reflection in the mirror, and was perturbed by it.

So typical of him, she thought, *to hog the mirror.*

Stone Coltrane turned to the beauty beside him and looked deeply into her sapphire blue eyes. "I know we can get control of Digitron if we can get Skylar out of the way," he said in even, modulated tones.

"But, she's having your love child!" Pageant Ragianni hissed back, turning away from him to stare moodily out into the dark. She was oddly pleased that as she turned her head, her newly cropped hair swished about her face with casual, but planned, abandon. When she shifted around in her seat, she happened to notice some unflattering wrinkling in her taupe leather miniskirt. She absentmindedly smoothed it out.

"You know she tricked me into sleeping with her after

Madison's funeral. She seduced *me!*" Stone said rigidly, his intense gray eyes taking on a steely cast. His eyes were the exact color of his pale-gray summer-weight suit. He had the jacket off and had loosened his paisley silk tie to allow him to breathe in the sea air. "Besides," he continued, "she thinks that she and I are together, which plays into our hands. I'll let her think I love her, get her shares of Digitron signed over to me, and then I'll leave her."

Pageant turned back to look at Stone, again swishing her hair about. "Oh, Stone," she breathed huskily, "when you talk like that, it gets me all . . . excited!" She began to unbutton her black silk blouse.

"Pageant, you know it's you that I love." Stone reached over to her, took her beautiful face into his large hands, and kissed her deeply. He kissed her with the passion of a caged animal finally set free. His hands dropped lower, and he slowly finished unbuttoning her blouse, pulling the soft, flimsy material down around her shoulders.

"Oh, Stone," gasped Pageant. "Make love to me! Make love to me *now!* Here! Here in your BMW!" She hungrily grabbed at him, wanting to feel his touch all over her body. . . .

"Cut!" Sam Michaels, *Sunset Cove*'s director, threw down his script. "Jack, you're blocking Cathy's face when you reach across her like that. Try it from the other side. Let's do it again!"

The darkened soundstage suddenly sprang to life. Grips felt free to scurry again, the extras left the stage to get a coffee, and the makeup artists were instantly ready with their powder puffs.

Wearing paint-splattered jeans and an ex-lover's old Double R. L. flannel shirt, art director Lefty Jannel surveyed his set. Lefty was just a shade under 5 feet 9 inches, and lately had taken to wearing his hair cut very short and dyed platinum blond. You could always tell where Lefty was in a crowd by his shock of white-blond hair. His brown, almost black eyes took in the activity in front of the camera.

The BMW was placed carefully on a contraption that he

himself had invented. He called it "the Rig." Originally built for a couple of sweeps-week episodes involving a tornado, Lefty had continued to use the Rig to great success.

The Rig allowed a large car or SUV to be driven up a ramp, and stopped when each wheel was over one of four risers, which were attached to four separate hydraulic units. After the emergency brake in the vehicle was set, all four wheels were chained to their respective risers. These risers and hydraulics were all connected to each other from underneath by a system of bolted steel cross-braces.

The ramp was removed, and grips would stand at each corner and push on a lever to drop the car slightly at that corner. A concentrated team effort of pushing the levers randomly would make the vehicle look either like it was bouncing slightly on a real road or flying wildly through the air in a twister.

The beauty of the Rig was that the camera could shoot into the car from any angle, simply by moving the camera around the car at will. A rear-screen projection of moving scenery completed the effect.

This day, however, the big BMW sedan was in the Rig to raise the car up about seven feet from the studio floor in order to achieve the feeling of being on a road above the ocean. The ocean was, in reality, a huge twenty-by-sixty-foot transparency photograph of a perfect California beach, which hung from the rafters of the studio. The potted sea grass was swaying gently due to the efforts of an old fan that whirred silently. The crashing surf and chirping crickets were both courtesy of special-effects recordings.

Lefty hoped this shot didn't take much longer, because he and his crew had to tear this set down and build the hospital hallway set for a scene to be shot later that afternoon.

"Dammit! I thought we really had it there, Sam. Sorry." Jack Benz, also known as Stone Coltrane, the rascally scion of the Coltrane family on the top-rated soap opera *Sunset Cove*, whipped out a tube of Kiehl's Lip Balm #1 from his shirt pocket and expertly applied the salve to his lips.

"Sam? Should I smolder more before I turn, or after?" Cathy Grant asked, rebuttoning her top. Her character, Pageant Ragianni, was *Sunset Cove*'s resident bad girl and the fans' absolute favorite character on the show. Even though the hot, hunky Travis Church, who played Stone's half-brother Cliff, was gaining on her in the popularity polls, Cathy was smug in her belief that the fans would always came back to revering her.

"Whatever works for you, darling," Sam replied. "Let's just try to get this in one take, please? We're running behind, and I need to break the crew for lunch."

Cathy returned her attention to her costar. "Jack," she purred, "Did you start smoking again?"

"Well, I'm trying to quit." Jack shrugged as he put away the expensive lip balm.

"Try harder. It's like kissing an ashtray."

You bitch, thought Jack.

As if her rum-soaked breath was a delight for him. She knew he was a two-year man in Alcoholics Anonymous. He swore she took a snort before every love scene with him, just to screw with his head.

"Anything you say. By the way, I love your new haircut," he offered casually.

Cathy's hands flew up to her new do and pulled at a few errant strands. "Isn't it fabulous? Frederick is a genius! He says it will be all the rage. He says they'll call it 'The Pageant.'"

Cathy smiled at the thought of thousands of women rushing out to cut their hair just like hers. It would be so much better if they would call it "The Cathy," but that probably wouldn't happen. After all, they hadn't called "The Rachel" the "Jennifer," had they?

"Yeah. It's great. Didn't Sandra Bullock just cut hers the same way last month?"

"What!? You mean it's been *done*?!" Cathy looked stricken. "I'll look like a copycat! Frederick! That *queen*!" To Cathy, appearing to be a follower, not a leader, was a fate worse than being on *Saved by the Bell 2003*. As she checked the snugness of her seat belt again, Cathy made a mental note to find a new hairdresser. Pronto. And cancel this weekend's upcoming *In Style* shoot until her hair grew out.

Knowing he'd scored a direct hit, Jack instantly felt better. *Just one more year,* he told himself. *Just one more year, then I'm out of here.* Features were where Jack Benz felt he belonged, and if Meg Ryan, Susan Sarandon, or Julianne Moore could make the transition from daytime to film, well, damn it, so could he. The fact that he could think of no male soap actor who had done it didn't faze him at all. In Jack's mind it was his world, and everyone else was just in it.

In fact, in order to prepare himself for the big time, Jack had, on his last vacation, checked himself into an exclusive "hotel," and had a minor face-lift. He also had some eye work done, and liposuction on his ass and stomach. It had hurt like hell, and no one had really warned him about how brutal the recovery process was (he'd had to wear a *girdle,* for Christ's sake!).

Quickly, though, he healed, and people began to comment on how fit and youthful he looked. Jack was all of thirty-seven years old, but everyone knew you had to have your first minor lift right around thirty-five, before the major ones at forty-five and fifty-five.

Fuck you, Travis Church, and *your thirty-one-inch waist,* he had thought one day after catching his newly svelte reflection in a store window on Rodeo Drive.

"Okay. Let's try it again. . . ." Sam resettled his wide rear in his specially ordered director's chair. "Ready . . . action!"

The grips quieted down, the extras drank their refreshed coffee silently, and the makeup artists went back to their makeup tables.

Lefty Jannel once again patted himself on the back for creating another amazing set out of nothing. He truly had a dream job.

Lefty had started out, not that long ago, as a Twyla Tharp-trained dancer. He arrived in Hollywood convinced that he was going to be the next Fred Astaire. It took a few years of starving while dancing as a go-go boy at the gay dance bar Rage on weekends, and only booking the occasional music video, to convince Lefty that Hollywood didn't want another Astaire.

An old boyfriend had been an art director, and Lefty had helped him out on a few jobs. He then booked a few on his own, and before he knew it, he had a thriving career as an up-and-coming art director. He began to get more work calls than the boyfriend, who promptly left him.

The previous summer, he'd been hired to take over the art direction for *Sunset Cove* by Joan Thomas, the show's tough-as-nails producer. He had impressed her with the luxurious sets he designed for a miniseries based on a novel by Dominick Dunne.

Now, at thirty-four, he still had a great dancer's body, and he loved to take the Salsa Sweat class at Gold's Gym, where he could once again be the center of attention and dance like he was Astaire.

As he watched Jack and Cathy begin the scene again, he looked at his sets. Lined up like ducks in a row on the left side of soundstage 24 were four separate sets. Pageant Ragianni's penthouse apartment occupied the first set. It was a two-story extravaganza decorated in the rich modern style of Mies van der Rohe and Le Corbusier. Next to that was her bedroom, which, when edited into the shows, looked like it was up-stairs.

Adjacent to that set was Stone Coltrane's Digitron office, a masculine enclave filled with chrome and glass and dark, sleek leather. This set was complete with a long hallway for the "walking talk" shots.

Finally, at the end of this opulence was the set they were shooting on now, the beach roadside set. This was also known as the "swing set," since it was the one changed out to other sets most often.

Directly opposite them, on the other side of the stage, where normally four separate sets would be, was the gigantic main set of *Sunset Cove*, the Coltrane family estate. Built at a cost of over a quarter-million dollars, this showcase featured a huge centralized living room with a sweeping staircase that led up to a gracious landing. A pair of tufted velvet George Smith sofas faced each other, and real European antiques and chandeliers were used to convey the immense wealth of the Coltranes. An enormous dining room and fully functioning kitchen were off to the left. On the right of the living room was a billiard room and bar. Balconies extended from the rear of the living room out over the "grounds," which were actually another enormous diorama photograph that showed extended gardens and a pool.

In this fashion the cameras and crew could shoot on one set, then move down or hop across the wide center hallway to a different set, and shoot another scene. It made for faster taping, since sets could be prepped for the next shot while shooting was still taking place on another set.

They just don't know, Lefty reminded himself. The fans. They just didn't understand the scope of the miracles he had created. The South of France. Tahiti. A Hawaiian luau. A London courtroom. An igloo. All done on these very stages. And all done under budget and on time.

Why wasn't he doing features yet? That's were the big money was. Fame. Fortune. Oscars. *One day,* he thought determinedly. One day, he and his hunky boyfriend would look back on the "soap days" and laugh.

Just as he was smiling at this thought, Lefty noticed that a small group of cast and crew had gathered behind him to watch the action in the car as well. The taping of sex scenes was very popular entertainment at *Sunset Cove.*

". . . Oh, Stone . . . When you talk like that, it gets me all . . . excited!" Cathy was saying. Jack moved in for the Big Kiss.

A loud cracking sound was heard, and at first, Lefty thought the old whirring fan had finally broke down. But his attention was soon drawn to the BMW. It began to lurch oddly over to the driver's side. Another loud *CRACK,* and the car dipped down more, passed the point of no return, and began to flip completely over.

Jack, startled by the sudden shift, tried to grab the steering wheel, but his hands were caught up in Cathy's silk blouse. In what seemed to be slow motion, he felt himself sliding about the cabin of the car, Cathy's shrieks ringing in his ear. As his hands finally tore free of her blouse, Jack slammed against his door, which now, for some strange reason he couldn't fathom, was underneath him. He felt himself start to slip out the open window.

Cathy grabbed onto the passenger door handle, breaking

three acrylic nails in the process. Since she was fastened tightly into her seat, she was hanging vertically, and loudly screaming bloody murder.

Jack was flipped out of the BMW like a rag doll, and his breath left his body in a *whumph* as his head slammed against the exterior of the car roof. In an instant, the full weight of the BMW rolled over Jack, and his last thought before the blackness was to wonder if this would damage his newly capped teeth.

Two explosive sounds shot out as the air bags inflated, then deflated. The car, completely upside down, was resting comfortably on top of Jack Benz, whose legs peeked out from under the roof like those of the Wicked Witch of the East in *The Wizard of Oz*. Inside the car, Cathy was hanging upside down and trying to push away the remnants of the air bags. Stunned quiet befell the sound stage.

"I certainly hope . . ." Speaking softly, Joan Thomas, the producer of *Sunset Cove*, broke the silence. ". . . That was a rental."

2

After the initial shock had worn off, pandemonium had broken out on Stage 24 at UBC Television City. After getting Cathy unstrapped and out, it took ten people to lift the heavy Bavarian car off of Jack Benz. What was left of Jack's once picture-perfect face was not a pretty sight. Cathy, who had positioned herself unfortunately close to Jack's body as the car was lifted, fainted dramatically in shock. Ambulances were called, and production halted on the five shows taping at the studio that day: the soaps *Sunset Cove* and *The Insiders*; two game shows, *One Hot Number* and *Jackpot!*; and a prime-time variety program, *The Stan Parish Show.*

Network suits and producers swarmed over the set while crew and talent were led away to offices and dressing rooms to wait and see what was next.

Clayton Beasley, twenty-eight, and one of the three extras working that day on the hospital scene to be shot later that afternoon, walked with his friend Cissi Stanton up to the *Sunset Cove* offices. The offices were accessible either by the main elevator bank or by hiking up a rickety flight of stairs that were hidden behind a large sequined bingo board that was to be used that day on *One Hot Number*, which taped on Stage 23. Clay and Cissi took the stairs. It was just easier.

"Oh, my God!" Cissi cried. "That was awful! Jack's dead! He was such a wonderful man . . . Oh, my God!" Cissi was *Sunset Cove*'s overweight but lovable assistant casting director and had the thankless job of working for Sylvia Sinclair, the talent coordinator.

Cissi was thirty-four and had a constant air of being perpetually unkempt. Her thick coppery hair always started out sleek and styled, but by the end of the day it was inevitably frizzed and unruly. Pretty green eyes were often overlooked because of the profusion of freckles that dotted her plain, pudgy face. She had a habit of wearing loose-fitting dresses that she thought hid her weight. Sadly, in reality, they only accentuated her body size.

Cissi's sainted mother had died in childbirth, so she had been raised by her father, who owned a small cab company in St. Louis, Missouri. Her dad, who was a good and honest man, knew little about bringing up girls, and did the best job he could. He raised her as he would a boy, so what little girlish refinement she had, Cissi had picked up own her own. Despite her lack of social graces, she was a devoted friend to all who knew her, and was one of—if not the—most popular person at the studio.

Clay grabbed her hand and helped her up the stairs and down a very beige hall where large framed posters of the cast members of *Sunset Cove* were evenly spaced. All the two-year contract players were represented. First came a beautiful Greg Gorman shot of Cathy Grant as the devious and sultry Pageant Ragianni. June Franklin and Burt Otter as the matriarch and patriarch of the Coltrane clan, Salome and Hark Coltrane, came next. Sadly, their storyline was back-burner, as the ratings proved the audience was much more interested in the younger cast members. Sofia Tacker was pictured next, as dowdy Delilah Tucker, the housekeeper. Then came a hot Herb Ritts shot of a half-naked Travis Church, as the handsome and rebellious Cliff Coltrane. Pretty Melina Michele, as good-girl-from-the-wrong-side-of-the-tracks Skylar Nelson, was next to last, with Jack Benz as Stone Coltrane the final photograph.

Cissi and Clay stopped briefly in front of the oversized Jack Benz glamour shot. The photograph of him showed a frankly sexy Jack, staring off into the distance, a devilish glint in his newly done eyes, his hair carefully blowing back off his face. He looked like he had the world by the tail.

Cissi renewed her sobbing, which made her plain face very blotchy, and Clay gently led her away from the print and to her office door. He truly liked Cissi and was grateful to her, since she was the reason why he was on *Sunset Cove* in the first place.

Six months ago, Cissi had called Clay in to read for the part of Brandon Slater, a new love interest for the character Madison Sloan, the young ingenue of the show. Cissi had seen Clay do a scene at an actors' workshop in the Valley and had remembered him when the part of Brandon came up.

Despite giving a good reading at the audition, Clay didn't get the part. It turned out just as well, since Madison suddenly died of yellow fever after contract renegotiations with the egocentric actress who played her failed. As a result, the character of Brandon Slater left town in grief after only twelve episodes.

However, Clay had made an impression with Sylvia Sinclair, and was hired to play "Intern #2" in all of the hospital scenes, which meant two or three shows a week at about $150.00 a show—union scale plus ten. He even had been given a few lines here and there, which made his day rate go up.

Clay never forgot that it was Cissi who had brought him in, and he made a point to seek her out and chat her up. Now he considered Cissi to be one of his best friends, and he knew she felt the same way. Even though she was several years older than him, they had an easy rapport that they both cherished. Clay had gone through a terrible breakup the year before, and talking it through with Cissi had been a great source of comfort to him.

When they got to the casting office, Cissi had left the door open. It was a typical production office setup. Her smallish outer office was in a constant state of flux as FedEx packages came in, scripts piled up, and faxes rolled out of the fax machine.

Her boss Sylvia Sinclair's larger inner office was tremendously overdecorated in a "shabby chic" style and heavily scented with too many aromatherapy candles. The whitewashed, canvas slip-covered easy chairs and sofa were always piled high with bags and boxes from the leading stores of Rodeo Drive. Whatever space was available on the strategically distressed and chipped pale-blue-painted consoles and sea-foam green breakfront was used for piles of scripts and headshots.

It truly looked like Rachel Ashwell had walked into a barren room and thrown up.

Cissi went to her desk, which was buried under a mountain of actors' eight-by-ten headshots and résumés. A stack of recent submissions, still in their envelopes, were in the guest chair.

"Can I get you anything? Some coffee?" Clay asked, glad to be in the comfort and security of Cissi's territory.

"How about a stiff drink? Got any tequila?" she asked, plopping down into her chair. Cissi's normally open and friendly face was clouded over by anguish, her green eyes periodically filling with tears.

"Well, no, not on me," Clay said. "But I'm sure I could find something in Cathy Grant's dressing room. She being *Sunset Cove*'s very own alcoholic, and all." He took a stab at humor, but Cissi waved him off.

"I was only kidding," she sighed. "But not really. Oh, my God! What are we going to do? Jack and Cathy's story is the prominent story line this sweeps period! This is going to screw everything up!"

Clay removed the stack of submissions from the visitor's chair and sat down opposite her. He sucked in his breath sharply.

The pants on the white intern's uniform he was wearing for that day's shoot were two sizes too small, and he had to shift around a bit to get comfortable. Wardrobe had been out of size thirty-twos, so he had been squeezed into a pair of thirties. The only upside to this situation was that it made his crotch bulge out provocatively, and he had noticed a few furtive glances in that direction that day.

"I don't think that's the big story here right now. A guy's been killed," he reminded her gently.

"Of course you're right," Cissi hurriedly said, her face blushing bright red. *God, I hope we don't recast,* she thought. *That's always a pain. Sylvia will be impossible to deal with.*

"But you know who is going to have to do all the grunt work on this. Me. Sylvia will push it off on me; just watch."

"I know, Cis," Clay agreed. "Everyone knows who really runs the casting department. Why you're not the head of it, I'll never understand."

"Oh, no. I don't want that responsibility!" she protested weakly. But in her heart of hearts, Cissi did feel that her hard efforts were either overlooked by upper management, or Sylvia simply claimed them as her own.

Sylvia was a bitch, no two ways about it.

Just as Cissi was thinking about her, Sylvia Sinclair walked briskly into the office. Sylvia had the overbearing demeanor of a woman who, at forty-seven, had fought many battles to get to where she was, but had lost her compassion on the way. A tall, full-figured silver-blond, Sylvia fancied herself a style maven and spent inordinate amounts of time shopping for new clothes online, nestled away behind her always-closed office door. A perfect size eight, she loved to find bargains, both new and used, from a multitude of different Web sites.

Sylvia paused briefly for effect upon entering the office, then dramatically tossed her coffee-colored pashmina shawl over the soft shoulder pads of her cream Armani pantsuit. Her low-heeled Manolo Blahnik mules matched the suit color exactly.

"Get me Jack's agent on the phone right away!" Sylvia ordered. "Joan and Peter need to speak with him." She sailed past both Clay and Cissi and into her office, leaving them awash in a cloud of Chanel No. 5.

Cissi snapped to attention and quickly picked up the phone and began dialing. One of the many great attributes that Cissi had was her remarkable memory. No phone number, once learned, was ever forgotten.

On the other side of her desk, Clay suddenly felt awkward at being there. "I guess I should go to the extras room," he whispered.

"Max Bickford, please." Cissi shook her head and motioned

for him to stay. "I have Sylvia Sinclair for you, Max," she said, then transferred the call to Joan's desk. She got up, walked over to the door separating the two offices, and closed it.

"Maaaaaxx . . . You've heard? . . . Yes, I'm so sorry! It's just simply too awful for words!" Sylvia's strident voice could still be heard through the flimsy door.

"Don't you dare leave me here alone. With her," Cissi said, jutting a thumb at the closed office door. "Oh, my God. I just can't believe it!"

"I know. I just keep seeing it over and over, that car rolling over on him like that. So freaky," Clay agreed. He had been off to the side of the soundstage, so he had not been particularly close to the set, but close enough to see most of the incident. "How in the world could that happen?"

"You know, I was standing near Lefty right when it happened! We both watched it together. . . . I wouldn't want to be him for a million bucks right now! I bet he's crapping in his shorts over the fact that his rig killed Jack," she said, shaking her head furiously to try and remove the mental image of the big car rolling over Jack.

"Well, Max, Legal will want to talk to you as soon as possible, I know," Sylvia's voice continued to drone on from the other side of the door.

"Listen, I really need to get to the extras room. I'm sure the police, or whoever, are going to want to talk to all of us who were there." Clay rose from the chair, carefully replacing the pile of submissions as he found them.

"Sure, fine," Cissi whined. "Leave me here when I need you."

Clay went to the other side of the desk and wrapped his arms around her and squeezed. "It'll be fine. Call me at home, later, if you need to talk, okay?"

"Okay." Cissi leaned one hand over, and opened the top drawer of her desk. She pulled out a large bag of peanut butter cups and spilled several onto her desktop. "Screw the drink. I need chocolate," she muttered.

Clay smiled and released his grip on her. At the door he

turned and said, "It's going to be okay, Cis. Honest. Call me tonight."

Stubby fingers were tearing off the wrapper of a cup. "I will. Bye, Clay," she said as she popped the chocolate cup into her mouth. She felt better immediately, and audibly sighed.

Clay left Cissi's office, turned left, and continued down the hall. At a cross junction, he turned left again and walked up to a door marked "Atmosphere."

He pushed it open and walked in.

Clayton Beasley was one of the thousands of young, handsome actors that roam Los Angeles, constantly in search of their big break.

He had moved to L. A. from Houston, where he left behind a beloved fraternal twin brother and not much else, four years earlier. Their parents had died five years before that, in a car accident, so the boys had been on their own for a while.

At 5 feet 10 inches, Clay was not tall, but he was not short. He weighed a trim 170 pounds, maintained with a usually strict diet and a strenuous workout routine.

Clay had warm brown eyes that sometimes turned hazel in bright light, and a straight nose that no one would suspect had been the work of Dr. William Denton, one of Houston's finest plastic surgeons and a family friend. It had taken Clay a solid year to pay off the nose job, but it had been worth every penny.

Clay's first job upon arriving in L.A. had been at the front desk of a Beverly Hills health club, where his remarkably worked-out body had attracted the attention of both female *and* male clients. His legs, defined and built up through years of biking and running, were the most commented-on part of his physique. That and his hair.

He had medium-brown hair, cut in a slightly longish style that he could wear curly—its natural state—or stick-straight. It just depended on his mood in the morning, and his willingness to stand under the blow dryer. And not that he would admit it to anyone, but he had his hair "kissed by the sun" every four weeks at Frederick's at $110 a pop. But hey, Cathy Grant went there, and she was as "in" as you could get, so what did it matter if sometimes the cell phone bill waited a month to be paid? In L.A., it was all about the appearance.

Square of jaw and light of fat, he was an ideal candidate for television stardom. It just hadn't happened yet. But Clay was determined that it would indeed happen—and on his own terms. More than once, a "producer" had offered him a small part in his next movie if only Clay would join the "producer" at his beach house/ski lodge/fill-in-the-blank for a quiet weekend.

Clay decided that the "quiet weekends" of the business were not how he was going to make it, and he politely but firmly declined all offers.

He had done a few commercials. Nationals, they were called, which meant big residuals. At least in theory. After taxes and agent's fees, the sum left was less than half of what he had earned. "Welcome to Hollywood, baby," his agent, Lucy Crater, had told him after noticing Clay's disappointed look upon seeing his first residual check.

Clay had also appeared in a few sitcoms, usually in a one-shot guest role as the boyfriend who got dumped at the end of the episode. He also did a lot of shows playing guys who wore a uniform. A bellman at a hotel. A security guard. A cop. A fireman. And, now, two or three times a week, an intern at a hospital.

Not that he was complaining. The money from *Sunset Cove* got him out from behind the counter at the health club, and he was pleased that he was making his living entirely from acting. Not that it took much acting to push around a gurney, but it sure beat checking ID cards at the gym.

"Man, do you believe this shit?" Scott Tyler asked Clay as he walked into the Atmosphere's dressing room.

"Squashed. Like a bug! Did you see the look on Travis Church's face? I though he was gonna hurl!" Josh Babbitt joined in. "And Christ! Cathy Grant stuck in that car? Priceless!"

Scott and Josh also played interns on *Sunset Cove,* though Josh had done double duty as a con in some prison scenes. Josh was a 225-pound party boy who never met a beer he didn't like or a pizza he couldn't eat. He lately had taken to wearing the scrubs that wardrobe put him in as his everyday wear. Josh swore it made women check him out more, because they thought he was a doctor at Cedars-Sinai, the major hospital complex that was near both the studio and Josh's apartment. It was a ruse he did little to correct.

Scott, short at 5 feet 6 inches, and only weighing 140 pounds had a deceptively deep voice, which was how he found steady work doing voice-over radio spots for a local grocery store chain. Scott had already removed his intern uniform and put back on his street clothes: jeans and a yellow T-shirt that read, "Big Things Come in Small Packages."

"Dudes, not cool. The guy is dead, you know," Clay chastised the pair as he slunk into a makeup chair, unbuttoning the top button of his too-tight pants.

"Fuck him," Josh snorted. "He was a dick, and you know it. You remember how he got you bumped out of that week when Skylar was in the coma?" Josh reached over to the coffee table and grabbed a stale doughnut from the morning. With a flick of his wrist, he tossed the doughnut up in the air and caught it in his teeth, just like a golden retriever.

As much as Clay didn't want to admit it, it was true. Jack Benz had been a world-class jerk, and he had indeed had Clay removed from the call list one week, a month ago, and replaced with a cousin who was visiting and had wanted to experience the "fun" of working on a soap.

It had been a real blow to Clay, because his Jeep Wrangler had been in the shop getting some very expensive new brakes, and he really needed the money. Cissi had later told Clay that when Jack had requested the change, he hadn't cared if this would cause a hardship or not—and had, in fact, specifically asked that Clay be the extra replaced.

"Yeah, I remember," Clay agreed. "But still. What a way to go. I just don't understand how it happened. Those metal braces under the car were, like, really thick. How could they just pop loose like that?"

"This is so gonna screw up the show. I wonder what they're gonna do," Scott pondered.

"Hey, we get paid for today, don't we?" asked Josh, his mouth still full of doughnut.

3

"Well. What the hell do we do now?" Joan Thomas, *Sunset Cove*'s producer, asked harshly. A high-level meeting had been hastily arranged in the director's booth, high above Stage 24. Joan, representing the production company that actually produced *Sunset Cove*, Klein Productions, looked at the other attendees.

Beside Joan sat director Sam Michaels, nervously rubbing his hands.

Sam was one of daytime's few African-American directors. He had started out as an actor in New York, but tired of always being cast as a drug addict or servant, he had deliberately drifted into directing. He won several daytime Emmy awards for his directorial work on *All My Children* and had been lured to L.A. and *Sunset Cove* with the promise of a huge pay raise and more creative control. His wife, a lovely woman named Naomi, was sick of the snow and was pressing to have another child to add to their brood of five. So he took the deal. So far, he'd gotten the money, but Joan Thomas rarely let him make any major decision. As a result, Sam had packed on more than fifty-five pounds since moving to California, and at only 5 feet 9 inches, he was often mistaken for Al Roker.

Next to Sam was a clearly miserable Lefty Jannel. Two network suits, Drusilla Gordon, vice president of Daytime Dramas, and Peter Dowd, production liaison, were sitting at a bank of monitors, looking at the activity below as shown on the many small screens. Each screen represented the view as seen through a camera on the sound stage. Two policemen had arrived and were doing some measurements near the pancaked BMW while the coroner was filling out paperwork. Jack Benz was in a large body bag on a collapsible gurney, getting ready to be wheeled out by two burly EMTs. A cleaning crew idled off to the side, waiting to clean up the area.

Baby-faced Peter Dowd was absentmindedly playing with his ebony Montblanc pen, clicking it open and closed, over and over. In the midst of a divorce, Peter had been having a hard time concentrating on his job lately.

Today was no different.

He had married his college sweetheart, as everyone thought he would, and had set out to conquer the television world. Unfortunately, Los Angeles was a far cry from Aurora, Illinois, and the urges that he had always resisted in his safe, ordinary life grew to full-blown temptations in L.A.

Being a normal, healthy man of twenty-seven, he had finally given in to them.

When his perky, blond wife came home early one day from her job as a personal shopper at Neiman Marcus, she was stupefied to find her 195-pound husband teetering around their perfectly decorated bedroom in her favorite Bob Mackie gown, the silver one she had worn when she won "Miss Greater Chicago." Even worse, he was stretching out her best pair of Jimmy Choo strappy sandals.

She quite literally freaked out.

In the ensuing fracas, Peter's carefully applied makeup had been slapped off, and his Marilyn Monroe wig was lying on the floor, a mass of crushed curls. He had checked into a hotel that night, only to be served with divorce papers the following day.

Now he had lawyer's fees, therapy bills, and sadly he realized he was going to have to give up half the money he had inherited from his grandmother's estate to his soon-to-be ex-wife. Plus, his new wardrobe tastes were breaking him. He was contemplating selling the Volvo and getting a Hyundai, and he wished that bitch Joan would shut up and let them go.

Jack Benz was dead, and there wasn't much he could do to change that.

He desperately wanted to get back to his office and look on the internet at a Web site he had found that sold only the best used designer dresses. The size eights always seemed to go so fast.

"Obviously, we have to issue a statement of some sort," offered Drusilla quietly. Her expertly tailored navy Donna Karan power suit showed off her remarkable body, the product of nightly spin classes at Crunch gym in West Hollywood. "Both the network and you, Joan, should issue statements," she concluded, nervously tucking a loose strand of her shoulder-length blond hair behind her ear.

"Fine. Then what? Are you willing to stop production for the next two days? It's going to cost UBC, you know," Joan said pointedly.

Never a beauty, Joan favored severely tailored dresses in shades of dark brown that caused her round face to seem constantly drawn and pale. She wore her lank gray-riddled brown hair in a simple pageboy cut and rarely, if ever, fiddled with it. Chunky black horn-rimmed Oliver Peoples glasses slightly magnified her already large brown eyes and had the curious effect of making her look owlish. If ever there was a person desperately in need of a makeover at the M.A.C. store on Robertson Blvd., it was Joan.

Her mind, however, was always five minutes ahead of everyone else's, and that was her secret strength. "I don't want you coming back to me later, trying to cut my budget because of this. I just want to be very clear on that, Drusilla," she finished.

"Please, Joan," Drusilla said quietly, "I've asked you repeatedly to call me Dru. You know I hate being called Drusilla."

"Oh, sorry, I keep forgetting, Drusilla. Or, Dru, or whatever your name is today. Klein Productions is not paying for network dictated shutdowns." Joan crossed her arms in defiance.

"Good God, Joan," piped up Peter. "That is . . . uh . . . a conversation for another time!"

"Just remember what I said."

"What I want to know," Dru interrupted softly, "is, how did this happen? Lefty?" All eyes turned to Lefty as he shifted his weight back and forth from foot to foot.

"I . . . I . . ." Lefty stammered. He had gone over it a thousand times. He knew that somehow he was going to take the fall for this. And, he supposed, that was fair. "I . . . I don't know. We've done this same setup many times before. Just last week, even. I just don't know what happened."

"Well, did you check it today before shooting began?" asked Joan pointedly.

"Today? Well, no. Chuck and I set it up last night before we left. We knew that would be the first shot today, and we thought we'd get a jump on the day. I guess I didn't check it today. I didn't have any reason to!" Lefty knew he sounded defensive, but he had always been conscientious on the job and had never had an accident before. His personal grieving for Jack was just going to have to wait until these people understood he thought he had done his job.

A phone on the console table began to ring, breaking the tension. Joan grabbed it on the third ring.

"Control room," she barked. She listened for a beat and then began to rub her temples.

"What . . . what is it?" Sam Michaels finally stammered.

"Shhh!" Joan hissed at him. She turned away from the small group and began whispering orders into the phone. Everyone stared at her back, not knowing what to do next. After a minute of hushed talking, Joan hung up the phone, turned, and faced the group, her owl eyes unblinking.

"Well. This just keeps getting better. There are news crews setting up out front. Apparently, someone here at the studio called the news division. I want to know who." She looked accusingly at each of the faces staring back at her.

Peter Dowd cleared his throat. "Uh, that was me. Well, I authorized it."

"*You* authorized it? Really? And pray tell, why?" Joan's sarcasm cut through the air like a knife.

"Well, Joan, as the executive liaison for the network, I felt it was best that we give the story first to our own network news team. I thought the network should handle the initial news break, rather than let some news crew we don't control leak it." Peter stood his ground. He was feeling less than comfortable, partly because the red lace Victoria's Secret thong he was sporting under his tan Hugo Boss double-breasted suit had ridden deeply into his butt crack. He bravely resisted the urge to tug it out.

"Huh. Well, I would have liked to have been included in that decision, Peter." Joan was like a terrier with a bone, and she would not let go.

"Well, that's really water under the bridge," interrupted Dru boldly. "We need to come up with a course of action." She turned to Lefty. "Lefty, let's look into hiring an attorney for you, just to be safe." Even though her tone was compassionate, Lefty's shoulders sagged.

"UBC will issue a statement of the facts: that this was a tragic accident, how we'll miss Jack terribly, such a tragic loss, blah, blah, blah," Dru continued, counting off the points on her fingers. "We'll shut down production on *Sunset Cove* today and tomorrow. The other shows can go back up now. This really doesn't affect them."

"I don't know if we can . . ." began Joan, surprised at the emerging take-charge tone coming from Dru, a woman she had always thought had slept her way into her job.

"You can, and you will," Dru politely but firmly cut her off. "Get the writers together, and come up with some plausible reason why Stone has left town. We'll decide later whether to recast or not."

"What a minute!" Joan was not happy with the way this was going. Who the hell did this woman think she was? "How do I explain the sudden disappearance of the main male lead of my show, *Drusilla?*"

Ignoring the obvious dig, Dru soldiered on. "It's a *soap,* Joan. Have him kidnapped by aliens. He suddenly got amnesia. I don't know. Isn't that your job? To come up with story plotlines? You had this very same problem when Lance Jackson died a couple of years ago in that car accident. You had to create a reason why he was suddenly gone, and you did a brilliant job by having him kidnapped by the mafia."

"This is a slightly different case. Lance wasn't in a front-burner story line. And, as I recall, we then pumped up Jack's part as a result of that," Joan caustically replied, her nostrils flaring in anger.

"I remember, Joan. The point is, you did it then, and I'm sure you can do it now."

"Who's that?" Sam pointed to the monitor for camera one, which was focused on the car set. A tall blond man in a blue denim shirt, navy knit tie, and wrinkled khakis was talking to the policemen and writing notes down on a small pad.

"Jesus Christ!" Joan gasped. "A reporter!"

All five of them bolted from the booth and descended the stairs to the stage floor. Joan's sensible brown Nine West pumps thudded across the cement floor as the rest of the group hurried to catch up with her.

"You! You there!" she screamed across the stage. "What do you think you're doing?"

The blond man, startled, looked up from his notes. He looked around to see who this lunatic woman was screaming at, and by the time he realized it was him, she was upon him.

"You have no business being here! This is a tragedy, and you need to leave! Go back outside with the other reporters! Now!" Joan shrieked.

The man's ice blue eyes twinkled a bit, and a slight smile crossed his lips. "I'm afraid there's some misunderstanding here," he started to say.

"You bet your ass there is! Chuck!" She called to a burly stage hand over by the BMW. "Call Security! Have the policemen toss him out of here!"

"Ma'am, you don't understand," the man tried to say.

"Chuck! NOW!"

The rest of the group had formed a semicircle around the interloper, with Lefty and Dru behind him, both of them appreciating the unobstructed view of his obviously rock-hard ass. This was a man who worked out.

Each began thinking thoughts of sexual acts that might be considered illegal in several Southern states.

"Chuck," the man called out, not taking his eyes from

Joan, "don't bother. I *am* the police." He reached into his left hip pocket, giving Lefty and Dru a secret thrill, and fished out his wallet. He flipped it open to reveal a badge and ID card. "Dave Parker. Homicide, LAPD, Hollywood Division."

"Oh, I, um . . ." Joan mumbled as she squinted at the ID card. "Sorry. Surely you must understand. We've had a day."

"Yes. It looks like it."

"Excuse me, but did you say Homicide?" Dru's heart skipped a beat. She wasn't sure if it was because of the incredibly handsome detective or the news he was saying. "Why is Homicide here? This was an accident."

"Well, I was called in by Officer Petty over there. Seems that the rigging for this car was tampered with."

"Tampered with? What are you saying?" Joan was just about at the end of her rope. This might actually give her the stroke she always feared she might have.

"The support braces were unbolted from two of the hydraulics. When the stress levels got to be too much, they snapped. Officer Gonzalez noticed it when he examined the rig. That's why they called me in. Who was in charge of this contraption?" Parker pointed to the Rig.

"Uh, it's mine—I mean, I built it." Lefty stepped forward. "I'm the art director. I do the sets. It was built to my specs. It's my special design. We've used it about twenty times so far, and nothing's ever happened." Lefty looked like he was on the verge of tears.

"Did you inspect it before the shot?"

"Well, no." Lefty just wished the ground would open up and swallow him whole.

"Hmmm. Okay. When did you set it up? When was the last time you checked it?"

"Last night."

"Who had access to this stage between the time you left this thing last night and the scene was shot this morning?"

"Well, we were out of here by nine last night then security locked down the stage right after that, and I got here at about seven-thirty this morning. Other than that specific locked-off time, gosh, anyone could come in here. We keep the stage doors open all day."

"Detective Parker, do I need to be here for this?" Joan asked impatiently, her owl eyes squinting.

"And you are . . . ?"

"Joan Thomas, Producer of *Sunset Cove*. This is my show, and we've had a catastrophic accident here today. I have things I need to take care of." She tapped a foot in annoyance.

"Tell you what. All of you give your names to that policeman over there. I'll need to talk to each of you. Find out where you were, that sort of thing." Parker caught the attention of one of the policemen. "Officer Gonzalez, please get all of these people's names." He then turned to Joan. "And, yes, Ms. Thomas, I will especially need to talk to you."

Parker put a hand on Lefty's shoulder and led him over to the Rig.

"I need for you to explain this thing to me. But don't touch it. We're going to have to dust it for prints."

The small group broke up after giving Officer Gonzalez their names. Sam went back up to the control room, and Peter Dowd practically broke into a sprint to get off the stage and back up to his forth-floor office, pausing only once to tug at his wedgie. Only Dru lingered on the set. She drifted over to Parker and Lefty.

"Uh, Detective?" she asked tentatively.

Parker and Lefty were kneeling in front of the Rig, looking at the shattered support braces. Parker looked up from Lefty and locked his gaze on Dru.

"I'm Dru Gordon, Vice President, Daytime, for UBC," she said while noticing for the first time the flecks of brown that spotted the irises of his blue eyes. "I . . . I just wanted you to know that anything I can do to help you, of course I will do. Do you really think this was a murder and not just an unfortunate accident?"

Lefty noticed that Parker's eyes slowly went from Dru's blond blunt cut all the way down to her navy Chanel slingbacks and back up again. Lefty understood the look. Mentally, Parker had just undressed Dru and was enjoying carnal relations with her.

Damn, Lefty thought. Score one for *their* team.

Dru blushed a deep red, as she too had understood the long look Parker gave her.

"I don't know yet. But we'll find out." Parker stood up and wiped his hands on his pants. He reached out and picked off a minute piece of fluff from Dru's left shoulder. "And thanks for the offer, Ms. Gordon. I'll hold you to that," he said with a slight grin.

At a loss for words, Dru nodded her head modestly, smiled, and walked away, giving Parker a chance, which he took, to study her backside.

Thank God for spin class, she thought as she crossed the stage floor.

Turning his attention back to the job at hand, Parker again knelt down. "Okay, Lefty, explain this part to me again."

4

Clay stood in front of Travis Church's dressing-room door and hesitated before knocking. Not sure if it was the right thing to do, he finally committed to the act, but only after looking up and down the hallway to make sure no one was around.

"Travis?" he said softly, as he rapped.

"Yes? What is it?" a deep voice responded from behind the closed door.

"It's me, Clay."

The door opened and Clay stood a mere two feet from soap opera's hottest superstar.

Travis Church had joined the cast of *Sunset Cove* a little over two years before as Cliff Coltrane, the long-lost illegitimate son of Hark Coltrane, the patriarch of *Sunset Cove*, and Delilah Tucker, the Coltrane family cook. Much drama and angst had accompanied his arrival to the oceanside hamlet of Sunset Cove, to the delight of viewers from coast to coast.

Travis had shoulder-length raven black hair and aquamarine blue eyes. High patrician cheekbones complemented his square jawline. His straight Roman nose ended at full, pouty, kissable lips that were put to good use at least once per episode. His face and body had inspired thousands of fantasies among the viewers of *Sunset Cove*, and he had graced the cover of *People* magazine twice: once as one of the "50 Most Beautiful People," and once as this year's "Sexiest Man Alive." At twenty-nine, daily two-hour workouts with a personal trainer gave him the body of a college gymnast, which was exactly what he had been.

He had food from the Zone Diet delivered to his Sunset Plaza house every morning at a cost of over four thousand dollars a month. Each of the three daily meals, plus snacks, was carefully calculated to the exact standards of his nutrition plan to limit carbs, sugars, and fats.

It worked.

"Hey. Come in, come in," Travis invited, letting Clay into his dressing room. He poked his head out the door and looked up and down the hallway, just as Clay had done. Satisfied there was no one there, he closed and locked the door.

Clay wandered to the center of the spacious dressing room. Travis had been allowed to decorate it in any way he chose, and he chose to let his decorator make the decisions. A rugged tan suede sofa occupied the farthest wall, flanked by two brown-and-black plaid horse blanket upholstered club chairs. The cocktail table was an old barn door, refitted with a glass top and iron base. Tasteful Western-themed art adorned the beige-tinted Ralph Lauren River Rock walls. It was unabashedly masculine, just like Travis.

"Anybody see you come in here?"

"No. I don't think so. . . . I checked," Clay answered. "I just wanted to make sure you were okay. This is all so bizarre, I just wanted to make sure."

"Oh, my God. It's fucking surreal! I just saw Jack . . . uh, this morning, in the parking lot. And then, I was on set talking with Melina, and I saw it happen! I thought I was going to throw up there for a minute." Travis left the door and stood directly in front of Clay, running his fingers through his hair to get it off his handsome face.

His plaid flannel shirt was half unbuttoned, showing a teasing glimpse of worked-out pecs. Tight faded Levi's fit perfectly, and his feet were bare.

The squawk box crackled to life. A square speaker box mounted on a wall in each dressing room and public area, the squawk box was an intercom system. Very similar to the kind that schools have, it blared out the action on the stage floor, but it was used mainly to page actors. "All personnel please stay off the *Sunset Cove* set," the disembodied voice of Joan Thomas said. "We will notify everyone when you can leave as soon as we have word. Thank you for your patience."

"Is there anything I can do?" Clay asked, ignoring the announcement.

Travis took only a second to think. "Yeah. Kiss me, I *need* you. I missed you! I hate waking up and you're not there." Travis snaked his arms around Clay's neck and pulled him close. They were the same height, so there was none of that awkward bending up or down.

The most famous male lips in the country were now firmly planted on Clay's. Their eyes closed, lips parted, and tongues began to explore. Travis groaned slightly, and the kissing got heavier. Hands started to roam, and Clay let his slowly move south, eventually reaching Travis's firm bubble butt, where they gently squeezed and caressed.

"Damn," Travis sighed. "You're getting me all going here . . ."

"Mmmm . . . maybe that's the plan." Clay began to kiss and gently tongue Travis's neck, searching for that spot that, when kissed hard, always caused the soap star to arch his head back and moan out loud. Travis began to breathe heavily.

"Oh, yeah . . . love that . . ." Travis reached down and began to rub Clay's hard bulge. Slowly. Up and down.

"Travis, should we do this now?" Clay asked, spreading his stance slightly as Travis's hands teased and rubbed.

"No, but I don't care . . . I needed you so damn much today . . . I can't help myself." Travis unbuttoned the top button of his partner's tight white pants. After unzipping them, his hand dug in and found what he was craving.

"God . . . I missed you, too . . ." Clay murmured, allowing himself to get carried away. Sex with Travis was unparalleled in his life, and each time was like a new discovery.

Travis sank to his knees and took Clay into his mouth.

Clay's hand gently stroked Travis's head as it bobbed back and forth. Travis had no gag reflex, and getting head from him was a five-star event.

All caution was lost now, and Clay roughly grabbed Travis by the shoulders and pulled him up. Kissing him hard, and often, Clay began to strip Travis's clothing from his body. He licked and kissed Travis's bare chest, giving special attention to his nipples, gently flicking them with his tongue and then teasingly licking them. Travis, in ecstasy beyond reason, welcomed his secret lover's moves. Travis was not that experienced, but he knew that in Clay he had found the perfect sexual partner.

Within moments, the two men were completely naked and rolling on the sand-toned, wool Berber carpeting that Travis's decorator had picked out. Flat, ripped abs were pressed up against flat, ripped abs, and muscular arms and legs were intertwined.

Clay twisted his body around so that they were inverted, head to toe, and each hungrily took the other in his mouth. They soon developed a pulsating rhythm that brought each of them very close to climax.

Pulling back from the brink, they began to kiss and lick each other's sweaty bodies again. Finally, Travis couldn't stand it anymore.

"God, I have to . . . you know I *have* to," he quietly pleaded.

Clay, wanting the same thing, offered no resistance.

Travis reached into a leather gym bag, opened a small zippered compartment, and took out a condom and a small travel-size bottle of lube. After slathering Clay's impressive erection with the lube, he deftly tore open the condom packet and slid it on Clay. More lube was stroked onto Clay, and soon Travis was on top of him, his muscular legs straddling Clay's hips. He began to slowly rise and fall on Clay, taking him deep inside.

Clay always marveled at his good fortune at these moments.

Here was the hottest man in daytime television, riding him, crying out his name softly. He could see the rapture Travis was feeling by the look on his face, his stunning eyes staring deep into his own, sexy lips slightly parted, a slight smile at the corners. The intense pleasure Clay felt from this connection with his lover was further deepened by the growing love he felt for him.

Travis began to buck harder, stroking himself with one hand while the other was pressed down onto Clay's chest. Explosive, short grunts escaped from Travis's mouth with each push down. His hair fell forward and hung loose, swaying with his movements. Clay reached up and grabbed his lover's melon pecs and gently squeezed.

"Oh, God Clay! I'm gonna come! I'm gonna shoot!" Travis gasped through gritted teeth.

"Shoot it, Trav . . . come on! . . . Let me see it!"

In a spasm of nirvana, Travis climaxed and, in doing so, so turned on Clay that Clay came as well. Both men gave heartfelt sighs and, drained from their exertions, began to slowly ratchet down their movements.

Eventually, they both lay on their backs on the plush carpeting, breathing deeply and enjoying the afterglow. Clay reached over and softly brushed away a damp lock of dark hair that had fallen over Travis's brow.

Travis turned sideways and spooned up next to Clay. "Say," Travis wondered. "Would it be really rotten of me to request Jack's parking space? I mean, it's way closer than mine to the artists' entrance, and I *am* a bigger draw than he was."

5

It was after ten o'clock at night by the time Clay got to his small one-bedroom condo on Sweetzer Avenue in West Hollywood, a street that had gained some notoriety a few years before for being the location where a popular young television actress had been shot and killed by a stalker.

Clay had lucked into a sweet deal on the condo, based on a tip from a buddy at the gym who was a real estate broker. The building had been an apartment conversion, and was going condo right when he had gotten an abnormally large residual payment on a Pert Plus commercial that he had done. Five hours standing in a cold shower with foam on his head had brought him the down payment on the place, and whenever he saw that commercial he smiled. He had practically stolen the apartment, getting an amazingly low price because the project hadn't been announced yet.

Clay then spent almost every waking moment fixing it up. Granted, it wasn't the Taj Mahal—just a few rooms composed of a large living/dining area, a good-sized galley kitchen, an adequate bedroom, and a perfectly serviceable bathroom. But the unit was on the top floor of a four-story building and thus had twelve-foot ceilings throughout.

Always good with his hands, Clay had done wonders to it. He had put in hardwood floors, added crown moldings and bead-board wainscoting, and replaced the carpeting in the bedroom with an upgraded soft beige pile. A pale khaki color by Ralph Lauren called "Rice" was on the walls, and the wood-work and trim were painted with a crisp white eggshell finish.

Clay spent many happy hours at the Hollywood Home Depot on Sunset Boulevard looking for new projects for the condo. On more than one occasion, he could have come home with more than a project, for the Home Depot was gaining notoriety as a cruising spot. It must be the arresting and intoxicating aromas of lumber and cement, Clay had always thought.

Clay furnished his place in a comfortable yet classic style he jokingly called "urban island." Enthused by the South Pacific, he combined modern dark woods with tropical-wood vessels and lamps. Subtle tropical prints on the curtains and throw pillows pulled it together. He bought on sale some good pieces of formal teak furniture from his favorite store on La Brea Avenue, Not So Far East. He had slip-covered his IKEA rolled-arm sofa with a sage green plaid, and made regular additions to the household from Pottery Barn, Restoration Hardware, and Crate & Barrel. The completed spaces had the calming effect of seeming as if a comfortable beach house from Hawaii had somehow landed in the middle of West Hollywood.

All his labor would pay off, too. His real estate buddy had recently appraised the place at double the price Clay had originally paid for it, not only because of the renovations but also because of skyrocketing Weho property values.

Bone tired and ready to fall into bed, he first checked his voice mail to see if he had any calls. Five calls. He had been so wrapped up in the events of the day, he hadn't called in once to check them.

One call was from his brother, Hayden, who was traveling in Europe on business and was just touching base with him.

One call from the Holloway cleaners on Santa Monica Blvd., to remind him he had six shirts that needed to picked up this week or they were considered abandoned property.

Another call from his commercial agent, Lucy Crater, giving him the details on a Dr. Pepper audition for the next day. Would he please wear jeans and a tank top and call back to confirm?

Next was a call from Travis.

"Hey, it's me. Just called to say that I just got home, and, uh, I'm heading to bed, and I wish you were here." Travis's deep voice sounded even sexier on the phone than in person. "I'd invite you over, but I have to get up so damn early tomorrow for a photo shoot and interview with *Soap Opera Digest*, so I need to sleep, and I wouldn't if you came over . . ." There was a slight chuckle, then he continued. ". . . so I'll call you when I get back, umm, about four. But, come for dinner and stay over tomorrow night, okay? and . . . well, come over tomorrow, okay? I'll call ya. Oh, by the way, thanks for this afternoon. Just what I needed. Bye, sexy."

Clay smiled. Oh, yeah. He'd come over.

The last message was from Cissi, asking him to please, please call her the second he got home.

Clay switched over the phone and, while scanning through his mail, dialed up Cissi. "Hey, it's me," he said after she answered.

"Oh, thank God." It sounded like Cissi had been crying. "I am just so upset! How long were you there? I didn't get out until seven. Just question after question!" she sniffed.

"Um, I just left. I think I was one of the last they interviewed. Low man on the totem pole, you know. The detective was a hottie, though." Clay could just picture Cissi sitting in her enormous Laura Ashley-covered bed, wrapped up in her favorite blue chenille robe, a bowl of potato chips on the bedside table.

"God! Wasn't he? I think I was actually sorry when my interview was over! So what did he ask you?"

"Oh, the usual stuff they ask people when a crime has been committed, though I just can't believe it was a crime. Where was I? Did I see anything? What time did I leave the night before? What time did I get there that morning? That sort of thing."

"Hmmm." There was a pause on Cissi's end.

"What?" Clay asked.

"He asked me the same stuff. . . . He really seems to think it was no accident. That means someone deliberately messed with that rig thing and caused the accident. Someone wanted Jack dead! Who would want that?"

Clay smiled slightly. "Just about every actress he's ever done a scene with, I imagine."

"Clay!" Cissi admonished. "Really! I know the two of you didn't really get along, but before I started to hang out with you so much, he and I used to be such good friends. I loved him, really."

"Look, Cis. I'm a nobody on that show. A glorified extra. So what I think about Jack Benz is absolutely of no importance to anyone. He always seemed to treat me like crap, and I never could figure out why. It was like I wronged him somehow. But even still, what makes you think he was the target? There were *two* people in the car, you know." Still sorting through his mail, Clay came upon the new pre-summer Pottery Barn catalog, and he started to flip casually through its pages.

"Oh! I never thought of that!" Surprised, Cissi digested this information.

"Exactly. I bet Cathy has just as many enemies as Jack ever did. She's so bitchy to people all the time."

"Well, you may be right about that . . ." Cissi agreed hesitantly. "So. Are you seeing the mystery man tonight?"

Clay laughed at the abrupt subject change. "No. Not tonight. Tomorrow night."

"I still don't know why you won't tell me about him. It's all very mysterious. I am your friend, you know," Cissi grumped.

"It's not that, Cis. It's just, he's not 'out' yet, and he's asked me to keep it quiet. I'm not happy about it either, you know, but I like this guy, so I'm gonna hang in there a bit and see if I can't loosen him up."

"He's married, isn't he? Oh, my God, you're dating a married man!" she hooted.

"No, sweetie, he's not married. Just a boy who's having trouble with the fact that he likes boys." While Clay could sound like it wasn't that big a deal, actually it was an important issue with him, and he resented the fact that he couldn't talk about it openly with his good friend. He did need advice about this relationship, but there was no one to talk to about it except his brother, to whom he told everything. And he couldn't get in touch his brother, who was unreachable somewhere in Europe right now.

"Well, just be careful. I don't want you to get hurt again."

Clay sighed. "I know. But he's the first guy since Matt that I've really been interested in."

Matthew was a painful memory to Clay. He was Clay's ex, the man who broke his heart.

After meeting cute at the underwear counter in Bloom-ing-dale's at the Beverly Center shopping mall, where they were both buying the same kind of Calvin Klein tighty-whiteys, the pair were soon headlong into a troubled two-year relationship.

In hindsight, Clay now realized that he had made many mistakes with Matt. He could have been more involved in Matt's life. He should have spent less time worrying about his career and more time on the relationship. It had been his first real relationship, and he had crashed miserably at it, but he had come to believe it was his choice of partner, more than anything, that had doomed them to failure.

No matter what Clay did to make it work with Matthew, it was never enough. According to Matt, Clay couldn't say, do, wear, or think the right thing. He constantly pointed out Clay's imperfections while he never examined his own. Matt loved nothing more than to remind Clay that he wasn't living up to Matt's impossibly high standards, standards that Matt himself seldom followed. Clay began to doubt his own character, when it was actually Matt who needed self-examination.

It didn't help that Matt was a compulsive liar. If he felt he could get away with telling a lie, if it put him in a better light, he'd lie. Then, when he was caught lying—which was almost always—he'd try to joke it off with "I'm just being a wise guy." As a result, Clay never knew when to believe Matt, and began to withdraw from him, shutting down emotionally. Sex was the first thing to stop. Clay just couldn't get sexually excited over a man he was constantly angry with.

Matt ended up leaving Clay for a twenty-year-old kid who worked at the local Starbucks. To add insult to injury, Matthew and "the kid" had taken an apartment together six buildings down Sweetzer, so Clay had to see them together *all* the time. It had been incredibly spiteful and painful, and it had taken almost a year for Clay to get over it. He and Matthew no longer spoke.

"Well, Matt was an asshole. I just hope this guy isn't, too," Cissi flatly stated.

"He isn't." For a brief moment, Clay thought of Travis, driving down the Pacific Coast Highway, top down on his silver Porsche Boxster, hair whipping around, a dazzling smile just for him.

"So. We're shut down tomorrow. I still have to go in, but what are you going to do? Were you scheduled for tomorrow?" A faint crunching sound coming from Cissi's side of the conversation meant that the bedside chips were slowly being eaten.

"I was, but I think it'll be pushed to Friday. I have an audition in the morning; then I think I'll take a bike ride at the beach."

"An audition? What for?" Cissi was always interested in the twists and turns of Clay's career. She was his biggest supporter and believed he had what it took to make it—he just needed "the break."

"Dr. Pepper commercial. Jeans and tank top," Clay answered.

"Oh, well, then. You're a shoo-in. Show off the pecs, baby. You got 'em!"

"I'm more than just a hunk of meat, you know," joked Clay.

"Please. Use it while you can."

"Don't I know it. Well, I'm sacked out. Bedtime for me. I'll give ya a shout tomorrow," Clay said, yawning.

"Okay. Sleep tight." Cissi smacked a kiss into the receiver, then hung up.

Clay turned his attention to his nightly rituals.

Every night he was home, he did two hundred and fifty crunches with his ab-roller while watching the eleven o'clock news with the handsome anchorman Rick Yung, a guy he knew from the gym. This night, he was amazed at the coverage Jack's death was getting.

After doing the ab work, he sauntered to the bathroom,

where he thoroughly washed and moisturized his face with the ridiculously expensive face products he bought at The Body Shop. Dental hygiene came next as he first flossed, then brushed his teeth with the special teeth-whitener toothpaste he bought in bulk at the Costco in Venice.

Finally, Clay climbed into bed with the latest issue of *Entertainment Weekly*. After reading for a bit, he started to feel drowsy and put the magazine down. He turned off the stylish Robert Abbey lamp he'd bought at Target, of all places, and settled back in the darkness, allowing himself to be swallowed up by his three hundred-thread-count sheets and summer-weight comforter.

With a smile on his face, he fell asleep thinking about Travis.

6

Clay first met Travis two years ago at an audition for *Friends*. They were both up for the same part, a four-episode stint as Lisa Kudrow's hunky but dim boyfriend. A natural competitiveness and mutual dislike was visibly noticeable between them, and they both went to the producer for the final audition.

Secretly sizing each other up in the outer office of the producer, they each pretended not to care that the other was there. Travis got to read first, and Clay's initial dislike for him didn't stop him from checking out Travis's ass as he walked past and into the producer's office.

Although Clay was the better actor for the part, Travis had the edge, since he was a "name," albeit a small one. He had just started a limited gig on *Sunset Cove*, and had the cocky air of an actor on the way up.

After his own reading, and on his way out of the building, Clay saw Travis leaving in his new red Jeep Cherokee. Travis looked at him, smirked, waved curtly, and was gone.

"What an ass," Clay had said to himself.

Travis got the part.

Clay had forgotten about the encounter until the episodes aired. Travis was passable in the part, but Clay recognized instantly that the choices he himself had made during the audition scene had been better, and that he, not the pretty-boy soap actor, should have been cast.

To make matters worse, the *Friends* episodes Travis was on

happened to air during May sweeps week and were enormously popular. The normally high ratings went into hyperspace, and it was thought that Travis's participation was part of the reason for that.

Suddenly, Travis was the "it" boy of Hollywood. His role on *Sunset Cove* was greatly expanded, and he was signed to a two-year contract. In weeks, he was on magazine covers everywhere and had landed a huge contract with Mennen to be the face of its new line of men's skin care products. He also became the new spokesman for Sears Diehard batteries.

Travis was photographed with all the hot young starlets at every A-list premiere and was getting a reputation around town as a party-boy lady-killer. The only bad thing that had happened to Travis that year was losing the "Best Actor in a Daytime Drama" Emmy to Jack Benz, who lorded it over him mercilessly.

Whenever he saw *Sunset Cove*, Clay would joke to his friends that Travis had stolen his career, and truth be told, he felt a real jealousy about it. Then, when Clay got the small recurring role as Intern #2 on the show, it was a mixed blessing. He would much rather have been seen by Travis as a contract player, an equal and not just as an extra, but a job was a job, and Clay hoped it would lead to more.

Fuck it, he figured. He doubted that Travis Church would even remember having met him.

It wasn't until his fourth time on *Sunset Cove* that Clay even saw Travis. Travis's character, Cliff Coltrane, was in the hospital in a coma (hastily written so that Travis could film a small part in Steven Spielberg's new movie and not have heavy duty on the soap), and Clay, as Intern #2, had to wheel him around the set. Travis had come down from his dressing room clad only in a pair of black 2Xist briefs and an open-backed hospital gown. Clay had noticed the stolen glances the women—and Lefty—took to check him out.

Once on the gurney and flat on his back, Travis turned his gaze to Clay.

"Hey. I know you from somewhere, don't I?" he asked.

Not wanting to remind him of the circumstances of their first meeting, Clay simply said, "Nah, man. I don't think so."

"What's your name? I'm Travis," he said, a quizzical look on his face.

"Yeah, I know," Clay laughed. "Hi. I'm Clay. Clay Beasley." The two men then shook hands. Travis had a good, firm grip. And in spite of himself, Clay had begun at that moment to think of Travis in a different light. Though he knew it was out of the question, the least of the problems being the fact that he thought Travis was straight, Clay allowed his mind to wander. Just a bit.

"I *know* I know you . . . wait a minute! You were up for that *Friends* gig, too! That's it, right?"

"Oh, riiiight . . . yes, that's right. We did meet once before." Clay tried to play it cool, all the while hoping the scene would roll soon so this embarrassment could end.

"I knew it. Ha! I bet you wish you had gotten *that* part, huh?" Travis gloated.

A long moment passed, and neither man said anything. Clay, red-faced and embarrassed, just stood on his mark and waited for his cue to begin wheeling Travis around. Travis, seemingly unaware of the slam he had just given, settled back on the gurney and shut his eyes.

Clay resisted all impulses to roll the gurney right into a wall.

After that, the two men rarely spoke. It was as if some unspoken rule had been formed, and they both honored it.

Three months later, Clay had been walking down the hall fronting the dressing rooms of the contract players, looking for Cathy Grant's dressing room so he could slide a birthday card under her door. He happened to pass by Travis's open door.

"Hey, Clay!"

Clay stopped short. Taking a deep breath, he backed up and stood in the doorway to Travis's dressing room.

"Hey," Travis began, toweling off his long wet hair. He had been shooting a scene set in a hurricane that day, and was soaking wet. "I, uh, wanted to talk to you for a sec. Got a minute?"

Uncomfortable but not wanting to seem rude to one of the

show's stars, Clay said, "Sure. What's up?" He could not help noticing how Travis's wet shirt clung to his chiseled body like it was painted on.

"Uh, can you come in?" Travis asked, and as Clay passed into the room, Travis shut the door. Turning to Clay, he fidgeted a bit with his towel and tucked his hair behind his ears. "Listen, I really just want to apologize to you." Noticing Clay's startled look, he hurried on. "I know we kind of got off on the wrong foot, and I think it was in my mouth."

Clay started to speak, but Travis cut him off. "No, really. The truth is, I knew who you were. And I don't know why I was such a dick to you."

"You knew who I was?"

"Well, yeah," Travis said sheepishly. "I think about that *Friends* audition a lot, actually. I remember everything about it. I remember the office; I remember the yellow dress the casting director had on. I even remember what you were wearing. Jeans. Red shirt. Black leather jacket."

Clay was, for the first time in his life, at a loss for words.

"The thing is, that's when it all really started to happen for me. I always wondered what would have happened had you gotten that part. Would you be here where I am?" he shrugged. "And, to be truthful, I thought you had the better look for it. I was so fucking nervous because I thought you had it in the bag. Believe me, no one was more surprised than me when I found out I got it."

"Well, to be honest with you," Clay admitted, "I knew who you were, too. And yeah, I think about that audition a lot as well. But you were the bigger name, so of course they picked you. I understand the decision. But if you ever tell that to my friends, I will have to kill you." Clay sat down on the most comfortable leather sofa he had ever been on.

"Well, I'd like to think I was more than just a name!" Travis laughed.

"Yeah, well, you know what I meant." Clay grinned, embarrassed again. "I mean, come on. Here you are, this big star now and everything, and sure, I think about the what-ifs, but my time will come."

"Of course it will!" Travis sat down next to Clay. Not too close, but not too far away, either. "And look, I'll see what I can do here. Get you some scenes."

"Wow, that would be awesome."

Travis smiled his signature smile that showed his perfect, even teeth.

God, he's handsome, thought Clay.

"One more confession," Travis said haltingly as Clay looked at him square in the eye. "I actually saw you about nine months ago, around Christmastime, at the Pavilions grocery store on Santa Monica Blvd. You and some guy were in . . . a . . . um, heated discussion, near the frozen foods." Travis looked down at his wet shoes.

"Oh, God. I remember that! That was Matt. A . . . friend. We had, uh, ended a . . . friendship and had run into each other there. We didn't end as buddies, so whenever we run into each other it can get kinda nasty. That incident was certainly not one of my finer moments. I can't believe you remember that. Or that you remember me."

"A friend, huh?" Travis teased. "I thought he looked more like your *boy*friend."

Well. Now it was out there in the open, Clay thought. "Uh, well, yes. He was. Key word being *was*. He dumped me for someone else. It was a nasty split. We don't talk anymore."

Where was this heading? he wondered.

"Hey, it's cool. I didn't know if you were, uh, gay, or not, for sure until then. When I saw you two together. That was definitely a heated conversation, not the kind that just plain friends have. Doesn't matter to me. I mean, I don't care if you're gay or not."

"That's mighty big of you," Clay smiled.

"Hey, it takes all kinds, right? Besides, the guy's a fool, letting you go. Fuck him." Travis said, his voice getting a tone deeper.

"Never again, thank you. Been there. Done that."

Travis laughed out loud. He then stood up and walked to the bathroom and tossed the towel in. "Listen, I have these two tickets to the Lakers game tonight. My date canceled. She

has to work late. She *says*. I just think she hates basketball.
You wanna go with me?"

"Uh, I . . ." Clay started to say, confusion distinctly written
on his face.

"Not as my date, you goof! I just thought, you seem cool; I
think we'd have fun." Travis smiled the dazzling smile again.

"Sure. In a purely nongay way, of course," Clay joked.
"Yeah, that would be cool. Let's go." Clay tried to ignore the
fact that he hated basketball with a passion. "I don't really
follow that game much, so if I ask dumb questions, cut me
some slack."

"Deal. We'll cut out of here when we're done shooting
today. Head straight to the Staples Center."

"Great." Clay got up from the sofa and went to the door of
the dressing room. "See ya later."

Travis had great seats on the floor of the Staples Center,
just two rows up from Jack Nicholson and one aisle over
from Danny DeVito. Clay had a hard time following the
game. He kept sneaking glances at Travis, who was completely involved in the action on the court. Clay had to keep
reminding himself that this was not a date, that Travis wasn't
into him, but damn! He was so hot, and he had those lips and
that body that looked so good in the tight blue Gap henley
and snug Levi's.

More than once he had gotten hard simply because he was
sitting next to Travis, and he hoped it wasn't obvious.
Whatever Travis's story was, it didn't matter. Clay liked him
and wanted him as a friend.

After the game, in Travis's Porsche Boxster, heading down
Olympic Blvd., the two men fell silent. Madonna's latest was
blaring on the stereo, and Clay noticed Travis silently
mouthing the words, his hair sexily flying around in the wind,
just like Tom Cruise's in *Mission Impossible 2*.

What straight man knew the words to a new Madonna
song? Clay wondered. What exactly was Travis's story? And
why did he have to be so goddamn sexy? And why did I wear
these baggy jeans that do nothing for me, today of all days?

"Hey, I have an idea." Travis broke the silence.

"What's that?"

"I just had some new sofas delivered today up at the house. I want your opinion. I don't know about that stuff, and my decorator says they're 'me.'"

"Hmmm . . . well, I have to wonder what a sofa would say about you, so, sure. I hear you have an awesome house. I'd like to see it."

"Great!" Travis gunned the motor, and Clay was pressed back in his seat.

In twenty minutes they were driving up a winding road, high above Sunset Plaza. A high-end retail area renowned for its expensive shops and quirky restaurants, the famous Chin Chin Chinese restaurant being the anchor, Sunset Plaza was *the* hip and trendy place to live. Not to mention expensive.

The homes up in this part of town were nestled tightly into the rising hillsides, and all had spectacular views of the city from downtown L.A. to Century City, and all the way out to the ocean beyond Santa Monica. The houses were stacked up the winding hillside, one almost on top of the other, as the ridges cut back and forth.

After several sharp turns, the silver convertible pulled up to an intricately designed wrought-iron gate. The beautiful and graceful gate was nestled into a long hedge of hot-pink bougainvillea bushes that had, over the years, overgrown and hidden the high stucco wall that surrounded the house and property. Travis pushed a button on his visor, and the gate silently slid open, allowing them access to the driveway. It was a very short drive to the house.

The good-sized residence was in a style now called "mid-century," which used to be called "fifties modern," which, of course, was another term for "ugly, with small windows."

Travis's architect had transformed this particular dwelling into a showplace. The uplighting along the inside hedgerow lit the house in a soft yellow glow. The clean lines and newly re-sized windows gave off an air of modern, sophisticated style. A flat-roofed slate gray porte cochere abutted the house, where a solid-glass door with chrome handles served as the entrance.

Parking the Porsche under the porte cochere, Travis hopped

out and motioned Clay to follow. After punching a few numbers on a barely visible keypad, Travis pushed open the glass front door with a slight whoosh, and the men entered the house.

Clay was taken aback. It was like a picture from *Architectural Digest*. The bamboo floors were polished to a high shine. The flokati rugs on top of them were large and spotless. The furniture was tasteful, expensive, and beautiful. Two camel-colored leather tuxedo-style sofas faced each other across a huge cocktail table and fronted a flat-manteled fireplace that was covered with a thick glass screen. A stainless steel wall rose from the top of the mantel to the pitched ceiling fifteen feet above. On either side of the centered fireplace were huge plate-glass sliding doors, through which the captivating lights of L.A. could be seen clearly. A beautiful and sleek ivory leather-tufted van der Rohe day bed was positioned in front of the glass on one side, accompanied by a large Fortuny floor lamp. The other side was left open and free. Large modern abstract paintings in the style of Jackson Pollock were framed with minimal fuss and hung, perfectly placed, on the walls.

"Jesus," breathed Clay. "It's beautiful." He walked into the living room, stepping neatly around the large square glass-and-stone cocktail table. "Who lives like this?"

"I guess I do. All courtesy of Sears Diehard. The ads I do for them paid for it." Travis shrugged. "Those are the new sofas. What do you think?"

"They're amazing," Clay whistled, sitting on one and luxuriating in its soft, supple leather. "Really, Travis, just gorgeous."

"Wait, check this out!" Travis walked over to a panel of switches on the far wall and pressed a couple. As he did, lights came on outside, lighting up a pool and jacuzzi located just a few yards down the hillside from the balcony outside the living room. He pressed a few more switches, and the recessed halogen lights in the living room dimmed, making the outside view even more clear and striking.

"Can I go outside?" Clay asked, leaving the sofas behind to go stare out the windows.

Travis walked over to one of the huge sliding glass doors and easily pulled it open. "Sure. Come on," he said as he stepped outside.

Clay followed and stood at the edge of the balcony with Travis, hands on the railing, staring at the city below them.

"Wow," Clay said, open-jawed.

Travis pointed to the front of the house and then up the hillside. "Do you see that house right there? The one with the lit-up balcony?"

Clay looked in the direction Travis was pointing, and locked in on another mid-century house that was built into the craggy hillside, one ridge above them.

"That's where the lovely Drusilla Gordon lives," Travis smirked.

"The network lady? She's your neighbor?" Clay asked, squinting up at the house.

"Well, yeah." Travis turned back to stare out over his view of L.A. "But, I never really see her. I've never even been invited up there."

Clay returned his attention to Travis's view as well.

"You must never get tired of this, huh?" Clay marveled.

"Not really," Travis acquiesced. "But, when I do, I use that," he said, pointing to a very expensive telescope standing off to the side. "It always perks things up a tad," he laughed.

"Skank! You're a peeping Tom?" Clay asked, surprised but amused. "I'm learning so much about the famous Travis Church today. I think my head may actually explode if I learn anything else."

Travis moved closer to Clay. "I don't 'peep.' But if something interesting should cross my line of vision, well, who am I to deny looking?"

Clay looked back out over the property. In the dim light of night, the water was reflecting up from the pool and covering them both in crazy fluid light patterns.

"And," Travis continued, barely audible, "at the risk of having your head explode, there is something else I want to tell you."

Clay turned to face Travis just as Travis raised a hand, placed it gently behind his neck, and pulled him close. "I've

wanted to do this since the first time I saw you at that audition."
Travis pressed his beautiful lips against Clay's. Tentatively at
first, then, as Clay responded, with more passion.

Clay's mind was reeling. He tasted Travis and liked it. No,
loved it. His hands found their way to Travis's back, and he
held on tight. Their bodies pressed together, and Clay could
feel Travis's hard-on rubbing against his own.

Travis broke away from Clay's lips and placed his hands on
either side of Clay's face. "Oh, God. I'm sorry. Not very smooth,
am I?"

"Works for me," Clay sighed. He leaned his forehead against
Travis's, and gently rubbed his back.

"I kept staring at you during the game. I couldn't even tell
you the final score. You're so handsome. I love your body,
your hair, your face," Travis confessed, his voice low and
soft.

"You were staring at me?" Clay asked, astonished. "I kept
sneaking looks at you! I was hard the whole time. I can't believe you didn't notice."

"I noticed." Travis smiled. "I just can't believe you didn't
notice I was, *too.*"

Clay started to laugh.

"What? What's so funny?"

"This. You. I've had a crush on you since, like, forever.
What's with all the 'my date's a girl, but she hates basketball'
bullshit?"

Travis blushed. "I didn't know what kind of man you were.
I kinda keep a low profile about this sort of thing, you know?
I have a career to consider: the soap, the contracts with
Mennen and Sears . . . I haven't been with that many guys,
and I just . . . I . . . it's hard for me." Travis struggled, trying
to explain.

"Yeah, I know. I can feel how hard," Clay replied as he
ground his hips into Travis's.

"Mmmm . . . I like that . . . I just needed to be . . . sure."
Travis looked deep into Clay's brown eyes, and they began to
kiss again.

Travis broke away from Clay again and pulled him back
into the living room, leaving the door open. He then silently,

slowly, deliberately pulled Clay's shirt off him. With a look of wonder, he placed his hands on Clay's bare, tanned pecs. He leisurely rubbed them, cupped them, and then let his fingers run down to Clay's abs, the fingers bouncing slightly as they found each depression created by the finely formed muscles. Travis's eyes greedily took everything in.

Clay moaned slightly and watched as Travis's fingers dropped down lower to find and grasp, through the loose denim, his hardness. Clay leaned his head back from the pleasurable sensations he was feeling. He then felt the button of his jeans pop open and the zipper being pulled down, all while Travis began kissing his neck.

"Oh, man . . ." Clay groaned

"Mmmmm . . . I know . . . so good . . ." Travis responded in between kisses.

Clay was now cupped in Travis's hands, which began to pull, tug, and stroke his shaft and head.

Clay reached his hands up and, making Travis stop for just a second, whipped his shirt off as well. Travis's hands went right back to their kneading. Clay let his hands roam free over Travis's magnificent chest and stomach, then dropped them to his crotch, and after a few tugs and pulls, he had Travis's jeans down around his knees.

Travis had not been wearing underwear, a fact that, for some odd reason, excited Clay even more. Travis also had the hottest Speedo tan line he had ever seen. Clay stared in lustful amazement at the striking contrast between the tanned skin of his body and the luminescent white of his pelvic area.

As an added bonus, on his right side Travis had a small tattoo of a lion, positioned in the joint where his thickly corded upper thigh met his torso. Clay had never seen anything so sexy in his life.

Well, except for the jutting erection Travis was sporting.

Soon they were rubbing their hard cocks together, and their hands began other explorations. Clay lowered his body position and began to lick Travis's chest, taking in his scent and feeling light-headed from the power of the act, as Travis murmured encouragement.

He went down to his knees to continue his tongue quest,

making a point of licking the lion thoroughly, and soon was going down on the soap star with an expertise that stunned Travis. The sensations he felt from Clay's tongue on his penis were like nothing he had ever felt before.

Most of the times Travis had had sex with other men had been rushed, drunken or drug-induced ruts that, while eagerly anticipated, had brought him no real satisfaction. This was a whole new ball game, and he eagerly wanted to step up to the plate.

Soon the two men were on the cool wood floor, carrying their explorations further. Travis quivered as he felt parts of his body being touched that he did not know he had, and he readily duplicated the movements back to Clay. Moans and groans were all that could be heard from them as each found the areas that caused his partner pleasure. Clothes were completely shed, and Clay eventually found himself facedown on the floor, with Travis kissing and licking his broad back. He slid his muscular arms under and around Clay and held on to his pecs, gently playing with his nipples. Clay spread his legs wider to allow Travis room to slide up between them and tease him with controlled, rubbing thrusts against his ass. This created a hunger in Clay that would not be denied.

"Son, you keep that up and you're going to have to fuck me," he gasped, pushing up his ass to match the motions of Travis.

"Oh, please . . . I want to . . . so bad . . ." Travis uttered between kisses.

"Do you have anything?" Clay asked, knowing that he had to feel this beautiful, sexy man inside him.

"Huh?" Travis looked up, confused. "Oh, rubbers! Yeah . . . hold on." He rolled off Clay and ran like a man possessed to another room, his large erection slapping in time against his lower abdomen like an erotic metronome. He came back with a box of Trojans and a bottle of Wet lube in his hands.

Within minutes, Travis had resumed his former position and was soon sliding in and out of Clay. Clay pushed back with each approaching thrust, wanting to take Travis in as deeply as he could. "Oh, God," Clay cried out. "You feel so good!"

Travis, feeling sensations he had only dreamed about, continued to pump, sliding his hands up and down Clay's back.

Clay pulled himself forward enough to let Travis slip out, and flipped over to his back. Heaving his meaty legs up over Travis's shoulders, he reached down, grabbed Travis's cock, guided it back in, and began his own stroking. Travis began his thrusting again, but now that he was face to face with Clay and could see the elation Clay was feeling, he slowed down and took his time, giving long, unhurried, deep thrusts that eventually caused Clay to arch back and groan noisily.

"Oh, God, Clay . . ." Travis sighed, then swallowed in air sharply. "I'm gonna come!" He quickly pulled himself out, whisked the condom off, and while crying out in ecstasy, let loose a thick spray that covered Clay's chest.

Clay followed suit soon after.

Breathing deeply, the two men stayed locked in their positions. Clay was on his back on the floor, smiling contentedly, with Travis mounted over him, staring at him in awe. Travis then leaned forward, letting his weight rest completely on Clay, compressing their mixed seed, and kissed him repeatedly.

"Hey," Clay interrupted. "When do I get to see the rest of the house?"

That night began their affair.

Clay would go up to Travis's house at least four or five times a week. Travis rarely came to Clay's condo, but that didn't really bother Clay, since Travis's house was so much nicer. They would lounge in the pool on the weekends, Jacuzzi in the evenings, and have sex every chance they got. Dinners out were a very rare occurrence, and always to restaurants that weren't labeled gay.

Mostly they just stayed in, watching DVDs on the huge Sony flat-screen TV in Travis's media room, snuggled up next to each other on the long, comfortable sectional. This inevitably led to hot sex on the media room floor, sofa, and side chairs.

Twice, so far, they had taken road trips.

One was a long weekend at the St. Regis resort in Laguna

Beach, where Travis had booked two side-by-side rooms. They only slept in his.

They spent the entire weekend making love, reading, eating incredibly fattening foods, and lounging by the pool. They caused quite the scene poolside just by being two gorgeous men, their sensually muscled bodies oiled up, tanning in their small Speedos.

A waiter, cruising them heavily, actually fell into the pool carrying a full lunch tray when he stared, drooling, at them so intently that he lost his footing on the slippery tile. Later, in Travis's room, they laughed at the memory so hard, they cried.

Each morning, Clay would dash back into his room and muss up the bed so the maid wouldn't know he hadn't slept there.

The other trip had been to Las Vegas, where they stayed at the Venetian Hotel. Travis had again booked two adjoining rooms. Walking through the hotel to get to their rooms, Clay had stared in fascination at the intricate fresco paintings and incredible marble work of the place.

They shopped in the mall over the canals, laughed at the tourists who constantly asked Travis for his autograph, took in the Siegfried and Roy show at the Mirage, and gambled. Clay became entranced with roulette, and won a bit at first. But he quickly fell prey to the gambling curse of not knowing when to quit, and he ended up losing over three hundred dollars by the time the weekend was over.

Each night was a marathon of sexual acts that left both men drained and sated. They had begun to truly know each other during this trip, and their lovemaking began to have the added layers of complete trust, devotion, and caring.

And again, each morning, Clay scrambled to mess up the bedding of his room before the maid got there.

Travis won eight thousand dollars at the craps table the last night they were there, and spent the entire amount on a stainless steel Rolex Submariner II watch, which he surprised Clay with, in bed.

But, to Clay, his best memory of the Vegas trip wasn't getting the watch, or the shows, or the meals, or even the mind-blowing sex. It was spending the four-hour drive, each way, alone in the Boxster with Travis.

Isolated in that German cocoon, they were totally at ease, laughing, singing along with the radio, and telling stupid jokes. Clay longed to go back to Vegas, just to have the long drive time with Travis.

Travis still squired women to the premieres and select parties; he just did it less and less as his relationship with Clay developed. He couldn't stand to be away from Clay, but knew he had to go through the motions of pretending to be straight for his career's sake.

Sex between them was consistently outstanding and actually increased in intensity as they went along.

They couldn't get enough of each other, and upon their return to L.A. from Vegas, their relationship had imperceptibly changed. An unspoken bond had grown between them, and they began to understand that they might one day think of themselves as a "we," not a "you" and "I."

Their comfort level with each other sexually had grown so great that they just knew they were a perfect fit. Each enjoyed the pleasures the other gave, and in turn loved to be the one giving pleasure. It didn't matter to either of them who was on bottom or top, just as long as they could share it together.

Although Clay did think it strange that Travis insisted on always using condoms. He longed to be inside his lover naturally and free, and wanted the same back. He felt that since they were both HIV negative (they both, it turned out, got tested every six months) and monogamous, it was all right to dispense with condoms. But Travis insisted, and it wasn't a point that Clay was going to argue. In fact, they rarely argued. They just got along so well that the need to fight had never arisen.

Every once in a while, Clay couldn't reach Travis at night when he was supposed to be home, but Clay didn't make much of it. Travis was entitled to do things without him, to go places with his straight friends, so Clay didn't bring it up. And while Clay did feel slightly constrained by Travis's paranoia about someone finding out he was gay, he chose to overlook it and concentrate on his affection for the man.

Once or twice, each of them had, in the throes of passion, cried out "I love you!" but it was never commented on again. At *Sunset Cove,* they acted friendly to each other, but not overly friendly.

No one at the show suspected a thing.

7

The morning after Jack Benz's untimely death Clay woke up at precisely seven o'clock. He groggily got out of bed and padded to the bathroom. Squinting into the bathroom mirror, he grimaced at the bed-head he was sporting. It looked like he had been electrocuted at some point during the night. He unsuccessfully attempted to smooth it down.

It was going to be a hat day.

After brushing his teeth, he pulled on a tight black Jocks wife-beater tank top and some Old Navy cargo shorts. He tugged on his new Nike Air Presto slip-on sneakers, grabbed his keys, and dashed out the door. Hopping into his Jeep, he took off for the gym a few blocks down Santa Monica Blvd.

Gold's Gym was located in downtown Hollywood, inside a renovated old television studio complex. Gold's had every piece of equipment you could desire, and the crowd was mixed. Celebrities getting in shape for future projects, worked out next to soccer moms. Circuit boys and butch lesbians sweated together in the spin classes held in the upstairs cardio area, and the occasional porn star would ask to work in with you on the bench press.

Clay had been a member since he'd moved to town, even when he worked at the gym in Beverly Hills. He just liked the atmosphere there—not quite as high-testosteroneish as the Gold's at Venice Beach, and not as businessman-ish as the one downtown. As Goldilocks would say, this one was just right.

And, as an added bonus, a lot of his friends went there, and it was a great way to catch up with people without actually having to call them.

After parking in the larger of the two gym parking lots, Clay confidently walked into the gym and ran smack into Kurt Farrar, a guy he'd known for about a year.

Kurt was one of the gym regulars, who looked like he spent every waking moment either at the gym or drinking Myoplex. He was a trust fund baby, being one of *the* Farrars, as in Farrar Construction, so he didn't have to work. All his time was spent on his physical appearance.

And it showed.

Every gay man at the gym had a thing for Kurt, and it was often fun to watch him shoot down man after man who approached him. Clay, too, had always wanted to date Kurt, but had never mustered the courage to ask him out.

"Hey, Clay. I saw what happened at your show on the news last night. You must all be in shock," Kurt said, his sparkling blue eyes giving Clay an appreciative once-over.

"Yeah, it was pretty upsetting. We're shut down today."

"Well, I just wanted to say hi and let you know I was thinking about you." Kurt shifted his weight from one massive leg to the other. Wearing a cutoff white tank top and tight electric-blue lycra shorts, there was little of his flawless body hidden.

"Really? That's so sweet." Clay smiled.

"Listen, I have two tickets to this new play at the Mark Taper tomorrow night. Would you like to go? With me?"

"Tomorrow?" Clay asked, a little startled.

"Yeah, well, I know it's late notice. I've wanted to ask you out before but never had a good excuse. You seem like the kind of guy that you need to take somewhere really great. Then these tickets fell into my lap last night, and I was hoping I'd see you here today so I could ask you." He blushed.

Kurt Farrar actually blushed, like a teenager!

Clay thought for only a moment. "Thanks, Kurt, but I'm seeing someone now, and it's new, and I don't want to screw it up . . . well, you understand, right?"

Clay could see the disappointment cloud over Kurt's eyes.

"Hey, no problem. I should have asked you sooner, huh? Ah, well. I get ten points for finally trying, right?" He braved a tight smile.

"Absolutely." Clay smiled back. "Listen, I gotta get started here. We're okay, right? I'd hate for this to be a problem."

"No, Sure, it's fine. I'll talk to you before you leave." Kurt stood awkwardly for a second, then wheeled around and walked away, giving Clay a good look at the rock-hard ass he was giving up.

Well. I must really be into Travis if I turned down a date with Kurt Farrar, Clay thought, as he began his workout.

Clay hurried through his routine, which that day was chest. He liked chest day, and though he worked up a sweat, he breezed through it. After riding the LifeCycle upstairs for thirty minutes, he flopped down on the mats and did a series of ab exercises that a trainer he once dated had shown him.

Thoroughly soaked with sweat, Clay left the gym, and drove home. Halfway home, he realized that Kurt hadn't talked to him the rest of that morning.

Must not be too often that he gets turned down, Clay thought. For some reason, that made Clay smile.

Kurt Farrar, however, was not smiling. He had walked through his workout, his enthusiasm for the training gone. Clay's refusal, no matter how polite, had upset him deeply. It brought up memories of long-supressed tortures when he was a gangly teenager who was always picked last in the school-yard dodgeball games.

Truth be told, Kurt wasn't all that into the gym and working out anymore. It was something he had started many years ago because it was a solitary endeavor that brought him to the attention of a man he admired. A bonus was that the results of his hard labor had finally gotten him the notice he'd never gotten as a child and teenager. He did it now because it was his routine. He didn't know anything else.

Kurt was the younger of his mother's two children. With an older half-brother, from his mother's first marriage, who could do no wrong, Kurt always felt inferior.

Paradoxically, he idolized his half-brother, wanting to do

everything he did. He was a drag to his brother sometimes, as only little brothers can be, but they always stuck together, forming a close bond that had remained to this day. His brother had tried to work with him, with his schoolwork, but it never helped. Kurt, eventually becoming so frustrated that he couldn't make sense of what he was reading, would usually quit and go watch TV.

His dyslexia continued to go undetected.

School remained a struggle, and even when he tried his hardest, Kurt couldn't keep up with the other kids. He fell further and further behind his classmates. Taunts of "stupid cootie Kurt" still ran through his head even now, years later. He'd finally been held back in the seventh grade, much to his mother's and father's embarrassment.

They then decided to send Kurt to a "special" boarding school, where he was correctly diagnosed and his education adjusted accordingly. His father, a stern, extremely successful man, seemed to give up on his blood son while allowing Kurt's older brother free rein.

It was at the high school for troubled boys in Arizona that Kurt started to work out.

Missing terribly his brother and the easy Beverly Hills lifestyle he was accustomed to, he became known as "the rich kid" and fell under attack as a gangly outsider. Twice he had been in fights, provoked by other kids, after classes. He had fought back the best he could, but he still got his ass kicked.

He distanced himself from his schoolmates and sought personal pleasure in solitary activities. Reading comic books because the pictures explained what the mixed-up words couldn't. Seeing movies alone every chance he could. Taking long walks around the campus, plotting his secret revenge against his taunters.

One particularly dismal day, he found himself near the school gym, which was surprisingly empty. Entering, he wandered through the maze of old equipment and weights and stared at the old posters of past Mr. Universes and Mr. Americas tacked up on the walls. He sat down on a bench press and did a few sets. It felt good, so he tried out some of the other equipment. Staring at the posters of the built gods that hung on the walls, Kurt figured no one ever picked on *them*. He wanted to look just like they did. Then, no one would pick on him, either.

He quickly became addicted to the ritual of working out, and came under the tutelage of one of the football coaches, a kind twenty-four-year-old named Billy Jake Hanson. Soon, more and more time was being spent in the gym, and less and less on other school activities. As the size of Kurt's body grew, Billy Jake asked him to try out for the school's football team. He joined the team, but not out of any special loyalty to the school.

He had fallen in love with Coach Hanson.

Billy Jake Hanson was married to the school nurse and never showed more than a friendly interest in Kurt, but Kurt didn't care. He lived for his workout sessions and football practice with the coach.

At 185 muscular pounds, Billy Jake had a blond buzz cut and an infectious grin. Sometimes Kurt would catch sight of the coach walking across campus, and he would get an erection just from staring at Billy Jake's butt as it moved under the navy blue coach's shorts he always wore.

As Kurt's body developed, so did his interest in males. At first confused by his increasing desire for men, particularly Coach Hanson, he was slow to grasp the cachet his developing hot, hard body was bringing him. It took a few furtive attempts at adolescent seduction by older boys before Kurt realized that he wasn't "the only one," and that he was desired.

Being on the football team brought him into the heady world of the school jocks, and he suddenly became "cool" for the first time. He liked it, and he didn't want to mess that up by being labeled a "fag." So he rebuffed any vague overture, even though he desperately wanted to accept them.

He didn't have his first sexual experience until he was a senior in high school. And the person who finally got him wasn't a student.

It was Coach Hanson.

Their affair had started one afternoon after practice, when

the handsome, worked-out coach walked in on the hot young man jerking off in the shower by himself, after all the other kids had gone back to the dorm. Mortified, Kurt had tried to turn around and hide his raging hard-on in the open-stalled shower, but Billy Jake walked slowly toward him, staring at Kurt's hard ass, his pink tongue quickly licking his lips.

"That's an impressive piece you have there, Farrar. Don't wear it out," the coach said jokingly, but nonetheless taking in the younger man's thickly muscled back and solidly built legs. "Mine's bigger, though," he added with a touch of manly bravado.

Kurt, who had fantasized so often about the coach, thought he recognized the intention behind the words but was afraid he could be wrong. When he turned around, he saw the older man subtly rubbing his crotch with his hand.

Kurt gulped and made a decision. He turned all the way around and faced the coach. "I doubt it. Mine's bigger than all the other guys. I've looked," he said, looking the coach in the eyes.

"I'll bet you have." Billy Jake grinned. "I've been watching you, too, you know. You have no idea how beautiful you are. Your body, it's . . . it's . . ." The coach struggled to find the words as he gazed at Kurt's abs, the happy trail of dark blond hair snaking down to his pubic area, the hair matting thickly around his still rock-hard, swaying piece. ". . . Perfect. I have to admit, I think about you sometimes. . . ." He let the sentence hang.

Feeling a shift in power, Kurt realized that he controlled the situation. The man standing in front of him, lightly stroking his engorged dick through his polyester gym shorts, was faculty. Coach Hanson could lose his job over this. All Kurt had to do was yell out.

He didn't.

"What do you think about?" he asked instead, stroking himself again.

"You . . . doing that," whispered Billy Jake, transfixed at what he was watching. ". . . And more."

"So, show me what you're touching there, Coach."

Like a dog obeying a command, Billy Jake pulled his coach's shorts down, allowing his rigid cock to spring free. He looked haltingly at Kurt.

"Nah. I'm bigger than you. No doubt about that," Kurt said dismissively, turning around again, slightly spreading his legs to give the coach a clear look at his wet ass.

"I don't think so, but the only way to really tell is to put them side by side and compare," Billy Jake said, finally.

"So, do it."

The coach walked over to Kurt and held his cock up next to Kurt's. Kurt's was bigger, thicker, and prettier, but the mere sensation of touching dicks so turned on the coach that he reached over and roughly grabbed Kurt's erection.

Kurt gasped, and before he knew what was happening, the coach was on his knees, sucking him off.

"Oh, man, I wanted to do this for so long . . ." Billy Jake whimpered, between head bobs.

Things quickly progressed from there. They ended up on the floor of the shower, Billy Jake sitting on Kurt's cock, which was buried to the base up his ass. Panting silently, Billy Jake rode Kurt like a bronco. Kurt, not believing what was happening to him, and having already come once before, when Billy Jake was blowing him, felt his balls seize up and he knew he was going to climax a second time.

"Oh, Coach! I'm gonna shoot again . . ." he gasped, pressing his hips up and down.

Just hearing Kurt say those words caused Billy Jake to climax, and Kurt quickly followed.

They secretly met two to three times a week after that. Soon the two young men were proclaiming their love for each other, but Billy Jake, constricted by his Catholic faith—and wife—knew he had to break it off.

At semester's end, with senior Kurt about to graduate, they both sadly realized their secret romance had to come to an end. They decided to meet one last time and then say goodbye. It was the night before Kurt's graduation. After the ceremonies, he was going back to Los Angeles with his parents.

The final fuck was held in the same shower, late that special night. Just as a shouting Billy Jake was about to come, his plain young wife walked into the supposedly empty men's locker room looking for her husband.

She found him.

Impaled, naked and gasping, on the hard cock of the hottest young man she had ever seen.

The sight of her husband getting royally fucked wasn't what really surprised her. It was the realization that she wished it were her.

Her shrieks of shock brought the school security guard, who happened to be smoking a joint behind the men's locker room, quickly to the scene.

The fallout of the now known faculty-student affair was all-encompassing. Kurt wasn't allowed to participate in his graduation ceremonies, as the school moved quickly, attempting to cover up the incident. Billy Jake was let go, and Kurt had later heard that his wife divorced him, taking their small daughter with her back to South Dakota, where she was from. The school wanted to withhold Kurt's diploma, and it was only after a tense meeting with his father that the headmaster relented and let Kurt have his diploma.

Kurt never asked how much it had cost his father.

Upon his return to Los Angeles, Kurt came out in a big way, much to the chagrin of his parents. He went to UCLA for a few semesters and fucked his way through all the frat houses, local gyms, and gay bars of West Hollywood.

He eventually dropped out of college. His grades had been dismal due to his poor study habits and the fact that he rarely went to class. He was spending all his time on his workouts, and school just didn't fit into his schedule anymore.

He became a fixture on the circut party scene, thinking nothing of hopping a plane to Miami for the White Party, or jetting to Sydney, Australia, for the annual gay pride celebration there. His Easter weekend bash in Palm Springs, where he rented out an entire gay resort for friends and aquaintances, was a highly coveted invitation. The three-day bacchanal usually ended up with Kurt having too much sex with too many people and abusing too many drugs.

But now, strangely, the excitement of those early party days was wearing thin. Kurt hadn't even gone on the last Titan cruise to the Caribbean and had let his subscription to *Instinct* magazine lapse.

He realized what he really wanted was to have feelings like those he'd had for Billy Jake, again. It would be so great to be able to share his life and financial security with someone he was in love with. He had no intention of becoming some twink's sugar daddy; he wanted a man who had a life of his own, but he wanted to share what he had with *someone*.

Kurt knew that somewhere out there was the guy he was supposed to be with. He just hadn't found him yet. And in what used to be so very cool but now was becoming a sore issue, most guys were only interested in having sex with him.

It was a cruel tradeoff. He worked out to be desired, but had grown to hate that he was only desired because he worked out.

Lately, he had really limited his exposure to men to seeing them at the gym, and maybe, every once in a while when he couldn't control his sexual needs, he would pick up a guy at a bar or online and invite him to his penthouse apartment.

They were never asked back.

Now, also, most guys who made a pass at him were rebuked. They just weren't what he was looking for. They weren't Billy Jake.

There were a couple of men who had potential, though. He had his eye on a select few, Clay Beasley being the main choice.

He had been watching Clay for a while. He liked Clay's personality, and there was no denying that Clay was a beautiful man. In fact, when Kurt was home alone, masturbating, Clay was the usual star of his fantasies. In his mind, as he frantically stroked, he allowed Clay to do things to him that he'd allowed no one to do.

That he had finally worked up the nerve to ask Clay out, only to be told no, had hurt deeply. Kurt had never been turned down. Not once.

And the fact that he had jumped through hoops to get the tickets, badgering his mother for two weeks to scrape them up, only made the refusal sting more. She finally came through last night, after making a large donation to some charity, and Kurt was thrilled that he could ask Clay out to a classy affair.

With Clay's polite decline, Kurt again felt twelve years old and awkward.

His mood getting darker by the minute, he decided to pack it in and go home. He was getting his car keys from the key box at the front counter when he caught the eye of a solidly built Latino man he'd seen around the the gym the past couple of months. The man was poised at the front doors, leaving also, when he had caught sight of Kurt, which stopped him cold.

Kurt, recognizing the look of desire emanating from the guy, sighed. What the hell. If Clay Beasley didn't want his dick, this guy sure did. And Kurt would give it to him. Hard.

"Hey," Kurt said, approaching the other man. "I'm Kurt. What's your name?"

"Dante," said the man, flashing a smile with teeth so white, Kurt wondered if he'd had them bleached.

"Hey, Dante." Kurt looked him up and down. He was hot, definitely. "Let's go," he nodded his head toward outside and walked past the hot Latino man.

Dante happily followed him.

After showering and shaving, Clay blew out his hair, using his secret weapon, Frizz-Ease. He pulled on a clean white Calvin Klein wife-beater, a pair of tight, weathered Polo jeans, and his ancient hiking boots. Taking a headshot out of the desk and sliding it into his black leather portfolio, he left the condo again. He practically leaped into the Jeep, and drove to the Dr. Pepper audition.

The audition was held at an acting studio on La Cienega, not far from the UBC studios. He had been called in by this particular casting director several times before and had always scored at least a callback.

He signed in and picked up the sides, which were the script copy and description of the commercial, and then sat down waiting for his turn. He smiled at a few of the friendly faces he saw of people he knew from previous jobs or auditions.

The sides were weak. A handsome guy sees a hot girl at a crowded bar and tries to make eye contact with her, but can't because of the crowd. He tries to talk to her but is stymied and eventually gives up trying. He orders a Dr. Pepper. Suddenly, the entire bar becomes silent in awe, and the hot girl rushes up to meet him, Dr. Pepper in her hands as well. He had done a variation of this "guy meets hot girl in bar" scene many times before, but usually for a beer ad.

A harried-looking casting assistant came into the room and began to pair men and women up together. She looked at the sign-in sheet and paired up the next available man with the next available woman, not caring if the couple were well suited or not. Luckily, Clay got paired up with Maggie Dawson, an actress he had worked with before, so that was good.

Maggie was a spitfire from Dallas, Texas, a former cheerleader at SMU. She had long, flaming red hair with big, buttery chunks of blond highlights that were meticulously maintained. She wore it in loose curls that bounced slightly when she walked. She had a pretty face, a face that was equally expressive and slightly suggestive. Her clear blue eyes danced when she spoke, and she worked a lot. Today she was sexily dressed in a bright-yellow Emporio Armani sequined minidress that showed off her shapely, tanned legs.

When it was Clay and Maggie's turn to go in, they each grabbed their eight-by-tens and strolled calmly into the audition room.

It was over in eight minutes, Clay and Maggie being pros at this sort of thing. The scene worked as well as it could in an empty room, with two actors pretending there was a crowd of a hundred around them, while an overworked casting director stared dully at them while manning an antique video camera.

As Clay was grabbing his bag to leave, Maggie sidled up to him.

"I think that went well. We'll be back." She winked.

"I think so, too. You were great."

"Thanks. Say, too bad about Jack Benz. You're on that show, right?"

"Well, sorta. Recurring extra. Nothing glamorous, but it

pays the bills." Clay shrugged. "And yeah, it is sad. I saw it happen."

"No!" Maggie exclaimed. "That must have been rough. I'm sorry."

They walked toward the door, left the building, and went out into the bright sunshine.

"You know, I went out with Jack a couple of times. He was nice enough, but . . ." Maggie hesitated, fearing she was talking out of school.

Clay perked up. "You did? When?"

"Oh, God, about a year ago. Believe it or not, we have the same manager. It was a setup thing for an awards show. He needed a date; I needed exposure. We went out to industry things a few times after that, but I don't think he was interested in *me*," she said dismissively as she whipped a pair of oversize red Gucci sunglasses out of her Kate Spade bag and slid them on.

"Really? I find it hard to believe a man wouldn't be interested in you," Clay said honestly.

"Well, not if he's *gay*, sweetie."

"What? You think Jack is . . . was gay?" Clay was shocked. He had never gotten that vibe from Jack. And at one time, he had looked. Hard.

"Honey, trust me, if after the second date a man hasn't made a play for these," she said, jutting out her cosmetically enhanced breasts, "then he ain't straight."

Clay laughed out loud.

"So that gave it away. That and the fact that he got a very intimate cell call from some guy once when we were at some party, and while he tried to speak low, I could tell he was talking to his boyfriend, or partner or lover or whatever the PC term is these days. Louie, or Lannie or Larry—something like that."

Clay thought for a minute. "Lefty?"

"Yes! That was it. What kind of name is that, anyway? On second thought, I don't want to know! See ya at the callbacks, sweetie," Maggie said, leaning forward and giving Clay an air kiss on the cheek. She hopped into her bright-red Mercedes C230 and was soon gone, lost in the lunchtime traffic.

Clay stood on the street corner digesting this bit of news. Jack and Lefty? Wow. He would never have put those two together, but you never knew. Why hadn't Lefty said anything? He must feel really bad with his rig causing the death of his boyfriend. Was this information relevant? Clay made a mental note to discuss what he'd learned with Travis that night.

"Hey, babe," Travis said, smiling as he pulled open the front door of his house for Clay. He was dressed in ratty Nike shorts, an old white V-neck T-shirt that was wet with sweat, running shoes and had pulled his hair back into a ponytail. Travis couldn't have looked sexier if he'd tried, Clay thought.

Once he was inside, they kissed warmly and walked through the stunning house to the kitchen. Travis held Clay's hand.

The kitchen was a modern mix of hard metal, cold granite, and soft leather upholstery. All the appliances were stainless steel and top of the line. Vast black granite counters rested beneath every possible gourmet kitchen accoutrement, and those gadgets not visible were cleverly stored in pullout cabinets. Recessed halogen lighting flooded the area with bright light. Chrome-framed counter stools that were topped off by rich beige ultrasuede seats lined up at the long front counter that broke the room into two areas: cooking and eating. A chrome-and-glass table designed by Makio Hasuike, complete with six ivory leather Mies van der Rohe Brno chairs, made up the dining area.

Travis punched at the light switch, brightening the room. "I just got back from my run," he explained as he pulled the elastic out of his hair, shaking the dark locks free.

"What are we doing for dinner tonight?" Clay asked, seating himself on one of the surprisingly comfortable counter stools.

"I thought we'd order in and just hang out. I haven't seen you hardly at all this week. Is Chinese okay?" Travis walked to the phone and picked it up.

"Fine with me. Only, you actually have to eat it, too. No Zone food tonight."

"You got it. I was thinking we'd order from Rice on La Cienega. They deliver up here." Travis pulled out a menu from a drawer by the phone and slid it across the counter to Clay.

"Perfect. But I know what I want. Lemon chicken with steamed rice. That's all. Um, maybe some wontons, too."

Travis called the restaurant and ordered the food. After hanging up, he walked over to Clay, came up behind him, and put his arms around him.

"It'll be here in thirty minutes. God, it's good to see you. What a bad few days, huh?" he said, squeezing Clay tightly.

Clay swiveled in the stool and faced Travis, wrapping his arms around him. "Yeah. Nuts. Eeeeww! You're all wet and smelly!" He pretended to be offended.

"Aw, just deal with it, crybaby. What did you do today?" breathed Travis softly, nuzzling his head against Clay's shoulder.

"I had an audition this morning and then took a bike ride at the beach. Was great. Cleared my head. How'd the shoot and interview go?"

"Fine. Lots of the same old questions. What's it like to be me? Who am I dating? Am I in love? The usual."

"What did you say?" Clay asked, wanting to know, himself.

"I said . . ." Travis paused dramatically. ". . . that I was fucking the hottest guy in Hollywood, that he had an amazing ass, the perfect dick, and I couldn't wait to see him tonight so I could fuck him some more!" He laughed out loud as he reached down and grabbed Clay's ass.

"Nice," Clay said, slightly hurt. "I guess I kinda hoped I was a little more than that to you."

"Oh, baby, you are! I was just kidding!" Travis rushed to smooth it over. "I told them my stock answers. That I was very lucky and that I just hadn't met the right person yet. That's what they really want to hear, anyway. Makes everyone think they have a chance with me."

"I see."

"Jack's funeral is going to be Sunday. You gonna go?" Travis changed the subject and nestled back against Clay.

"I don't know. I guess so. One thing's for sure: Lefty will be there," Clay murmured.

"Lefty? I don't think so. He killed the guy!"

"He didn't. His rig did. Big difference," Clay admonished.

"Whatever. Same thing," Travis blithely said as he tucked his damp hair behind his ears.

"Say, what was your take on Jack?" Clay asked seriously.

"My take? What do you mean?"

"Well, what kind of guy did you think he was? Nice? Mean? What?"

"Hmmm. He was a fucking ham, that's for sure, and he didn't like it when they pumped up my part." Travis broke away from Clay and went to the Sub Zero refrigerator. Pulling out a sport bottle of water, he refocused on Clay. "And he certainly didn't like all the press I've gotten this year. Actually, he made some really snide comments, now that I think about it. I think he was jealous of the endorsement stuff, too. He would always rub his Emmy win in my face. I think he was a complete asshole. A rude, fucking asshole that this world is better off without." Travis got a hard gleam in his eyes as he spoke about Jack.

"Wow. I didn't realize you disliked him so much," Clay said.

"Disliked him? I fuckin' hated his guts! It was all I could do to be civil with him . . . on set. I gotta tell ya, if anyone had to bite it, I'm actually glad it was him. Not a nice man," Travis said forcefully.

"I've never seen this side of you before," Clay said, staring in mild disbelief at Travis.

"Clay, I'm not a box. I don't have *sides*. I'm just a guy who likes some people, like you, and hates others. Like Jack Benz. Not a big deal," Travis said dismissively.

"Well, it *is* a big deal when that guy you hate ends up dead as the result of murder! You better not let the police know how you feel, or it'll be the interrogation room for you." Clay got up and went over to Travis and playfully boxed at him. "You'll end up in prison, and making all kinds of new friends."

"That'll be the day," Travis said coldly, pushing Clay away.

Feeling that the atmosphere had changed, and not quite sure why, Clay retreated a bit. "I ran into a friend of mine today, Maggie Dawson, and she says she went out with Jack a few times," he finally offered.

"So?" Travis asked in a petty tone.

"Well, she says Jack was gay. And get this: his boyfriend? Lefty!"

"Huh? What's all this about, anyway? Who gives a fuck what Jack Benz did? Or who? I sure don't, and I'm sick of talking about him!" Travis sputtered, actually getting testy.

"Hey, hey. Relax. I'm just telling you what Maggie said." Clay tried to calm him down.

"Well, don't! I don't give a shit what some fake-titted actress says." He turned his back to Clay and placed both his hands on the dark-granite counter. He clenched and unclenched his fists.

"Okay, okay," Clay patronized.

"You know what? I'm getting a really bad headache. Maybe we should do this another night," Travis said, still turned away from Clay.

Clay was unprepared for that. Confused as to what had just happened, he stood still for a moment. When Travis said nothing else, Clay grabbed his keys from the table.

"Fine. I'll see you tomorrow on set. I hope you feel better." He left the kitchen and was walking to the door when Travis called out.

"Hey! Wait up."

Clay stopped in his tracks and faced Travis. "Yeah?"

"Look. I'm sorry. I don't know what got into me. It was a long day, and I'm taking it out on you. I'm sorry," Travis said sincerely, his eyes beginning to well up with tears. He went to Clay, put his arms around his waist, and pulled him close. "Face it. Your boyfriend's an ass," he sniffed.

"Is that what you are? My boyfriend?" Clay asked directly as he rubbed Travis's back.

Travis was silent for a moment. "Yeah, I guess I am. You know that I'm in love with you. I'm just not very good at saying that stuff." He could not hold back any longer, and great sobs racked his body.

"Hey, hey. What's this all about? Are you okay? Travis?" Clay asked, concerned. He reached up and stroked his lover's head in a gently soothing fashion.

Travis struggled to regain his composure. "I'm just so glad that you're in my life. I don't know what I'd do if I didn't have you to hang on to right now. Please don't ever leave me. I love you, and I need to tell you that more often. I'm so sorry. . . ."

The raw emotion of the moment was getting to Clay as well, and he could feel his eyes watering up. "Travis, listen to me."

Travis pulled his head away from Clay's shoulder and gazed at him with trusting eyes. If Clay had been even slightly ambivalent about his feelings toward Travis before, he now knew that he was deeply, hopelessly in love with him.

"I love you, Trav," Clay said. "I don't think I realized how much until this very moment. I'm not going to leave you." He hugged Travis hard and kissed him deeply. He wanted to crawl inside Travis and curl up there forever.

Travis reluctantly broke free of the kiss. "How much time you think we have before the food gets here?"

Clay gave a glance to his new Rolex. "Umm . . . about twenty minutes. Why?"

"Mmmm. Just enough time," Travis said as he resumed kissing Clay and unbuckling his belt buckle. He had never wanted to have Clay inside him as much as he did now.

Clay closed his eyes and let his lover go to work. Travis worked his hands inside Clay's pants and then inside his snug underwear, taking a firm hold of his cock. As he kissed Clay, Travis gently pumped and squeezed his hand, getting the desired reaction from Clay. He slid his other hand into Clay's pants and, after digging down, cupped Clay's balls.

"Do you like it when I do this?" he whispered between kisses on Clay's neck.

"Oh, yeah," Clay uttered.

"Me, too," Travis said, deftly pulling Clay's piece out of his pants and into the cool air of the kitchen.

Clay couldn't ignore his own yearning anymore, and he slid his hands into Travis's shorts and freed his hard-on. They rubbed cocks together for a minute.

"Get on the floor," Travis ordered, pushing Clay down. Clay eagerly obeyed and, after pulling his shoes and pants off, settled down on the chilly tile floor, a slight shiver going up his spine. Despite the coolness, he pulled off his shirt and threw it aside. Now, completely naked, he looked up at Travis, wanting him to get down on the floor with him.

"Oh, man, you look so damn good right now," Travis said. He slid his damp shorts all the way off and peeled off his T-shirt, throwing it next to Clay's rumpled pile of clothes.

Clay was staring intently up at the man he loved. Travis's position over him gave Clay a direct view of his thickly muscled legs, protruding cock, and shaved balls. His ass, pale white where his Speedo swimsuit covered it, was like two pasty orbs hovering above him.

Travis placed one leg on either side of Clay and lowered himself onto his lover's chest. He slid back so that Clay's dick was pressing up against his ass. He reached back and rubbed it against his skin. Clay stretched up and gently played with Travis's nipples, getting them hard and causing Travis to squirm and moan.

Travis had a lock on Clay's cock and was slapping it against his ass. Sighing heavily, he suddenly stood up and ran into the other room, leaving Clay on the floor.

"Hey!" Clay called out, confused.

"Hang on! I'm coming back!" Travis yelled, laughing.

He returned quickly with his small gym bag, and after a few seconds of frantic tearing, pulling, sliding and squirting, he repositioned himself over Clay's now sheathed and lubed cock and pushed back on it, taking Clay inside him fully. Clay pushed up in a slow rhythm that allowed Travis to rise and lower on him using his thigh muscles to support his weight.

Both men groaned, and cried out professions of love and lust while Travis rode Clay. Clay knew Travis was close to climax, and he reluctantly stopped his upward thrusting.

"Don't come, yet, baby," he breathed. "It's my turn."

Travis flopped over his partner and they kissed for five full minutes, Clay still inside him. Travis then raised himself a bit and let Clay slip out. Clay lifted his big legs up and spread them wide for his lover.

"Now. In me, now," he begged. Travis quickly complied. They made love for over three hours, each taking turns, each giving, each taking. They cried, laughed, and shouted out in pleasure together. It was the night that they finally became one, and neither of them would ever forget the depth of feeling he felt for the other during those magical hours when the world went away and they were the only two souls alive.

The delivery man from Rice rang the gate buzzer six times before cursing, giving up, and going back down the hill to the restaurant.

8

Clay was in a great mood as he walked up to the artists' entrance of UBC studios the following day. He heard the unmistakable whine of Travis's Boxster roaring in behind him. Turning to look, he saw Travis pull into his new parking space, closer to the artists' entry. Someone had painted over *Jack Benz* and replaced it with *Travis Church*.

Clay had left Travis's house at about five that morning, gone to the gym, and done an hour of weights, a half hour of cardio, and twenty minutes of abs. He had then gone home, showered, shaved, thrown on a pair of baggy cargo pants and a red long-sleeved T-shirt, and driven to the studio. He was slightly tired from the night before, since he and Travis had stayed up making out and talking until falling asleep together around two in the morning. But it was a good kind of tired.

Cissi appeared from nowhere and poked Clay in the ribs. "Stop gazing at hottie-boy over there. I don't think you're his type."

"Uh, I know. Damn!" Clay said, taken aback but playing along.

"Please. Leave us straight girls someone, would you?" Cissi sighed, adjusting the shoulder strap of the oversized brown leather satchel she carried everywhere, while trying not to spill her Starbucks Mocha Valencia all over her loose white Mexican peasant dress.

"So, how are you today? You okay?" Clay asked, hurriedly changing the subject.

"Yeah, I'm all right. Hey, did you happen to talk to Josh either last night or today?" she asked, a hint of annoyance in her expression.

"No. Why? Should I have?"

"No, it's just I needed to get in touch with him, and I can't seem to find him. Oh, well. His loss."

With a hefty pull, Cissi opened the entrance door and walked through. Clay, closely behind, stole one last look at his lover. Travis, getting out of his car, spotted Clay, locked eyes with him and gave a small wave and a warm tight smile.

Clay glowed with pride just from his boyfriend's glance. Funny how a simple thing like that can make you deliriously happy, he noticed. He threw Travis back a broad grin and passed through the door.

Cissi and Clay went directly to her office so they could catch up with each other. It was standard procedure with them now. Cissi's first chore of the day was to make Sylvia's coffee, a special blend that Sylvia had found on the Internet. It was made in Brazil and shipped over. To Cissi, it tasted like cow manure—she herself preferred the Starbucks brand—but by now it was simply the routine to make it. After that was done, she and Clay could sit down for a few minutes and catch up on the latest dirt that was flying around the studio.

"So tell me," Clay began after Cissi sat down, "how are they going to explain Stone?"

"You won't believe this. He's had a brain aneurism! They'll cut to Pageant calling 911, then Stone will be in the hospital after surgery with bandages wrapped all around his head so you can't see his face. We'll just use a body double for those. It's still up in the air as to whether he'll live or not. The network wants to judge the public reaction before deciding that. Joan, of course, is having a fit! She wants to recast, and recast *now*. Isn't that a little heartless, don't you think?" Without waiting for a reply, Cissi reached into her desk drawer and brought out a peanut butter cup. "And you know what all this means, don't you?" she asked, a curious smile on her lips.

"No, what?"

"Hospital scenes! Lots of them! And maybe a surprise if we don't hear from Joshie soon," she triumphed.

Clay's first reaction was one of elation. He wanted to retile the kitchen counters of his condo, and now maybe the extra days would pay for it. But almost immediately, he felt a tad uncomfortable feeling good about personally profiting from a situation that was so tragic. "Um, yeah, that's really cool," he finally allowed.

"Hey! This is good news! I think you'll find that this will all play to your advantage," Cissi continued, noticing his less than enthusiastic reaction.

"No, that's great. I'm just a little upset about the circumstances, that's all." Clay gazed down at the carpeting. He noticed that a tiny crumpled foil wrapper from one of the many peanut butter cups Cissi ate had fallen under her desk.

"I understand. It's upsetting for everyone, but at least some good will come out of it for you," Cissi said finally. She reached into the drawer for a second cup.

"Look, thanks. I'm sorry. It is great news." Clay forced a smile.

The office door flew open, and Sylvia Sinclair made her impressive entrance. Dressed head to toe in black Prada, she wore a black pashmina loosely draped around her arms, shawl-style. She had pulled her hair back into a severely tight bun and had used minimal makeup. A single fragrant gardenia was pinned to the slight lapel of her power dress.

"Good morning, Cissi. Why, hello, Clay. Such a sad day, isn't it?" she asked imperiously.

"Hello, Sylvia," Cissi and Clay said at the same time.

"Clay, you simply must forgive us, but we have so much work to do today! Cissi, I need the revised scripts for next week now, and I'll need to talk to Joan as soon as she gets in. Is Josh in yet? Oh, and be a peach and fetch me a cup of my coffee? I so desperately need it today!" Sylvia waltzed through Cissi's small office and into her own, slamming the door behind her.

"I suppose I'll leave you to the duchess," Clay said sympathetically as he rose to leave.

"Ugh." Cissi grimaced, knowing that she was about to have "a day."

Clay smiled at his friend brightly, waved good-bye, and went to wardrobe to get dressed for his scenes that day.

Two stories up, in Dru Gordon's immaculate corner office, Joan Thomas, wearing her signature brown, was fuming.

"What do you mean I can't begin casting for Jack's replacement?! This is sweeps time, and I need Stone and Pageant's story line to propel us into the next story arc!" she seethed, pacing about the room.

"Joan, I understand—" Dru started to say before Joan cut her off.

"No, you don't understand! If I don't have a Stone, then I have nothing for the next four months! I need Stone! If it can't be Jack, then we need to recast! As soon as possible!" Joan was literally shaking in her fury.

"Joan. Calm down! The network simply will not move forward with a replacement at this time. It would be a slap in the face to our fans, not to mention to Jack Benz's memory. Don't you understand that a beloved actor has died?" Dru was tired of trying to reason with this impossible woman. Ever since she had been promoted from Development, Dru could sense that Joan Thomas had it in for her. At every opportunity, Joan criticized her decisions, belittled her position, and made rude accusations behind her back. Dru had endured it for the sake of the show, but she was fast reaching her breaking point. She wanted to pick up her beloved Herman Miller Aeron ergonomic chair and hurl it at Joan.

"Do *you* understand that I spent a hundred and fifty thousand on sets and costumes for the trip-to-Paris storyline that Stone and Pageant are supposed to take? Sets and costumes that I can't use if I have no Stone?" Joan countered.

"I don't recall approving that kind of budget for the Paris storyline. You submitted a budget of around a hundred thousand. That's what I approved." Dru was shocked. If Joan had overspent her budget and had not cleared it with her, that was a direct assault on her position. "Let's see," she continued as she rummaged through some papers in a file folder on her desk and pulled one out. "To be precise, you asked for ninety-seven-five. I have it right here." She waved the sheet of paper at Joan.

"There were overruns," Joan quickly said, owl eyes blinking rapidly. "Sue me. So now I have these beautiful sets sitting on the scene dock, waiting, and no one to use them! Lester Jarvis won't like that much, I can assure you." *That'll teach the young bitch*, she gloated. Lester Jarvis was the president of UBC, and a legendary pain in the ass.

"Joan," Dru said, trying mightily to control her temper, "you deliberately kept me out of the loop on this, didn't you? You knew what they were going to cost, and you hid it from me. Now I'll look like an idiot when I have to explain this to *my* bosses."

"I did no such thing," Joan protested, knowing that was exactly what she had done. "I'm the producer of *Sunset Cove*, and as such, I can make those sorts of decisions."

"You are the producer for Klein Productions, a company hired by this network to produce *Sunset Cove*. At a specified cost. And as such, you *do* have to answer to the network. And that's me. Do I need to remind you—again—that I am the Vice President of daytime dramas? You work for me. Those overruns will have to be taken from somewhere else. I suggest you start looking as to where," Dru replied coolly. "*Sunset Cove* will be on budget this year. I will see to that." She made a mental note to review the books of the show as soon as possible and find out what other surprises Joan had in store for her.

"Well, if you won't let me recast Stone, then what in the hell am I supposed to do with those damn Paris sets?" growled Joan. She was not used to being challenged. Even her immediate boss, Jake Klein, the president of Klein Productions, let her have free rein, since she made him a mint of money each quarter, and he never asked how.

"Figure it out. We will not recast Stone yet. It's too soon," Dru said impassively, trying to bring the tension down. "Leave him in the hospital for a few weeks, and then we'll see. I suggest you have the writers come up with some other couple who gets to go to Paris. How about Travis and Melina? They're white-hot now, and should be the two we focus on, anyway."

Joan's reply was silenced by the sudden ringing of Dru's phone.

"Yes, Carole?" Dru asked her assistant after she picked up the phone. She listened for a moment. "Well, please put him through."

Joan quit her wild pacing and flopped down into a guest chair opposite Dru.

"Hello, Detective Parker," Dru said, overly cheerful.

"Hello Ms. Gordon. I'm sorry, may I call you Drusilla?" Dave Parker's resonant voice flowed through the earpiece.

As soon as she heard him say hello, she felt warm all over. "No, please, call me Dru. I hate Drusilla. It sounds like a maiden aunt." While saying that, she looked squarely at Joan, who put on an indifferent air.

"And you call me Park, ok? Everyone does," he said smoothly.

"Ok, Park. What can I help you with?"

"I need to come down and get some correct Social Security numbers from some of your employees that were there the other day, so I can run some checks. I also need to speak with Lefty Jannel again, and I'd like to do it informally, there at the studio, but he now has a lawyer, who is making that difficult. I was hoping you could smooth the way on that." His voice, while merely relaying his needs, had a hint of something more.

"I don't think that should be a problem. I advised Lefty to seek counsel, as I'm sure there will undoubtedly be liability claims against UBC made by Jack's family." Dru noticed that Joan was listening unabashedly to every word. "Um, excuse me just a moment, Park," she said, pushing the hold button. "Joan, I think we are through here for now. I'll come down to the set later, and we can continue our discussion about what to do with the Paris sets then." She looked Joan evenly in the eye and waited for the protesting to begin. Oddly, there was none.

"Sure, *Drusilla*. Whatever you say," Joan said sweetly as

she rose from the chair and walked to the closed office door. "By the way, Drusilla, Detective Parker has upset a lot of people here the past two days with his baseless accusations of foul play," she said, opening the door. "Jack's death was an accident. An unfortunate accident. Perhaps you could use your infinite charms on him and convince him of that. It would be to everyone's advantage. Especially yours. He looks like he'd be a hot fuck." Having gotten the last word, Joan spun around and left the office, slamming the door behind her.

Outraged and angry, Dru sat for a moment composing herself before reconnecting with Parker. "Hi. I'm back. Sorry about that," she said halfheartedly.

"No problem. Anyway, I have to advise on a shooting on Westbourne, near the studio, and I should be done with that around noon, so if you don't have any plans, maybe we could have lunch." There was a hesitant note in his voice.

Unsure of his motives, Dru was cautious. "I believe I have an eleven-thirty meeting. . . . I should be done around twelve-thirty or so. Will that work for you?"

"I'll make it work."

Dru smiled in spite of herself. "Okay, then. I'll call Lefty and make sure he's available for you. His lawyer will probably want to be present, however." In spite of her ridiculous growing infatuation with Park, Dru had imperceptibly returned to her business mode.

"Not a problem. I would expect no less. I'll see you later, then. Should I come to your office? Or do you want to meet on the set?" Park asked.

"Uh, how about you come up here? Suite number four-seventeen. Fourth floor."

There was a brief silence as Parker was obviously searching for a pen and paper. "Four . . . one . . . seven. Got it. See you at twelve-thirty then. Bye." After waiting a beat, he hung up.

Dru held on to the phone for a second or two before hanging up herself.

There was definitely an interest on his part, she concluded. After all, she was a beautiful woman. Why wouldn't there be?

And, Lord knows, it had been a while since a decent man had shown some interest in her. Dru got hit on all the time, but usually by men she just wasn't attracted to, and therefore she'd had more than her fair share of Blockbuster Saturday nights at home, alone. She'd actually won a Sony TV last year with all her video points.

And frankly, she couldn't remember the last time someone else had been in the room when she came.

Wistfully, though, Dru knew that nothing could come of his interest. It would be bad business all around to become involved with the detective who was investigating an accident—that could be murder—on one of her shows.

She could lose her job over something like that.

She got up from behind her neatly organized desk, walked over to a large silver-leaf-framed mirror that hung over an easy chair by her closet door, and looked long and hard at herself in the mirror. She was pleased that she had worn her dark-gray Gucci dress. Through its simple lines it showed off her exquisite body to perfection. As an afterthought, she had quickly thrown on a simple strand of rare black pearls before leaving the house, and her hair was in its usual tousled style. Her face was made up with minimal cosmetics, since she was naturally stunning. Had she chosen a different path, she could have been *on* the soap instead of producing it.

Yes, she thought, *I look good today*. No harm in letting the guy eat his heart out over her just a little bit.

Dru smiled in spite of herself.

After getting his costume, which today was blue scrubs, from wardrobe, Clay went to the extras' dressing room to change. There were already a few people there, eating stale donuts and drinking lukewarm coffee. Scott Tyler was there, but as Clay looked around the room, he didn't see Josh. It wasn't like Josh not to show up for work. Actually, Clay couldn't remember him ever flaking out like this. In fact, Josh was usually in the dressing room early on his workdays because he liked to watch the live network feed from the New York morning show.

Additional extras had been brought in that day, and one,

a dark-haired man who was roughly the same size and build as Jack Benz, was obviously there to be his body double. He was wearing a duplicate outfit of the one Jack had been wearing in the car scenes, and he introduced himself to Clay.

"Hey, man. I'm Bill. Bill Garrett," he said, pumping Clay's hand up and down in an overly friendly way.

"Hi, Bill. I'm Clay. Nice to meet you," Clay answered as he pulled his hand away. "I guess you're here to be Stone for a while, huh?"

"Yeah. Tough break for him, lucky break for me," Bill said affably.

Clay was taken aback by the callousness of the remark.

"Well, uh . . ." Bill stammered, realizing he had just committed a faux pas. "I mean, I'm sorry and all for the poor bastard, but a job's a job, right? Someone had to do this, and I'm glad it's me."

Clay gave him a thin smile and walked into the men's bathroom to change his clothes. After he had changed into the scrubs, he went back out to the larger room and sat down to wait until he was called. He looked up in surprise when the door to the dressing room opened, and instead of Josh, there stood Sam Michaels, the director. Sam had some pink papers in his meaty hand and looked very stressed.

"Good morning, Clay," Sam said, looking about the room. "Is Josh Babbitt in yet?"

"No, sir, I haven't seen him," Clay answered.

"Goddamn it! We're doing scenes today with Stone in the hospital, and I wanted to use him for . . ." The director's voice trailed off as he looked Clay up and down, as if for the first time. He seemed to make a mental decision. "Congratulations. You're now a doctor." He held out the pink papers, which were actually the newest script revisions. "Learn these fast and report to makeup. I need you on set in twenty minutes." He handed the pages to Clay and quickly left the room. Scott instantly joined Clay's side.

Clay's heart was racing as he and Scott tore through the new scenes looking for his lines. He was now to be called Dr. Chase Kendall, and he had three really good scenes with

Pageant. Thrilled beyond belief, he grabbed the dressing room phone and punched in Cissi's extension.

"Sylvia Sinclair's office," Cissi pleasantly answered on the second ring.

"Hey, Cis, it's me," Clay said excitedly. "You won't believe it! I just got a real part!"

"Dr. Chase Kendall, I presume?"

Clay could almost feel her smile through the phone. "Did you have anything to do with this?"

"A minor role, at best," Cissi answered cagily. "When we got the new pages yesterday, I suggested we use someone from within for that role instead of trying to get it cast this morning. Sylvia agreed, surprisingly enough. I said you would be perfect for it, and again she agreed. Apparently, Travis Church had already said something to her about getting you a few scenes," she said, her curiosity apparent. "I didn't realize that you two were that friendly."

"Uh, we're not, really," Clay covered while glancing through the pages. "I guess I must have mentioned I'd like more to do, that's all." Scanning down, he read that the scene was an emotional one for Cathy Grant, as she had to play hysterical with much crying.

This is really going to be a challenge, he thought as he read through it again.

"Huh. But then Sam, our beloved director, didn't agree with us," Cissi continued. "He said he wanted to use Josh. But I can't seem to find Josh. He hasn't answered the phone or his pages, so we have no idea where he his. Since the part shoots this morning, I again said let's go with you. Sam is *so* pissed at Josh!"

Clay was slightly dazed. Cissi had really gone to bat for him. She was truly an amazing friend. "I hope I don't screw it up and make you look bad," Clay joked.

"You won't. I think you are going to be brilliant in the part and prove me right," she said confidently.

"I don't know what to say. Thank you!" he practically shouted.

"I'll call Lucy Crater and hammer out the money. It's not a contract part, *yet*, so don't expect the moon. You'll have to sign some paperwork before the end of the day, too, so don't forget."

"I won't! Cis, I owe you big-time!" Clay whooped.

"Okay, okay, get going; you have to get the lines down. I'll try to break away and come see you shoot. Bye, baby, you deserve this chance," Cissi said with true conviction in her voice.

"Bye. Thanks again!" Clay hung up the phone, high-fived Scott, and ran out the dressing room door, pink pages in his hands.

After sitting in the makeup chair for what seemed like an eternity, Clay dashed down to Stage 24, arriving just in time for camera blocking. The beach road set was still up, but it was marked off by yellow police tape warning that it was a crime scene and not to be tampered with. A single beefy security guard stood nearby, craning his head around to see as much of the action on set as possible.

Pageant Ragianni's penthouse apartment set was gone, however.

In its place were now sections of the Sunset Cove hospital. A front lobby with institutional-styled furniture, a hallway, a hospital room, and an operating room comprised the extent of the sets.

Lefty and his crew had worked through the night to dismantle Pageant's apartment and install the hospital sets. Last-minute touches were being put in now. Lefty was barking into a walkie-talkie, ordering more props from the enormous prop room on the second floor. Already there were beds, trays, gurneys, and every other kind of apparatus a hospital needs scattered about the four rooms.

Stuart Harper, the wardrobe supervisor, came over to Clay and stuck a name badge that read *Dr. Kendall* on his scrubs, then placed a stethoscope around his neck. He handed him a clipboard with some phony documents on it and, as a final touch, slipped a doctor's mask around his face, and paper shoe covers over his shoes. He pulled the mask down so it hung loosely about Clay's neck.

"There. Ready for surgery," Stuart said with a smile.

"Thanks, Stuart," Clay responded, slightly overwhelmed by the rush of activity but trying to study the dialogue on the pages.

Clay was so absorbed in learning his lines, he didn't even see Cathy Grant walk onto the set. Wearing the same black-and-taupe outfit as she had the day of the accident, she looked wan and tired. She was talking to Sam, getting her personal direction for the scene.

Clay finally looked up when he heard his name being called. Looking around, he spied Travis hanging out across the hall in the vast Coltrane living room set. He was wearing his wardrobe for the day: a pair of khaki jeans, a white spread-collared shirt, and a great pair of dark-brown leather sandals. Hair and makeup had put a touch of pomade in his hair to make it slightly greasy and mussed. He looked so attractive, it almost took Clay's breath away.

Travis gave him a warm smile and winked. Clay suddenly felt ten feet tall and knew he would ace the scene as long as Travis was there.

Sam and Cathy walked up to him, and Sam held his hands out wide in appreciation. "Clay, you look great. Very doctor-ish," he said. "I just want to go over some direction with you and Cathy about this scene. . . ."

The next few hours went by in a rush. Clay and Cathy rehearsed each of the three scenes a couple of times and worked out the blocking with Sam. It was actually a simple setup.

Pageant was to rush screaming and crying into the hospital, grab Dr. Kendall, explain that her boyfriend was passed out in the car outside, and drag him out the hospital lobby doors. The next setup would take place in the hallway as Stone was about to be rushed into emergency surgery. Dr. Kendall would explain the complications that could arise to Pageant, who would then reach new heights of hysterics. The final scene would show Pageant in Stone's hospital room, vowing to be there for him, however long it took.

They were demanding scenes for all involved, and Clay was impressed by the range of Cathy's talent. She went full throttle during each rehearsal, giving an Emmy-winning performance of a woman in shock and terror each time. Clay found that he rose to the occasion simply by the company he was with. He played Dr. Kendall as compassionate and determined to do his best for his patient. His line readings hit exactly the right balance, and he could see that Cathy was realizing that he was a talented professional, too.

After calling a ten-minute break to make sure all the cameras were ready to go, Sam walked over to Clay and put his arm around his shoulders. "Clay, my friend, you're doing a great job! I'm really quite pleased. I'm glad we had you around." He squeezed Clay's shoulder lightly and then took off for the booth upstairs, where he would direct the actual taping of the scene.

Cathy sauntered up to him next. "Really Clay, who knew? You're actually quite good. It's nice having some new blood around here," she said, tugging at her strategically disheveled hair.

"Well, not quite new blood, but it sure is great to be working with you, Cathy. You're amazing! You totally make it all work," Clay complimented her sincerely.

"Why, thank you," Cathy smiled. "But do me a favor? In that last bit of business by the gurney thing? Could you step back a few inches? I can tell you block my face from the camera, sweetie, and we can't have that, can we?" She patted him on the head like she would a puppy. Then, surprisingly, she leaned in close to him. "You realize, of course, that if you play your cards right and support me on set, give me something that I can really act off of, then the sky's the limit. Now that Jack's gone, we *all* have a chance to really shine." She winked at him conspiratorially and spun off to find her personal makeup artist. She wanted to make sure that her face was tear-streaked, but not *too* tear-streaked.

After she had left his immediate vicinity, Clay noticed the lingering scent of alcohol. Was that rum?

After taking the break, everyone went back to work, this time to actually put the scene on tape. Some daytime dramas did all the scene blocking in the morning, then shot all afternoon. But at *Sunset Cove,* they blocked a scene, then shot it, then blocked out the next one, then shot that, and so on.

During the second take of his first scene, Clay noticed that Cissi had joined Travis on the Coltrane set to watch him. He saw them whispering to each other and laughing quietly.

Pushing all thoughts of each of them out of his head, he concentrated on the work at hand, and it went relatively smoothly. He flubbed his lines only two times, and Cathy had been cool about it. She was, of course, pitch perfect each take, like a robot.

After the scenes were done, Clay went over to Cissi and Travis.

"Well?" he asked expectantly.

"You were great! Good bedside manner. You can be my doctor anytime!" Cissi joked as she gave him a big hug. Clay glanced at Travis, who merely smiled at him.

"Good job," Travis said blandly. "Well, I've got scenes shooting next, and I need to answer nature's call, so if you two will excuse me . . ." He nodded slightly toward the men's room and walked away.

Clay waited a minute. "I need to go myself, actually. Be here when I get back?" he implored Cissi.

"Yes, but hurry. I have to get upstairs. Sylvia's probably put an APB out on me."

Clay hurried to the restroom and, after walking in, spied Travis washing his hands at the row of sinks. A quick glance around let him know that they were alone.

Travis rushed at him and gave him a huge bear hug. "Baby! I'm so proud of you; you were terrific! Just the right note of urgency. Really, so good! Even the queen bitch Cathy was impressed, you could tell," he raved.

"Really?" Clay was smiling ear to ear.

"Really." Travis gave him a big, wet kiss to emphasize his honesty. "Though I did notice you upstaged her on that first shot. I'm surprised she let you get away with that." Grinning, he pulled away.

"She almost didn't. But I was feeling cocky, so I did it anyway."

Travis's right hand dipped low. "Speaking of feeling cock . . ." he leered.

Clay laughed out loud, dropped his own hand down as well, and rubbed it up against an already hard Travis, imitating him. He laughed again, stopped his own rubbing, and pushed Travis's hand away.

"Jesus. How cliché," he giggled. "Two gay men feeling each other up in a men's room. All we need now is George Michael to join in."

Travis snickered at this.

"And besides," Clay said, pouting playfully, "for someone who acted like he didn't care if I was dead or alive out there on the stage thirty seconds ago, you're sure awfully friendly now." Nevertheless, he held on to Travis's hand warmly.

"Oh, come on. Cissi Stanton is the biggest gossip on this set! I know you two are great friends, but still, you can't be too careful."

"Please. Cissi has been the best! If you knew what she did to get me this part, you think differently. I hate not being truthful with her."

"Well, if you ask me, I think she's in love with you," Travis said half-seriously. "And I don't think I like it."

"Oh, jealous, are you? Good," Clay answered in fun.

"Completely. And not ashamed to admit it. You be *my* man. Don't you ever forget that!" he said as he again landed a deep kiss on Clay. "And besides," he said when they parted, "I had a little something to do with you getting this part, too."

"She told me. You *did* say something to Sylvia, like you promised you would. So if you let me, I'll thank you personally, tonight. In bed." Clay had a quick flash of the two of them locked in each other's arms, rolling around Travis's big bed.

"Deal!" Travis quickly agreed, having exactly the same vision.

They had just let go of each other when Lefty Jannel barged into the men's room. "Hey, boys," he said, heading straight for a stall. Blushing as if they had been caught, the two men left and went their separate ways, Travis up to makeup for a touch-up, and Clay back to find Cissi, who was waiting impatiently by camera number one.

"Jesus! Did you fall in?" she asked, clearly irked at having been kept waiting.

Blushing, Clay shrugged. "Sorry. Got to talking with Travis."

"I'm sure. Slide him your number, did you? Trust me, he isn't interested. In fact, all through your scene, he kept talking about Cathy's tits."

9

All through her meeting with Peter Dowd and the other UBC network executives, Dru found she could not concentrate on the business at hand, which was how to minimize the damage caused by Jack's death. Her mind kept wandering to a place it shouldn't: wondering what Dave Parker looked like naked. She would unconsciously drift in and out of the conversations the other suits were having. It was an incredibly dry discussion on whether the accident was indeed the result of someone's tampering with the Rig, and if so, what plan of action would have to be in place when that news was released.

Dru nodded her head at appropriate intervals and finally forced herself to put thoughts of Parker out of her mind. It was hard to do.

The execs at UBC were not unaccustomed to dealing with the deaths of its stars. Three years earlier, they had all been shocked by the sudden death of Lance Jackson, who had played Rock Coltrane, the oldest Coltrane son. Lance had been killed in a one-car accident late one night, up on Mulholland drive. He had apparently fallen asleep at the wheel while driving to his hilltop home and had plunged off a cliff and crashed three hundred feet into the backyard of an enormous estate owned by the Sultan of Brunei.

Little remained recognizable on the car, and Lance had been killed instantly. UBC had run a special memorial program during that week, recalling Lance's life and triumphs, his two daytime Emmy wins as Bart, and his successful marriage and two beautiful children. It had been the tasteful way to say good-bye to a favored actor, and UBC wanted to do the same for Jack Benz.

The problem was, Jack Benz's death may have been the result of murder, and it was hard to have a feel-good sendoff when the cause of death was still undetermined. And until Detective Parker had a suspect, there was much hand-wringing as how to proceed.

The minutes ticked by like hours until finally the meeting was adjourned. Dru hurried back to her office to find Park already waiting for her. He was standing with his back to her in her office, looking at her various diplomas and achievement awards that she had hung on the wall with pride.

He was wearing a worn brown leather blazer that fit his broad, V-shaped back perfectly over a white button-down shirt, and a pair of aged chinos. Brown suede Gucci loafers were on his feet, she observed. That struck her as odd. *How could a detective with the LAPD afford Gucci loafers?* Dru wondered.

"I'm so sorry I'm late. My meeting went long," she apologized, tucking a loose strand of her hair behind her ear. It was a habit she'd had since grade school: whenever she got nervous or flustered, she would play with her hair.

And being in Park's presence made her nervous.

Park turned and smiled appreciatively at her. "Oh, no problem. I just got here myself." He held out his hand to her, and she stepped close to him to shake.

He smelled good, she noticed. And he was wearing a stainless steel Rolex watch.

"Did you find my office all right? It can get a bit confusing around here. Lots of hallways to get lost in."

"I managed," he grinned. "So . . . where shall we go eat?"

"There's a cafeteria here at the studio, or there's a great little place a block up the street. We could walk it," she offered. "Though I must confess, I'm not quite sure what this lunch date is all about."

Park's grin shrunk a little. "Well, first off, it's not a date. I just thought that I, as the lead detective on this case, and you, as the network executive in charge of the show, should have a friendly working relationship. I'm probably going to get in the way around here, and I don't want any trouble from the network. Lunch seemed like a good way for us to set some issues straight. Is that all right?"

Slightly deflated, Dru recovered quickly. "Of course, of course. Good idea."

"As for where we eat, you pick. Though I'd like to go somewhere we can really talk."

"Up the street it is, then," she laughed.

She has a great laugh, he thought. And, as previously noted, a knockout body.

Park had not been entirely truthful just now. He was very interested in this woman and *had* wanted this to be a date. But he knew it was bad news. She was, after all, still a suspect in what he was positive was a murder. He could only imagine the entanglements dating her would cause for him at work. It would be just the excuse they were looking for to can him. Nope, he sadly decided, this was one he was going to have to pass up.

After walking the short block to the diner, they were seated immediately, Dru being a regular. They sat in a window booth and began to study the menu.

"They make an amazing caesar salad," Dru commented, pointing to it on the menu.

"Yeah?" Park said distractedly. "Fine. I'll have that. Is it big?"

"Huge. You really won't need anything else, but I'm just guessing." She stole a glance at him over the top of her menu. "We could split one."

"Sounds good to me."

The waitress took their order and quickly returned with their two iced teas. Park seemed a little distant suddenly, Dru noted. Like he had something on his mind. He was staring out the window with a grim look on his face. After an awkward silence, she finally spoke up. "Bad couple of days?"

Park snapped back to the here and now. "I'm sorry." Genuinely contrite, he looked her full in the eyes. "As if Jack Benz's death isn't enough to deal with, I now have this other case. A new one. I mentioned it earlier? A drive-by shooting, early this morning. Near here, actually. Just a couple of blocks away. The guy wasn't a gang-banger; he was a doctor. It was a nice neighborhood. I just can't seem to get it out of my mind. Something about it just rings wrong. . . ." He took a long sip of tea, then paused.

"Please, go on," Dru urged.

"A guy's out in front of his building, maybe getting his paper, about six o'clock this morning. A car pulls up and fires twice at him, hitting him both times and killing him. Of course, nobody saw anything. All we got was a halfway decent skid mark. Hopefully, we can ID the tire through that. That might lead to the killer's car. Crazy." Park shrugged helplessly.

"Who was this man?"

"Don't know yet. Hopefully we'll have an ID by this afternoon." Another long swig of tea. "But enough about me. How about you? How are you holding up, dealing with Benz's death?"

"Me? I'm fine, but the network is going crazy. Everyone is convinced Jack's death was an accident, but you seem to have other ideas," she said, broaching the subject boldly.

"Well, I do have a few promising leads."

"Oh? Can you tell me about them, or is it 'top secret' stuff?" She looked at him coyly. She impulsively wanted to flirt shamelessly with this man.

Park sat in silence for a second. "Did you know that Jack Benz was heavily in debt? He bought a house last year, got a great deal on it, then went way over budget on the remodel. He also took a beating in the stock market this year. Lost almost a million dollars. His contract is up for renewal, but he didn't want to continue on the show. Had designs on being a movie star." Park stopped and took another long sip from his tea, then continued. "He had landed a contract with a beer company to be their spokesman. It was going to be big money. He felt he could afford to quit the show. His agent, a rather slick character named Max, was doing all he could to get him to continue on at *Sunset Cove* for another two years."

"Yes." Dru nodded. "That's true. I've been involved with

the negotiations. Max was asking for a substantially revised contract for Jack. The sticking point for the network was all the time off Jack wanted to pursue film roles. It would have made it really difficult for us to schedule the story arcs. Not to mention the hefty raise they were asking for."

"Well, now you understand why Jack needed the money. He was running a deficit with the banks. Overdrawn, late on loan payments. Then, curiously, two months ago, Jack makes two fifty-thousand-dollar cash deposits in his account two days apart, which he promptly spent paying off debts, one of which was to a Dr. Smith Jeffries, a plastic surgeon. Seems Jack had a little face work done last fall."

"Wow" was all Dru could say.

"Then he loses the contract with the beer company. Turns out our buddy Jack is a recovering alcoholic, and somehow, the beer company got wind of that. Not wanting a former lush who can no longer drink to be their spokesman, they pulled out and went with another actor. As for his personal life, he was having an affair with someone you know rather well." He paused dramatically.

"Well, don't leave me hanging, Detective. Who was she?"

"*She* is Mr. Lefty Jannel." Park took in the stunned look on Dru's face with bemusement. "His fingerprints are all over Jack's house. There's a closet full of men's clothes there that aren't Jack's size. Photos of the two of them looking quite cozy. Not to mention a very revealing message that Lefty left on Jack's answering machine, telling Jack exactly what sexual acts he planned to perform on him that night. So I did a little checking on Mr. Jannel, who, by the way, is also a stock market investor—only he's successful at it—and I discovered that Mr. Jannel made a fifty-thousand-dollar withdrawal from his primary savings account. Two months ago. I don't think it's a coincidence," he added flatly.

Park was a little surprised at himself. He had no idea why he was telling this woman all of this, but for some odd reason, he just kept talking. She had the most beautiful face. Maybe that was why he kept gushing on like a schoolboy with a crush.

"I'm stunned. I had no idea about the two of them!" Dru's

head was swimming. If it turned out that one of UBC's own staff had indeed killed Jack, this was going to get worse by the minute. She had just assumed that Jack's death had been an accident, and not really considered the ramifications of a true murder. "So you suspect Lefty? I just can't picture that. He's such a sweet guy. A great employee. Just because they were boyfriends doesn't mean Lefty killed him."

"Well, I've also found out that randy Jack was seeing someone else on the side."

"What?"

"Jack kept a diary of sorts on his home computer. He had started to see someone else, though 'seeing' may be too strong a word. From what I can tell, by the way Jack writes about it, it was just a sex thing. And a little on the rough side, if you know what I mean. I think Jack had something on this guy, who he never calls directly by name. He just called him 'the fuckboy.' It's all very secret and sneaky. Don't ask me why, but my gut tells me that Jack was blackmailing this guy into sleeping with him."

Damn, she is so beautiful, he thought, shifting around in his vinyl seat.

"So Jack was two-timing Lefty. Maybe Lefty found out. Maybe Lefty got tired of hiding his relationship. From what I noticed, Lefty doesn't hide who he is very well." He grinned.

The waitress brought them their salads. After grinding on some black pepper, she retreated back to the kitchen, leaving the two of them alone again.

"Well . . ." Dru had a huge forkful herself and was holding it absentmindedly in midair. "Maybe the new squeeze was a tad upset over being forced into doing something he didn't want to do, and killed his blackmailer."

Park nodded. "Maybe so."

"I just can't believe Jack was gay. I would never have guessed! Lefty, sure. But, not Jack."

"I found quite a stash of pornography at Jack's house. All gay. Trust me on this one. He was gay."

"Well, poor Lefty."

"Why 'poor Lefty'?" Park wanted to know.

"Well, not to be disrespectful to the dead, but Jack wasn't a very nice person, was he? I mean, I always suspected he was a bit of a—what's the word?—'user.' Doesn't seem like humanity lost anything great when he died, does it?"

"While it's true that the more I learn about Jack Benz, the less I like him, I'll pretend I didn't hear you say that. Might make me think *you* had something to do with all this." Park smiled.

"As if I had the time!" Dru laughed. "So, who do you think the other man was?"

"I don't know yet. I'm banking that it's someone who has something to do with *Sunset Cove*. And blackmail would explain where Benz got the other fifty grand."

Dru finally ate the forkful of salad. After a minute she looked at Park. "Some people are saying that Jack wasn't the intended victim. *If* it was a murder. You know, Cathy Grant is not well loved by many, either."

"I looked into that. But, she's extremely well off financially, got a great house and a nonexistent personal life. Has a drinking problem, from what I can tell, but otherwise, her life seems to be the show. I understand she can be a tyrant on the set, but no real enemies that I could find. So far," he allowed. "No, all signs seem to point to Jack being the target. The cast and crew knew who was shooting that morning and where, thanks to the call sheet, which spells all that stuff out. And it seems those call sheets are freely given out, so anyone connected with the show could have planned this," Park said, noticing that Dru had a small smear of dressing on her upper lip. He reached across the table and gently wiped it away. He felt an electric jolt the instant he touched her skin, and let his thumb linger a beat too long on her upper lip.

Dru felt the same energy and was warmed to her core by his touch. She was actually a bit disappointed when he drew his hand away. "Connected to the show?" she said, returning to the topic at hand. "I'm really going to hate it if that's the case."

"Our killer also has some mechanical experience," Park continued with difficulty. "I've checked out that rig several times now, and only somebody who really knows about that stuff would know precisely which bolts to loosen."

"Oh, my God!" she said suddenly.

Startled, Park stopped in mid-bite. "What is it?"

"That means that there is a killer loose on the show! A real killer!" The thought seized her, and a stab of fear began to fester.

"That's what I've been saying," Park patiently said.

"But what about the personal safety of our cast and crew? We need to protect them."

"That would be a good idea. I can recommend a good security firm. It would be wise to have some security on set." He pulled out a small pad and scribbled down a name and a phone number.

Dru whisked out a cell phone and, after reading off the number, punched it in. "I'm doing it now."

Park nodded and went back to eating. He felt a familiar vibration in his pocket and reached in to get his cell phone. He disliked ringing cell phones and always set his to vibrate.

"Parker," he answered flatly into his phone. While Dru had a conversation with the security firm, Park had one with his office. Two people eating at a table having two completely separate phone conversations. Typically L.A.

As Dru was getting the details for a bodyguard team to cover *Sunset Cove*, she heard snatches of Park's conversation. "Uh-huh," he was saying. "Yes . . . not a doctor? . . . what's his name? . . . We're sure about this? . . . Okay . . . Thanks . . . Bye." He wrote a few quick notes in his pad, put away his phone, and sat waiting patiently for her to finish.

When she was done, she looked at him. "What is it? Bad news?"

"No. They ID'd the victim of the drive-by." He went back to eating.

"Oh? What was his name? Are you allowed to tell me?"

"Joshua Rabbit." Another forkful of salad found its way home. He glanced at his pad, stopped, and looked closer at his scribbling. "Oops, no, sorry. That should be Babbitt."

Dru stared at him, confusion written across her face.

"What is it?" he asked, concerned.

"There's a Josh Babbitt who works on *Sunset Cove*. He's one of the permanent extras. Oh, my God! Is it the same guy? Is that possible?" Her voice rose several decibels.

"Jesus!" Park was up in a flash, waving the waitress over by making a large check motion in the air, the international symbol for "bring me my bill." "Sorry, Dru, I need to get back to the studio. . . . I need to use your fax machine, okay?"

"Sure, of course," Dru said as she rose. She grabbed her bag while watching Park throw some bills down on the table. "You think these two things are related, don't you?" she asked, not really wanting to hear the answer.

"Pretty big coincidence if they're not," he replied bleakly.

"Oh my God. This just can't get any worse, can it?"

"I hope not. Come on, let's get out of here." He took her by the arm gently and led her out of the restaurant. The bright sunshine caused each of them to put on their respective designer sunglasses: hers, Gucci; his, Ray-Ban.

"Listen, I'm sorry about the abrupt end to our lunch date," Park said kindly.

"I thought you said it wasn't a 'date.'" Dru reminded him, wagging her fingers in quotation-mark movements.

Park hesitated and chose his next words carefully. "Well, officially, no it wasn't. I'm a police officer investigating a murder, which, theoretically, you're a suspect in," he said, watching Dru's eyebrows shoot up quizzically. "However, speaking off the record, and as a man who has just met a beautiful and interesting woman that I know I would want to see again . . . I think I'm headed for trouble."

The corners of Dru's mouth turned up a hair.

"I just think the timing's off. It wouldn't be smart for us to get involved right now. Maybe after all this is over with." He suddenly stopped short, a curious look of displeasure on his face.

Dru stopped as well and looked at him expectantly. "What is it?" she asked, a slight touch of concern in her voice.

"Nothing. It's just a sad day when I let the job get in the way of my pursuing a gorgeous woman."

Dru blushed three shades of red and stood inches from

him, wondering what it would be like to kiss him right here in the street.

She didn't have to wonder for long.

Park slipped his arms around her and pulled her to him. He knew this was wrong, that he was breaking all the rules, but he could not control himself. He had been accused of thinking with his dick before, and now, as he leaned down slightly to meet her upturned face and kiss her, he realized they had been right.

It was a slow, soft kiss that actually caused her to feel weak in the knees. Park didn't break contact and continued to kiss her, a little more urgency building up as she felt his tongue slide into her mouth and begin explorations. She eagerly returned the gift, and soon they were lost to the world, a small island of raw emotion, alone at the corner of La Cienega and 3rd Street.

After what seemed like a few seconds but was actually over four minutes, they broke from each other, breathing hard. Breathing wasn't the only thing that was hard, Dru noted.

A telltale bulge was definitely noticeable against the soft chino fabric of his trousers. A large, well-packed bulge.

Damn, it felt good to cause that reaction in a man! Hell, she herself was now wet and wanted nothing more than to have him take her right here, right now. But instead, she smiled and said nothing.

"I'm sorry. I didn't mean . . ." Park fumbled, feeling like an awkward teenager.

"Don't be. I wanted to do that as much as you did," Dru responded, oddly calm. "Now what?" she asked, looking him square in the eyes.

"When can I see you again?" Park sighed, giving in.

"Tonight? I've got spin class at six, but will be done by seven-ish," she answered quickly.

"You got it. I'll take you to dinner."

Before Dru could respond, they heard a car horn honk nearby. Looking over to the street, they both saw Joan Thomas returning from lunch in her black Mercedes S 500. Smirking, she waved a brief hello and continued on her way to the studio parking lot.

"Oh, great," moaned Dru. "I hope old eagle-eye didn't see that. It'll be all over the studio before two o'clock."

"I'm so sorry. That was stupid and clumsy of me. I got carried away." He looked away from her. "Look, this is gonna cause us both some problems, and maybe we'd better back off. In fact, I know we should," Park decided.

He was treading on shaky ground, and he knew it. It went against all his instincts to become involved in any way with a possible suspect, no matter how attractive he found her. Even though he knew in his gut she wasn't involved in the death of Jack Benz, it still wouldn't look good.

This was exactly the type of thing defense lawyers looked for when defending a criminal.

Dru thought hard for a beat before she responded. "I know we should back off, too," she allowed. "But somehow, I think we're both going to ignore that. We'll just have to be discreet and careful." She thought she saw relief in Park's eyes. "And don't worry about Joan Thomas. She's just a pain in the ass who's convinced I slept my way into my job instead of earning it." She held up her hands. "Don't ask. But that's not your problem. I'll deal with her myself, so don't worry." A hard shadow seemed to fall over Dru's eyes.

Shaking off the dark thoughts, she straightened her dress and looked brightly at Park. "Oh, I almost forgot. I set up a time for you to talk to Lefty again. Three o'clock this afternoon? At his office on the first floor. His lawyer will be there, just so you know."

"Thanks. Great," murmured Park.

They began the walk back to the studio, enjoying the rush of excitement they were feeling at having found each other. Park wanted to slip his big hand into Dru's delicate one and hold it tightly. He didn't. Instead, they walked in silence the rest of the way to the studio.

As she parked her car, Joan was beside herself with glee. At least the little bitch had taken her advice and was gonna fuck the cop into falling into line—something, she had to admit, she wouldn't mind watching. That truly was the only thing Dru was good for as far as Joan was concerned. This whole "homicide" thing would go away, and Joan would save the day by brilliantly steering the show back on course, thereby making her upcoming contract negotiations swing heavily in her favor.

Joan idly wondered if a twenty-five-percent raise was out of the question. She almost floated into the building.

Yes, it was good to be the queen.

She couldn't wait for the day she could quit this lousy business and retire to a beach house in Tahiti. She cracked a smile as she imagined herself tanning on a sun-drenched slice of heaven, propped up in a chaise, with several tight young brown boys waiting on her every whim.

She had been taking care of her end to make her Tahitian dream a reality, and in just another year or so, she would be set. Well off enough financially never to have to worry about money again. She would become the kindly lady who lived in splendor on the beach, and all would love her.

She waved good-naturedly at staff people all the way up to her third-floor office. They all seemed to be taken aback by actually seeing Joan Thomas attempt a smile. Joan realized she had never felt so good.

Her high lasted about fifteen more minutes.

On Stage 24, Clay and Cathy were finishing up their last scene of the day. Their scenes had gone remarkably well, and Clay had impressed all who were there. Cissi had sneaked back down for a quick minute to watch and was bursting with pride. The intensity of the scene where Pageant vows to remain by Stone's side no matter what brought tears to the eyes of many who were on the stage watching.

It was an Emmy-winning performance, a fact that did not escape Cathy's notice. All the while she was acting the scene, she was mentally figuring out how best to use this to her advantage come voting time. She would make sure that this tape was sent to everyone who could help her. She'd make the necessary phone calls and do the photo shoots. Whatever it took.

There was no way she would lose to Susan Lucci this year!

When he heard Sam yell "Cut!" for the final time that day, Clay felt a strange letdown. He didn't want it to end. He was feeling so high, knowing he was hitting each note just right. He felt in his bones that this was the beginning of something great; he just didn't know where it would end.

Out of the corner of his eye, he saw Rick Yung standing calmly to the side of the stage, whispering something to Lefty, who had a stunned look on his face. Lefty's hand went up to cover his gaping mouth.

What is that about? Clay wondered.

Rick Yung was the local UBC noon and eleven-o'clock news anchor. A graduate of UCLA, he had risen quickly through the ranks of reporters and had landed the anchor desk due to his good reporting skills and his extremely handsome and photogenic face. At 6 feet 1 inches and a very lean 165 pounds, he was often called the Asian Brad Pitt, due to his hot looks, self-effacing humor, and ready smile. He went to Gold's Gym religiously, where Clay saw him all the time.

In fact, he had seen more than he wanted to of Rick Yung one day in the showers. Rick was getting out of his shower stall when Clay was stepping into his. Rick smiled slyly at him, beckoning Clay to join him by giving a clear view of his wet, ripped body and jutting hard-on.

Clay declined politely and went about his showering, but he always thought it was a rather tasteless gesture, and it had colored his opinion of Rick. While he was always polite to Rick, he didn't seek him out or go out of his way to speak with him.

Rick, by way of contrast, thought that Clay was playing hard to get, and doubled his efforts to sleep with him. When he saw Clay at the gym, he would adjust his workout so that he was doing the same muscle group, in the same vicinity, as Clay. He would often wander down from the UBC Action-News studio, on the second floor, to Stage 24, on trumped-up business to look for Clay and talk with him. To Clay, Rick was a minor but harmless annoyance.

"Clay! Clay!" Rick called loudly from his position with Lefty.

Curious about what he had been telling Lefty, Clay went over to the two men. "Hey, Rick. What's up?"

"I'm afraid I have some bad news. It just came out over the police band. Josh Babbitt was killed this morning in a shooting in front of his apartment," Rick said sympathetically. He secretly hoped Clay would be upset and need major consoling.

"What? Are you serious?" Clay was stupefied.

"Yes. He was shot around six this morning." Rick reached out to place his hand on Clay's broad back. He gently applied pressure in a comforting manner.

Clay stood there, digesting this news. "Oh, my God, this is unreal."

"I just can't believe it! What is going on in this world, where a man is shot and killed in his front yard?" Lefty wondered aloud, shaking his head.

"Do they know who did it?" Clay asked, searching Rick's face for answers Rick didn't have.

"No. They're calling it a drive-by, though I've never heard of a drive-by shooting in West Hollywood. No witnesses. I understand that the detective that's investigating Jack's death also has this case."

Lefty wandered off, now dreading his upcoming meeting with Detective Parker even more, leaving Clay and Rick alone.

"Listen, Clay, if you need to talk, I'm always here for you," Rick said in husky tones. "I'm sure you're upset. Let me take you to dinner, and you can talk it out," he suggested smoothly, still rubbing Clay's back but lowering his hand, bit by bit, toward Clay's ass.

"Thanks, Rick," Clay replied, stepping back a few paces to break the physical contact. "I can't tonight. Maybe some other time." As soon as the words came out of his mouth, he regretted saying them. Now Rick would *never* leave him alone.

Rick, thrilled at hearing a "maybe," thought that at the least there was hope for some other time. Good enough for him. "Sure. Anytime. I'll talk to you about it later. I have to get back upstairs," he said, suddenly filled with hope.

Clay merely nodded and walked away, heading over to Cissi, who was listening intently to Lefty.

"Oh, Clay! It's just so awful! It's like we're cursed or something," she blurted out. Clay gave her a good hard hug, much to the envy of Rick, who watched the scene from afar, a look of intense frustration clearly visible on his face.

"I know; I know. I have to get some air. Let's take a walk."

"I can't. I have to get back upstairs. I shouldn't even be here now, but I wanted to watch you. You were so good! I knew you would be," Cissi said proudly.

"I'll walk you back, then. Let's get out of here."

They left the stage, and Clay escorted Cissi to her office, kissed her good-bye, and meandered slowly back down to his new dressing room. He had been given one of the three unused dressing rooms that were kept available for day players and select guests. There was even a sign on the door now that read *Clay Beasley*. How and when that had appeared, Clay didn't know. It was just suddenly there. It was a little strange not to be back in the comfort of the large extras dressing room with Scott, and he realized he missed being there.

A gentle beeping woke him from his funk, and he went to his cell phone and saw he had two messages waiting. The first was from Travis. "Hey, bud," he said. "You were great today. I can't wait to see you. Come over tonight and let me treat you like the star that you are. Bye, babe."

The second message was from Lucy Crater. "Clayton! What a day you're having!" Lucy's raspy voice was ebullient. "I got you five hundred a day on the soap, and featured billing. They won't guarantee you a number of days per week, but from what I can tell, it should be about three to four. Congratulations! And to add a pretty bow to that package, you got the Dr. Pepper commercial. The director has a time crunch and just cast you off the audition tape. You and Maggie." Maggie was also a Lucy Crater client, so this was doubly good news to her. "It shoots on Sunday, so that's double time, golden time! You'll need to do wardrobe tomorrow at noon at Paramount Studios in the Lucille Ball building. Use the Gower

entrance. Call me when you get this, okay? Good job, Clay.
I'm proud of you!"

Clay was always amazed at the nature of the business.
Yesterday, no real prospects; today, a good part on a soap,
and a national commercial, to boot.

Crazy.

10

As word of Josh's death spread through the studio, no one was more vocal in disbelief than Joan Thomas.

"You're shitting me!?!" she shrieked at Peter Dowd after he told her. "What the fuck! Who did that moron piss off so bad that they picked him off in front of his house? Jesus Christ! This is the last thing I need!"

Unconsciously Peter backed up, away from the frothing woman in front of him. "Uh, Joan, I'm sure it was the last thing Josh needed, too," he said meekly.

"Oh, shut up! Who asked you?" she spat. "Well, obviously this has nothing to do with us. He was probably screwing some gal whose husband got even." She started to pace around her office. "Is that brain-dead detective still in the building? Is he still with Drusilla?"

"I don't think so. I just saw him on three, in Cissi Stanton's office."

"Good. I'm gonna nip him in the bud right now." Joan marched out of her office, leaving Peter alone.

Exhaling with relief that the dragon lady was gone, Peter allowed himself to look around Joan's large office. She had plain, serviceable furniture placed in a sensible arrangement. Her heavy oak desk was loaded with papers, scripts, books, and two laptops, but was orderly. In the front corner of the office was a large standing coatrack, where Joan had casually tossed her simple brown Ann Taylor blazer. Quietly closing her office door, Peter walked slowly to the rack. Lifting the jacket off, he studied it for a second, sniffed it, then quickly slipped it on. He closed it tightly about him and twirled in a circle. He enjoyed the sensation of being naughty, and he liked the feel of the silky lining against his body. He made a mental note to get a blazer just like it but in his size.

Joan dashed over to Cissi's office but was irked to find that she had missed Park. On a hunch, she drifted over to Dru's office to see if he was lurking around there. Nope. Neither Dru nor the detective was there. Now, completely frustrated, Joan started to storm back to her own office.

"Joan! Joan, do you have a minute?" It was not a question but a command, and it came from Cathy Grant, who was standing in the open doorway to the snack room.

"Yes, Cathy. Of course. What is it?" Joan toadied.

"Well, now that poor, dear Jack has . . . has . . ." Cathy started to tear up and actually wrung her hands together. "Passed on, I just hope that . . . that . . ." she struggled to find the words.

Joan observed her distress and, deciding it was genuine, reached out a comforting hand. She had always coddled the talent, and today was no exception. "Cathy, what is it?" she asked kindly.

"Well, I just hope that my poor Pageant doesn't get lost in the shuffle. Jack and I had a big story line coming up, and I don't want to lose my—er, *our* momentum."

Joan's eyes narrowed. "Uh-huh . . ."

"So, be a love, and make sure my Pageant gets the lion's share of scenes. Get me a new Stone. Or if you don't, I like the new guy, Clay what's-his-name. Give me some action with him. I'll act the shit out of it and win . . . you . . . the Emmy." Cathy dropped all pretenses of being upset. Her naked ambition was on full display.

Joan inwardly smiled. Cathy was a shark. She had only her own interests at heart. But Joan was a shark, too, and she liked that quality in others. Others whom she controlled, that is. "Don't you worry, Cathy, dear. I'll take care of you."

Cathy beamed. "Thank you, Joan." She backed up and let

Joan continue on her way. After Joan had turned the corner and disappeared, Cathy slyly grinned.

It's all going to work out perfectly, she thought happily.

On her way back to her office, Joan walked by the elevator bank, where she happened to pass Peter Dowd, who purposely looked away from her.

Upon reentering her office, she immediately felt that something was out of place. She scanned the room and finally noticed what it was. Her blazer was hanging neatly on the coatrack, arms carefully tucked into its pockets. It was clearly not the way she had left it, and she wondered what Peter had been looking for when he had so obviously rifled through it.

Hmmm, she thought. *I'm gonna have to keep an eye on that one, too.*

Unbeknownst to Joan, Park was at that very moment asking Lefty Jannel some hard questions in Lefty's ground-floor office.

"So you say the last time you saw or spoke to Jack Benz was here, on set, during the afternoon prior to his death?" Park asked.

Nervously Lefty eyed his attorney, a slightly dweebish man by the name of Dexter Blass, who was seated in the corner of the office. Beside a large drafting table that was covered in blueprints, papers, and magazine clippings, Lefty sat in his bright green ergonomic chair.

"Yes, that's correct," Lefty agreed.

"And you did not see or speak to him again until the next day, when you placed him in the Rig for the shot?"

"That's right."

"Lefty, I have a problem with that," Park said slowly. He was sitting in a rather plush club chair, facing Lefty, in an office that had more magazines, fabric swatches, wood finish samples, and carpet remnants than any contractor's office he had ever seen.

Sketches of past and future sets were pinned up on a giant bulletin board that stretched across the width of the room.

Paint chips were taped to the wall, and small props such as lamps, bowls, and candlesticks cluttered the space.

Lefty looked surprised. "What do you mean?"

Dexter Blass shifted in his chair.

"I think you were more involved with Jack than you're letting on."

Lefty's color left his face, and he looked at the attorney in a panic.

"Uh, I believe . . ." Blass began.

Park cut him off. "Why aren't you telling the truth, Lefty? Did you have something to do with Jack's murder?"

Lefty's mouth dropped open, and the attorney rolled his eyes.

"We've found clothes at his house. They're your size, not his. One of the shirts, a personalized bowling shirt, has your *name* on it. We have your fingerprints all over the place. There are photographs of the two of you, framed, in his study."

"My client did extensive decorating for his good friend, Mr. Benz. That would explain his fingerprints all over the house," the lawyer finally managed to say.

"Lefty, I know that you called Jack at exactly nine-forty-five the night before he was killed, and left a message for him. Do you want me to remind you of what you said to him?"

"That's impossible! Jack always erased each incoming message!" Lefty bolted upright.

Dexter Blass, stunned, looked at his client, who slunk down into his chair.

"I believe you left a laundry list of the sexual acts you wanted to perform with him that night, including, if I'm not mistaken, something involving Ecstasy, handcuffs, and a pair of leather chaps," Park pressed on.

"Now, wait a minute! My client will not answer any more . . ." the lawyer started to say as he rose to his feet.

Park ignored him. "You were having an affair with Jack, weren't you, Lefty? The two of you were lovers and kept it quiet; isn't that right?"

Tears welled up in Lefty's dark eyes, and he nodded.

"Lefty," Park said in soothing tones, "it's very important

that you be honest with me. When was the last time you saw or spoke to Jack? Did you see him the night before his death?"

"No." Lefty shook his head and wiped away his tears with a red bandanna that was lying on his desk. "I called him, like you said, but he never called me back. Yes, we were in a relationship, but he didn't want anyone to know, so I had to keep it secret. I hated that. I've never been a closet case in my life, but he was."

"Lefty, please. Say no more," Blass interrupted. He turned to Park. "I need a moment to consult with my client, Detective."

"No, it's all right. I want to talk about it. I'm glad it's finally out in the open," Lefty said. The attorney sat down and crossed his arms in frustration.

If the guy wanted to hang himself, so be it, Dexter thought.

"I loved him, you know. He was a complete shit, but I loved him," Lefty sighed. "I think he loved me back, but he was a complicated man. He would get crushes on other men and fantasize about them, tell me what he wanted to do with them. We were together for over a year. I got used to it. He bought the house, and I helped him fix it up. I hoped it would bring us closer together; I even loaned him some money when he was short, but after it was done, he began to shut me out. He wouldn't let me move in; I always had to call before I came over. That sort of thing."

Park was writing everything down on his pad.

"I tried to win him back. When he asked me to dye my hair this ridiculous color, I did. It was something he'd seen on somebody that he liked, and he wanted me to copy it. I did everything I could, but I could tell he was losing interest. So," Lefty continued, "it became obvious that there was someone else. Who, I don't know, but there was somebody. It hurt me. A lot."

Park looked at Blass, who simply shrugged.

"Did you kill him, Lefty? Were you so mad at him for screwing around on you that you needed to get even?" Park asked in composed, even tones.

"God, no!" Lefty shouted. "I didn't do any such thing!

How do you think I felt when my Rig killed him? I feel terrible, and I'll have to live with that for the rest of my life!"

"Okay, really, that's enough. Lefty, for Christ's sake, shut up! This interview is over." The attorney stood up for the last time and seized his briefcase. "We're done here, Detective. Lefty, let's you and I have a chat, shall we?" He waited until Lefty got up, and the two of them left the office.

Park sat in the office for a while, digesting Lefty's information. Lefty certainly had motive. And as art director, he was responsible for making sure the Rig was safe. It would have been very easy for him to have tampered with it to maim or kill his lover, then feigned innocence. So he also had means. And knowing when the stage would be empty, he had opportunity. Three strikes.

Park breathed a little easier now. He felt he had his man. How the death of Josh Babbitt fit into this was something that had to be figured out. But Park was confident there was a connection between the two murders. He would have to look a little more closely at Josh to find a connection with Lefty. He would request around-the-clock surveillance on Lefty and soon would have what he needed to put him away.

II

Clay arrived at Travis's house shortly after seven that night. Dressed in a pair of black jeans and a tight ribbed white tee that showed off his upper body, he looked better than he felt. He just couldn't shake the feeling that there was something terribly wrong with the timing of Josh's death. There had to be some reason for it. Random acts like that just didn't happen to people he knew. Or did they? It was all so confusing, and truth be told, he was in no mood to go out and celebrate the fact that he scored a job because his friend had died.

Travis opened the door in his skintight Jocko underwear, the head of his lion tattoo peaking out of the elastic waistband—a sight that always gave Clay a flash of excitement. "Hey! I'm running late."

He ushered Clay into the house, and once they were a safe distance inside, he leaned over and kissed him. "Mmmm. *So* good to see you."

"You, too."

"I thought we'd try Valentino's Steakhouse in Hollywood tonight. How's that?"

"Good, fine. Whatever," Clay said vacantly.

Travis stopped kissing him and looked Clay in the eye. "Okay. What is it? Would you rather go somewhere else?"

"No, it's not that," Clay meekly answered. "Josh's killing has me, well, kinda spooked."

Travis put his arms around his lover. "Clay, nothing like

that's gonna happen to you. It's just one of those weird things that you can't explain."

"No, it's not that. I feel bad about him being killed. And getting his part on top of it."

"Well, I wouldn't feel so bad about that," Travis said lightly. "You should have had the part in the first place. Don't let the bad in this overshadow the good, okay?"

"Yeah." Clay glumly nodded.

"So give me five minutes, and I'll be ready to go." Travis paused for a beat. "Unless you'd rather fool around first." He winked as he reached down and squeezed Clay's crotch tantalizingly.

Tempted and, to be honest, getting slightly aroused, Clay thought for a beat. America's hottest daytime stud was standing in front of him in his underwear with his hot little tattoo peeking out and was wanting to take him to bed. He sighed. "No, let's go eat first. I'm hungry, and I'd rather have you when I'm in a better frame of mind. Is that okay?"

Travis smiled. "Of course. Just give me a minute." He spun around and ran off to the bedroom to get dressed.

Clay plopped down onto one of the new leather sofas and picked up the current issue of *Men's Fitness* off the coffee table and lazily thumbed through it. He stopped short when he came upon Travis's picture.

It was one of his ads for Mennen.

He was shirtless, lounging on a spacious bed, the top button of his pants undone, his legs spread slightly, his crotch full and enticing. He was looking up with an expression of desire at a beautiful nude woman standing in front of him, who was holding a can of shaving cream and a razor behind her back. The whole point of the ad was to get the viewer wondering what, exactly, she planned on shaving. It was erotic, sensual, and humorous all at the same time.

The photographic image of his hot lover looking so damn sexy had an immediate affect on Clay. He had to shift around to give his erection some room. After staring at the picture for a few seconds more, Clay stood up, threw down the magazine, and practically ran to the bedroom.

"Trav? Brace yourself, I've changed my mind!" he whooped as he ran through the house.

He quickly covered the distance to Travis's bedroom, and upon reaching the opened double frosted-glass doors that were its entrance, he stopped, mouth agape.

Travis was lying on the king-size bed, completely naked, stroking himself. He gazed at Clay with lust in his eyes and spread his legs a bit farther apart.

It was an almost duplicate image of the one Clay had just seen in the magazine.

"I'm sorry, but I'm so horny right now. I just need the release," Travis explained, licking his famous lips.

Without saying a word, Clay stripped his clothes off and climbed on the bed. He crawled on all fours until he was directly over his lover. His own hard-on hung heavy, almost touching Travis's. He leaned his head down and began kissing the now-squirming man beneath him. He kissed his lips, his nose, his eyelids. He then worked his way down, kissing his neck, getting his favorite response of Travis groaning out loud.

Clay worked his way to Trav's chest, taking time to suck and tease each beautiful, erect nipple, then he slowly licked and kissed Travis's stomach, erotically tracing the outline of each cut in his six-pack with his tongue.

He took hold of Travis's rock-hard member and slowly, with his eyes locked on his gorgeous partner, let his mouth slide over the mushroom head and down the thick shaft. On the return up, he made sure to tease the head with some minor tongue-flicking that made Travis twitch.

He brought his right hand down and began to stroke it in the opposite direction his mouth was moving, so Travis never had a second's respite from the sensual pleasure he was giving.

Travis, watching the man he loved with all his heart going down on him, thought he would explode at any second. Just watching his dick slide in and out of his handsome lover's talented mouth was enough to do it, but when you added in the sensations he was feeling, it became too much.

Clay sensed Travis was close, and finished him off with his

hand, smoothly moving it up and down as Travis, grunting loudly, shot in a high arc that nearly caught Clay in the eye.

Clay continued to stroke Travis, rubbing his thumb over the head of his wondrous dick, and grinned as he watched Travis spasm in rapture.

"Stop! Stop!" Travis cried out, laughing.

"Hey, you wanted it," Clay responded, not stopping.

"Oh, man . . ."

Eventually, Clay slowed down and then stopped. Travis lay motionless on the bed.

"I'm spent," he said, eyes closed, grinning from ear to ear.

"God," Clay said quietly. "I love to watch you come. You get this look of absolute joy on your face. It's truly amazing to witness."

"Come here," Travis asked, gesturing for Clay to lie on him.

Clay obliged.

"Mmmm. This is the best. Just holding you after sex, just feeling your heart beat, hearing you breathe," Travis said dreamily, wrapping his arms around his lover.

"I know. I always feel so connected to you at these times. Like we're the only two people in the world."

"Exactly."

The two men let the silence fill the room as they lay together.

"Hey," Travis asked in a placid voice. "What about you? You want to come?"

"I'm happy like this for now," Clay sighed, squeezing Travis slightly. "But ask me again after dinner."

"It'll be my pleasure."

One ridge up the hillside, Dru stood in her closet and stamped her foot in frustration. She had tried on six different outfits, and nothing seemed right. She wanted to look refined, yet sexy. Her face was flushed with heat, and she was afraid she'd have to reapply her makeup. Park was due in fifteen minutes, and she still didn't have a clue what to wear.

Calm down, she told herself. *It's just a date.* A secret date. A could-lose-her-job secret date. No big deal.

"What the hell am I gonna wear?" she asked herself aloud. The TV was on in the bedroom, and she peeped her head out of the closet when she heard the anchorwoman begin a story on Josh Babbitt.

"Still no leads in a fatal drive-by shooting early this morning in West Hollywood," the carefully lacquered anchorwoman said in dulcet tones, staring straight into the camera. "Joshua Babbitt, twenty-five, was shot and killed outside his apartment building at 1346 Westbourne Avenue, at approximately six o'clock this morning. Witnesses said that they heard two shots fired, and then a car speed away. Joshua Babbitt was an aspiring actor who was recently working as a featured extra on this network's daytime drama Sunset Cove. LAPD Detective David Parker had this to say about the investigation into Babbitt's death . . ."

Dru smiled in spite of herself when the image of Park came on the screen. Dressed in his clothes from that afternoon, he looked slightly peeved at having to answer questions from the reporter.

"We are investigating Mr. Babbitt's death to the full extent of our resources," he growled. "We will find the perpetrator of this crime, and we urge anyone who has any information to come forward and call us." The screen then cut back to the overly blond anchorwoman. "Detective Parker would not comment on whether this case is related in any way to the accidental death earlier this week of Jack Benz, the Emmy-winning star of Sunset Cove. In a related story, Jack Benz's funeral is scheduled to take place on Sunday at Forest Lawn Cemetery in Burbank. The funeral will be closed to the public, but the UBC network has set up a large condolence card at the UBC studio gates at 356 La Cienega Blvd. in Beverly Hills, which fans may sign. The card will then be displayed for a short period of time before being forwarded to Mr. Benz's family."

The card had been Dru's idea, and she was glad to hear it mentioned. She tuned out the newscast after that and returned to her more pressing issue: clothes. Finally settling on wearing the first thing she had tried on, a tight black-and-white floral print Diane von Furstenberg classic wrap dress, she quickly threw it on. She opted to forgo the hose and bare-leg it. Slipping on a pair of black Manolo Blahnik mules with a lethally thin heel, she twirled once in the mirror and watched the skirt float up, then down. Yep. This was it. She twirled again just for fun.

The doorbell stopped her in her mid-twirl. "Jesus! He's here already," she muttered to herself.

Park stood at the door, holding an exquisite bouquet of pink roses. He heard the clattering of Dru's heels on the terrazzo floor, and when she opened the door, he sucked in his breath. She looked stunning. She was slightly panting from her race to the door, and her hair was in perfect disarray. His eyes automatically roamed down to her breasts, which pulled at the fabric of her dress, tempting him with their fullness.

"Hi," she said, opening the door wide for him to enter.

"Hi. These are for you." He handed her the bunch of flowers, and she took them gladly, bringing them to her nose to inhale their fragrant aroma.

"That's so sweet of you! I don't think a date's brought me flowers since senior prom," she laughed.

"Well, sorry, I left the blue-ruffled tux at home. I hope this will do," he said, holding out his arms. He was wearing a Ralph Lauren navy blazer over a cream-colored merino wool polo shirt. Cream pleated linen trousers by Hugo Boss ended, cuffed, at a pair of highly polished black loafers. No socks.

"Oh, yes. You'll do very nicely," she sighed as she leaned in for a kiss.

After kissing for a few minutes, she took Park by the hand and gave him the grand tour of her house.

"Kinda, um, empty, isn't it?" Park asked.

That was an understatement.

Most of the rooms were completely bare. Dru had bought the house six months earlier but hadn't had the time to furnish it. She had previously been living with a Pi Phi sister from college who had a completely furnished condo on Wilshire Boulevard near Westwood, so she hadn't ever bought any of her own furniture. When the sorority sister and her boyfriend decided to get married, Dru had to move out, and she bought the house, actually the first one the realtor showed her.

"Sad, isn't it? I just haven't had the time. I don't even know what style I want," she sheepishly replied. Still holding on tightly to Park's hand, she led him through the large living room and out the sliding door to her deck. A spectacular view of Los Angeles was spread out beneath them. A large telescope was situated off to the left side of the balcony, next to a large bright-red Weber kettle barbecue grill. The telescope had a large yellow bow attached to it. "Housewarming gift from my father," she explained. Re-entering the house, she took him past the dining room, which had a card table and two folding chairs sitting alone in the center of the room.

"Cozy," Park quipped.

"Be quiet." Dru led him through to the big kitchen. She placed the roses in a crystal vase, filled it with water, and then placed the bouquet on the slate counter. She and Park exited through another doorway back to the living room. At a set of stairs, she led him below. "The bedrooms are downstairs. It's an inverted house," she said.

"Cool."

There were two bedrooms, each with its own bathroom. One bedroom was fitted out as a home gym/office complete with LifeCycle, treadmill, Bowflex machine, and a large TV mounted up on the wall so it could swivel around to wherever Dru was working out. There was also a desk, where a new iMac sat, along with a printer, fax, and other bits of office equipment.

The other bedroom was hers and was furnished only with a plain queen-size bed, a couple of nightstands, a side chair, and a large whitewashed pine armoire that held the TV, which was still on. The sheets on the bed were pulled back, and it looked damn inviting, Park noticed.

"Well. At least you have the necessities," he said, gesturing toward the bed.

Dru laughed out loud. "I guess I have neglected the house a

bit. Maybe I'll go look at furniture this weekend. Care to join me?" she asked, a suggestive cadence in her voice.

"Anything to spend time with you, m'lady."

"Smooth talker."

"You have no idea." He pulled in close to her.

Suddenly aware that she was in her bedroom with this incredibly sexy man, Dru knew that if they didn't get out of here now, they never would. "We better get going, don't you think?"

"Sure. Let's go."

Dru flipped off the TV, grabbed a thin black cropped cashmere cardigan, and led Park back upstairs.

When they left the house, Dru stopped short at the sight of Park's car, parked right behind her own silver Audi A4 3.0 Avant wagon.

"Okay, Buster. What gives?" she asked him.

"What do you mean?"

"Let's be real for a sec, okay? You were wearing Gucci loafers today, I noticed. You have on a Tag Heuer watch now. Earlier, you had on a Rolex. And you drive a Mercedes Benz G 500? On a cop's salary?" She looked at him hard, hands on her hips.

"I have a few nice things, so sue me," Park said flippantly. Seeing that Dru wasn't buying that, he softened a bit and spoke sincerely. "Let's just say I have other income." He opened the passenger door to the black SUV for her and stood there waiting for her to get in.

"Not so fast. Are you on the up-and-up? I mean, this is all a little too odd." She wasn't going to give an inch.

Park sighed. "Look, I have family money, okay? Happy? I'm an honest cop, don't worry about that. So honest, in fact, that I feel guilty about going out with you, knowing I'm jeopardizing my career. Now, would you please get in? I'll explain it all to you at dinner, okay?" he pleaded.

Dru hesitated for brief moment, but deciding to give him the benefit of the doubt, she climbed in.

Park pulled up to a beautifully redone building on Hollywood Boulevard. He tossed the keys to the valet and took the claim check. He took Dru's arm, and together they entered the restaurant. Wonderful high ceilings were covered in beautifully hand-painted crossbeams. The huge open dining room was bathed in warm subdued lighting, with a massive mahogany bar to the right. Up a raised flooring area, large high-backed leather booths were lined up on the left. Small, intimate tables for two were scattered about the rest of the floor space. The pretty hostess seated them quickly at a booth far in the back, where they could see everything but not really be seen.

After ordering two cocktails, Park turned and faced Dru, who was looking at him in anticipation.

"Okay. Show-and-tell time, I guess," he laughed.

"Please."

"I was born right here in L.A. Hard to believe, but true," Park began. "There are a few of us native Angelinos around. My dad was a beat cop in Los Feliz, and my mother was a nurse. She met him at the hospital she worked at, when he was knifed by some punk. They dated, then married, and planned on living a happy life together. I came along, and my mom started to pressure my dad to take his detective's test, so he would get off the street. He loved being a flatfoot, but to please my mother, he applied, and was accepted. On his last day of foot patrol, he stopped at a fast-food joint on Western Avenue to get a Coke, and interrupted an armed robbery." Park's face took on a hard edge as he told the story. "Long story short, he was shot and killed by some loser who got away with seven dollars."

Dru placed her hand over Park's. "I'm so sorry. Did they catch the . . . man who did it?"

"No, they never did. I was only two when it happened, so I don't even remember him. My mom was pretty messed up for a while, and had to quit her nurse's job. Eventually, she took a job as a secretary and ended up marrying the boss, who became my stepfather. Maybe you've heard of him? Charles Farrar?"

Dru looked startled. "The construction guy? As in Charles Farrar Construction? As in Farrar Stadium? As in Farrar Boulevard in the Valley?"

"As in."

"Jesus! Your dad, uh, stepdad is one of the most respected—and richest—men in town!" Dru was clearly impressed.

"I'm glad you approve. And he's actually a nice guy. Treated me well, for the most part, even though he's always just thought of me only as his wife's son from her first marriage. Of course, when my half-brother, Kurt, came along, I really faded into the woodwork as far as he was concerned, but all in all, a decent man," Park said simply.

"Do you not get along with your half-brother?"

"That's the funny thing. We get along great. Always have. We've been best friends since the day he was born. I'd do anything for Kurt. I love him. I don't think of him as a 'half-brother'; he's just . . . my brother." Park's devotion to Kurt was obvious.

"Well, that's great."

"Of course, when Charles found out Kurt was gay, that kind of dampened dear old Chuck's love for his son. But that's another story."

"Oh, my. How do you feel about that?"

"Me? Oh, hell, I don't care. I think I always knew Kurt was gay, even when we were kids. He could whip out G.I. Joe fashions on this little sewing machine our nanny had, so fast it was scary."

Dru laughed, and Park joined in. "When Kurt had the affair with his high school football coach, I thought Chuck was gonna have a stroke! They got caught in the locker room shower by the coach's wife. It was quite the nasty scandal."

"I can imagine!"

"So suddenly, Chuck realizes I'm around and starts to pal me up. I think he decided that I would carry on the family business, and not his gay son. He set me up with an obscenely large trust fund. He even wanted to officially adopt me and have me change my name from Parker to Farrar. I wouldn't do it. By that time, it was too late, and I felt it would be disrespectful to my father's memory."

"I can understand that." Dru nodded.

"So, I graduate from Stanford, and then—to please my mother more than me, I think—I went to Harvard and got my law degree. After that, I decided to do what I wanted to, and that was to join the LAPD—much to my mother's horror. Given my family history, I don't think you need a Ph.D. in psychology to figure out why," Park said dryly.

"No, you wanted to emulate your dead father. You want to finish what he started. It's very noble," Dru said, patting his hand again.

"I don't know about noble, but I enjoy it, and it makes me feel good. So I keep at it, though Chuck is at me constantly to quit, take the bar, and join the firm."

"I can't imagine your buddies on the force are quite so blasé about your extra income as you are. Doesn't that make your job harder?"

"Well, to be fair, I really do live beneath my means. I don't drive the Mercedes to work; I have an old Bronco that I use for that. I try to keep the money thing as low-key as possible, but they all know who my family is and what I have. Sometimes it's an issue, and I get some crap because of it, but if they don't like it, my attitude is 'fuck 'em,' " he honestly replied. "But believe me, I'm the first guy they come running to when their kids are having a raffle or cookie sale."

Dru laughed. "So tell me. What does Kurt do now?"

"Not a damn thing. He lives off his even larger trust fund and works out. He's big into the whole gay circuit thing. That's about it," Park laughed. "It's his way of getting back at the old man. I think Chuck's virtual abandonment of him because he was gay has messed him up some. They rarely speak to each other. Kurt has some pent-up anger at Chuck, and I don't blame him. To Mother, of course, he's still 'the baby.' "

"I'm sure Kurt'll come around one day."

"Maybe. We'll see. He really is a good man. I keep hoping he'll meet someone and settle down. That's what he needs: a stable home life, and to end all his party-boy ways."

"And what about you? You ready to settle down?" Dru teased.

Park took a deep breath. "Actually, I thought I was, once. I was married before," he said, studying her face for a reaction. Outside of a slightly raised eyebrow, she remained calmly attentive. "It was right after college. The daughter of one of my mother's best friends. A debutante. I thought I was in love with her, and since it made my folks happy, I married her. It didn't work out."

Dru took a sip of wine and let him talk. For some insane reason, she was slightly jealous of his ex-wife.

"I date, but I guess I just haven't really met anyone that I was truly interested in. Until now." He cast his eyes downward. "Even though this is the dumbest thing I could possibly do." Finished, he sat back and let out a deep breath. It felt good to come clean, and he reached over and took her hand firmly in his.

Across town, in his Doheny Drive penthouse, Kurt Farrar threw the TV remote down and sighed. He was idling, watching *Trading Spaces* on his large flat-screen TV, but he was incredibly restless.

He had called Park a little while ago to see if he wanted to go out for dinner or to a movie, but he'd gotten the answering machine. Kurt was disappointed, not just because he was feeling lonely, but because lately he'd felt like he and his brother had grown apart. It bothered him. They had gone through a rough patch a few years back but had come out of that rift the better for it. Kurt considered Park to be his true best friend, even if they didn't see each other every day.

Kurt had always idolized his older brother. He'd followed him around like a puppy when they were kids, and always knew Park had his back.

Kurt just wished that Park would find a measure of happiness. Park had let on that his family position was a hurdle at work, and Kurt could tell it really had started to wear the detective down. Kurt had suggested he quit the force and go into private practice. "Be a private eye. Or use your law degree for some good," he had told Park, during one particularly moody night when Park had stopped by to vent his anger. Park had demurred on that and was still fighting it out at headquarters every day.

Kurt felt that was foolish. What was the point of having all this money if you didn't exploit it in some way? He himself, while always keeping a careful eye on his "egg," as he called it, certainly allowed himself to enjoy the fruit of his father's labors. He knew it pissed off his father that he did nothing but work out all day and party, and that knowledge actually increased Kurt's desire to continue to do just that.

Fuck the old man, he reasoned.

Turning his attention back to the plasma-screen television, he ruefully wished he'd made plans with Park earlier. He made a mental note to call him tomorrow and set up a dinner. Kurt idly wondered where he could be now.

I bet he's out with some hot babe, getting off, while I sit here on my lonely ass on a Friday night, he thought glumly.

Kurt could have joined his parents at a dinner party at A-list socialite Betsy Bloomingdale's if he had wanted to. His mother had called earlier in the day with the last-minute invitation, but Kurt had declined it. Spending time with his father was the last thing he wanted to do.

So here he sat, alone, in his million-dollar condo, which overlooked West Hollywood on one side and Beverly Hills on the other. He picked up his remote, and clicked through the channels aimlessly, coming to a stop when he came upon a newsbreak airing on the local UBC affiliate.

The hot news anchor Rick Yung was reporting on a low-speed police chase happening live on the 405 Freeway. Kurt found himself drawn to the articulate man on the television screen. Something about him compelled Kurt to continue watching, and he set down the remote.

It wasn't because the anchor was such a good-looking man, or that the story was so fascinating. It was something else. It was as if the anchor was speaking directly to him. Kurt took in Rick's expressive eyes, sexy mouth and broad shoulders, and realized he was attracted to him in a big way.

He had seen Rick Yung at the gym on a few occasions, but had never really paid him much attention. His interest now piqued, Kurt made a mental note to get to know the hunky anchor personally next time he saw him.

The news flash ended all too soon, and Kurt picked up the remote again and continued his channel surfing, once more bored and restless.

He'd spent the day as he usually did: working out, tanning, a quick stop at his money manager's office to check on his accounts, and small meals every three hours. He hadn't seen Clay Beasley at the gym today, thank God. Though just thinking about Clay now made him realize that he was "in the mood."

Antsy now, he wanted to get out of the house, so he decided to go to the Virgin Megastore on Sunset Boulevard and get some new CDs. He got up off his leather sofa and went to his massive bedroom to get something to wear.

Travis's Boxster pulled up to the valet stand, and he and Clay got out. After getting the stub from the valet, they entered the newly reopened restaurant. Valentino's Steakhouse & Bar had been completely renovated the year before and was on the verge of becoming too popular.

Hollywood itself was going through a major transformation from scary tourist trap to high-end retail area. The recently built—and enormous—Hollywood & Highland shopping mall had set the tone.

Built to replicate the gigantic sets from D. W. Griffith's famous silent film classic *Intolerance,* the mall had thirty-foot-high elephants on pedestals in the center courtyard, and mosaic floor tiles telling stories of Hollywood's early days. It was also the new home of the Kodak Theater, where the Academy Awards were given out, and the newly refurbished Grauman's Chinese Theater.

Other businesses besides Valentino's were following the renovation suit. Where Hollywood used to be a place where no one would be caught dead, now it was struggling to regain some of its old glamour and mystery and was becoming cutting-edge and hip.

Upon entering the heavily carved front doors to Valentino's, Clay gaped at the beautifully redone restaurant. The amazing painted crossbeams, the incredibly lush leather booths: it was all very cool and very "old Hollywood." He approved of Travis's choice immediately. They were shown to a booth near the front of the restaurant by the hostess, who recognized Travis and flirted brazenly with him.

Travis was, as he always was in these situations, kind, and he flirted a bit back at her, making her blush. After she left the table, the two men simply enjoyed being out together and, in the dimmed light, paid no attention to the other diners.

Sitting far back in the booth, Dru noticed Clay and Travis enter. Surprised, she nudged Park and nodded in their direction. Park, who was in the process of buttering a roll, looked over, puzzled, before he recognized them.

"That's Travis Church, and Clay . . . um, Beasley, right?" he asked, recalling their names from the interviews he had conducted with both of them.

"Yes. Odd that they're here together, don't you think?" Dru whispered.

"Why are you whispering? They can't hear you," he smiled. "And what's odd? Obviously, it's 'date night.'" Park went back to buttering his bread.

"*Hello?* Travis Church is *straight.* Clay, I always suspected was gay, but not Travis!"

"And your point being . . . ?"

"Nothing, I guess," she sighed. Was every hot man in L.A. gay? "I'm just surprised; that's all. And how do *you* know it's date night for them?"

"Trust me. I've been out with my brother and his dates enough times to know. Those two are having a *big* date night. And by the looks of it, I'd say they're in love, to boot."

Suddenly, Dru had an awful thought. "You're not . . . um . . . I mean, you never . . ." She couldn't finish.

Amused, Park took her face in his hands. "Am I now, or have I ever been, gay?" he laughed. "No, sweetheart, I'm as straight as they come, and I'd like to prove it to you tonight. Over and over, if you'll let me."

"I think that can be arranged," she whispered just before he kissed her. She felt his tongue probe her mouth, and she reciprocated eagerly. They only stopped when the waitress brought their entrees.

"Funny that we should see Travis Church, of all people," Dru said after they started to eat.

"Oh? Why is that?"

"He lives right below me. Next ridge down. You can see his whole house from my balcony. He probably thinks I'm a bitch, because I've never invited him up. But you've seen my house. I'd be too embarrassed. His house was in a magazine last month."

"You know what? This is all very interesting about Travis Church," Park said, pointing his fork at him. "But I'd much rather talk about you. So, tell me about your family. . . ."

Across the restaurant, Travis and Clay only had eyes for each other, and had not noticed Dru and Park. The two men were comfortable enough with each other to be able to talk about anything. Their conversation tonight rambled from Travis's high school prom to Clay's first car. The food was excellent, the atmosphere romantic, and the setting perfect. Every so often, one of them would put his hand on the other's thigh under the table. Occasionally, that hand might wander up to a thickening bulge, and caress, but only if the coast was clear.

Despite Clay's initial misgivings about the evening, he was pleasantly surprised to discover that his good humor had returned. Of course, making Travis come so gloriously hard earlier had a lot to do with his tension release.

They actually finished dinner rather quickly and decided to pick up a DVD at the Blockbuster on Sunset. Travis wanted to jump in the pool for a quick swim, maybe a jacuzzi, and then settle into bed with Clay and watch a good movie. To Clay, it sounded like a perfect evening. Travis picked up the check and paid it.

Just as they were leaving the restaurant, the hostess came over to Travis and slipped a small white card into his jacket pocket. She winked at him and, in a low voice, said, "I'm Shari. Call me. Anytime." Travis winked back at her.

They waited only a minute for the valet to bring the car around. Gently nudging Clay forward, Travis laughed out loud in pure joy as they hopped into the Boxster and drove away down Hollywood Blvd.

One-point-four miles away, Kurt parked his British racing green Range Rover in a surprisingly close parking space in the underground parking garage of the Sunset 5 Plaza. He pressed the alarm button on his key and walked to the elevators.

When the metal doors opened, he stepped in and noticed there was another man in the elevator car with him. Kurt casually glanced over at him and saw that he was about twenty-six, wearing very tight black Lycra bike shorts and a fitted tank top from Los Angeles Sporting Club. He had awesome legs and a toned, cut-up upper body. The two men smiled briefly at each other, and Kurt was momentarily drawn to his clear green eyes and handsome face. Crunch Gym was also located in this plaza, and that was where the hot guy was obviously going. Kurt turned back and faced the doors, but the stranger kept giving him the once-over, but good.

After the doors opened on the first floor, Kurt headed over to Virgin, while the other man walked around to the escalators heading up to the upper level, where the gym was located. He never took his eyes off Kurt.

Inside Virgin, Kurt took his time looking at the new releases, listening to new artists with the headsets provided, and checking out the promotions. He selected a few CDs; then he wandered upstairs to the video area and picked up a couple of hot new DVDs. There was a line at the upstairs register, so Kurt went back downstairs to pay.

Just as he reached the landing, he happened to see the hot guy from the elevator standing at the new-release rack at the front of the store. He wasn't looking at the CDs, however. He was scanning the store.

Kurt smiled to himself and walked to the register, taking care to pass within inches of Hot Guy.

"Lose somebody?" Kurt said as he passed him.

Hot Guy whipped around in surprise, then, flustered, tried to think up something clever to say. Failing that, he tried honesty.

"Yes. You," he said to Kurt's retreating figure.

Kurt grinned and walked up to the register. He paid for his selections and rotated around to find Hot Guy standing behind him.

"I was wondering if you'd like to get a cup of coffee or

something. Buzz is right outside," Hot Guy said sheepishly, green eyes flashing his interest.

Why not? thought Kurt. He was definitely cute, and if coffee led to something else, then fine. What else was he going to do tonight? Clean his sock drawer?

"Sure. I'm Kurt," he said, holding out his hand.

"I'm Gage. Nice to meet you," Hot Guy said, obviously relieved.

"Gage. That's a cool name," Kurt said, holding open the plate glass front door for Gage and letting him pass through first. Gage had an amazing ass, and his hamstrings were unbelievably tight, Kurt observed.

"It was my mother's maiden name. Family tradition."

"Well, traditions can be good."

They entered Buzz Coffee and ordered their cups. Kurt found an empty table outside, and they sat down, each nursing his beverage.

"I take it you go to Crunch," Kurt said, indicating Gage's clothes.

"Yes. Well, actually, I teach spin class there." Gage took a sip of his coffee. "But there was a busted water pipe, and the room got flooded. They canceled my class, only no one bothered to call me at home and tell me," he shrugged.

"Ah. You teach Spin. That explains your legs," Kurt nodded.

"Yup. Once a day. Every day."

"Well, it pays off. You have a hot body."

Gage blushed. "Not as hot as yours. I mean, your arms! They're huge! I could never get mine that big."

"Yours look pretty good to me," Kurt said.

"And your pecs! They look like two pillows. I just want to lay down on them," Gage laughed.

Kurt smiled in response.

"So let me," Gage said boldly.

"What?"

"Let's cut to the chase, Kurt. I'm obviously into you. I think you're into me. Let's get the hell out of here and go back to your place." Gage leaned in close and dropped his voice. "I want to see you naked, on top of me, my legs wrapped tight around you, as you fuck me into next week."

Well, give the guy ten points for directness. Kurt smiled. "Let's go, then," he said, rising up from his chair.

Park and Dru had been so involved in their own conversation that they didn't notice Clay and Travis's departure. Some time during their after-dinner coffee, Dru looked over at their table and noticed they were gone.

"So. You done?" Park asked her, breaking into her thoughts.

"Yes. Just a quick trip to the ladies' room while you settle up, and away we go." She got up and went downstairs to the bathroom.

Park was handing his stub to the valet when Dru joined him at the curb. When the SUV was brought around, they got in and Park began the short drive back to Dru's home. He reached over and took her hand and held it, squeezing slightly. She reached over with her other hand and placed it on top of his, completely blissful. They drove all the way to her house in contented silence.

Dru unlocked and opened her front door, then walked in. Park was trailing slightly behind her, his eyes cast down, studying her excellent ass. As soon as the door shut behind him, he could resist the temptation no more, and he reached out and cupped her buttocks with his hands. Dru gasped in surprise but did not pull away. Park allowed his hands to roam in small, tight circles. Dru's heavy breathing let him know that what he was doing was fine by her.

She turned around, and face-to-face with Park, she boldly reached out with her right hand and began to fondle his crotch. His response to this was instantaneous. They began to kiss deeply. Their hands began to rove, and they felt each other's bodies. Alternating between gripping hard and touching softly, they allowed themselves to be felt and to feel, neither one caring that what they were doing had such potential for disaster.

Dru finally extracted herself from Park and walked to the boom box in the corner of the living room. She flicked it on, and smooth jazz filled the room. She had just come so close to letting this man take her on the barren living room floor, and she needed a minute to regroup. Park followed her with his eyes, drinking in her graceful way of movement, something he felt he would never tire of doing.

She went to the sliding glass doors and slid one open to let in the cool summer air. Enjoying the sensation of the air blowing around her body, Dru stepped out onto the balcony. Park decided to follow her. As he stepped outside, he saw her looking over the railing toward Century City in the distance. The silence of the night was suddenly broken by splashing sounds coming from somewhere, but he couldn't figure out the direction of the sounds. Dru, too, had heard the noises, and looked down.

"It looks like the boys are home," she said to him, directing his gaze to the house below. "That's Travis's house," she explained.

Park walked to her side and looked down the hillside. He could see another beautiful house with a thick stucco wall around it. But from their vantage point high above, they could see over the wall into the sloping backyard of Travis's house, where two men were splashing around in the bubbling Jacuzzi that was adjacent to a small swimming pool. A pile of discarded clothes was lying next to some towels and a small leather gym bag.

"Are they naked?" Dru asked, slightly titillated by the sight.

"I can't tell from here, but I assume so," Park responded, glancing down briefly at the pool, then returning his gaze to Dru. He reached out and caressed her face.

"You're going to think I'm awful, but I just *have* to see this," she whispered conspiratorially as she moved to the telescope with the ribbon on it. Dragging it over closer to Park, she peered through the eyepiece and focused the lens.

"You are one twisted lady." Park grinned.

"Shut up! I am not . . . but this is just *too* good! Travis Church, naked, practically in my own backyard!"

"Whatever works for you, baby," Park uttered as he slipped behind her and began to run his hands up and down her body.

Through the telescope Dru could see Travis and Clay clearly. They were hotly kissing each other, their hands touching and stroking each other's slick, wet bodies. The sight was strangely erotic to her, and she found herself becoming completely turned on by the sight of the two men making out. She felt Park's warm hands upon her own body, snaking around her, cupping her full breasts, and then slightly squeezing them. She groaned involuntarily and felt Park's hot breath on her neck as he began to kiss her. She reached her free hand back, found Park's hardness, and began to rub it. He felt good in her hand, and she heard him murmur loving phrases, then felt his tongue flick in and out of her ear, which drove her crazy with desire.

Yet she could not pull herself away from watching the two men down below.

She saw Clay lift Travis out of the water and lay him on his back, on a yellow terry-cloth towel, by the side of the Jacuzzi. Travis spread his legs in a wide V and lifted them slightly up in the air while Clay enthusiastically buried his head in Travis's crotch. After a few moments of furious head-bobbing, he repositioned himself and began to deep-tongue Travis's ass. She could clearly see that Travis was going crazy with pleasure, and she barely noticed that her wrap dress was being undone by Park.

So she was slightly surprised when she felt Park's hands on her bare breasts, though she welcomed his touch. He alternated between gently squeezing her hardened nipples and smoothly running a finger over them, back and forth. She arched her head back and cried out in a soft whimper, urging him on for more.

Park's hands left her for a brief moment, and she heard rustling as he pulled off his shirt. She next heard his belt buckle being undone, then the sound of his zipper being pulled down, which was quickly followed by the soft whoosh of his pants dropping to the Mexican paver-tiled flooring. She reached back again and grabbed his full-blown erection with her hand and squeezed hard. Park stiffened, moaned, and pressed his naked body up against her.

A distant, muffled shout of passion came up the hillside

from below, and Dru couldn't resist looking back at the men below. She saw that Clay had climbed up between Travis's spread legs, his hard, wet buttocks moving back and forth, his shaved balls slapping against Travis's ass. She noticed out of the corner of her eye that the leather gym bag was now half open, and a torn-open condom wrapper was lying next to it.

She felt her thong panties being pulled down, and as they fell to her ankles, she lifted one leg slightly, then the other, and shook them off. Park's hand found her mound and began to caress and tease her. She spread her legs farther apart and felt his fingers enter her, causing her to shudder. With a soft cry of release, she came.

Still, she kept her eyes glued to Clay and Travis. Travis's legs were now thrown over Clay's shoulders, and Clay was slamming into him with a fury that she herself wanted to feel.

She was to get her wish.

She felt her dress being taken from her body and with her peripheral vision saw it float to the tiled floor. She was now completely nude, except for her spiked Manolo Blahniks. Park removed her hand from his cock and took himself in hand.

"Oh, God, Dru . . . I want you so bad. . . . You're so beautiful . . . I want to be inside you," he whispered into her ear, as he positioned himself behind her.

"Yes . . . yes . . ." Dru gasped. She felt him begin to enter her and, widening her stance, welcomed him completely. He fit inside her perfectly, and she ached for the sensations he caused in her as he pulled out and pushed back in.

"Oh, God . . . you feel so good . . ." he whispered into her ear while licking and kissing it.

"Just don't stop fucking me!"

"Don't worry . . . Oh, my God," he moaned.

She drew her hands back, grabbed his ass, and slammed him against her, driving him deeper into her. She cried out sharply, "Oh, yes!"

Again she looked through the viewfinder of the telescope to find Clay still banging it to Travis. She could see by the eager expression on his face that Travis was encouraging Clay on.

Park found a solid rhythm, and she began to anticipate his

thrusts, so she pushed back against him to bring him deeper inside her. She found herself saying things she had never uttered before, carnal things, and she loved how freeing it felt.

The effect her words had on Park was noticeable. He did what she asked, when she asked for it, and then some. He simply couldn't get enough of her. He wanted this to last forever.

Dru's last look into the telescope at Clay and Travis showed her their most private moment. Travis's mouth was hanging open in wonder, love written on his face, and she knew he was climaxing.

The moment felt too intimate for her to watch, and she felt a slight blush of shame that she had intruded on their privacy. She pushed the telescope away and let Park carry her away with the intensity of his plunges. She could sense the moment arriving, and with a loud shout, Park came inside her, his body racked by quivers. She, too, climaxed with such force and power that she thought she would black out. Park's strong grip on her held her up as she tried to catch her breath.

"Baby," he said slowly, trying to regulate his own breathing, "anytime you want to stargaze, be my guest. Damn!"

Dru giggled like a schoolgirl and turned around to face her lover. "Let's go inside. I'd like to try that again, only horizontal."

"Jesus, dude! *Fuuuuck!*" Gage yowled, throwing his head back and clutching the mussed sheets with his hands.

"Yeah, you want it," Kurt said, slamming his hips back forward.

Gage was flat on his back on Kurt's lush bed, his beautiful legs spread wide and bent at a forty-five-degree angle. Kurt was pushing in and out of his ass like a jackhammer, an opened bottle of lube tangled in the sheets beside him.

"Give it to me!" Gage shouted, thrashing about as much as he could, given his position.

Kurt gave it to him. He'd *been* giving it to him for the past forty-five minutes, and still Gage kept going like a freaking Energizer bunny.

Gage had jumped on Kurt the second they entered his posh

apartment. Gage's hands had roamed everywhere they could, while he frantically kissed Kurt with a passion that could only be described as frenzied.

Kurt initially got into the spirit of the occasion, but soon he felt his motions were becoming automatic, not heartfelt. He was just screwing this guy, and he slowly came to understand that he had no real connection with him on any level. That sad realization made it difficult for Kurt to maintain his erection, and Gage had eagerly taken it upon himself to fix that problem.

He had expertly blown Kurt for a solid half hour before getting Kurt hard enough to sit on. Which Gage did, as fast as he could.

Instead of being a sexually erotic encounter with a hot stranger, the whole escapade had only underscored Kurt's loneliness. As he was fucking Gage, Kurt found himself wondering why he was doing this.

"Oh, yeah! That's it! I'm coming!" Gage finally shouted.

Kurt practically shouted, himself. In relief that it was over.

Twenty minutes later, Gage was gone, and Kurt was alone again, sitting in front of his flat-screen TV watching the eleven-o'clock news. The substitute anchor tonight was that good-looking guy who was usually on the six o'clock newscast, Rick Yung. Never one to let a handsome man pass in front of him without close inspection, Kurt found himself watching the entire program. He liked the way Rick composed himself, and he discovered that the anchor's dynamic personality practically leaped through the screen.

After the news was over, a *Friends* rerun came on. It was one of the ones with the hot actor from Clay's soap in it. Kurt watched it for a few minutes, then was surprised to find himself crying.

He felt empty and lonely and wished that he had someone in his life so badly, it ached. As the gang on *Friends* teased and joked with each other, Kurt buried his head in his hands and sobbed like a baby.

12

Dru woke up at nine o'clock the next morning and instinctively reached over to the other side of the bed for Park. Her searching fingers felt only bedcovers. He wasn't there. Surprised, she sat halfway up; then she inhaled the smell of coffee wafting through the house. She could hear footsteps squeaking on the floorboards above her, and she realized he was up in the kitchen. Plopping back down into the bed, she pulled the covers up over her gloriously naked body and hugged the sheets close.

A broad smile appeared on her lips as flashes of the night before passed through her mind. Park on top of her. Park under her. Park below her. It had been an incredible night, and even though she was a tad sore this morning, the four times they had had sex that night were definitely worth it.

A personal best record, in fact.

"Good morning, sleepyhead." Park was bringing in a makeshift bed tray made from a silver platter he had found in one of her cabinets. He had made toast and coffee and had stuck a red rose from her small garden into a water glass. The paper was folded neatly and tucked next to the plate.

"Wow." She reached up for the tray. "I could get used to being served breakfast in bed by my handsome houseman."

"And I could get used to serving it to you." He sat down beside her and tenderly rubbed her leg. "Sleep okay?"

"Who remembers?" she laughed as she ran a hand through her hair, trying to get it into some sort of style.

Park grinned and reached for a piece of toast. "Well, what are your plans for the day?"

"I was going to go to a ten-o'clock spin class. It's Gage's class, and he's my favorite spin teacher. But, I don't think *that's* going to happen. After that, I *was* going to go to the office and try to get some work done, but now I don't feel like it. And you?"

"I want to run by the station and see if anything new has turned up, but nothing much after that. Want to have lunch later? Maybe go look for some furniture?" he gently kidded her.

"Not a bad idea. Let's do it."

"Good. I've gotta go home, get cleaned up, do my thing, but I'll be back around twelve-thirty?"

"Okay."

Park took her face in his hands and leaned close. "Listen. I had a great time last night. You are an amazing woman, I'm glad we decided to . . ." He left the sentence hanging and kissed her. They locked lips for a few minutes, and then Park let go and stood up. With difficulty. "Damn," he muttered, looking at the rise in his chinos. "Ready to go again. You will kill me, you realize."

"Mmm . . . I hope so," Dru smugly said.

"Bye."

"Bye. See you in a few."

Park left the room, went upstairs, and walked out into the bright sunshine, a contented look on his face. He hopped into his truck and drove away, already looking forward to his return that afternoon.

A few hundred feet down the hillside, in another bedroom, Travis and Clay were in bed cuddling, idly watching a cartoon on the flat-screen TV that hung on the wall opposite the bed.

"See? I just don't get kids today," Clay said languidly.

"What do you mean?"

"This stuff. It's awful." He pointed vaguely to the TV. "How can they watch it? Where's Scooby Doo, man? Where's Penelope Pitstop? Speed Racer? Now, those cartoons had heart and soul."

"Spritle! Chim-Chim," Travis remembered.

"Trixie and Racer X, exactly. Now, that was animation! Not this crap," Clay pontificated, pulling in close for a kiss.

"Well, for every *Speed Racer,* there was a *New Ghost-busters,* don't forget," Travis reminded him, kiddingly pushing his face away.

"True. Ah, well, I still think we had it better as kids."

"Jesus! You're turning into an old man...." Travis laughed. "You're all, like, 'In my day'..." he said, affecting the accent of an old geezer.

"I'll show you an old man!" Clay yelped as he rolled over on top of Travis and playfully grabbed his wrists and started to pin him down. "Say 'uncle'! Say 'uncle'!"

Travis barely put up a fight and allowed himself to be restrained. "Or what?" he asked, enjoying the weight of Clay on top of him.

"Or I'll have my wicked way with you!"

"Promise?"

Clay leaned forward and began to sensually kiss Travis, who responded blissfully. Clay felt he would, as long as he lived, never tire of kissing the amazing lips of Travis Church. As the necking got more passionate, he released Travis's wrists and allowed himself to be held tightly by him.

"Oh, shit!" Clay suddenly remembered.

Travis, lost in the moment, was startled. "What? What is it?"

"I completely forgot! I have a fitting today!" He leaned over Travis and studied the bedside clock. "Jesus! It's after nine-thirty! I gotta get moving." He rolled off Travis and jumped to the floor, heading for the bathroom. He looked about the room wildly. "Where did I leave my clothes?"

"In the living room. On the sofa, I think."

"Right. Thanks!"

Travis rolled over to his stomach and sighed. "Do you have to go? Now?"

From the bathroom Clay answered back, vigoriously moving his toothbrush around in his mouth. "Thwarry. I'm stuppothed to be there at noon. I have to hit the gym firthed, thaower up, and change clothes. Am I theeing you later today?"

Travis thought for a minute, mentally sorting out the day ahead of him. "I'm having lunch with my agent at Newsroom Cafe on Robertson. Then I have to tan and get a haircut this afternoon. Then the trainer. And I have . . . something . . . I have to do this evening. If you want to make it late, I should be home by ten," he called back.

"Oh? What are you doing tonight?"

"Nothing that would interest you."

Clay peeked his head out of the bathroom door and looked at Travis. "The other man again? Well, tell him I won't share you anymore!" he half joked.

A thin smile appeared on Travis's lips. "Hardly. Nah, just something . . . personal."

Sensing that Travis wasn't going to tell him anything more, Clay decided to let it go. "Okay. Call me when you get home." He disappeared back into the bathroom.

"You got it."

After putting on his clothes from the night before, Clay gave Travis an intense kiss good-bye and dashed out the door to his Jeep.

The second Travis heard the door close behind Clay, he jumped up out of his luxurious bed and quickly walked over to his closet. He pulled open the doors and stepped into the huge walk-in room.

His interior designer had outdone himself with the space. He had taken a spare bedroom, knocked down one wall, re-configured a couple of others, and created a sumptuous closet and dressing area. It was a study in blond wood and nickel hardware. Clothes racks were built staggered, one on top of the other, into the walls. Hanging shirts were carefully iso-lated from folded shirts, and dress slacks meticulously hung separately from the stacks of pressed and folded jeans. One full wall was filled completely with pair upon pair of well-tended shoes. Another wall was floor-to-ceiling drawers. A large three-way mirror like the kind found in better depart-ment stores was centered on the far wall, and racks of belts and ties hung nearby.

Travis went straight for one of the built-in dressers and

pulled open the top drawer. After rummaging around a bit, he found what he was searching for and held the object tightly in his hand. The cool metal had a calming effect on him.

He had decided on a course of action, and he had to follow through with it, no matter how hard. Too much was at stake. He silently prayed he wouldn't get caught, and leaving the closet, he hoped the day would pass quickly. Nighttime was a long way off, and he wanted to get this over with.

13

Clay arrived at Paramount Studios on time. He had hustled through his morning since leaving Travis's bed, and now that he was at the appointment, he could finally breathe.

Maggie was already there and in one of her outfit choices, a baby blue suede miniskirt and crop tee. She waved at Clay as he entered the two-office suite where the wardrobe fittings were to take place. Clothes racks lined three of the four walls of the outer office. The inner office was used as a changing and fitting room. Two wardrobe stylists were buzzing around, taking out and hanging up clothes from shopping bags titled with names like Fred Segal, Maxfield, Kate Spade, Gucci, and American Rag Company. When they spotted Clay they quickly began to size him up.

"Forty-two regular," confidently said the tragically thin, tall man with bright-green hair cut in a Carol Brady shag. One hand on hip, the other pointing at Clay, he turned to the equally thin woman beside him and began to point at various items of clothing. "Thirty-two inch waist, right, sweetheart?" he directed at Clay. The rather horse-faced woman, dressed head to toe in chic black, was pulling clothes as fast as her counterpart pointed at them.

"Yes. Thirty-two, thirty-two."

"I knew it. I'm Thorton, the head wardrobe stylist for the

shoot tomorrow. You're our hero, right?" His fingers flew over the lines of shirts, deftly pulling one from here, tugging one out from there.

"Yes, I'm Clay. Clay Beasley." He had to smile at the "hero" reference. In the world of commercials, "hero" meant the lead, or most important.

"Of course you are," he nodded. He turned to the woman next to him and tilted his head in her direction. "Penny? I'm thinking celedon."

"Brilliant," Penny replied simply, the lilting tones of England barely noticeable.

"Chocolate pants. I think I got some from Prada. Look in that bag by the chair." He waved vaguely in the direction of a pile of bags and boxes.

Maggie emerged from the inner office, clad only in flesh-colored bra and panties. "What next?" she asked.

"That Miu Miu dress over there. I'm not sure about the print, but I think you can pull it off."

Maggie pulled the vividly striped dress off the hanger, sniffed in indifference, and slid it on over her head. The silky fabric clung to her body in all the right places. She pulled the spread collar wide and left the top four buttons undone, showing more than a daring glimpse of her enhanced cleavage, which strained against the thin fabric. The dress was both sexy and understated. It simply would not have worked on anyone but Maggie, and she knew it.

Penny dashed over and buckled on a thin vintage brown leather belt that hung loosely about Maggie's hips. Realizing this outfit was a keeper, Maggie struck a few provocative poses, to the delight of Thorton and his assistant.

"Perfect!" Penny exclaimed. "Absolutely brilliant!"

"Where are those knee-high Roberto Cavalli boots? I want those to go with it. Then Polaroid it, darling; it's perfection!" Thorton crowed.

Penny rooted through some shoe boxes, found the brown suede boots, and gave them to Maggie, who struggled briefly to pull them on. Again striking some great poses, Maggie threw attitude while Penny grabbed a Polaroid camera. She snapped off two shots of Maggie in the complete outfit, to be used later as reference points on set.

Thorton handed a bright-green shirt and pair of brown pants to Clay. Clay walked into the inner office and dropped his trousers.

After putting on the new clothes, he emerged and spun for Thorton.

"Hmm," Thorton pondered, looking at Clay intensely. "Here. Try these on." And he handed over several other shirts to Clay.

Seven costume changes and two rolls of Polaroid film later, Clay's wardrobe was finally approved. The celedon shirt made the cut, as did a pair of flat-front black Gucci slacks. A pair of black Ralph Lauren Soho boots completed the look. Maggie's outfit was a no-brainer. The Mui Mui dress and Cavalli boots were easily the best of the lot, and Maggie loved it.

In fact, she offered to buy them after the shoot. But only at cost.

Clay escorted Maggie to her car, parked in the garage several blocks away from the office building. Walking across the studio streets, they drank in the quiet of a Saturday afternoon on the lot. There was almost no hustle and bustle, and the air was clear because the Santa Ana winds were blowing through town.

"I told you we'd get this one," Maggie gloated.

"Yes, you did. Let's just hope they run the shit out of it," Clay prayed. The more times the commercial aired, the more money they would make in residuals.

"Please, God. I want to buy this house I've had my eye on in Studio City. So cute."

The pair entered the district of the studio known as New York Street, a section of buildings and alleys that were made up to look like brownstones and skyscrapers simulating the busy, crowded streets of New York City. In constant use, they had appeared in countless movies and TV shows and were currently dressed in a turn-of-the-century style for a much anticipated miniseries based on a Stuart Woods thriller.

"Good for you. You'll love the tax breaks." Clay walked

along for a few minutes in silence. "Say, do you remember telling me that Jack Benz had a boyfriend?"

"Uh-huh," Maggie answered absently. She was mentally trying to figure out if the check she had just written for the dress and boots would bounce, or did she need to transfer money over from savings?

"I mentioned it to a few friends. No one believes it."

"Just can't keep a secret, can ya?" Maggie joshed.

"No, it wasn't like that . . ." Clay tried to explain.

"I'm kidding with you," she said good naturedly. "I don't know what to tell you, except I know what I know. Oh, my God!" Maggie suddenly remembered something. "I forgot to tell you! I thought about it after I left you the other day. I did see Jack about two weeks ago, with another guy. I remember thinking at least he found himself a hot one."

"Oh? That must have been Lefty. A really blond guy?"

"No, it wasn't anybody named Lefty," Maggie chuckled.

Clay was confused. "How do you know? Have you ever seen Lefty?"

"Honey, I wouldn't know Lefty from Righty. But, I do know Travis Church when I see him," she snorted.

Clay literally stopped in his tracks. "What?"

"Yeah, broke my heart, too. Such a hot-lookin' man! Why are all the hottest men gay? It gets so discouraging! Anyway, they were having lunch at Chin Chin. Looking quite intimate, though Travis did look a little uncomfortable. Seemed like they were having a lovers' spat. Oh, you gay men. So dramatic."

Clay was at a loss for words.

What the fuck?!

Travis was seeing Jack? He *hated* Jack! But he did act funny the other night when the subject of Jack Benz had been raised.

Things that had caused some minor concern for Clay suddenly fell into place. Of course! That's why Travis was sometimes missing at night when Clay called him. The mystery lunches Travis wouldn't bother to explain. The way he would never play his incoming messages when Clay was around.

That would also explain why Jack always treated him so

badly, Clay realized. Why Jack had him replaced that week on the show. Travis must have told him they had been seeing each other, and Jack didn't like it. Everything suddenly made sense.

Maggie, who noticed everything, saw the color drain from her suddenly silent friend. She zeroed in on the problem immediately. "What's the matter, honey? You having a thing with Mr. Church, too?"

Clay didn't know what to say. His head was swimming, and he was finding it hard to breathe.

Act cool, he told himself. *Act cool.*

"Oh, no, nothing like that. I just, uh, well, you think you know someone, and then, you don't, really. That's all," he put forth lamely.

Nobody's fool, Maggie saw through Clay like glass. She put a comforting hand on his shoulder. "Honey," she said softly. "I don't know what you're going through, but I'm sorry if what I said hurt you just now."

"I just can't believe it." Clay came clean. "I thought that we . . . I mean, I love him. I thought he loved me. He told me he did!" Hot tears of betrayal started to well up in Clay's eyes, blurring his vision.

"Oh, sweetie, I'm so sorry! Me and my big mouth! Maybe it wasn't what I thought. I could be wrong," she said hopefully.

"No. It all makes sense. Some stuff has gone down, and it fits."

Now Maggie was at a loss for words, so she just did what any friend would do. She reached out and, taking Clay in her arms, gave him a good, long hug. She could feel his tension start to ease. After a long moment, he pulled away.

"Thanks, Mag. I'm sorry. It's just a shock; that's all—yet somehow I guess I knew," he said, wiping a tear away from his face.

"Honey, men are for shit. Take it from me. If this guy was two-timing you, *dump* his worthless ass! You deserve better."

Thoughts of Matt suddenly filled Clay's mind. After all he had gone through with him, he had finally found a new man to trust and believe in, and this man was screwing around on him, too? It really was too much to bear right now, in the middle of New York Street on the Paramount Studios lot.

Maggie placed her arm around Clay's shoulder and walked with him to their cars in silence. As he was about to get into his Jeep, she brought up her purse.

"You going to be all right?" She dug into her bag and pulled out a small white business card. "Here's my card. That's my new number. You call me tonight if you need to, okay?" she said tenderly.

"No, I'll be all right. Just have some thinking to do. I'll see you at the location tomorrow. We'll have fun, right?" he asked, putting on a brave face.

"Of course we will."

"Cool. Okay. Well . . ." Feeling awkward now, Clay gave Maggie a quick hug and got into the Jeep. He started it up, backed away, then drove off, leaving Maggie standing in the parking lot, wanting to kick herself.

It was after six by the time Dru and Park got back to her house up Sunset Plaza. Park carried in the to-go dinner they had just picked up at Chin Chin, and he went straight to the kitchen to put down the bags and boxes. Dru went into her empty living room and turned on the boom box that sat on the floor.

"I don't know about you, but I am worn out." Park leaned against the doorway, watching her, and popped the remains of an egg roll in his mouth.

A sly smile formed on her lips. "I hope not *too* tired," she said suggestively.

"Oh, I think I can rise to the occasion." He walked to her and slipped his arms around her waist. They kissed for a few minutes. Dru giggled and pulled away.

"I'm hungry. And you taste like food."

"Then let's eat." He took her hand and led her to the kitchen. They dug into the bags and pulled out the various dishes they had splurged on. It was far too much food for two people, but they hadn't been able to decide on anything simple. Dru pulled a couple of dishes down from the cabinet and decided to forgo utensils. Chopsticks, it would be.

"I really like the sofa you picked out. Very comfortable," Park mumbled between bites of broccoli beef.

Park had picked her up earlier that afternoon and, true to his word, had taken her furniture shopping. They had hit all the trendy stores down La Brea Avenue, and Dru had found a terrific sofa at Plantation. She had also picked up a beautiful dark-wood armoire and a cocktail table there. She had also bought two great side chairs at another store a few doors down. They would all be delivered in the next few weeks.

She was glad he had suggested she finally go out and get some things for the house. She also appreciated the fact that Park let her wander about the stores, eyeing the fabrics, testing every drawer, touching the finishes without one word of complaint. It was rare to find a man who could power-shop with her and still be standing at the end of the day.

"I know. It's perfect. I can't wait for it to get here. I can't decide on the dining room table, though. I liked that one we saw, but it seemed too traditional for me."

"As opposed to the classic card table and chair you have now," he laughed.

Dru blushed. "You're right. I know. You'd think I have some idea of what I want here."

"I wouldn't sweat it. It'll all fall into place soon enough."

They took their time eating their meal, feeding each other from their plates and the cartons spread out before them. They sampled everything they had bought, laughing at the clumsy way they used their chopsticks. Almost as much food hit the table as actually went in their mouths.

All in all, a great time.

After eating, even though it was still early, they sauntered down to Dru's bedroom, where she flicked on the TV. He decided to take a shower. There was an unspoken understanding that he would stay the night, and they fell into a strangely comfortable routine.

While he was showering, she pulled down the bedcovers and changed into a sheer nightgown she had bought at Neiman Marcus a few weeks before. She walked into the bathroom to go about the business of flossing and brushing her teeth.

She could see Park through the glass shower door, though

his form was a bit hazy from the steam. She could see that his lean, hard body was tinged slightly pink from the hot water and vigorous scrubbing he was giving himself. His blond hair was plastered to his head, and he shook it, sending out a halo spray of water drops. His thickly corded shoulders were flexing with every movement of his arms. The whole scene had the effect of completely turning her on, and almost before she knew she was doing it, she had slipped out of the nightgown, quietly opened the shower door, and stepped in to join him.

"I was wondering what was taking you so long," he whispered, and he pulled her close, the slick soap on his body quickly covering her.

Clay finally reached up and turned on the lamp next to his sofa. He had been sitting there for hours, trying to sort out what he was feeling and what he needed to do. Dusk had come, and he had been so wrapped up in his thoughts that he hadn't noticed he was sitting in fading light until now.

That he was in love with Travis was obvious. He just didn't know what the next step was. He knew he was going to have to confront Travis with the information that Maggie had given him, but in what way? If it was true that he had been screwing Jack as well, then how could he continue to see him?

Clay had been through this before, with Matt, and had no desire to go through it again. With Matt, after his cheating became known, Clay had given him an ultimatum.

The Starbucks kid or me, he had said.

Matt choose the Starbucks kid after much tortured drama. One day he was going to leave Clay. The next day he wasn't so sure, and so it went, and all the while the kid was calling Matt constantly on his cell phone to pledge his undying love. The whole situation had gotten so twisted. Matt finally moved out, taking only one suitcase, leaving all his stuff behind, so Clay had had to pack up his ex-lover's belongings for him just to get them out of the house. It was one of the hardest things Clay had ever had to do.

On that awful day when Matt actually packed his one bag and left, Clay remembered sliding down to the kitchen floor and crying like he had never cried before. Gut-wrentching sobs that racked his body and caused him to curl up in a whimpering ball. He had lain on that cold tile floor for over six hours. The worst had been yet to come.

When Matt first told Clay that he'd found a great apartment but could never take it because it was right down the street, and he knew that would be miserable for Clay, Clay agreed that that would be the worst thing Matt could ever do, and how could he even *consider* it? That had led to a big argument, and just to spite Clay, Matt signed a year's lease on it and moved in. The Starbucks kid moved in with him a few days later. The pain of constantly seeing them together was like nothing Clay had ever experienced. He felt completely replaced.

They, however, seemed very happy together. Two of a kind, apparently.

All in all, it had taken Matt only three months since first meeting the kid to end up living with him. His nonchalance at the pain it caused Clay proved what a small, vindictive man Matt had always been.

The whole sad experience with Matt had shown Clay what was acceptable to him and what was not, and Travis's sleeping with Jack Benz was definitely not. Clay had to face the fact that he had been so wrapped up in the excitement of his relationship with Travis, that he always put off considering the ramifications.

Travis was closeted and absolutely opposed to being public about his feelings for Clay in any way, shape, or form. Not that Clay was marching down the street with a banner screaming "I'm Queer!" but he felt there could be a middle ground on the issue. He had hated not being able to tell his closest friends that he was in love with a great guy, and going over the minutiae of the relationship, as friends do.

The phone rang and broke his concentration. He answered it to find Cissi on the other end.

"Hey, sweetie. How's the hottest new star on daytime tonight?" she asked cheerfully.

"Um, okay," he replied cautiously, wanting to tell her everything but still feeling that he couldn't.

"Humm. Sounds like it. You wanna go see a movie tonight? There's that new Julia Roberts thing at the Chinese."

"Oh, sorry, Cis, I can't tonight. I have . . . plans."

"Oh. The mystery man again? I don't think I like this. I never really see you anymore except at work. I miss you," she said frankly, clearly annoyed.

"Don't give me a hard time, okay? I was just sitting here, trying to figure it all out in my head, when you called."

"Well, I just hate that I never see you anymore. What time are your 'plans' tonight?"

"After ten, I think. It was kinda up in the air," he admitted.

"Well, that's perfect! There's a seven forty-five showing. we'd be done by ten. Come on . . . let's go. Please?" she pleaded.

What the hell. Why not? *It would sure beat sitting here stewing by myself,* Clay thought. "Sure. Let's do it. I'll pick you up in ten minutes."

"Great! Hurry," Cissi said; then she hung up the phone.

14

Jack Benz had lived in a very nice house located in Hancock Park, a rather normal-looking neighborhood by Los Angeles standards. In fact, the houses in Hancock Park were often used to double as other typical American cities such as St. Louis or Chicago in movies and television shows. There was always a film crew shooting somewhere within its borders, because the houses there had the look of Anytown, U.S.A.

The homes of Hancock Park were large and roomy and had that most prized of all assets: land. The lots were large and deep. It wasn't unheard of to have a five-bedroom home, detached garage with servant's apartment, pool *and* tennis court, and still have yard left over for the obligatory rose garden. Though not as well known as Beverly Hills or Bel-Air, some of the larger homes here could easily match and surpass the standards for those higher-priced and more staid neighborhoods.

Jack's house was not among the largest but certainly was one of the loveliest. A big, rambling English tudor, it had what those in the L.A. real estate trade call "curb appeal." Crossed timbers set in thick ecru-toned stucco decorated its sturdy facade. Multipaned windows allowed light into its interiors, and tall, healthy rose bushes grew next to and over the honest-to-God white picket fence that enclosed the property. A beautifully tiled pool anchored the backyard, where instead of the usual tennis court, surprised visitors would discover an exquisitely designed croquet court.

Jack had paid below-market-value price for the house be-cause when he bought it, it was termed a fixer-upper. A fading rock diva had owned it before him and had neglected the house as her cocaine habit became all-consuming. Finally forced to sell, she had taken the first offer that had come in—Jack's—and with the money had bought a small, elegant condo on the Wilshire corridor before checking into Betty Ford.

After sinking untold thousands into it, Jack had restored it to its original grandeur. He had felt it was his due to live in a grand house, and he did nothing halfway during the remodel.

Under Lefty's careful supervision, the peg-and-groove pine floors were sanded down and refinished. The bathrooms were updated with fixtures from Waterworks, and the kitchen was completely renovated. Stunning Baccarat crystal chandeliers were hung in the foyer and dining room, where a twenty-four-carat gold-leaf ceiling softly glowed above Jack's imported English dining table, which could easily seat sixteen. The house was a testament to Jack's ambition and Lefty's taste.

Now finally completed, its owner would never enjoy the splendor of the world he had created.

It was half past nine when the back mud-room door opened slowly. It creaked rather loudly, but there was no one in the house to hear the squeal of the antique hinges. A stab of light clicked on as a flashlight was put to use. The concentrated beam of light moved carefully around the walls and lo-cated the alarm sensor that it had been seeking. A sigh of gratitude escaped the lips of the intruder on seeing that the alarm on the back door was still broken.

The trespasser slowly shut the door, leaving no trace of entry, thanks to the surgical gloves, and continued through the mud room and into the new kitchen. Using the flashlight as a guide, the intruder quickly walked through the expertly decorated house to the front hall and started to climb the stairs. Halfway up, the beam from the flashlight momentarily caught the serene image of Jack Benz staring straight down the landing.

"Jesus!" shuddered the interloper.

The oil portrait of Jack Benz in a full English riding costume, complete with hounds lying loyally at his feet, was a recent acquisition and had been hung with great pride on the landing of the stairwell, just above an antique console. A large floral arrangement of now-dead flowers was directly beneath the painting, its fallen, dried petals a melancholy reminder that this was now an empty house.

"Pretentious prick," muttered the trespasser, eyeing the portrait as the ascent up the stairs began anew.

At the top of the stairwell was a broad hallway that ran the depth of the house. Several oak doorways led off this hall, and the intruder went straight to the one that led the way to the master bedroom. Again using the flashlight as a beacon, the trespasser followed a direct course through the lavishly decorated room.

An enormous four-poster bed covered in Porthault sheets dominated the room, as various settees and antique side chairs created small conversation areas around the room. A thick armoire wall unit that used to be a vestments closet in an abbey in Surrey, England, stood sentinel on the far wall, which housed Jack's impressive and intricate television and video equipment. The beam of light focused on this area as the intruder began a search.

If Jack had splurged on redoing his home, he had truly gone overboard with this home theater system. The largest flat-screen TV Sony made was placed prominently in the middle of the massive armoire. The best stereo speakers money could buy were hidden behind the carved fly walls of the wall unit, as gilded screens allowed the sound to come out in decibel levels that would rival the Chinese Theater on Hollywood Boulevard. Other speakers were hidden around the room to create a surround sound that was equal to none. Two DVD players, three VCRs, and a highly sophisticated stereo were all housed in close proximity to the TV.

In two matching side pieces were stored hundreds of DVDs and video cassettes. And while to the casual observer, this would not seem odd at all, upon closer inspection it could be quickly ascertained that Jack Benz had one of the largest collections of gay pornography anywhere in Los Angeles.

And it was this collection that had the attention of the interloper. After first checking each VCR, including one in an open and unlocked cabinet at the bottom of the armoire, and finding nothing in any of them, the trespasser began quickly scanning the labels, tapes, and DVDs. They were pulled out and tossed aside in an increasingly frantic search. Videos with titles like *Jocks and Cocks, Spank Me, Daddy!,* and *Mission InProbe-able* began to pile up on the one-hundred-year-old Aubusson carpet.

The intruder's frustration began to mount as the search took longer than anticipated. The videos and DVDs began to fly from their shelves, and some spilt open, adding their contents to the growing mess on the floor. In desperation, the intruder began to look at each tape box individually, opening them up and pulling out the tape to verify that it was indeed the same as the title on the box. The minutes ticked by, and still the intruder searched.

After every video had been thoroughly opened and searched, the trespasser sat breathing heavily on the floor, surrounded by a huge pile of tapes and now-empty boxes. Scanning the room, the intruder decided to check every conceivable storage space. Closet doors were pulled open and the contents rifled through, the carefully placed clothing joining the ever-growing pile on the floor.

Both of the multidrawered bedside tables were ransacked, and while no more tapes were found, a dizzying array of sexual toys, from handcuffs to an impossibly large double-headed dildo, revealed that Jack's sexual tastes were quite varied. The intruder actually had to stop and pause to try to figure out what some of the devices did, but time being an issue, they were quickly thrown out of the drawers and onto the floor as well.

"It's fucking got to be here, Goddamn it!" the intruder cursed out loud. "Where would the sick motherfucker put it?"

Completely stymied, the intruder stopped for a second to regain control. It was here, but just where? Where would Jack have hidden the cursed thing?

Suddenly, the room was filled with light, and a deep voice called out, "Don't move! Put your hands in the air where I can see them! Get 'em up!"

The intruder whirled around to face two armed policemen, who were aiming their service revolvers straight at him. He quickly did as they said and raised his hands, not realizing that in his gloved right hand he was still clutching a large, cherry red dildo.

Later, when the two cops told and retold the story to their cohorts down at the station, they would always get great guffaws of laughter describing the stunned look on Travis Church's face when he finally noticed what he was holding in his upraised hands.

15

Clay had been home from the movies for hours, and there was still no call from Travis.

Alternating between anger and worry, he had called Travis's house every fifteen minutes, hoping each time to get a response. He just kept getting put into voice mail. After the fourth call, Clay had stopped leaving messages and simply began hanging up.

He knew Travis had caller ID and would know he had called him repeatedly, but he didn't care. It seemed so ironic to Clay that when he most needed to talk to Travis, to find out what, exactly, had been going on between him and Jack, he couldn't get hold of him.

He finally reached the conclusion that his only options were either to go to bed and deal with it tomorrow, or drive over to Travis's house.

He chose to deal with it tomorrow.

Suppose he went over to Travis's house and found him there with some other guy? What would he do? Throw a fit? Punch Travis out? He knew he wouldn't be able to handle that scene, so it made more sense just to go to bed and try to get some sleep, since he had to be on location in Santa Monica for the commercial at eight A.M.

Clay walked through his home, lost in deep thought. He locked up and cut short his nightly rituals to simply brushing his teeth, then climbed into bed. He set the alarm for 5:30, and, suddenly extremely weary, he fell asleep within seconds after his head hit the pillow.

He slept deeply and without dreams.

An irritating beeping woke Park up with a start.

What the hell is that? he wondered, his mind still in a sleep-induced fog.

He was, for a moment or two, confused about where he was. He pried open his sleep-encrusted eyes and glanced to his right. He saw the sleeping form of Dru, on her side, facing away from him, one hand tucked under her head, the other hugging a pillow. Smiling briefly at the beautiful sight she presented, he was again annoyed by the beeping sound.

He realized that it was his pager, still clipped to his belt, buried in the pile of clothes heaped on the bathroom floor, where he had left his pants. He sat up, swung his legs over the side of the bed, and willed himself to get up.

He stumbled over to the bathroom and, after digging through the pile of clothes, found his pager. He clumsily punched the *light* button and read the blinking number on the tiny screen. Groaning audibly, he again rummaged through the clothes to find his cell phone, clicked it on, and dialed the number he knew by heart.

The call was answered on the second ring. "New Hollywood Police Station, Detectives' division, García speaking. How can I help you?"

"Hey, García, it's Park. I have a page?" Park ran a hand through his thoroughly mussed-up hair.

"Oh, sure. Parker. Nice to finally hear from you. We've been paging you for two solid hours," García grumbled. "Where the hell you been?"

Memories flooded through Park's mind of the sexual acts that had taken place between Dru and him in those two hours, and despite himself, he felt a familiar stirring between his legs. "I'm at home," he lied. "The batteries must be fading. So what's so important?"

"Oh, not much. Just the usual, you know. Got some hookers in, and a car jacker. Oh, yeah, we did arrest Travis Church a few hours ago for breaking into Jack Benz's house in Hancock Park, but hey, you go back to sleep."

"What?!" he practically shouted into the phone, waking up Dru.

She groggily turned to see him framed by the bathroom doorway, kneeling, animatedly talking on his cell phone. He was naked and sporting a half erection.

Not a bad view, she thought dreamily.

"You heard me. Mr. Church was caught . . . red-handed, so to speak." García broke into a small fit of unexplained laughing. "He was ransacking Benz's place. A neighbor called it in when she saw lights flashing around a supposedly empty house," he continued after he had stopped chuckling. "He's here, in the cell, but he won't talk to us. We were wondering, if it wouldn't be too much trouble for you, if you could come down and show us poor boys how a real, live detective gets a murder suspect to talk." García's sarcasm cut at Park like a knife.

"I'll be there in fifteen minutes," Park said. He snapped shut the phone and tossed it down on the pile. He looked back at Dru, who was now propped up on her elbow, chin in hand. Wide awake, she searched his face for information, and finding none, she finally spoke. "What was that about?"

"You're not going to believe this, but they've just arrested Travis Church for burglary. He apparently broke into Jack Benz's house. For what, or why, I don't know."

Dru's mouth dropped open, and she slowly sat upright, the floral printed sheet falling down around her waist, exposing her breasts. Either not noticing or not caring about her nakedness, Dru sat there, stunned.

"Oh, my God. Does the press know?"

"I have no idea. I just found out myself. I don't know how you want to proceed with this, but I suggest you get the man a lawyer—and fast." Park stood up and began to grab at his clothes, pulling them on hurriedly. "I'm sure the papers are going to have a field day with this when it gets out, if it hasn't already. They monitor the police bands, you know."

"Oh, shit!" Dru was up and out of the bed in a flash, grabbing a T-shirt and a pair of men's boxers from a dresser drawer. She quickly slipped them on and then ran out of the room and into the other bedroom, to her home office.

Park got to the New Hollywood Police Station in seventeen minutes flat.

Since the new revitalization of Hollywood had caused major new construction in the Hollywood area, a new police station had been built to go along with the general sprucing up of the formerly rundown area. It was generally felt that a stronger police presence on the Boulevard would help keep down crime, therefore increasing pedestrian traffic, therefore increasing the coffers of the local merchants and businesses.

So, while the old station at Wilcox and DeLongpre had been adequate, it certainly didn't have the panache of the new structure located in the very heart of the new Hollywood, at the corner of Hollywood and Cherokee. Built at a cost of over $200 million, the four-story structure boasted the latest state-of-the-art features a police station could have. Holding tanks, offices, reception areas, interrogation rooms, jail cells, crime labs, and more were all master-planned to keep the business of crime-fighting moving.

Built in a fluid modern style to complement the new Hollywood and Highland center that was several blocks down Hollywood Boulevard, the police station even boasted a street-front Krispy Kreme donut shop that was open twenty-four hours a day. Much derision and ridicule had accompanied the decision to lease out that space to a donut shop, but since the city got a percentage back from sales, and sales were phenomenal—and not just those to police officers—it had proved to be a valid and profitable idea.

Park shared an office on the third floor with two other detectives. There was actually room for four, but ever since Park's last partner retired five months ago, a replacement had not yet been found, so Park worked his caseload alone.

Though no one had come out and said it to his face, he knew that no one wanted to be his partner. He was still the odd man out here. It was never directly said to his face, but Park knew his Stanford and Harvard education, coupled with his family connections and trust fund, caused intense jealousy in the office.

No matter how hard he worked, no matter how many hours he put in, no matter that he had an 87-percent success rate with his caseload, it was never good enough. The other cops always felt like he'd gotten a break somewhere, paid someone off, or lucked into an arrest. It actually didn't bother Park that much that he wasn't really accepted at work, because he loved his job and took great personal satisfaction from doing it well.

His superiors, aware of the animosity toward Park but powerless—or unwilling—to do anything about it, had let slide the fact that one of their best detectives had no partner. There had actually been several high-level meetings to discuss the "Parker Problem," as it was known, and while it was generally conceded that Park did his job very well, it was also felt that perhaps the department would be better off without the fractiousness his presence caused.

Park knew in his gut that they would be only too glad to see him leave the force, and one small slipup on his part would gladly be used as an excuse to get rid of him.

Police Sergeant García was sitting at the night desk when Park walked in. He looked up from his magazine and gave Park a withering glance.

"Ah, Park, glad you could join us. Another debutante ball tonight keep you up late?" he razzed him.

In no mood for it, Park ignored him and went straight to his office, grabbing a pen and a notepad. After emerging from his office, he gave García an icy stare. "Where is he?" he said brusquely.

"Interrogation room three. Bancroft is in there with him. I'm sure he'd love to pass it off to you and go home."

Nodding so García would know he'd heard him, Park strode over to the stairwell. He quickly went down the stairs to the second floor and entered the interrogation room.

The room looked like most other interrogation rooms across the country. A steel table was centered in the space, a row of switches and dials set into its face. Rather industrial-looking chairs were on both sides of the table. A large steel-framed mirror hung on one wall, while plain chalkboards and cork boards covered the other three walls.

What was unusual about this room, however, were the high-tech recording devices that were placed in it. A whispered conversation would be recorded as if it had been shouted. Video cameras were strategically placed in all four corners of the ceiling, so not a square inch of the room was left out of the video coverage. They were the same type of cameras that the Las Vegas casinos used for surveillance. These cameras could pivot, pan, and zoom in tight to view any object in the room.

Behind the framed mirror was, of course, an observation room. But, more than just an observation room, it was also the media center for the interrogation room. Monitors hung from the walls, since each camera's images were recorded on one of five VCRs. The voices and sounds that the microphones picked up were taped on three different machines. It was as sophisticated a system as you could get.

Park entered the room to find Detective Dan Bancroft sitting at the desk, arms folded across his chest, a sour look on his face. A manila file folder was unopened in front of him. Across from him sat Travis Church, who nervously drummed his fingers on the cold steel desktop. A microphone and a yellow legal pad and pen had been placed in front of Travis, as well as a glass and a pitcher of water.

Bancroft looked up at Park as he came into the room, sighed, stood up, and passed off the interview. "He's all yours, but he's not saying anything. He called his lawyer, but the guy's on vacation. I think the law firm is trying to dig someone up to come down here." He grabbed his jacket from the back of his chair and started to leave.

"Anyone manning the machines?" Park asked, nodding his head in the direction of the mirror.

"No, man. It's three o'clock in the morning. You're on your own. The machines are all on; just use the control switches there"—he pointed to the row of buttons set in the tabletop—"and start or stop at your leisure. Good luck with this one." Giving Travis one last scowl, he strode out of the room.

Wanting to wait a minute or two for the tension in the room to ease, Park sat down, opened the file, and began to read silently. Travis looked at him balefully.

"Okay, Travis," Park began slowly, placing the file back on the tabletop. "This file here says you're being arrested for breaking and entering, vandalism, and resisting arrest. Just so you know, I've spoken to Dru Gordon, and she is in the process of getting you an attorney. It is your right not to say anything until an attorney is present, and I will respect that right. But I have to warn you now that this, um, robbery puts you in more trouble than just this." He tapped the file for emphasis.

Travis's eyes grew larger.

"The very act of breaking into Jack Benz's house puts your name at the top of a very short list of possible suspects in Jack's murder. And that's what I want to talk to you about."

Travis bit his famous lip in nervous tension. "I didn't break into Jack's house. I have a key," he finally said.

"A key?" Park looked through the papers in the file and found a list of the contents on Travis's person at the time of arrest. Among the various items was indeed listed *1 house key on plain silver ring*. Park noticed that there was also a separate notation about a much fuller set of keys, those being on a sterling silver Porsche-logo key fob. "And where did you have this key?"

"It was by itself. On a plain key ring. I'd hide it in my closet drawer at home."

"Okay. How is it you come to have a key to Jack Benz's house?"

Travis squirmed.

"Travis, when I interviewed you last week at the studio, you stated that you and Jack Benz were not close, or even particularly friendly. I find it odd then, that you would have a key to his house." He looked at Travis hard. "So tell me. Where did you get it?"

Travis sat tight-lipped for a full minute. He was obviously making some sort of mental decision, and Park hoped it would swing in favor of cooperating.

"He gave it to me," he finally whispered. His shoulders sagged, and he suddenly looked very young and lost.

"And why would he do that?"

"Look, if I tell you, and it has nothing to do with his murder, can we keep this between us?" he asked hopefully. "I'm serious. If this gets out, I can kiss my career good-bye."

"Travis, I can't really promise you that, and you know it. Tell me what's going on. Let me try to help you. If you're not involved in Jack's death, you've got to be straight with me right now. I'll do my best to help you, but you have to help me."

Travis knew he was in a tough spot. His worst fears were about to be realized, but he had no choice. He would come clean. The nightmare was over, and it would be good to finally tell someone about it.

"Oh, man. How did I end up here?" he mumbled painfully to no one in particular. He looked up at Park. "Okay. Here's the truth, and I swear to God, it's the truth, okay? I didn't kill Jack Benz, but I can't say as I'm upset that he's gone. He was a rat bastard and deserved every rotten thing that happened to him. I only wish I'd had the balls to do it myself!" he spit out.

Park sat silently and let Travis vent.

"I've worked so hard the past four years, so hard, and no one helped me. You know how I started out? I was an underwear model for Calvin Klein. Do you *know* how many former Calvin Klein underwear models there are? Hundreds! I managed to overcome that. I did it all myself. You think it's easy to be a success in television? Think again. The odds are against you. You make one little mistake, one fuck-up, and they'll take it away! I'm a spokesman for Sears, for God's sake! I'm gonna lose everything when this gets out." Travis began to cry softly. "Okay. Okay. Here it is. About ten years ago, right out of high school, I came to L.A. for a summer to visit an aunt. I was just a young punk, a gymnast and surfer who didn't know anything. I ended up partying a little too much. Too much alcohol, too many drugs. I'd do things when I was out of it, and not remember the next day what I had done."

Park listened intently, trying to see where he was going with this.

"So one night, I'm up at this party at this dude's house in Malibu—some rich guy I had met at the beach. He gives me a few snorts of coke, and I drink a few drinks. It was a party, you know?" Travis paused for a second to wipe away a tear from his eyes. His voice lowered to barely audible, and he hung his head in shame, his long dark hair falling forward, covering his face. "Only, he must have slipped something in the drink," he continued. "The next day, I wake up at his house, naked, and I'm sore all over. And I mean *all over.*" Travis looked up and shook his hair out of his way. He stared directly into Park's eyes to make sure Park got the point.

He did.

"So I got the hell out of there, and I never saw him again. Until just before I'm supposed to go home, probably two months later. I saw him drive by in his convertible Rolls Royce. I asked a buddy of mine, who was with me, about him, not saying that I knew him or anything, and my buddy tells me that the guy is some big-shot closet case and likes to make homemade porno." Travis began to pull at his sleeve in nervousness. "Well, I freak out, cause then I click, and I realized what happened up at his house, and I'm thinking I'm gonna get AIDS or something. So I go and get tested. Waiting for those results was the worst time of my life, but everything turned out fine, so I kinda just pushed the whole thing to the back of my mind. But you know, to this day, I absolutely will not have sex without a rubber."

Park had heard a lot of stories in his time, but he really felt for this man. He had been abused and afraid for his life. Pretty scary stuff.

"So time goes by, and after college I got the Calvin Klein gig, then I move out here, and I break into the business. All goes swell. I get the soap. I get a great chance on *Friends;* I get endorsement contracts; I meet someone who I care very much for; everything is great. Then, out of the blue one day, Jack Benz invites me up to his house for dinner. He'd given me shit since the day I started on the show, so I think he's trying to be nice. Make peace, right?" Travis looked imploringly at Park. "Only after dinner, he's giving me a tour of his house, and we go into his bedroom. . . ." Travis's voice faltered.

"It's all right, Travis, tell me what happened," Park calmly assured him.

Travis breathed deeply. "So we're in his bedroom, and he flips on his TV. He's got this huge TV system, and I look at the screen, and I see me. Only it's not me, now. It's me from ten years ago." The tears were freely running down Travis's cheeks, and he made no attempt to wipe them away.

"I had really short hair then, and I bleached it really blond—you know; I was a surfer dude. And there I am, naked as hell and flat on my back, getting . . . gang-banged by all these guys. I mean, you could see everything! Just one guy after another, fucking me . . . and the sad part is . . ." He again faltered, his voice weak. He took a deep breath and exhaled slowly. ". . . the sad part is, I look like I'm enjoying it. I mean, you can tell I'm out of it, but I look like I'm having a fucking great time!" he spat out.

Park reached across the table and poured Travis a glass of water. He handed it to him, and Travis drank slowly before putting the glass down.

"So I'm standing there watching this disgusting thing, stunned, and Jack comes up behind me, puts his hands on my ass, and tells me that he's had this tape for years and that he always fantasized about the guy in it—that he just realized recently that it was me, and if I didn't want this to get out and end up on *Entertainment Tonight* or in the *Enquirer,* then I was going to have do whatever he asked." Travis's humiliation was complete.

"What do you mean he *just* realized it was you? He didn't recognize that it was you on the tape, after working with you for a couple of years?" Park asked.

"I didn't look really like I look now. It was ten years ago! My hair was really curly then, bleached blond and cut super short, and I've had my nose . . . fixed since then. It's a grainy tape, and you can really only tell it's me because of . . ." He stopped. Sighing, he bravely continued. "I have a distinctive tattoo, here," he said, pointing to his hip flexor. "Jack had seen me naked when I was changing clothes for a scene at the studio one day. He saw the tattoo and put one and one together."

Not wanting the detective to think he was gay, and therefore would have enjoyed having a sexual relationship with
Jack Benz, he quickly added, "I mean, I'm straight, so the idea
of having some gay guy fuck me was, well, you know, I
wanted to punch his lights out."

"Uh-huh, but in this tape you saw, you were doing that
very thing," Park gently reminded him.

Caught, Travis thought fast. "Man, I told you! I was out of
it! I don't know what they gave me, but I don't remember it,
and I certainly didn't ask for it!" he shot back hotly.

"Okay, okay. Relax. I didn't say that." Park retreated.

"So, seeing as how I didn't see that I had any options . . . I
figured I'd get drunk, let him do what he wanted, and it
would be over with," Travis continued, calming down a bit.
"But, what I didn't count on was what a sick, twisted fucker
he really was. He didn't want to have *sex* with me, he wanted
to *control* me. He had me do the most . . . disgusting things. I
had to crawl around the floor naked in a dog collar and leash,
while he led me through his house barking orders at me. I had
to eat dog food off the floor, just fucked-up shit like that. One
time he made me . . . put on full leather gear—Chaps, arm
bands, hood, the whole thing—and he spanked me for over
an hour while he jerked off. He just wanted to humiliate me in
any way he could." Travis's voice had become a flat mono-
tone as he recalled the anguish he had suffered. "I was
trapped. I had to get the tape back, but once I started down
this road, he wouldn't let up. I never understood it. He was a
good-lookin' guy, you know? He could have had anybody he
wanted willingly, but instead, he had to blackmail me into . . .
well, anyway, he'd always play that tape when this was happening. I had to watch myself getting fucked by those guys
over and over. Countless times. Every time I thought it
couldn't get worse, it did. He held that damn tape over me
and would tell me, 'You do this one last thing, and I'll give it
to you.' But he never did." Travis's posture was telling. His
shoulders were slumped over, and his head hung low, like a
whipped dog. "He had to sneak around because he had a
boyfriend, Lefty Jannel, the art director on the show. So most
of the time it was all really rushed, because Lefty was due to

come over. I hated every fucking minute I was with him. Whenever he wanted to see me, I had to go. He gave me a key so I could let myself in, go upstairs, and find him naked on the bed. It was just a game to him, but it was ruining my life, and that's what got him off, the sick bastard."

"Why didn't you pull a 'snatch and grab' and yank the tape out of the VCR?" Park asked.

"Have you seen his VCR setup? He has, like, four of them, and one is in a locked cabinet under the others. That's where he played it from. I couldn't get at it. Believe me, I tried. You know, his very touch made my skin crawl so much that I had to pop a few pills and knock back a few drinks just to be able to stomach him. By the time 'the training session,' as he called it, was over, I was usually half gone. The only good news was that he had got the videotape from the guy that shot it, and it was the only copy."

Park continued to nod slowly and let Travis talk. He didn't want to interrupt his free-flowing speech. But he had to admit, the more he heard about Jack Benz, the less sad he was that he was dead.

"The whole thing made me sick. I thought I was going to go crazy! I was living this double life, and I have this amazing . . . woman . . . in my life that I care so much about, and I had to hide this awful thing."

"Travis, normally, I wouldn't care about your private life," Park said, finally breaking in. "I just want to solve a crime. But unfortunately, your private life has something to do with that, and I'm truly sorry. I'm sure that this is painful for you, and I can't imagine how you withstood all that." He paused for a beat. "But you're lying to me. I know you're gay, so if you're going to lie to me about that, then how can I believe anything else you say? I mean, this is a pretty fantastic story you're telling me."

"What? I'm not gay, I told you. I just did what I had to do. Made me feel like a whore." Travis was incredulous. It never occurred to him that people might actually conceive of his being gay. Even after telling a story in which he was the sexual toy of men, he was confident enough in his masculinity to think that Park would obviously be able to differentiate between sexual desire and just doing what he had to do. He knew that people always wondered about actors, but he didn't put that vibe out there, and whenever he was caught scoping another man, he always managed to cover it.

"Not gay? Really?" Park pressed, eyebrows raised. "Odd, then, that I saw you and Clay Beasley out having dinner the other night. You two looked pretty tight," Park said. "Besides, the lap massages you were giving each other kinda gave it away. A word of advice, Travis. If you're going to play straight, you might want to reconsider feeling up your boyfriend in public restaurants," he said flatly. He wasn't going to embarrass the man more and tell him that he had also witnessed him getting his lights fucked out Jacuzzi-side.

"Oh, hell," Travis finally admitted, his cocky air evaporating. "Okay. Yeah. I'm gay. So what? I'm sorry I wasn't truthful about that, but I didn't want you to think I wanted or encouraged Jack in any way, because I didn't. I also have a career to consider, and . . . I'm sorry. I *am* telling you the truth about everything else, though. I didn't ask for this to happen, but it did, and I tried to handle it the best way I knew how."

"Why didn't you go to the police? This guy was blackmailing you!"

"Oh, yeah? And, tell them what?" Travis snorted contemptuously. " 'Gee, officer, there's this tape of me, daytime's hottest dude, getting screwed to the walls by a bunch of guys, and someone else is blackmailing me with it'? It would have validated the tape, and it would have gotten out in the papers. I couldn't risk that. I had to handle this myself."

"I see your point," Park agreed.

"Look. I didn't kill Jack Benz. I hated him, but I didn't kill him. If I was gonna kill him, I had plenty of time alone with him to do that. I didn't. The only thing I ever did to fight back was anonymously let this beer company know that their new spokesman was a recovering alcoholic." He smiled grimly at the memory. "That fucked him good. He really needed the money. They pulled his contract, and he was so pissed. He never could figure out how they found out. What an idiot." He stopped to catch his breath. "Look," he implored Park. "I'm guilty of only trying to protect myself from the man. I just wanted to go into his house, find that fucking tape, destroy it, and never have to worry about it again."

"Wasn't too smart to do that so early in the evening, then, was it? Why didn't you wait until later, when the neighbors were asleep?"

"Because Jack has a security patrol cruise by the house every half hour starting at ten o'clock. I had to get in before they started coming around."

Park digested this and sat in silence for a moment. "Is there anything else you want to say about Jack Benz?"

"Not really, except he also extorted some money from me. I guess he figured he had me over a barrel, and he did."

Park perked up at this. "How much did you have to pay him?"

"Fifty thousand bucks. He promised me he'd finally give me the tape back if I paid him that. I paid him, and he didn't keep his word. Big surprise."

"Anything else?"

"Nope. Now what?" Travis asked quietly. "Am I under arrest, or what?"

Park thought for a moment. Most of Travis's story matched up with what he already knew, so outside of trying to protect his sexuality, he hadn't been caught lying. And he had been through a lot at Jack Benz's hands. Of course, he had an excellent motive for murder, but there was no evidence to hold him for that now. And Travis was right about one thing. It stood to reason that had he wanted to kill Jack Benz, he would have done it when they were alone together. A thought came to Park.

"Tell me, Travis. Where were you the afternoon and evening before Jack's death? At our initial meeting you said you didn't work that day and were running around town doing errands."

Travis sighed and looked down. "Okay, yeah, I saw Jack that afternoon. He called me and told me to come over. I was supposed to see Clay that night for dinner, but I ended up canceling because Jack wouldn't let me leave. I was at his house from about three in the afternoon until after eleven. It was one of the longer 'sessions,'" he said distastefully.

Park rubbed his temples. If that was true, then Travis couldn't have screwed with the Rig on set, because Lefty hadn't set it up until after four, and the studio guards locked it up at nine. But was Travis telling him the truth now? Could he prove he was with Jack the whole time?

"Is there anyone who can corroborate that?" Park asked.

"Not that I can think of. The house was empty. Just me and Jack."

"Okay," Park decided. "I'm going to do you a big favor, and you're going to owe me one. Because you had a key to the house, I'm not going to charge you with breaking and entering, since you had previous permission to enter the house. I'll drop the vandalism and resisting arrest charges, but you have to make yourself available for a lie detector test as soon as I can set one up. Probably tomorrow, or Monday at the latest. If you lawyer up and stall me on that, I'll reinstate the charges, and I guarantee you'll be sitting in county for a long time; is that clear?"

Travis nodded vigorously.

"I can't do much to help you with the media, and they're going to get wind of your arrest, so be prepared for that. I suggest you get with your attorney, and maybe the network, and figure out how best to handle it. I don't care what you say to wiggle out of the bad press this will cause, but if you scream police brutality or police misconduct of any kind, I'll slap your ass in jail on the original charges so fast, it'll make your head spin, okay?" He glared sternly at Travis, who was in no position to argue.

"Yes, sir," Travis agreed.

"Then you're free to go. Stop by the sergeant's desk out front, and get your belongings. You'll need to sign out for them, so make sure everything is there. Do you have someone who can pick you up?"

Travis immediately thought of Clay but couldn't think of what he would say to him. In fact, he didn't want to talk to anyone until he could think up a good cover story. "Not really," he said.

Park actually felt bad for the guy. He'd been in a jam and had done what he had to do. Maybe it wasn't the choice he himself would have made, but could he fault Travis? Not really, he decided.

Travis had been used and abused, and now he didn't seem like he could face anyone until he'd had time to sort through it all. Park understood that and was surprised to find that he wanted to help the guy out.

Again, knowing it would be against police policy, he decided he would have to help Travis. He'd figure out some way to get around the rules. He always did.

"Tell you what. Get your stuff; then wait here for a few minutes. I'm gonna wrap some things up, and then I'll drop you off at your house. We'll leave through the underground garage, and you duck down. That way if there's press out front, they won't see you."

A wave of gratitude came over Travis, and he felt his eyes start to well up again. "Thanks. I'd appreciate that," he croaked.

Park gave his shoulder a comforting squeeze, and started to leave the interrogation room. He stopped suddenly. "Hey, Travis," he asked. "Did you ever see that rich guy again? The one who taped you?"

Travis blinked back his tears and shook his head. "Nope, and I hope I never do."

Park absorbed this, nodded, and left the room, going into the empty observation room next door. He closed and locked that door behind him.

16

Sunday would eventually pass in a blur for Clay.
His alarm went off precisely at 6:30 A.M., but he had been wide awake for hours. He wearily reached over and punched it off.

Sighing heavily, he plopped back into his soft down pillows, and his thoughts again returned to Travis. He had not really slept at all and was a little angry at himself for allowing his emotions to rule him. So much had occurred over the past few days, his head actually hurt trying to keep it all straight. Still not having heard from Travis only made it worse. With no information to go on, he could only recycle the info he did have. His so-called relationship with Travis had come to a crisis point. He had to figure out what he wanted and what to do. He knew going back down the path of dealing with a cheating lover was not going to be an option, but didn't Travis deserve the benefit of the doubt? All night long, mentally he'd tried to work out all the scenarios that could happen, having imaginary conversations with Travis and answering himself back as he felt Travis would.

It was a no-win game, and the imaginary conversations always ended the same way: Travis admitting he had lied, and Clay saying good-bye.

And why hadn't he called? It was so unlike him. But then again, how well did he really know Travis?

Clay shook his head in frustration, sat up, and decided to get out of bed. Today was a big day for him, and he needed to clear all thoughts of his fucked-up relationship out of his mind. He headed slowly to the shower and faced the unalterable fact that it was going to be a long day.

He arrived on set for the Dr. Pepper commercial shoot on time, eight A.M., and was in hair and makeup fifteen minutes later. A rare early-morning rain shower had sneaked into town, and as a result, the start of filming had to be pushed back until afternoon.

The location, a trendy open-air bar on the Third Street promenade in Santa Monica, had to be completely wiped down and the floor squeegeed after the rain stopped, eating up valuable time. The sun finally came out about ten, which helped the drying process. As the crew frantically tried to get the wetness under control, Clay and Maggie cooled their heels in their respective trailers.

Which, unfortunately, gave Clay far too much time to ponder again the ramifications of Travis's apparent unfaithfulness. He simply could not stop thinking about it. It was as if his mind was stuck on some sort of loop. Over and over he thought about Travis. He racked his brain to sort through the information that Maggie had given him, and organize it in some logical way, a way that would make sense, and get Travis off the hook. Failing to achieve that, Clay was convinced that he had been played again, and he didn't know what to do about it. The more he thought about it, the more convinced he became that Travis had deceived him.

And it hurt like hell.

He was pulled from his thoughts by an urgent banging on his trailer door. Maggie flew into the trailer and rushed to the TV set. She was completely decked out in the Miu Miu dress and Cavalli boots.

"You are not going to believe this! Have you seen the news?" She didn't wait for an answer, snatched up the remote, and pushed buttons frantically.

"Maggie, what in the world . . . ?" Clay began to complain before she cut him off by holding her hand up in a "stop" position.

"You are going to flip out!" she promised excitedly as she

clicked through the various TV stations. Finally finding the news channel she was looking for, she noticed with triumph the perplexed look on Clay's face as he stared at the mug shot of Travis displayed on the TV screen.

". . . And in entertainment news today," the announcer was droning on, "daytime TV star Travis Church was arrested late last night for allegedly breaking into the Hancock Park home of former fellow castmember, Jack Benz. An Emmy-winning actor, Jack Benz died last week in what investigators are now saying was a suspicious accident on the set of the top-rated UBC soap opera, Sunset Cove."

Various images were used as tape filler for the story: shots of Jack Benz; his home, cordoned off by police yellow tape; a studio still of the cast of *Sunset Cove;* and shots of the new Hollywood police station, where several cameramen were seen standing around waiting to shoot video of Travis.

"Mr. Church was arrested while still inside the home," the announcer continued, "and taken to the Hollywood division police station, where he was detained for several hours, sources say, and questioned not only about his alleged break-in but also about a possible connection to Jack Benz's death. Church's attorney, Hank Blumberg, firmly denied those reports this morning at a press conference held at his office."

Clay sat openmouthed and unblinking as the newscast cut to a shot of an overfed lawyer standing in front of a tidy office building in Beverly Hills, clad head to toe in white tennis clothes. There was a slight breeze, and his comb-over hair style was coming slightly loose, threatening to expose his bald spot.

"My client was not trespassing in Mr. Benz's house," the lawyer calmly stated. "This is a simple misunderstanding and will soon be resolved. Mr. Church had full

*and complete permission to enter Mr. Benz's home, and
all charges have been dropped. And to my knowledge
Mr. Church is not now, nor has he ever been, a suspect in
any continuing criminal investigation. Thank you."*

"Do you believe this shit?" Maggie asked, laughing.

"Shhh!" Clay whispered, not wanting to miss a detail from
the TV.

The newscast cut back to the anchor, who was, not surprisingly, Rick Yung.

*"Police Detective David Parker, who is leading the investigation into Jack Benz's death, would not comment
on Travis Church's arrest, except to say that all avenues
were being explored in solving what could turn out to
be a very tragic murder. And now, with a look at our
weather . . ."*

Rick continued on, but Maggie clicked the TV off.

"What the fuck!?" Clay exclaimed.

"Honey, he's bad news. I'm tellin' ya."

"Had full and complete permission? By who? Jack? What's
that all about?"

Maggie laughed again. "What a loser! He might as well
walk down Santa Monica Boulevard with a sign taped to his
back reading 'Number One Suspect'! Is he for real?"

"I need to call him," Clay said as he reached for the phone.
He was interrupted at that exact moment by the assistant director peeking her head through the door of the trailer.

"Excuse me, you two, but we're ready for you on set. And
a word to the wise: our director is a little agitated this morning. The delays and all." The dead look in the young AD's
eyes indicated to both Maggie and Clay that she had been on
the receiving end of a nasty rant.

"Then let's go be brilliant and make his day!" Maggie
chirped. She reached over, took Clay's hand, and led him out of
the trailer. Clay, ever the professional, pushed thoughts of Travis
to the back of his mind and refocused on the job at hand.

* * *

Dru had spent most of the morning on the phone, consulting with lawyers and other UBC brass to try to decipher what Travis's arrest meant to the network. Joan had gone almost apoplectic in her anger. It had taken almost an hour just to calm her down so they could make some decisions.

They decided to wait it out and see which way the wind blew.

In the meantime, UBC would stand cautiously by Travis unless new details came out that would put the network in a bad light. In that case, they would ditch him and protect their own interests.

Dru also had to deal with the media, because no one could find Peter Dowd, who on Friday had mentioned he was going out of town for the weekend. Promising to get back to every reporter she talked to with the details as she found them out put Dru in the awkward position of currying favor with them, something she was loath to do.

She demanded to know from the attorney she had hired for Travis, Hank Blumberg, what the actor's story was. Blumberg had told her what little he knew, based on a rushed phone conversation he'd had earlier with Travis, and promised to report back to her after meeting with his client that afternoon. Dru had no choice but to wait, since she had to attend Jack's funeral that same afternoon. It was something she dreaded now, knowing that the press would be crawling all over the place.

Jack's funeral was a more stately affair than Dru had thought possible, given the circumstances. The media had been kept at bay behind the gated iron fence and could only videotape the arrivals of the mourners and dignitaries as they got out of their cars. The graveside service itself was dignified and short. Jack's family were closest to the casket as it was lowered into the ground. His mother, so identifiable because she had exactly the same pair of eyes that her famous son did, wept silently as her only child was placed in the open grave.

Dru shifted her weight from one leg to the other. The heels of her shoes kept sinking into the ground, and she was sorely tempted just to step out of them. She was wearing a V-neck dress in black jersey that gathered at the neckline. It was somber and dignified, yet with different jewelry it would be a great date dress. She had hurriedly bought it the day before at American Rag Company, during a quick break from the furniture shopping with Park. She had needed something to wear at the funeral, and it was the first thing she had spied.

As for her golden hair, she'd sleekly pulled it back and gathered it at the base of her neck with a silver-and-onyx hair clasp.

She gave a cursory view to the attendees and spotted mostly familiar faces. Lefty, dressed all in black Calvin Klein and standing with the family, nodded solemnly at her as she gazed around. She saw Sylvia, complete with black pashmina, Cissi, Scott Tyler, and Sam Michaels all clumped together on the edge of the small crowd. Joan Thomas stood alone, clad in her usual dowdy brown, scowling. She repeatedly looked at her watch, giving the impression that she had other, more important funerals to go to that afternoon.

Dru also noticed a strikingly tall woman way in the back of the crowd, wearing a beautifully cut navy Chanel suit. She had on a demure hat complete with net veil, which covered her face enough so that Dru couldn't get a good, solid view of her facial features. She seemed oddly familiar, though Dru couldn't think who she was.

Turning her attention away from the statuesque woman, Dru looked around some more and became far more intrigued by those people who didn't show up. Travis Church was an obvious no-show, as was Cathy Grant, Jack's love interest on the show. That seemed odd. She didn't see Clay Beasley either, and thought that strange until she remembered he had a commercial shoot that day—something his agent had advised her about on Friday.

Looking over her right shoulder, she caught her breath when she spotted Park, hanging back from the rest of the mourners, surveying all who were present, too. He was in his rumpled khakis but had put on a dark-gray tie and a navy blue blazer. She tried to catch his eye, succeeded, and smiled slightly at him. He winked back at her but made no effort to join her side. She returned her attention to the service, and when she looked back for him a few minutes later, he was gone.

When the service ended, the crowd dispersed, with the cast and crew of *Sunset Cove* quietly converging on Jack's family to offer their condolences. One by one, they said hello and struggled to find something nice to say about Jack as they filed past. Once that tedious chore was over, they each hurried back to their cars in the parking lot.

As she left the crowd behind and walked away from the graveside, the tall woman Dru had spotted earlier began to breathe easier. She wasn't sure if it had been a good idea to come to the funeral, but she felt the need to be there, and it was also a good test. So far, so good. She'd gotten nervous when Dru Gordon stared at her intently, obviously trying to figure out who she was. It became clear that Dru couldn't place her when she had returned her attention to the funeral and never again looked in her direction. Reaching up to scratch her nose, Peter Dowd felt a rush of relief to know he could pass.

This opened up a world of possibilities for Peter, and he smiled to herself.

Blumberg drove up to Travis's house, parked his black Escalade on the winding street, and boldly walked past the four cameramen positioned at the gate. Ignoring their shouted questions, he entered the gate when it buzzed open, and confidently strode up to the massive glass door. Letting himself in, he gave a last look to the jackals who were videotaping him, and smiled expansively.

A chastened Travis met him in the living room, and after exchanging banal pleasantries, they got to the business at hand.

After discussing the issue for over an hour, Blumberg knew his client wasn't being honest with him on most of the events that had happened. Lawyers knew a lie when they heard one, and this kid's story was full of them. Not having reached his position as an entertainment powerhouse by being stupid, Blumberg saw through Travis's feeble story as quickly as it fell out of his lying mouth. He correctly guessed that this pretty-boy actor was shtupping the dead guy and wanted to get something of his that was in the house back. But instead of calling Travis on it, he played along.

Ultimately, after another hour of back-and-forth, together they had managed to cobble together a somewhat plausible story. It held up, Blumberg decided.

If you didn't look too hard.

Travis had gone to check up on his deceased good friend Jack Benz's house, as he used to do when Jack was on vacation. After letting himself in with a key that Jack himself had given him, an elderly neighbor lady, who was a dedicated viewer of *Sunset Cove* and loved Jack dearly, noticed suspicious movement in the house and had called the police, as any concerned citizen should do. When the police arrived, they had walked in and found Travis straightening up Jack's home after it had been put in shambles following a search by the police the day before. Not understanding the situation completely, they did their job and arrested who they thought was a burglar. When it was discovered that Travis was not a burglar but rather a grieving friend, the police had quickly dropped all charges. And, as a gesture of good faith on Travis's part, he was sending a sizable check to the policemen's fund to show no hard feelings, and a bouquet of flowers to the neighbor to thank her for her diligence in watching Jack's house so closely. Case closed.

Filming the Dr. Pepper commercial had been long and tedious but ultimately rewarding. Racing against the clock, Maggie and Clay gave the director exactly what he wanted, over and over again. After countless retakes, they still maintained their energy and focus. They set the example for the rest of the cast and crew, who, realizing they were dealing with two actors who knew their craft, quickly quit the petty bitching and carping that happens on every set. To a person, they each rose to the occasion and gave their all for the shoot, which miraculously, even with the time delays, ended on schedule.

When they wrapped for the day, Clay did his customary rounds. He went to each crew and cast member to thank them for their time and effort, and let them know what a great job they had done. A warm hug here, a firm handshake there. He knew that he would be working with these people again someday, and he wanted them to remember him as a solid professional. Many an actor's career had been hurt by backstage talk of rudeness or callousness, and it was something he never wanted to happen to him.

After kissing Maggie good-bye, he got into the Jeep and began the drive back to West Hollywood. Using the cell phone, he checked his voice mail at home, but there was no word from Travis.

It irritated Clay beyond belief that not only had Travis stood him up the night before, but he had also been arrested and *still* hadn't called him. If that didn't tell Clay where he stood in Travis's opinion, then what would? He desperately wanted to know what had happened the night before and what it meant, but he was also afraid of the truth.

Travis's being in a dead man's house, particularly since he had sworn he hated the occupant, pretty much proved that he had something going on with Jack and had lied to Clay. Clay truly prayed that there was a logical explanation, but wasn't confident there was.

Irked that he hadn't heard from Travis, he resolved as he was pulling into his parking garage that he was not going to be the first to call.

Upon her arrival back home, Dru heard what Blumberg had come up with. She didn't buy it. It was a paper-thin story, but being the company gal that she was, she called each reporter back and trumpeted it to all who would listen. She actually managed to control the story by the end of the day.

Travis would owe her one big-time.

Finally, at around eight in the evening, she hung up the phone for the last time that day and turned off the phone's ringer. Any other calls could go to voice mail, she decided. She had tried to get hold of Park but only got his answering machine. It was just as well. She was bushed from the day's events and just wanted to draw a hot bath and soak for an hour before going to bed.

She did just that.

17

Clay was off from the show on Monday, so he allowed himself the luxury of sleeping in late and took his sweet time getting to the gym. There was no word from Travis, and it was the longest they had gone without speaking since they started to see each other. Clay was mad and upset and sad all at the same time and wanted to focus his inner rage at the weight machines.

Not even conscious of the gym clothes he was wearing that day, he didn't realize that he had a tear in the seat of the baggy cargo shorts he had slipped on just before he walked out his door. When he got to the gym, Rick Yung gladly pointed out the tear to him. Mildly curious as to how he did it, but not particularly bothered by the hole, he thanked Rick for showing it to him, and tried to continue with his work-out.

"You can see your underwear," Rick said, fingering the rip in the shorts, the tip of his finger subtly caressing Clay's ass.

Kurt, who had confidently strode into his domain, the gym, not thirty minutes before, saw Clay from across the busy floor. Deciding he should go say hello, he was stopped short by the sight of Clay having his ass squeezed by the hunky news anchor he had watched on TV the other night. The news anchor must be the guy that Clay was seeing, he realized. His brow furrowed at this revelation.

Typical, he thought morosely. *The only two guys I'm remotely attracted to are dating each other.*

Deciding not to embarrass himself in front of Clay any further, he changed direction and headed upstairs to run on the treadmill.

"Here," Rick said, pulling off his gray sweatshirt. "Tie this around your waist; that way it'll hide the hole." He handed the sweatshirt to Clay, who took it and tied it so it covered his ass.

"Thanks, Rick," Clay said, trying to be polite.

"No prob! I guess you heard about Travis getting busted, huh? What's going on at your show? Is it a full moon, or what?" Rick joked.

Trying to muster up a half smile, Clay didn't want Rick to know that any of it bothered him. "I guess so. Well, thanks again for the sweatshirt. I'll get it back to you before I leave."

"Sure, whenever. I don't need it," Rick smiled brightly and walked a few paces away to the triceps pushdown machine he was working on. Clay idly watched him do a set and had to admit that Rick did have amazing arms. In fact, upon closer inspection, his whole body had a sinewy sexiness to it that, in different circumstances, Clay would find quite desirable.

Maybe I've been a little too judgmental of him, Clay thought. *I should lighten up.*

In a show of friendship, Clay playfully squeezed Rick's shoulder as he walked past to get to the biceps machine he needed. Rick looked up, surprised, and beamed.

Clay worked out hard and long, trying to tire himself out. He did double ab work because he felt he needed the push. Just as he was finishing up his routine, he glanced at one of the many TV monitors that hung suspended from the ceiling.

There was Travis, in a news video obviously taken that very morning, personally delivering flowers to some old lady who seemed thrilled to be the center of such attention. Travis looked good in the tight jeans and John Varvatos leather blazer, and he seemed not to have a care in the world. He even chuckled happily as the old lady kissed him on the cheek.

Fuck him, thought Clay. *He can go deliver goddamn flowers to some old bag, but he can't pick up a fucking phone?!*

Whatever good humor he had achieved at the gym was now gone. Sullenly he grabbed his car keys from the storage cubicle, and stormed out of the gym. It wasn't until he got home and discovered that Travis hadn't called that he even noticed he still had Rick's sweatshirt tied around his waist. Pulling it off, he threw it angrily in a heap on the sofa and began to pace. His rage started to build.

Who the fuck did Travis Church think he was, anyway? he fumed.

All that he had put up with! The secretiveness. The hiding his feelings. The not being able to share this part of his life with his friends. And this was what he got in return? Another loser guy who fucked around on him? *And* didn't call?

The more Clay stewed about it, the angrier he got.

Dru sat at her desk, her head in her hands. Thoroughly annoyed, she didn't know what to do. She had been off the phone with Lester Jarvis, the president of the UBC network, for over an hour, and she replayed the conversation over and over in her mind.

"Dru, darling, how are you?" Lester had asked cordially.

"I'm fine, Lester, considering the circumstances. I've had a busy weekend, as I'm sure you can imagine."

"Yes, I'm sure. I saw the coverage on Jack's funeral. Very dignified. Made UBC look good . . . So tell me, how bad is this Travis Church thing going to be?"

"I think we've got that under control, Lester. *Entertainment Tonight* called and wants to interview him regarding his great attitude after his wrongful arrest. I think we take advantage of that, milk it for all we can, and spin the story into positive publicity for the show." Dru rubbed her temples. It was only ten in the morning, but she already felt like she had put in a day and a half so far.

"Well, that's certainly good news," Lester said. "Listen, Dru, I had an interesting phone call this weekend from Joan Thomas."

Dru sat up straight. Suddenly filled with dread, she braced herself for what was about to come. "Oh?" she managed to say calmly. What had Joan told him? Something about Park? Was she going to be fired?

"Yes. You may not know this, but Joan and my wife went to Sarah Lawrence together. Roommates, in fact. So, we consider Joan to be like family. Now, I know she can be a bit . . . direct sometimes, but she has always delivered for us, and we take her advice very seriously."

Oh, Christ, Dru thought. *Here it comes. Good-bye corner office.* She quickly began to calculate what her severance package would be.

Would the Aeron chair fit in her car?

"Joan seems to feel we must recast Jack's character. The network's made a substantial investment in his story line, and she feels it would hurt the show to pull focus away from Cathy Grant's character. I understand that Cathy's been asking Joan to ramp up her role, so perhaps this is a blessing in disguise. I know you feel Travis and Melina are the direction to go in, but in light of recent events, that might not be the most prudent thing to do right now." Lester continued in his fatherly manner.

"Uh-huh." Dru nodded into the phone.

"I think our audience will understand if we recast Jack. We need a Stone Coltrane, and I want you to make it happen."

Dru thought for a minute before answering. Finally, she decided to speak her mind. Wasn't that what they paid her for?

"Lester, you know I'm a company girl," she began. "Whatever you say, I'll do. But I want to go on record as saying this is a bad idea. I don't think you give our audience enough credit. Daytime fans are rabid! This will not go down well, and I beg you to reconsider."

"Dru," Lester started to say.

"Please, Lester, let me finish," Dru interrupted. "Travis Church and Melina Michele pull in the demographics we want. We have turned Travis's little hijinks this past weekend into a plus, which can only help viewership, and I must say, I am very disappointed that Joan chose to go over my head. She knows how I feel about this." Dru had worked up a good head of steam and had to struggle to control her voice.

"Dru, Joan raised a concern with us—I mean me, and I have to agree. But to be perfectly honest with you, I have heard some rather disturbing reports about the way you've been handling your duties. It would not be wise of you to press this point with me. Do I make myself clear?" Lester's fatherly voice had turned to steel.

Defeated, Dru barely whispered her reply. "Yes, sir."

"Good. That's settled. Begin the recasting process as soon as possible. I'll be out to the coast next week. Let's take lunch, you and I, and see if we can't come to some agreement as to how we can do a better job. How's that sound?"

"That's sounds just great, Lester. I look forward to it." *Could I be more of a hypocrite?* Dru thought.

"Terrific! See you then." Lester had hung up the phone before Dru could reply.

Now, an hour after the phone call, Dru could see the handwriting on the wall. Her days at UBC were numbered. Joan would win this one, she thought bitterly.

Or would she?

An idea began to form in Dru's head, and instinctively she decided to follow it. She picked up her phone and punched in a few digits.

"Accounting. This is Kyle," answered a thin, reedy voice.

Kyle. Who was Kyle? Dru racked her brain. Oh, yes, the new hire who had the worst case of acne she had ever seen.

"Kyle! It's Dru Gordon; how are you?" she said cheerfully.

"Oh, hi, Ms. Gordon. I'm fine, thanks." There was an awkward pause. "Um, what can I do for you?"

"Kyle, how's your morning look? Are you very busy?" she said casually.

"Well, we have payroll, and I was going to get a jump on the invoices for next month. Why?"

"Kyle, I need a huge favor from you. A special project."

Clay was sitting on his sofa, moping, when the front door buzzed and pulled him out of his funk.

Maybe it was Travis!

Figuring that Travis had forgotten to bring the key that he had recently given him, Clay pressed the button that let the visitor into the building, and quickly he raced to the mirror to check his hair and appearance. In a few minutes, he heard his doorbell.

He was caught off guard to see Rick Yung standing there, a workout towel over his shoulder, and wet hair indicating he had just showered. He was holding a paper bag, and two cups of Seattle's Best coffee in a paper tray.

"Hey," Clay managed to say.

"Sorry about just dropping by, but you left the gym in such a hurry, I didn't get a chance to ask you if you wanted to go have breakfast, so I took a chance and brought it to you here." Rick blushed. He looked a little nervous and kept rubbing one of the coffee cups with his index finger.

Opening the door wide so Rick could enter, Clay took the tray from his hands. "Wow. Thanks, Rick. That was really nice of you. Come on in."

Rick, relieved to have been asked in, walked over to the sofa and noticed his sweatshirt lying in a pile.

"Oh, sorry about that!" Clay moved quickly to pick it up and tried to fold it with one hand while still holding the coffee tray. "I forgot to get this back to you. I'm so sorry," he said.

"Oh, no problem."

"How did you know where I lived?"

Rick turned red and shyly grinned. "I looked up your address at work a while ago. I'm not an investigative reporter for nothing, you know."

Clay lost his balancing act. The two cups of coffee popped out of the tray and fell to the floor, creating a large, brown puddle on the polished hardwood. "Damn!" Clay uttered as he dashed into the kitchen to get a dish towel.

Rick was already on his hands and knees trying to mop up the coffee with his workout towel when Clay returned. Clay dropped down to join him.

"Oh, Rick, I'm so sorry! Not the most graceful person on the planet, am I?" he mumbled feebly.

"So, you're not perfect after all, are you?" Rick razzed him. Their faces were almost touching as they swirled the towels around to soak up the liquid.

"Hardly," Clay responded, finally getting the last of it wiped up. He looked at Rick.

"Well, I think you are," Rick whispered as he brought his face even closer to Clay's and closed his eyes.

And then Clay did something that surprised him.

He kissed Rick Yung.

His anger and resentment toward Travis were clouding his judgment and made him feel like turnabout was fair play. If this incredibly hot man wanted to have a go with him, why not?

Having made the decision, Clay committed.

Fully.

He not only kissed Rick again, he dropped the wet towel, reached up, placed his hands on Rick's face, and pulled him down to the floor. Rick went ardently, and soon Clay was straddling him, pulling, tearing, and ripping his clothes away. Rick adjusted and maneuvered his extraordinarily lean, ripped body to make his clothes' removal as easy as possible, and was soon left wearing only a surprisingly sexy leopard-print thong that barely contained his raging hard-on.

Clay wanted to feel loved, and he knew that at that moment, Rick loved him. He stroked Rick's beautiful body, grabbed at his erection, and squeezed. Rick groaned loudly and, with eager fingers, got Clay out of his clothes.

Rick had the most wondrous skin that Clay had ever touched. Velvety smooth, soft, and warm, it drove Clay wild with a longing hunger, and he allowed his tongue to travel to places that it rarely went. Flipping him freely onto his stomach, Clay used his hands to lift Rick's backside up into the air, pulling him into a kneeling all-fours position, and he began to kiss and tongue Rick's astonishingly hard ass cheeks. He slowly peeled down the thong, and while Rick whimpered in pleasure, he dove in.

Rick reacted strongly to the sensual assault he was receiving. He tried to spread his legs as far as they would go, yet still keep his ass in the air. He never wanted this to stop. He shouted out the delight he felt, and urged Clay on, not to stop, don't ever stop! He actually began to twitch with the intense feelings he was experiencing, and before long implored Clay to enter him.

"Please! . . . Oh, man, I . . . gotta have it! . . . Please!" he gasped in short, staccato bursts while pushing back his ass into Clay's face.

"You want it? You want me inside you? Is that what you want?" Clay demanded, completely turned on by the bucking he was causing in the exceedingly hot anchorman beneath him.

Dirty talk and role-playing were not something that Clay did that often, but for some reason, in this situation it felt right. Clay didn't know if it was a need to lash back at Travis for shutting him out, or a compulsive desire to control someone else as he felt he had been controlled. In any event, he was completely turned on by the erotic reactions he was causing in Rick.

"Oh, yeah! YES! Now! Don't make me beg!"

"Yeah, that's exactly what I want you to do. I want you to beg! Tell me how bad you want it! Tell me!"

"Oh, God, so bad! So bad! I WANT IT! Give it to me! Please!"

Within moments, Clay was sliding in and out of Rick, whose shouts of gratification encouraged him on. Clay brutally slammed into Rick with hard thrusts that he took willingly. He took a firm hold of Rick's hips and pulled him back into each thrust, causing a loud, excited grunt to come out of Rick's open mouth each time.

"Oh! . . . Yeah! . . . Oh! . . . That's it . . . Oh! . . . Just like that!" Rick panted.

Clay lost all sense of time as he was fucking Rick. In his mind he was fucking Travis, taking out all his frustrations and fears and anger in the pounding he was dishing out. He was carried to another place, a zone in his head where he and Travis were welded together as one.

He never heard the door open.

Time stopped as Travis stood still, locked into place in the open doorway, shock and disbelief flooding his face. In one hand was his key ring, containing the key to Clay's building. In his other hand was an even grander bouquet than the one he had been convinced by his lawyer to give to Jack Benz's nosy neighbor.

"What the fuck?!" was all he could muster to say.

At that exact moment, Rick could not contain himself any longer and climaxed, arcing out a stream that hit the coffee table, easily several feet away.

Clay and Rick both turned to the direction of the voice, and seeing Travis, Clay gasped. Rick, spent, fell forward onto the floor, puffing heavily.

Travis just stood there, staring at his naked lover, who stared back defiantly. Neither said a word.

"Do you mind?" Rick finally said between deep breaths. "We're kind of busy here." He gave Travis a wink.

Travis, stunned, looked at Clay with hurt eyes, dropped the bouquet to the floor, and turned around. Without saying a word, he walked out, closing the door quietly behind him.

Clay sat back on his haunches and covered his face with his hands.

This did not just happen, he told himself. *This did not happen.*

"Jesus! What was that about? How'd he get in here?" Rick asked, rolling over on his back.

Clay said nothing.

"Good God. That was the most intense, satisfying fuck I ever had!" Rick closed his eyes and smiled. His still rock-hard erection throbbed noticeably at the same rate as his pulse.

"I'll be good to go again in a few, if you're up for it," he suggested, reaching out and placing a sweaty hand on Clay's thigh.

Ashamed, humiliated, and dejected, Clay didn't answer Rick. Instead, hot tears fell from between his fingers and gently splattered onto the floor.

18

Dru and Kyle sat on her office floor, surrounded by open ledger books and countless files. Papers were placed in various piles around the room. Kyle had a pencil stuck behind his ear and was pulling even more papers and receipts out of several large manila envelopes. Every once in a while, he would punch up a long column of numbers on an adding machine next to him and then compare those numbers to those he had found in the pages.

Dru had kicked off her shoes and was looking through stacks of invoices. Every so often, she would pull a file folder over and compare papers. She scribbled notes down on a pad, organizing her thoughts.

Her phone rang, and since she had given strict instructions to her assistant not to interrupt her unless it was Park, she reached up to the desk and picked up the receiver.

"Dru Gordon," she said into the mouthpiece.

"Hey, it's Park. Have you got a minute? What are you doing?" he asked, his voice oddly detached.

"Oh, a little detective work of my own. What are *you* doing?" she said, a warmth of affection overcoming her tone.

"Packing up my desk."

"What?"

"I'm on suspension. My chief just called me into his office. 'Gross dereliction of duty and bad judgment' are the official reasons," he said tightly.

"Oh, my God, Park! Why?" Dru was shocked.

"Apparently, someone called my supervisor and informed him I was sleeping with a suspect in the Jack Benz murder investigation. Any ideas?"

"Joan. That bitch!"

"That's what I figure, too. Plus, I didn't help myself by giving Travis Church a break the other night. My chief says I have loyalty issues. Can you believe that shit?"

"Oh, Park. I'm so sorry!"

"This is not about you or Travis; I guarantee it. It's about me being a rich man who was never really accepted here. They found a loophole, and they're using it to get rid of me. It's been coming for a long time, and I'm not surprised."

"I'm so sorry," Dru said again.

"Don't be. Meeting you was the best thing that's happened to me in a long time. I'd do it all over again in a heartbeat."

Dru didn't know what to say.

"By the way, good spin."

"Huh?"

"Travis Church. Your spin. Took the heat right off him, didn't it? Made everyone look good, even the neighbor lady. Good work," he conceded.

"Well, that is part of my job. He's got a good lawyer, too. That helped."

"Apparently."

"Say, now can you tell me what really happened at Jack Benz's house?" she asked.

"Didn't you catch the news? It was all a great big misunderstanding."

"Please. That's bullshit, and you and I both know it. You'll talk. I have ways of making you talk, you know," she purred. She glanced at Kyle who was lost in his papers, adding up numbers and paying no attention to her conversation.

"You're on. I'll never crack, but I'm willing to let you try," he played back.

"Deal. By the way, Travis told me what you did for him, letting him go, taking him home. That's was above and beyond, Detective Parker, and I'm so sorry it cost you your job. I . . . just wanted to thank you."

"Please do. Thank me into unconsciousness," he said suggestively. "And I'm not fired. Yet. I'll have a hearing in a month. I'm just on paid suspension. But I'm sure they'll figure a way to make it stick. I won't be welcomed back; that's pretty obvious."

"So now what?"

"Gonna get my box of personal effects—and me—the hell out of here, go home, have a cold beer, and figure it out."

"I'm here if you need me"

"Look, I think it's fair to warn you. Lefty was my number one suspect. The guy they gave my cases to? His name is Bancroft. He's a dick, and he's sniffing around Travis. He smells blood and thinks he'll get a promotion if he makes a case stick. Now, I don't think Travis did it, but he does have a pretty good motive. Fortunately for Travis, I, uh, 'forgot' to mention that fact to Bancroft. If he finds it on his own, then Travis is going down. So as someone who wants to help you and Travis, out, I'd advise him to keep the lawyer. He'll probably need him. Soon."

Dru sighed. "Oh, God, Park. Are you sure? I just can't see it. Lefty? Travis? It's just so hard to believe."

"Trust me on this."

"Okay. Please, please, is there any way you can give me a heads-up when the police plan to move on this? I have people that I have to answer to, and I need to be prepared. Please, Park. Can you do that?" she pleaded.

"Dru, I can't. . . . I'm officially not involved with it anymore," Park started to say. But he stopped and marshaled his thoughts. "Tell you what. I do still have one or two friends around here. I'll see if I can stay in the loop on this, and I'll let you know what I find out, okay?"

Dru held on tightly to the phone and closed her eyes in relief. "Thank you."

"Listen, I gotta get out of here. I'll call you later," Park said, and in an instant he was gone, having hung up the phone.

Dru stared out her window for a moment.

"Dru," Kyle interrupted her thoughts. "This doesn't add up."

"What doesn't?"

"I have an invoice from Klein Productions for costumes in March, but the actuals show a different number, almost ten thousand dollars less."

Dru crawled over to where he was and looked at the figures. "Good. Note that down."

"You know, it would really help to have Klein's books," Kyle said, rubbing his temples. "We're picking at pieces here. If we had theirs, we could marry up each invoice and bill to their actuals. I have a feeling what you really want is in those other books."

"Yeah, but we don't have them. And I can't very well call Jake Klein up and ask for them," Dru said dejectedly.

"But you don't have to."

"What?"

"Joan has them in her office," he explained. "I was in her office on Friday, getting some approvals, and I saw her looking at them. I think she's been reviewing their quarterlies."

"Kyle! That's perfect! We have to get them." Dru began to formulate a plan. Her faced brightened, and she smiled slyly at him. "Feel like doing something a little risky?"

Kyle had not had this much fun since he'd arrived at UBC six months before, fresh out of USC. Frankly, he was bored stupid by his dull job and had been thinking of quitting. He was up for anything that would make it more interesting. He nodded vigorously.

Dru got up and ran to her office door. She pulled it open and leaned out into her assistant's office.

"Carole, get me Joan Thomas on the phone."

When her phone buzzed with Joan holding on the other end, she calmly picked it up. She took a deep breath before speaking.

"Joan, how are you?"

"I'm fine, Dru. What is it? I'm in the middle of a meeting." Joan was her typically charmless self.

"Well, I just got off the phone with Lester Jarvis."

Her interest now piqued, Joan changed her tone instantly. "Oh, really?" she asked sweetly.

"Yes, and I'd like to take you to lunch today. Perhaps I've

been wrong; I'd like to discuss some things with you," Dru said appealingly.

Wild horses wouldn't have kept Joan away from that! "Well, Dru, I'll have to see . . . I know I have a lunch already . . ." she lied.

"Please, can't you reschedule? It would mean so much to me. I really could use a mentor right now."

Joan's mind was racing. *It would not be bad to have the little bitch as a lackey. In fact, it could prove useful,* she thought. "Why, for you, of course, Dru. Say, in an hour?"

"Perfect. I'll come to your office and met you there. Goodbye, Joan. And thanks." Dru replaced the receiver on the phone and turned to Kyle. She was smiling broadly.

Travis drove in endless circles, not even caring where he was. He drove past the Beverly Center and UBC studios five times before he pointed the car toward his house. It wasn't seeing Clay screwing the anchorman that so hurt him—though that was bad enough; it was the look he had caught on Clay's face. A look of such intensity and determination he had never seen before, and it made him feel that all the times they had been together were nothing compared to the fuck on the living room floor he had just witnessed.

The tears came now, hot, heavy, and salty. They clouded his vision, and he had to blink several times to be able to see the road. When he thought about all he had been through the past six months with Jack Benz and that goddamn tape—the degradation, the shame and guilt, being arrested—the only thing that had kept him sane was knowing he had Clay.

He knew that Clay had trouble with the secrecy of their affair, but he had always counted on it working itself out. He knew Clay loved him, but Clay truly had no idea of the depth of emotion and love Travis felt for him.

But now this! How was he supposed to handle this? Ignore it? Challenge Clay? He was clueless about what to do, and to make matters worse, the only person he could talk to about it was his best friend, who, of course, was Clay.

The phone was ringing when he walked in the front door,

and he knew instantly who it was. As he picked up the phone, he saw there were ten numbers on the caller ID list. He was positive everyone of them was Clay's.

"Hello?" he shakily answered.

"Travis? Oh, God, I'm so sorry!"

"What the fuck was *that*? I come over to see you, and I find you fucking that goddamn weatherman?!" Travis shouted.

"I'm sorry! I'm sorry!"

"Sorry, my ass! You sure didn't look sorry when he shot his load all over your fucking coffee table!"

"Trav, baby, I—"

"How long, Clay? How long have you been screwing him? Huh? How long? Answer me!" Travis demanded.

"I swear to God, that was the only time. I . . ."

"The only time? Right," Travis snorted sarcastically. "Well, you sure picked a hell of a moment!"

Clay took a deep breath. "I'm sorry."

"You say that one more fucking time, and I swear, I'll kick your ass!" Travis threatened.

"Wait a minute! Who the fuck are you to yell at me?! How long were *you* fucking Jack Benz? Huh? Got an answer for *that*?" Clay retorted hotly.

The question came out of left field, and Travis was taken aback. "What?"

"Don't play stupid with me! You've been doing him all along, haven't you? Don't bother to deny it; I know it's true."

Travis dropped the phone and wildly punched at the air, contorting his body in rage. "God damn it!" he screamed at no one. The air-fighting allowed him to release a small measure of his pent-up anger. The hot tears began to flow freely again. Partly regaining his composure, he reached over and picked up the receiver. "Clay, you don't understand. I had to . . ."

"Had to? *Had to*? That's fucking rich! Had to! 'Gee, Clay, I just couldn't help myself; I just *had* to cheat on you and fuck daytime television's biggest slimeball!' You asshole!" Clay mocked him.

"You have no idea what you're talking about! And you're the last one to talk about fucking around!" Travis shot back.

"Yeah? Well, at least Rick wants to be seen with me! He'd be proud to have me by his side and let everyone know how he feels about me. Can *you* say the same?"

As if slapped across the face, Travis fell silent.

"Yeah, thought not! And where have you been the past couple of days? I haven't heard from you. You get arrested and don't even bother to call me? What's *that* all about, huh?" Clay's anger was overcoming his regret, and he lashed out at Travis. "No answer for that, either? Funny! You expect me to answer all your fucking questions, but you can't answer one of mine!"

Travis dropped down to the floor as if punched in the gut. He could barely breathe, he was crying so hard. He grabbed his knees with his free arm and hugged them close, trying to make himself as small a ball as possible.

Hearing the racking sobs of his lover coming over the phone line, Clay's anger instantly dissolved. He, too, slid to the floor and tried to calm himself down.

"Travis?" he asked, quietly. There was no reply, only the steady sounds of sobbing. "Travis, please. Talk to me. I'm so sorry. It kills me to know that I hurt you, but you hurt me, too."

"I know I did. I just . . . you don't . . ." Travis couldn't find the words.

"I know it sounds so . . . trite, but it didn't mean any-thing. In my mind I was fucking you! I was so mad, and so angry at you for shutting me out, that I kinda took it out on him. But in my head, I was fucking you," Clay tried to ex-plain. However true, his words sounded lame even to him-self.

"Is he still there?" Travis quietly asked after a moment.

"God, no! I asked him to leave right after you left. I'm sure I hurt his feelings, but I'll deal with that later."

"Oh, God. Seeing you and him . . . like that . . ." Travis started to cry again. "The look on your face! You were so . . . intense," he whispered.

"I was thinking about you. I wanted it to be you." Clay sighed heavily. "I'm sorry."

Travis felt another wave of tears coming and knew he had

to get off the phone. "Look, I can't do this now, okay?" he pleaded, speaking slowly so he could get it out. "I don't know what to do or what to think, and I don't want to say the wrong thing. Can I talk with you later? Please? I just need to calm myself down."

"Sure, I understand." Clay let out a deep breath. "I could use a time-out myself. You're not working today?"

"No."

"Me either. Okay. Let's get off the phone. Let's talk tonight when we've had a chance to think things through."

"Okay."

"Travis . . ." Clay felt another strong rush of emotion course through his body. "I love you with all my heart; you know that, right? I love you so much, and I know that you love me. But I just don't know if that's enough. You only show me certain parts of yourself. It's like you're hiding something. I always feel like you're holding back, not letting yourself go, and I can't help but feel I deserve to be with someone who can. Let go. Does that make any sense to you?"

Travis digested that for a moment before answering. "Yes," he said finally. "It does. And you're right. You do deserve that."

A long silence fell between them as they both began to understand the gravity of what they were saying.

"Clay, I have to go. I'll call you later. I love you," Travis said in a whispered rush; then he hung up the phone, not waiting for Clay's response. He hugged his knees with both arms now and cried the lonely tears of the lost and afraid.

It took Clay only a few minutes before he decided to call Cissi. He knew she was on her lunch break. If he wasn't around for her to have lunch with, she either ate at her desk alone or went up to the roof of the studio to eat there and enjoy the sweeping panoramic view of West Hollywood in solitude. He breathed a sigh of relief when he reached her at her desk.

"Hey, sweet pea," she said, happy to hear from him.

"Hey. Listen, Cis, I need to talk to you about something really important, okay?"

"Sure, anything. Shoot."

"No, I'm serious. This is really important, and I need for you to be understanding and listen, and above all, promise me that you won't repeat what I'm about to tell you," Clay asked.

"Are you all right? Is anything the matter?" Her voice went up an octave as she began to get nervous.

"No. I'm not all right. I mean, yeah, I'm fine, but I'm not."

"Sweetie, you're not making any sense."

"Are you alone? Is Sylvia there?"

"No, she's gone to lunch with the suits to plan and scheme."

"Okay. I haven't been entirely honest with you," Clay began. "And I'm sorry. I hope you'll forgive me when I explain everything to you."

"What do you mean?" Her curiosity was killing her now.

"You know the guy I'm seeing, the one I won't really talk about with you?"

"Yeah," she said.

"It's Travis. We've been dating for months, and I'm completely, hopelessly in love with him. And, he's in love with me. It's just so fucked up now."

At first, Cissi didn't think she heard right. "Travis? *Our* Travis?"

"Yeah. Travis Church. I'm sorry I couldn't tell you before. He wanted to keep it secret, and I stupidly agreed. It was the worst thing to have to keep it from you. I'm so sorry, Cis," he said sincerely.

Nonplussed, Cissi was still peeved. "I can't believe you didn't tell me! After everything I've done for you, you keep this from me? Wow. Some friend!"

"Cis, please don't be mad at me. You have to understand the position I was in. Please?"

The truth was, Cissi could not be mad at Clay for more than two minutes. She forgave him completely. "Okay. I'm over it. So what's the problem?"

Clay told her the entire story. From the way he and Travis met back at the *Friends* audition to what their dating life was like, and how hot the sex was, to the events of this morning. Clay spoke frankly and openly, not afraid to put himself in a bad light when he had to, and for once, Cissi was so enthralled in the story that she didn't interrupt him.

". . . And so, now I have to decide what to do," he wrapped it up.

"What does your heart tell you?" she asked softly.

"I love him; there's no doubt about it. Not like I thought I loved Matt, but really, truly, deeply in love with him, as in, I could spend the rest of my life with him. But this whole thing he had with Jack—I mean, what does that say about him as a man? And on top of that, he's closeted! How can I be with a man who can't really acknowledge who—and what—he is?" Clay asked, not really expecting an answer back in reply.

"Oh, sweetie, I'm so sorry," Cissi comforted him.

"And all I can see happening is yet another guy breaking my heart. I didn't think I would live through the whole Matt fiasco, but I did, and I thought I would have learned more from it. But here I am, in another mess, with another guy who doesn't play fair." Clay started to cry, despite his best efforts not to.

"Oh, sweetie," Cissi soothed.

"I'm sorry, Cis, but I don't know if I can take having my heart broken again. I swear, this time it will kill me."

"No, it won't. You'll be fine. It's Travis who deserves a slow death for doing this to you," she half joked.

"Yeah. Fuck him, huh?" Clay managed a small laugh.

"And the horse he rode in on!"

"And that would be Jack Benz!" Clay snickered, amazed that he could laugh.

Cissi laughed out loud. "My lord. All you gay boys right here under my nose, and me without a clue. What kind of fag hag am I, anyway?"

"The very best kind."

"Obviously not. Seeing as how I didn't even know it. Oh, well," she sighed. "What are you going to do?"

"I don't know. I really just needed to talk to someone

about it. Thanks for listening. You're the best, and I love you very much," Clay spoke softly.

"Aww, I love you, too sweetie. You know I'd do anything for you."

"Yup. I know. And you have."

"You want to come down here and hang out with me while I interview possible replacements for Jack Benz? We just got the word this morning they want to recast."

"Do me a favor. Hire an ugly one this time, okay?" he joked. "No, really, I'll be fine. I just need to think. I think I'll take a bike ride at the beach. That always clears my head."

"Good idea."

"Okay, then. I'll call you later and fill you in. And Cis," he said, "I'm so sorry not to have clued you in to all this as it was going on. I really feel bad about it."

"Oh, don't. You've told me now; that's what matters. And I'm going to help you with this any way I can, okay?"

"Deal. Bye."

"Bye, sweetie."

Clay hung up the phone and had to admit he did feel better. It was so great just to have someone to talk to about it. Made him feel less alone. He stopped for a second and wondered if Travis had someone to talk to.

He hoped so.

Kyle stuck his head in the outer office of Joan's assistant, a pretty girl named Melody. She wasn't there. Her computer screen was dark, and there were no open papers or files on her desk, so Kyle assumed she was at lunch. All he needed was five minutes in Joan's office.

He opened the door silently and walked in, surprising Peter Dowd, who was twirling around in circles wearing Joan's brown blazer, arms outstretched.

Peter caught sight of Kyle out of the corner of his eye and stopped spinning. Too stunned to speak, his mouth opened and closed, but no sounds came out. Kyle stared at him, slack-jawed.

Without saying a word, Peter peeled off the jacket slowly, rehung it on the coatrack carefully, and walked out of the office, back straight, head high.

What the hell was that about? Kyle thought to himself, not quite sure he had just seen what he knew he'd seen.

He wanted to laugh, but then remembered why he was there. He quickly crossed over to Joan's desk and started to root around, looking for the thick binder.

"Come on, come on," he urged himself on, peering under papers, looking in desk drawers, and rifling through her file cabinets. The binder he had seen Joan poring over last week was nowhere to be found. He was almost about to give up when he noticed her black Coach briefcase on the floor, tucked away under the desk.

A quick search of its contents revealed the binder, sandwiched between some contracts and several scripts. He pulled it out and slipped it under his arm. At the door to Joan's office, he peeked into the outer office to see if the coast was clear. It was, and he practically ran down the hall to the copy room.

He slammed the binder down on a counter, snapped open its rings, and lifted out the heavy pages. Breaking it up into manageable sections, he fed them through the self-collating copier and pressed *Start*.

The copying process took about fifteen minutes, and Kyle was sweating from nervousness when he sneaked back into Joan's office to replace the original binder in her briefcase.

He had just cleared her office doorway when Joan's assistant returned, carrying a Diet Coke and a Snickers. She looked happy to see him loitering around her office.

"Can I help you?" she asked pleasantly. She put the soda and candy bar down on her desktop.

"Um . . . uh . . . is Joan around?" was all he could think to say.

The assistant shook her head. "Nope. She's at lunch with Dru Gordon. She should be back within the hour. Should I call you when she gets back?" she offered helpfully, unconsciously smoothing her skirt.

Clutching the newly copied pages under his arm, Kyle

backed away. "Uh, no. That's okay. I'll come back later. Thanks!" He turned and raced down the hall to the elevator bank.

"Well, come back whenever you want!" the assistant called after him. "Maybe we can take a snack break together some time." She leaned around her desk to watch his retreating figure.

Kyle, startled, smiled awkwardly, waved, and stepped into the elevator.

19

The warm air felt good rushing against Clay's face, and it had the added bonus of helping to dry the sweat as it poured down his brow. Occasionally, he would reach up a gloved hand and wipe the dampness away before it could drop into his eyes, stinging him. The beach was relatively uncrowded for a Monday afternoon in the summertime, and Clay was able to really push himself on the bike.

He raced down the paved bike path that hugged the shoreline, and passed the slower bikers with ease. The bike path ran all the way from Marina del Rey to the edge of Pales Verdes, a total trail of over ten miles. Clearly marked and well maintained by the county, it was Clay's secret refuge from the world.

He tried to ride the bike path at least three times a week—more if he could swing it—and he found it was not only excellent exercise but also a great time to think and plan. He valued the time he spent pedaling, because it always helped clear his head. Unlike taking one of the numerous spin classes offered at every gym in West Hollywood, he could be outdoors, by the beach, as he worked his body out.

A blur in his tight black fitted bike shorts, black tank top, and red bandanna do-rag wrapped around his head, he flew down the trail, his mind a million miles away.

Travis.

He was all he could think about. That and the awful scene that had happened just a few short hours ago.

Rick had actually been pretty cool about it and didn't protest when Clay told him it was probably better that he left. He just quietly put his clothes back on, told Clay again how much he had enjoyed their time together, and slipped him a card with his home number written on it in pencil.

"Call me anytime you want. I'll be here in a flash," he told Clay. "I'm sure it's pretty obvious to you that I have a thing for you, and having you . . . well, what we just did, it's something that I've wanted to do for a very long time."

Clay hadn't known what to say, so he said nothing.

"And again, for the record, it was the hottest fuck I've ever had. I'd like to repeat it, but somehow I don't think that's going to happen, is it?"

Clay demurred and looked at the floor.

"Hey, it's okay," Rick smiled. "I know you're not that into me. And given the interruption we had, I'm guessing you already have a thing going on with Travis. I hope it works out for you, but if it doesn't . . ." he said hopefully.

"Thanks, Rick. You're a classy guy."

Rick then gave him a soft kiss on the lips and left. Clay had felt terrible.

He immediately called Travis on his cell phone but got only the voice mail. He then tried Travis at home but again kept getting the voice mail. He called Travis over a dozen times, pleading with him to call him back. And then, when he finally did talk with Travis, their conversation had been completely unsatisfying.

Clay still couldn't believe that Travis had walked in on him.

What were the odds? he asked himself.

Although he wasn't going to deny he had strayed, he still felt slightly justified. It just was too much that Travis had actually *seen* the straying. And as loath as he was to admit it—even to himself—the sex with Rick had been amazingly hot, and he was surprised by how easy it had been to fuck him. What did *that* mean? He knew he had been thinking only about Travis while he was fucking Rick, but he could not deny that Rick was a sexy man, whom he had treated poorly the past few months.

All these thoughts flooded Clay's mind as his feet spun around and around in a steady rhythm, the pavement underneath sailing past him.

Dru returned to her office about one-thirty, her stomach in knots. Her lunch with Joan had been the most trying ordeal she had ever had to go through. Joan had pontificated on and on about how indispensable she was, that Klein Productions would not be the company it was today if it hadn't been for her very hard work. Joan was quite full of herself, and Dru let her ramble on, knowing that egocentric people like nothing better than to talk about themselves. All she did was nod every once in a while and utter phrases like "Then what happened?" and "Oh, really?"

Dru forced herself to listen to Joan blather on, but she kept thinking about the events taking place at that moment back at the office. She hoped Kyle had found what he was looking for while she bravely kept Joan away.

Joan talked so much, she never even got around to asking why Dru had wanted to have lunch with her.

"Hey," Dru said to Kyle as she entered her office, "did you get it?" She braced herself for bad news.

"Yup! I've only been looking through it for a few minutes, and already I have some things to show you." He beamed.

"Oh, thank God! Kyle, my friend, you are *so* getting a raise!" She was delighted. Throwing her bag onto the sofa, she kicked off her shoes and joined Kyle on the floor. They started to compare notes, lists, invoices and ledgers.

They spent the next two hours studying the various pages.

When Clay got to the Redondo Pier, he slowed down, then braked and hopped off the bike. The pier was a favorite biking destination for him. An enormous U-shaped structure, it extended out over the water, the waves sliding past its thick wood pylons and crashing onto the beach it hugged. Restaurants, markets, and shops filled up its inner core, and broad, pedestrian-friendly walkways fanned out farther over the water.

Clay gripped the bike's handlebars and walked it over to the soft-pretzel store that was built in the center of the pier. He ordered his usual, a fresh-baked pretzel dipped in melted butter and lightly salted, carbs be damned! He took his pretzel and bottle of water and walked the bike over to a bench that faced the blue Pacific. Lining the rails of the pier were dozens of anglers, casting their lines over. About four hundred yards offshore was a buoy that gently bobbed in the swells of the surf, its warning bell clanging with each dip. On its base, a pair of seals were sunning themselves, content to enjoy the hot sun and cool water.

Clay sat down and began to eat his pretzel.

The seagulls were squawking and swooping low overhead, hoping for a morsel to fall from his hands, while small children and their parents strolled along the pier. He turned his gaze out to sea and again returned to his thoughts of Travis. He ached to see Travis, to talk to him. He realized he missed him badly, but strangely, he felt like he would never see him again.

"Is this seat taken?" a familiar deep voice asked.

He looked up and was bewildered to see Travis, wearing a blue Adidas track suit and a black Nike ski cap pulled down low, standing there looking down at him through his mirrored sunglasses.

"What . . . what are you doing here?" Clay asked, completely flummoxed.

"You always stop here for a pretzel on your bike rides, and it suddenly seemed very important for me to be wherever you are. Can I sit down?"

"Of course!"

Travis walked around the bench and plopped down next to Clay. For a moment he was silent as he, too, stared out to sea.

"Trav, I'm so sorry about today. I never wanted to hurt you," Clay broke the silence.

"I know." Travis removed his glasses, revealing eyes reddened from crying, and stared deeply into his lover's eyes.

Clay felt a strong surge of emotion that made him want to sweep the soap star into his arms and kiss away his pain.

"And I guess," Travis continued, "I don't blame you. I can see how you would feel that I cheated on you, but you need to listen to me," he said as he took Clay's hands in his own. "I love you. I never wanted to lie to you or hurt you. But, I realize now that I did you—and me—a disservice. I wasn't honest with you, and I should have been."

Clay saw the pure sincerity on his lover's face, and his heart melted.

"So I'm going to tell you the truth. All of it—now," Travis resumed. "I just want you to listen to me and really hear what I'm saying."

Clay agreed readily, and for the next forty-five minutes Travis spilled out the entire saga of the gang bang, the videotape, and his time as Jack's sexual puppet. He cried when he told the story to Clay, not because of his shame, but because the compassionate and wounded look on Clay's face told him he should have confided in his boyfriend months before.

When he was done talking, the two men just sat, still and quiet. Travis felt like an enormous weight had been lifted from his shoulders, and was glad that it was out in the open. He held on to Clay's hand like it was a lifeline.

Clay was in a state of shock. How had Travis kept this from him? How awful it must have been for him to hide this, not only from him but from everyone. The guilt and shame that Travis must have been feeling for months! Clay couldn't comprehend what it must have been like, and he prayed he'd never find out.

"So there. Now you know it all," Travis whispered.

"Are they serious about considering you a suspect in Jack's death? I mean, that's just crazy."

"I really don't know. I know I look good to them, but Detective Parker was really cool to me the other night, so I don't know. It's 'wait and see.'"

"And the show? Have you talked to them? How's Joan dealing with your weekend escapade?"

"I haven't talked directly to her. My agent got an earful. I did talk to Dru Gordon this morning, who saved my ass with the network, and I think the flower thing and the public explanation seems to have taken, and it's all behind me . . . so far," Travis said wearily.

"Trav, why didn't you tell me all this right away? How could you think you could deal with this by yourself?" Clay pressed.

"I don't know. I guess I figured if I just got the tape back, no one need ever know about any of it."

"And you never fucked him? Or he you? I find that hard to believe."

"I swear it. Never. He was a sick fucker, and I often think that would have actually been easier to deal with. He had me try to suck him off a couple of times, but he couldn't keep a hard-on. It was all about control and power with Jack. Not sex." Travis sighed. He was still holding Clay's hand, and he gently squeezed it, never wanting to let it go again.

"My God. I had no idea. When Maggie told me she saw you two together, it just fit that you two were sneaking around. You were so weird about us, so private, so I figured it had to be true. Who wouldn't?"

"I know. I'm sorry." Travis paused. "Now, what about you and Rick Yung? Are you seeing him? Are you in love with him?" he asked.

"I'm in love with you! I just felt that you'd ditched me. I didn't hear from you all weekend. You got arrested, for God's sake, and never once called me! I was so hurt, and he just happened to be in the right place at the wrong time. I can't deny what I did," Clay said unabashedly. "But you have to know that I had a weak moment, and I regret it, and I'll probably regret it forever. And for you to walk in and see us! My God, I was completely humiliated. I never felt so bad in my life—like I had done something dirty, and I want to just forget it ever happened."

"Forget it? Seeing my boyfriend, the man that I love, plowing away at another guy?" Travis's voice broke. "It's all I see. When I close my eyes, I see it. When I look at you now, I see it. It's like it's seared into my brain. And you want to know what the worst part of it is?" he asked.

"What?" Clay said quietly.

"You looked so . . . I don't know, *complete*, as you were doing it. And all I remember thinking while watching you fuck him was that I wanted to be Rick. I want to see you look like that when you're inside me."

"But that *is* what I look like when I'm inside you! Trav, making love to you is the most amazing, intense, wonderful feeling in the world for me! I don't think I would ever be able to be with another man without thinking about you. That's what you saw. I was imagining that it was you. I wanted it to be you."

Travis looked out at the sea again and watched the buoy bobbing in the bay, the seals honking at each other. He sighed. "Why him, Clay? Why Rick Yung? Of all people! We have to see him at the studio every day. Is he going to talk about this? It's all so . . . low-rent."

"Trav," Clay whispered, ignoring the question. "What do you want now? What do you see happening with us?"

"What do I want? I want to go on like none of this ever happened."

"I don't think that's possible now."

"Then I guess I don't know what to do, except I know I don't want to lose you. I love you, and I just want that back. I don't want anything to change."

"But sweetheart, it can't be the same. This whole thing has shown me one thing, and I just can't get around it."

Travis looked at him imploringly.

"Trav, our whole relationship is built around your needs. Not mine. Yours. You're so afraid of being 'outed' that we don't live a normal life. I had that before, and that's what I want. A normal life. With you."

"But we're not normal people. We're not mailmen or store clerks. We live in a fishbowl, and that's a fact."

"No, *you live* in a fishbowl, I don't, and you're only there because you like it. You like being the hot new guy; you like being the celebrity. You like the fact that while you forget meeting Jane Doe from Arkansas the minute you sign your autograph, she remembers meeting you for the rest of her life. I'm not in your league, and that's fine by me. I just want to work, and my work happens to be acting. I truly believe you can be a working actor and have a private life. You don't."

"Clay, that's not reality." Travis shook his head. "I just have to be careful; I thought you understood that. I've got only a few years to get set and move on to feature films. You know that's what I want. It's what I've been working at for years. I can't risk my dreams. It's so close! I can almost taste it! I love you, but please, can't you just bear with this for a little while longer?"

Clay looked at his lover and pondered what he'd heard. His heart was telling him one thing, but his mind told him another. "I don't know. I really don't. I love you, Trav. I'm proud to be with you, I want to shout it to the world, but you make me feel like I'm some dirty little secret. I just have a huge problem with that."

"That's not true!"

"It *is* true, Trav. You just don't see it the way I do. I don't know if I can go on this way." Clay sighed, then turned away from Travis.

"You don't mean that. You're just upset—and mad—and I don't blame you. Can't we talk about this later? Please? Stay with me tonight. Don't make any rash decisions now," Travis pleaded, squeezing Clay's hand hard. Out of the corner of his eye, Travis spied a small girl and her mother staring at him and Clay. The mother obviously recognized him from *Sunset Cove* and was in the process of walking over.

Clay noticed the woman approaching them, too. As she got closer, he could see her eyes drift downward and focus on their interlocked fingers. A look of puzzlement crossed her face; then her mouth dropped open as she realized what she was seeing.

Travis must have noticed her reaction as well, because he dropped Clay's hand like it was a hot plate. He stiffened and turned his attention back to the buoy with the seals on it. The woman took her daughter's hand and hurriedly led her away.

Clay wanted to cry. Travis's response had been to let him go. When he most needed to establish a bond with Clay and pull him closer, he'd let it drop.

"I have to go. I need to finish my ride," Clay said, his heart breaking.

"Can't you throw the bike in the back of the Boxster and let me drive you home?"

"No. I want to finish the ride. And the Jeep's at the other end, anyway. I need the time alone. I'm sorry." Clay stood up, grabbed his bike, threw a beefy leg over the center bar, and prepared to ride away.

He stopped and slowly turned back to his boyfriend. "It's not that I don't love you, Travis, because you know I do. With all my heart. But you just don't get it. You make me feel like I should be ashamed of what I am. That it's wrong, and that I need to pretend you don't feel the same way. You're asking me to hide who I am, and I can't—no, I *won't*—do that."

With those final words, he hopped up and pedaled off, leaving Travis sitting by the bay alone.

When Clay got back to his condo, it was after four, and he spied a manila envelope leaning against his front door. Ripping it open, he found his pages for the next day. He had been told that the studio would deliver the next day's script each night, but he was still a little surprised to find it there. He was a real working actor on a daytime drama, he had to remind himself.

He quickly looked the script over. He was in several scenes with Cathy Grant again. His prognosis for Stone was going to be bleak.

Clay was flipping through the pages, searching for his lines, as he entered his place and leaned the bike up against the dining room wall. He walked through his home turning on lights, all the while scanning through the pages. As he read the last page of the script, he stopped short.

"What?!" he said aloud, shocked.

His character, Dr. Chase Kendall, and Cathy's character, Pageant Ragianni, were to have a lingering kiss over the inert, comatose form of Stone Coltrane.

The phone rang and brought him out of his stupor. It was Cissi.

"How are you? I'm worried about you! Did you talk to Travis?" she asked breathlessly.

"Yeah, I did. Cis, I just don't know what to do."

"Why don't you come over to my house for dinner? You can tell me everything, and we'll figure out a plan of action. How's that sound?"

"That sounds perfect. Thanks for being there for me, Cis," Clay said warmly. "We'll order in. My treat."

"Deal."

"Have you seen the pages for tomorrow?"

"Yeah. Why?"

"Did you read them all?"

"No, I skimmed them. Why? What's up?" Clay could tell she was looking around her desk, hunting for the new pages.

"I make out with Pageant! What's that about?" He still couldn't get over it.

"What? Really? Well, that's good! That means you're going to stick around a while! How did I miss that?" He heard pages flipping and knew she was searching through them.

"You think? I shouldn't worry?"

"No! Maybe they're making you a new love interest! Wouldn't that be great?" Cissi's voice was filled with excitement, and it was contagious. Clay began to feel happy. "Come by around seven. See you then, sweetie," she said, hanging up.

Well, the personal life may be for shit, thought Clay, *but the professional life seemed to be doing great.*

Carole, Dru Gordon's assistant, was a little irked with her boss. A dedicated worker and a proven team player, she felt left out of the loop.

Something big was going on in her boss's office, and she was dying to know what. Dru, whom she loved working for, and pimply Kyle from Accounting, had been locked up in her office all day. Carole had been instructed to hold all calls except those of that unbelievably hot detective and not to let anyone disturb the two of them.

Every once in a while, she would hear a hoot of joy coming from behind the closed door, followed by mumbled chatter.

She had tried her best to listen in, even placing her ear on the door, but hadn't been able to pick up anything of value.

The mystery was further deepened by Dru's asking her to place several calls, asking a few key people connected with *Sunset Cove* to an early-morning meeting, set for tomorrow. Now, she felt compelled to stick around, even though it was after quitting time. Dru and Kyle were still locked away and might need something, and she was loath to interrupt them to see if she could leave.

Finally working up her resolve, she timidly knocked on Dru's door.

"Yes?" Dru called out.

Carole cracked open the door and leaned her head in. "Um, hi. I was wondering if you were going to need me anymore tonight?"

"Oh, no, Carole. Did everyone confirm for the meeting tomorrow?" Dru was seated at her desk, typing on a computer keyboard, while Kyle was sitting on the floor, surrounded by neatly stacked piles of invoices.

"Yes, although Joan insisted that you call her and explain what it's about."

"I'll do that. Thanks, Carole. Have a good night!"

Carole shut the door and went to her desk. She flipped off the computer and got her bag, which was hanging from the back of her chair. Just as she was walking out of the office, she heard Dru yell out another joyful whoop.

20

Clay and Cissi sat on her flounced floral sofa, picking at the remains of their pasta. They had ordered from a small family-owned Italian place around the corner from Cissi's apartment on Citrus. Both were starving by the time Clay got to her apartment, and as soon as the food got there, they had attacked it with gusto.

They each also had a few beers from Cissi's fridge, though Clay had three to her one. Clay wasn't a big drinker. In fact, he so rarely drank, he would get drunk off two cocktails. Tonight, however, he felt the need to unwind, and the beers were the answer.

Slightly buzzed, Clay looked around Cissi's apartment and smiled. It was as "girlie" as you could get. It was as if she had tried to make up for the lack of feminine guidance in her formative years and had gone overboard with it in her adult life.

The walls were painted a pale pink, and the furniture was old-fashioned and slip-covered in tea-stained floral chintz. The hardwood pieces were painted a crisp white, and ruffles and bows ruled. Numerous cute stuffed animals were placed here and there, and her walls were covered with gilt-framed family pictures. Down a short hall was a door to her bedroom and the small bathroom. Busy floral curtains hung from ceiling to floor over all the windows in the apartment and made the rooms quite dark.

Clay had cried when he told Cissi about his conversation with Travis on the pier. He was in such pain and conflict, and he didn't know what to do. Cissi had been sympathetic toward him and madder than hell at Travis.

"He's such a dick!" she had said forcefully. "I mean, whatever do you see in him? You could do so much better than him."

"I love him, Cis. I just don't know if I can live his way of life."

"Well, I think you should dump his ass. What a dick!" she repeated vehemently.

They had gone back and forth like that during the entire meal. Now, with dinner finished, they sat back and simply enjoyed being in each other's company. Cissi was noticeably happy that Clay was there.

A flash of anger flitted across her features when the phone rang, interrupting the evening. Before she could tell Clay to let the machine pick it up, he had snatched the phone receiver out of its cradle and handed it to her.

"Hello?" she said, subtly irritated.

"Cissi? It's Sylvia. I'm at the office. I have been looking for the under-five file all night. Where is it?" Sylvia, as usual, sounded overly dramatic.

"It should be in the file cabinet. Look under the 'U's," Cissi answered, perceptively testy.

"I did. It's not there. Could you do me a huge, huge favor? Can you pop down here and dig it up? You know I'm useless when it comes to those things. I have a very important meeting in the morning, and I need it. You're only ten minutes away."

It wasn't a request.

"Um, sure. I'll be right there," Cissi said tightly. She hung up the phone and quietly seethed. Then, in a flash, she broke out into a broad smile and told Clay she had to leave for just a few minutes.

"I'll be right back, so just make yourself at home. Here, watch TV," she said as she clicked on the remote. A small TV situated in a wall unit opposite them blinked to life. She grabbed her large satchel and her keys and was gone out the door.

Clay sat there, a little taken aback. Her mood swing had

been so fast and dramatic that it had seemed almost unsettling. Shaking off the feeling, he popped open another beer and took a long swig.

He took the remote and flipped through the channels, trying to find something good. Of course, he came across a Sears Diehard commercial starring Travis. He quickly changed the channel again.

He let his gaze move around the room. Cissi had a large grouping of family pictures clustered on the wall by the dining table, and, curious, he got up and walked over to look at them.

They were enlargements of various old photos of Cissi and her dad. There was one of the two of them sitting on the top of one of his cabs, smiling at the camera. There was another one of her, at around age seventeen, sitting behind the wheel of a taxi, a cabbie hat cocked to one side of her head. The best photo was one of her, completely covered in grease and oil, peeking out from under the hood of a cab, obviously doing some repair work, a huge grin on her smudged face.

Clay smiled, looking at his friend in her happy youth. He had completely forgotten that she had worked part-time at her father's taxicab company and was also a great mechanic. She even did the tune-ups on her own car. He made a mental note to ask her more about her childhood when she returned.

The beers he had drunk had filled up his bladder, and he felt the need to use the bathroom. He walked unsteadily down the short hall to the bathroom but noticed that one of the curtains covering a window in the hallway had slightly parted. Instead of the expected window, he saw a door. He reached out and pulled the curtain open, completely revealing a door.

Clay curiously opened the door and saw that it was another darkened bedroom. His first thought was one of astonishment. Cissi had told him she lived in a one-bedroom. But here was a second bedroom. Why would she lie about that?

He put his hand on the wall to feel about for a light switch. After a minute of drunken fumbling, he found it and flipped it on. He audibly gasped.

The small bedroom had been fitted out as a home office, with bookcases, a desk, a chair, and a large computer system.

That wasn't what surprised him. It was the pictures. The entire wall facing him was covered from ceiling to floor in eight-by-ten glossy photos.

Of him.

They were all five of the different headshots he used. Just row after row of him. There were also childlike renderings of him that had been thumbtacked up. Hundreds of smaller personal-sized pictures of him were taped up as well.

There were shots of him at the studio Christmas party the previous year. Candid shots of him on set, in the cafeteria, in the parking lot. Cissi had obviously used her own camera and shot numerous rolls of film of him. Clay had never noticed her taking his picture.

As if the whole thing weren't surreal enough, he then saw something really disturbing. There was a whole section of pictures of him at home. Obviously shot through his windows with a long-range zoom lens, he could see himself sitting on the sofa, cooking in the kitchen, even napping in his lounge chair. How had she taken those?

Like a zombie he wandered into the room and looked at all the images of himself. The room began to sway under him, and he had to hold on to the desk to focus for a minute. When he looked up, he saw that there were dozens of large scrapbooks lining the shelves of the bookcases, and, almost afraid, he pulled one out at random and leafed through it.

More candid pictures of him. A shot of him and Travis chatting on set came loose and fell out. Clay bent over, head swimming, and picked it up. Staring intently at it, he folded it and slipped it into his pants pocket.

He replaced that scrapbook and pulled out another one from lower down the shelves. To his surprise, this one didn't contain a single picture of him. Instead, it was full of shots of Jack Benz. Page after page of the same type of candid pictures of Jack. Him at home, him at the gym, him on set. A few had Lefty in them, who was always looking at Jack with complete adoration.

One picture in particular caught Clay's eye. It was a candid shot of Jack and Cissi, locked in a tight hug, broad smiles on their faces, looking like the best of buddies.

Clay returned the book to its place on the shelf. Reaching over to the lowest self on the farther bookcase, he pulled one out. At first he didn't recognize the man in the pictures. They were the same type of secret shots that had been taken of him and Jack.

The man was good-looking, and Clay knew he had seen him somewhere before, but couldn't place him. He turned the pages and realized that the shots were a few years old and had been taken on the old *Sunset Cove* set. There was a much younger Cathy Grant with long blond hair talking to the man who was the focus of the photo album. Another was a shot of the man and Jack Benz together, arms around each other, laughing at the camera.

Clay suddenly remembered who it was. Lance Jackson. He had been on the show a few years before, as the oldest Coltrane son.

The beers he had drunk were really beginning to make Clay woozy, so he replaced the book on the shelf and backed out of the room. His mind was reeling from what he had seen, but it was fast becoming clouded by the effects of the alcohol. He pulled the curtain tightly closed again to hide the secret door and stumbled into the bathroom. He relieved himself and barely made it back to the sofa before the exhaustion of all the day's events, and the relaxing effects of the beers, finally overcame him.

He quickly slipped into an alcohol-induced unconsciousness that came over him in ever-increasing waves.

Peter Dowd took a deep breath and pushed open the door of the lesbian bar, Rack. He was dressed in a chic form-fitting vintage Pucci dress that he had bought online, and strappy Chloe sandals graced his freshly shaved legs. He had carefully applied his makeup, and the wig he wore, a long dark auburn that made his limpid eyes shine, was as good as any ever made. The transformation was remarkable; he looked completely like a real woman. He had shaved his light beard three times to get as close a shave as possible and had adjusted his gait to more closely mimic a woman's walk.

As he entered the club and took his time getting to the bar, he surveyed the crowd. It must have been fem night at Rack, as almost every woman there was a lipstick lesbian. Peter was pleased to note the attention he got on his walk through the club. He could sense the buzz he was creating, and it made him get slightly hard, which was a huge problem, seeing as how he had tucked back his penis severely, and any erection would prove not only disastrous, but painful.

At the bar, he selected a stool, placed his Chanel chain bag on the countertop, and ordered a cosmopolitan from the pretty bartender.

Peter had accepted the fact that he was transgender. He felt free and normal when he was in drag, and only when he had to wear his men's wardrobe did he feel freakish. He knew he was a woman trapped in a man's body, and as soon as his divorce was final, he would begin the long and expensive process of having a complete sex change.

He wanted to live life as a woman, and he had already begun to make small changes. He was growing his own hair out. He had adjusted his workout routine to slim down his masculine body shape and had lost over thirty pounds since his wife had left him. He read every book he could find on the subject of transsexualism and transgenderism and took the advice given in these books seriously. He wore women's undergarments all the time now. He had made some preliminary phone calls to see about starting hormone shots. But he had also begun to despise his penis, and could not stand to even look at it. He longed for breasts of his own, not to mention the other vital female anatomy.

The catch was, Peter wasn't gay. Of that, he was certain. He had tried to have sex with a man, a good-looking guy in his apartment building, but after some minor fumbling and trying to give the other man head, he'd had to stop. He just wasn't turned on by, or sexually attracted to, men. He was excited by women, fantasized about women, and wanted to sleep with women.

It was women he wanted, so he realized that he was going to have to become a lesbian.

And that's why he was in Rack on a Monday night. He wanted to experience what the lesbian scene was and just wanted to get his feet wet on a slow night. It was his first foray into the lesbian world, and he didn't plan on picking up anyone, for obvious reasons. Peter just wanted to start developing a comfort level with the lifestyle.

He hadn't been seated at the bar for more than five minutes when he sensed he wasn't alone anymore.

"Hey, I've never seen you here before. Are you new in town?" a slightly slurred voice asked him from behind. It was oddly familiar, and he almost had time to place it. Before he could, a striking blonde stepped next to him, pressing close. "I said, I've never seen you here before. Are you new in town?"

Peter recognized the woman in front of him instantly. Flustered, he didn't know what to do. "I . . . uh . . . yes," he finally stammered, remembering to lighten the register of his voice.

Cathy Grant winked suggestively at him and turned to the bartender. "Get this beautiful woman another of whatever she's having. In fact, make it two. I'll have one, also." She then locked her dazzling blue eyes on Peter. "You are stunning. I'm sure you hear that all the time," she said, emboldened by her slightly inebriated state. She was dressed in a tight yellow cropped tee. A wide, worn brown leather belt was strung through the belt loops of her low-rise jeans.

"Actually, no," Peter said, looking down at the bar counter.

"I find that hard to believe. I'm Cath. It's a pleasure to meet you." She held out her hand. Peter daintily shook hands with her.

"Hello. I'm Petra," he managed, giving the name he hoped one day to officially adopt as his own.

"Petra? What a fascinating name. It suits you." Cathy oozed charm.

Peter was amazed at the difference in her. On set, she was all business, tough as nails and a royal bitch to work with. Here, even though she'd had a bit too much to drink, she was in her element. Cathy was hot, sweet, charming, and, he had to admit, quite sexy in the dimmed smoky light of the bar. He'd had no idea she was a lesbian. And to his complete amazement, he was finding himself attracted to her.

They chatted together for the next hour. Then, Cathy brazenly asked him to dance. Having had a couple of cocktails, Peter agreed, and they went to the small, crowded dance floor.

Girl-girl couples were rubbing up against each other; groping each other; fondling, teasing, and kissing each other. It was the single most erotic thing he had ever seen. He was quite amazed to discover that women could be just as horny as men and didn't seem to worry about hiding it. He truly had to concentrate on not getting a hard-on.

Cathy wasn't helping. She was rubbing up against him suggestively, thrusting her face up close to his, wet lips parted and teasing. He wanted to kiss her so badly, but was scared she would discover his secret.

"You are so sexy," Cathy whispered into his ear. "I want to make love to you. Right now. I could eat you out right here on the dance floor," she said, then flicked her tongue deep into his ear, wiggling it about.

Peter gulped, spun around, grabbed Cathy, and pressed his lips to hers, hard. He could taste the rum she had been downing. They let their tongues roam free in each other's mouths, and Peter cupped Cathy's beautiful big breasts in his hands and squeezed, taking care to gently pinch her nipples in the process. Cathy's eyes flew open in grateful surprise, and she let out a muffled cry of pleasure.

Peter continued to tease her nipples with his fingers and was completely turned on by the rapid panting he was causing in her.

"Oh . . . my . . . God . . ." Cathy could barely speak. Her hands were clutching at his back, opening and closing in the grips of passion. Peter dropped one of his hands down to her pubic area and let it rub up and down against the snug denim crotch of her jeans.

The lights of the dance floor had dimmed down considerably, and no one was paying them any attention. Peter, motivated by the strong reactions he was getting from Cathy, teased and rubbed harder. Cathy began to undulate her body in rhythm to his touches, and her flushed face was shiny with sweat.

"Oh! . . . You can't . . . I . . . Oh! . . . That's it! Yes! Oh,

God," she hissed through pleasure-clenched teeth. "Oh, God! I want your fingers inside me!"

She pressed her body against his and, by sheer physical power, pushed him into a darkened corner. There were several other couples hotly making out in the area, but no one so much as glanced at them.

He quickly slipped his hand down into the front of her jeans and was thrilled by the soft, silky mound he found. Cathy adjusted her posture, allowed him to part her, and let him slip his long index finger inside. She sucked in a gulp of air and exhaled it slowly. She moved her body back and forth as Peter explored her.

Cathy arched her head back, closed her eyes, and let herself go. Her breathing became panting again, and tiny cries of pure joy came forth from her open mouth. Her whole body was alive and quivering, and she felt sensations she didn't know were possible. She could not believe that she, America's daytime favorite, was in her favorite lesbian bar, in public, getting finger-fucked, and finger-fucked *well,* by the hottest woman she had ever met. It was so unlike her.

But she liked it. A lot.

Oh, screw it, and enjoy the ride, she reasoned through waves of pleasure. Tomorrow she'd just blame it on having had to much to drink.

"Oh! . . . Yes! . . . Yes . . . That's it . . . Oh! . . . I'm . . . Oh! . . . I'm gonna . . . !" Before she could finish her sentence, she shuddered, and Peter felt a small warm gush of fluid on his fingers, and he knew she had come.

Slowly Cathy came back to earth. Peter let his hand linger just a moment before withdrawing it. Cathy lowered her head and opened her eyes, looking up at Peter. "Oh, Petra! That was amazing! I've never . . . I mean, I have never . . ." She let the sentence hang.

"Me either. Trust me," Peter puffed.

"Oh, my God. I hope no one saw! Damn! Imagine what we would be like in bed!" Cathy chuckled.

Peter had to adjust himself because his erection was entirely painful.

"Look, I never do this. Honest! But you are so beautiful.

Let's go back to my house. I want to give you back what you've given me," Cathy said, determined not to let this mysteriously wonderful woman get away.

Her words only made his situation worse. He didn't think he was going to be able to walk, and he knew he had to leave before he made another mistake.

"I can't tonight.... I'm so sorry ... I have ... to go to work early tomorrow," he lied.

Obviously disappointed, Cathy went with Plan B. "Then give me your number. We can go out later in the week."

"I don't have a phone yet." Peter was thinking fast. "But, give me your number? I'll call you."

"Promise you will?"

"Of course!"

Cathy walked away to the bar to find a napkin and a pen to write her private number down.

Wiping the sweat from his brow, and slightly smearing his base, Peter exhaled slowly and tried to become unexcited.

It was very difficult.

21

Travis was beneath him, soaking wet, lying on a towel next to the Jacuzzi. He cupped Clay's face in both hands, repeatedly telling him that he loved him. Clay looked down at him and drank in his physical beauty: his perfectly formed and rounded pecs, the cut abs, and the meaty legs spread wide for him. Clay loved being inside his lover and rode him hard, not ever wanting it to end. . . .

"Clay!"

Distracted, he looked away from Travis. Who was calling him?

"Clay! Wake up! You're going to be late!"

He carefully opened his eyes and felt a throbbing pain as his vision slowly unclouded. Cissi was standing over him, holding out a cup of coffee and glancing at her watch. He groaned.

He wanted to go back into his dream about Travis. At least the last one had been good. He knew he'd had a really bad one earlier. He couldn't remember it, but he knew it had been bad.

"I let you sleep in a little, but now you're going to be late. We've got to go!"

Clay groggily sat up and tried to focus. Now he remembered why he never drank much. A bad memory of a fraternity mixer and ten trash-can punches flooded his mind, and he had to breathe deeply, so he didn't hurl.

"Oh, my God. I can't move; I think I have polio," he muttered, holding his head in his hands.

"I came back and you were totally passed out. I just put a blanket over you and let you sleep," Cissi explained, slightly laughing at him.

"Just shoot me."

Cissi took one of his hands and pulled him to his feet. "Hurry up—go pee, and let's hit the road. You have an eight-o'clock call. It's seven-thirty now."

Clay wobbled to the bathroom and did what she said. On his way out, he noticed the curtained window opposite the bathroom door. There was something about it that bothered him, something flitting on the outskirts of his memory, but he couldn't quite put his finger on it.

Oh, well. It'll come to me, he thought as he walked back out to the living room.

Cissi practically dragged him out of her apartment and wouldn't let him drive to work. Instead, she sat him in her passenger seat and drove them both to the studio.

Clay couldn't shake the feeling that he was forgetting something about the night before, but his head hurt so bad, he let it slide.

Peter pulled into the UBC parking lot in his new used Hyundai Sonata. He parked and was walking into the building when he noticed that Cathy Grant was also arriving. A happy grin on her face and a spring in her step made it obvious that she was in a rare good mood.

Peter's face flushed, and he looked down as she walked past him.

"Good morning, Peter. Beautiful day, isn't it?" she called to him cheerfully.

"Um, yeah, sure is," he replied, still looking down.

"Have a good day!" With a smart wave, she entered the studio.

Peter exhaled slowly. He had fantasized about her all night, and felt a stirring in his lacy panties.

Nuns and dead kittens, he thought to himself. *Nuns and dead kittens.*

That killed the stirring.

Clay walked to his new dressing room and, once in, flopped down on the sofa there. He saw that Stuart, from wardrobe, had placed his costume, another pair of hospital scrubs along with a lab coat, on the hook on the back of the door. He quickly stripped off his clothes and changed into them.

He still had to learn his lines for today, and he was really mad at himself for drinking so much the night before. He would need to be on his toes today during his scenes with Cathy, and he forced himself to focus on the script. He started to memorize the dialogue.

A gentle knock on his door caused him him to look up from the pages. "Come in," he said loudly.

The door slowly opened, and Travis leaned in.

"Can I come in?" he asked softly. He looked terrible, too, Clay noted. He had dark circles under his red eyes and, like Clay had been, was wearing the same clothes he'd worn the day before. His usually immaculately clean-shaven face had a pretty heavy five o'clock shadow going.

"For a minute. I have to learn this," Clay said, holding up the script. He wouldn't admit it, but he was very happy to see Travis.

"I won't stay long. I have to get to makeup myself. I just wanted to tell you again that I love you, Clay. I didn't sleep at all last night. I missed you so much. I called you at least ten times, but you never picked up."

"I stayed at Cissi's last night," Clay said.

"Oh. I know we can work this out, can't we?" Travis pleaded.

Clay sighed. "I don't know. I thought I knew who you were, but I didn't. I don't know what to do, Trav."

Travis nodded and placed a hand on the doorknob.

"Look," Clay said as he rose to face Travis eye to eye, "I love you, too. Let's have lunch together today, okay? You're right. We should be able to figure this out and compromise somehow, right?"

Travis's face brightened considerably. "Yes. Yes!" He rushed at Travis, and they hugged each other tightly, pulling only slightly apart to kiss each other repeatedly. They each were, between kisses, saying, "I'm so sorry."

"Trav, I've have to learn these lines," Clay finally had to remind him.

"Okay. Okay. I'll go. See you at lunch." Travis walked to the door and opened it. Turning back to Clay, he winked at him and was gone, closing the door behind him.

His good humor having returned, Clay say back down and tried to concentrate on the script.

Joan marched up to Carole's desk and leaned over the computer monitor. "Are we ready to go? I do have other commitments this morning."

"Oh, Joan, the meeting is in the small conference room on three. I thought you knew. I'm sorry," Carole responded calmly.

Joan stomped a foot in exasperation. "Ugh!" she seethed. "Why didn't someone call me?"

"I'm sorry. I thought someone did." Carole remained impassive.

Joan spun around and stormed out of the office, her anger building.

This is intolerable! Joan thought to herself. *I took a lunch with that bimbo, and this is what I get in return? Who is she to order me to a meeting?*

The more she stewed about it, the madder she got.

Joan decided that she was going to have to step up her get-rid-of-Dru program. She just wasn't going to be at that bitch's beck and call. She'd place a call to Lester Jarvis the second she got back from this mystery meeting. Dru would be gone by the end of the week. Just like the detective she'd gotten canned.

She actually cracked a smile as she stomped down the stairs one flight to get to the third-floor meeting room.

The door to the conference room was closed when Joan got to it, and she purposely flung it open hard, prepared to take charge. She was stopped short by the collection of people that Dru had assembled.

Dru sat at the head of the long mahogany table. To her right was Peter Dowd, then, next to him a lawyer she knew was UBC general counsel, then there was her own attorney, Hank Blumberg. On Dru's other side was the follicularly challenged Jake Klein himself. Next to Jake was some guy from Accounting whose name she didn't know, but, damn! he needed to visit a dermatologist. Next to him was a man she didn't know, but from his plain dress, he seemed to be some sort of policeman.

What was going on? She instantly was on high alert and entered the room cautiously.

"Ah, Joan. You're the last to arrive. I believe you know most everyone here," Dru said magnanimously. She indicated the stranger. "This is Detective Bancroft. He's taking over the investigation in Jack Benz's death. He's here purely as an observer."

Bancroft stood and offered a callused hand to Joan.

Very wary, Joan ignored the proffered hand, barely nodded to him, and took a seat next to Hank Blumberg. She noticed that in front of each person was a binder full of pages. In the center of the table was a speaker pod, and the steady red "On" light indicated it was in use.

"Who's on speaker?" she shrewdly asked.

"Hello, Joan! It's Lester. How are you today?" came Lester Jarvis's disembodied voice.

"Oh! Lester, hello! I'm . . . good. But I must admit that I'm at a loss . . . as to what's going on," Joan stuttered, completely thrown by Lester's presence.

"Actually, me, too. Dru, what is this all about? I called in as you requested. What is the problem out there?" Lester's voice testily demanded.

"Well, Lester, we seem to have some minor accounting irregularities, and I felt you should be aware of them." Dru was cool.

"*Minor* accounting irregularities? What do I care about that? Dru, I canceled lunch with Katie Couric for this. . . ."

"Please, bear with me, Lester," Dru continued. "I've been going over the invoices from Klein Productions regarding costs from *Sunset Cove*. If you will all open your binders . . ." There was a scurry of activity as all in the room opened their binders. "Lester, I FedExed yours out yesterday. You should have it by now."

"I have it here."

"Good. You'll notice I have a copy of the invoices that UBC was billed from Klein Productions for various fees over the past year. Production costs, costumes, sets, scenery—that sort of thing. But opposite each page you'll notice another page which represents the actual amounts paid to Klein. The numbers don't match."

"What?" Jake Klein leaned in closer to study the pages in the binder.

"Yes, Jake, I'm afraid UBC was being charged a higher rate than you were actually billing. And as you know, all checks from UBC were paid to a Klein Production corporate account. It seems once the funds were deposited, a dummy invoice was generated, and the lesser, correct fee was entered as paid." Dru looked directly at Joan. "The overages were then electronically transferred out of that account and into another account."

Joan was growing noticeably uncomfortable.

"I don't believe this! I assure you, Dru, and you too, Lester, that there must be some mistake!" Jake was flustered.

"Dru, is this true? We were being overbilled? How much?" Lester's voice was all business now, all traces of peevishness gone.

"Well, going back one year? A total of seven hundred, eighty-five thousand."

"What?!" Jake and Lester said at the same time.

"I'm afraid so. And that's just this past year—those figures I can prove with these Klein documents. I have no idea what was misdirected last year. And, it must be noted, that as the dates go further back, it's harder to uncover the missing funds. The person who did this was clever at first but then got careless. There most likely has been more money siphoned off, and a full audit is warranted, but I don't think we'll ever find out how much."

"How did you get these, Drusilla?" Joan archly inquired, her voice tensely shrill.

Dru smiled sweetly. "Oddly enough, Joan, I received them anonymously from a concerned party." *Well, it was almost true,* she reasoned.

"Well, surely there is a logical reason," Joan said quickly. "Jake, I just need some time to sort this all out. But I assure you . . ."

"Lester," Dru went on, ignoring Joan. "If you look at the approval signatures on each of these invoices, you'll see that they are all signed by Joan."

Everyone at the table studied the signature scrawled on each document. It was indeed Joan's bold script. Every person then looked up in unison and stared at Joan, who was turning a very unattractive shade of red.

Dru turned to Jake. "Actually, we know where the missing money is, Jake."

The balding man had begun to sweat profusely. "You do?" he said, relief filling his body.

"Yes, we do," Bancroft said. All heads now spun to look at him. "Ms. Gordon? May I?" he asked courtly.

"By all means," she replied.

"Mr. Jarvis, I'm Detective Dan Bancroft, LAPD. I've taken over the Jack Benz and Josh Babbitt murder investigations. When it came to Ms. Gordon's attention that there was some possible embezzling going on, she contacted me. Feeling it might lead to a motive in the two homicides, I had the various bank accounts checked out. And I found something interesting."

Joan was squirming in her seat. Peter was watching her closely and enjoying every minute of her discomfort.

Payback's a bitch, he thought. *And so are you, Joan.*

"It seems that the exact amounts that were overbilled to UBC and taken from the Klein Productions account matched the exact amounts of deposits into an account held at the same bank, Beverly Hills Bank & Trust, in the name of a J. S. Thomas."

Joan's eyes blazed fire at Dru.

Dru spoke up. "Joan? Your middle name is Susan, isn't it?"

Joan sat silent.

"Lester, Joan has been embezzling small amounts out of almost every invoice. The amounts were small enough not to cause scrutiny, but when added up, well, you get the picture," Dru said to the speaker.

"You bitch," Joan hissed. She then stood up so quickly that the chair she had been sitting in was kicked back with enough force to knock it over.

"Joan." Jake looked her hard in the eyes. "Did you do this?"

"Jake, no! I am . . . I never . . ."

"Oh, drop it, Joan," Dru cut in. "We have the documentation. We have your signatures. Detective Bancroft has copies of your electronic deposit transfers. You stupidly left a paper trail a mile wide. You're busted. Admit it."

Joan looked at each person in the room, hatred blazing in her eyes.

"You idiots!" she said haughtily. "I'm not saying a word until I speak with my useless attorney here. You can all go fuck yourselves! I made you all so much money. This is the thanks I get? Accusations? Lies! Half-truths! Who do you think brought this show in under budget each day? Me! Not this piece of ass." She pointed at Dru. "Me! I did! I made this show number one. Me!" Joan was slamming her hands down on the table to emphasize her points.

"Joan. Sit *down*." Dru's tone was one of steel. The sheer forcefulness of it shut Joan up, and she moved to the next available chair and sat.

Dru pulled out a document from her binder and slid it across the table to Joan, who ignored it. "Lester, the money is all in her account. She didn't touch it."

There was silence from the speaker box.

"I want her outta here!" Jake Klein said forcefully. "I want her prosecuted! Detective, can you arrest her?"

Bancroft looked at Dru.

"Jake, Klein Productions was paid the correct and true amounts, it's UBC that took the hit here. It would appear she was saving for something," Dru said.

While Joan shot daggers at her, Jake digested this and settled back in his chair.

Dru focused on the speaker box. "Lester, I don't think it would be to our benefit to arrest Joan and let this get out. We have enough trouble right now with Jack—the deaths—and I don't think any of us want any more negative ink on UBC and *Sunset Cove* than necessary."

"What do propose, Dru?" Lester asked.

"I've taken the liberty to draw up a resignation letter." Dru looked hard at Joan. "In it, Joan agrees to return the money from her secret account back to UBC. She will resign her position from Klein Productions, effective immediately. . . ."

Joan snorted.

"In exchange for UBC not prosecuting her to the full extent of the law, Joan agrees to all terms and conditions set forth in the resignation letter, which include a nullification of her severance package, an admittance of her guilt, an agreement to no litigation in any form against either UBC or Klein Productions, and a nondisclosure clause that will not allow her to discuss the terms and conditions of her resignation."

Joan could not believe what she was hearing. All that money gone. No severance! She couldn't sue. No beach house in Tahiti. No tight brown boys waiting on her, hand and foot.

She was screwed, and she knew it. The only good thing was that they didn't seem to know about the other account. While it wasn't as much as she had planned on, she still had that, at least.

"I won't sign it," she said defiantly.

"Then you will be arrested and prosecuted on over five counts, which will include fraud, grand theft, larceny, and so on," Dru warned. "And I guarantee you, UBC will stop at nothing to see that you do from ten to fifteen years in state prison. I will see to that!"

"Lester." Joan changed tactics and turned to the speaker box and began to plead. "I made a mistake! I'm sorry. I can fix this! You need me here. . . . Don't do this!"

"Joan," he hesitantly answered, his voice sounding faint, "I can't tell you how upset I am to find out that you have stolen from us—from me, Joan, a friend! I don't know what to say."

Hank Blumburg spoke up for the first time. "Joan, let's take a minute out in the hall." He stood up and waited for Joan to get up. She did. They walked out of the conference room.

No one in the room said anything until they returned five minutes later. Joan had been crying. Without a word, she took a pen offered by Hank and scribbled her name on the resignation letter. She then stood up tall and started to walk out of the room.

Two security guards materialized from nowhere and escorted her all the way from the conference room to the parking lot, not even letting her stop at her office for personal effects. They would be boxed up and sent to her later, she was told.

She cried the entire time.

Back in the conference room, the meeting was breaking up. Lester had praised Dru twenty times before hanging up, and she was at the door, thanking everyone for coming. Bancroft hung back, looking out the windows at the parking lot below. He watched as Joan bitterly got into her Mercedes and drove away.

"Thanks, Hank. Yet again, you save UBC from scandal," Dru said, shaking Hank's hand warmly.

"My pleasure. All this UBC activity this past week has been quite exciting." he replied. "And I understand from Detective Bancroft that Travis's problems aren't over yet."

"Yes, well, that's what I've heard. Just be prepared," Dru warned.

Hank nodded and left, followed by the UBC attorney and Kyle.

"Kyle, thank you so much for your help. I promise, you won't be sorry you helped me out." Dru winked at the young man, who turned beet red and smiled wanly as he left.

"Dru, hats off. Thank you for helping keep this under wraps," Jake Klein said as he pumped her hand up and down. "Should I authorize an audit?"

"I would. Just to know. I don't think we'll recover anything more, but you never know."

Klein nodded. "I'll have my accountants get on it immediately. I'd like to talk to you about something else, in private, later. Are you free for lunch today? I'll come back and pick you up. We'll go to the Ivy."

"Okay, Jake. That's the least I can do for you today," she smiled.

"I'll call you in a few. Good-bye."

After he was gone, only Dru and Bancroft remained in the large room, separated by the enormous table.

Dru crossed her arms and stared at the detective. "Thank you for your help here."

"My pleasure. But I don't believe your theory that Ms. Thomas is behind the two murders. I agree, she's a thief, but I just don't see what motive she had for killing those two men. In fact, killing her leading man would only hurt the show, not help it. I think I'll still concentrate on Mr. Beautiful there," he said, pointing to a copy of the Herb Ritts shot of Travis that hung on one of the walls.

"Maybe Jack discovered she was embezzling. Isn't that possible? Isn't that your job? To investigate all leads? She's a thief! It doesn't take a huge leap to think she'd be capable of killing," Dru passionately insisted.

Bancroft's eyes narrowed. "I don't need you to tell me how to do my job, Ms. Gordon," he said archly. "I believe that was my predecessor's problem. He listened a little too much to you, didn't he?"

Enraged, Dru said nothing.

"So go ahead. Tell your boy Travis to watch his back. But I'm coming after him. Soon." With that, he grinned an oily smile and started to leave the room. He stopped short when he almost ran into Park, who had silently entered the office moments before.

"Ah, Dan. Charming as always," Park said, a tightness in his throat.

"Huh," Bancroft grunted. "Can't keep away from her, can you? Please. Fuck up your career. We won't miss you."

Dru and Park watched him leave the conference room. Dru sighed loudly.

"Well. He seems to have a bug up his ass, don't you think? Why does he dislike you so much?" she asked.

"Oh, it's hardly worth mentioning. We've never gotten along ever since I wouldn't loan him twenty-five grand to buy some bad Internet stock he wanted. He's badmouthed me ever since, all over the station. Fuck him. He's an idiot."

"Well, he does have a point. Us being together did screw up your career."

"I told you last night, I don't care. I'm glad I met you. In fact, I wonder if I can throw you on the table here and ravish you repeatedly," he said as he took her in his arms. They kissed passionately.

"I wish," she sighed after they broke apart. "Why are you here?"

"I thought my girl might need a little support after this meeting, and I wanted to invite you to lunch."

Dru glowed at the words. "I'm so glad you came by. I was so nervous. Even though I had Joan nailed to the wall, I was still a little scared."

"I'm sure you handled it all very well," he said. "Wonder what that Klein guy wants to talk to you about," Park asked.

"You heard that? I'm sure it has to do with money recovery. And I'll bet he's hoping UBC doesn't sue him for any lost monies. His company would be responsible."

Park kissed her lightly again and walked with her to the door.

"Sorry we can't have lunch together today. I'd much rather be with you than with Klein," she said honestly, enjoying the sensation of his arm around her waist.

"No problem. Actually, I won't be eating alone, either. My stepfather is taking me to lunch today. I thought you could join us, and thus spare me the lecture. He and I are due for one of our regular 'come work for me' lunches. Maybe now I'll have to." Park held open the door for Dru, and they walked out into the hall. "I'm not looking forward to it."

22

Clay again placed the stethoscope on the barely moving chest of Bill Garret, who, as Stone, was swathed in head bandages and lying in the hospital bed. A beautiful young woman with bright-red curly hair tucked under a nurse's cap was standing next to him holding a pen and clipboard.

"No change," Clay, as Dr. Chase Kendall, said seriously. "Make a note of that, Cindy," he continued.

"Yes, doctor," she replied quickly. She pressed the pen down too hard on the metal clipboard and accidentally dropped the clipboard to the fake-tile floor with a loud clang. "Oh, shit! Sorry!" she giggled nervously.

"Cut!" Sam Michaels called out. He sighed.

It was the fifth take of this scene, each take ruined by the idiotic girl in the nurse's uniform. Worse than that, she erupted into the most irritating giggle each time she screwed up. It had the same effect on him as fingernails on a chalkboard.

Why had he agreed to let Jake Klein's daughter have this part? he wondered. But, he knew the answer. Because Joan had told him to.

However, things change. *Ding-dong, the wicked witch is dead!*

The news had spread like wildfire that Joan had unexpectedly resigned that morning. No reason was given, and the rumors were flying. Frankly, Sam didn't care why; he was just thrilled that she was gone. He had wanted to wrest some control of the show back and now felt free to do it. Starting now.

"Honey?" he said to the nervous, giggling girl. "Tell you what. You just stand by the door and don't say a word. Clay, make the notations yourself, okay?"

"Sure, Sam. Whatever you say," Clay agreed, wanting to do anything to help get this scene in the can.

Jackie Klein's face fell, and she silently walked over to the door of the hospital-room set and stood quietly, crimson-faced.

They reshot the scene with Clay ad-libbing the notation-taking, and the scene worked beautifully. Clay did to perfection the long facial hold that always comes just before a commercial interruption.

"Cut! Great, Clay. Perfect. I think you have a career ahead of you," Sam joked, his good mood restored.

"Thanks, Sam. I hope so!"

"How was that, Mr. Michaels? Was I okay?" Jackie piped up, eager for praise.

"Uh, yes, dear, that was perfect. Thank you," he patronized her. She would not be returning. "Lunch, everybody. Let's be back in one hour. Clay, we won't need you until after we shoot Travis and Melina's kitchen scenes."

Everyone began the rush to the doors to leave. Clay spied Travis hanging by the craft services table and hung back. Soon they were the only ones left on the stage.

"Hey," Clay said, strolling up to Travis.

"Hey."

"Where do you want to eat? I don't want to eat in the commissary. I want to be able to talk freely," Clay stated, reaching out to brush a straggling strand of hair off his boyfriend's brow.

"I don't care. Anywhere. That Italian place up the road?" Travis suggested.

"Perfect. Let's go."

Park and his stepfather were seated at a booth in the very restaurant that Clay and Travis were headed to. They had both been on good behavior since they had met in the parking lot of the eatery.

As always, Charles Farrar cut an impressive figure. Tall, lanky, and exquisitely dressed in expertly tailored brown slacks, ecru Hugo Boss knit shirt, and a tan Carroll & Company private label light wool blazer, he moved with the air of the very privileged. His salt-and-pepper hair was conservatively cut, and he had a color-coordinated hankie peeking out of his breast pocket. A pair of Gucci loafers, just like Park's pair, graced his sockless feet.

"So," Charles said, after they had ordered. "You've been on the TV a lot with this latest case of yours. Did you know that I actually knew Jack Benz? He was on a committee with me for a charity fundraiser a few years ago. Nice man, for an actor. Your mother, however, is quite distressed by all the publicity this case has caused."

"Why? It hardly affects her, you, or the family," Park said.

"Anything you or your brother does affects the family; don't you realize that?"

Oh, Christ. It's going to be one of those kinds of lunches, Park thought. He suddenly wished he'd ordered a Jack Daniels instead of the iced tea. He had no idea how, or if, he was going to broach the subject of his suspension.

"And since we are now on the subject, I want to talk to you about Kurt."

Park smiled slightly. *It's a Kurt discussion day. I'm off the hook,* he realized.

"You must speak to him. This rootless life he leads has got to stop. Your mother is worried sick about him. As you know, I have completely given up on him ever amounting to anything, but your mother insists that he can achieve great things," Charles smirked as he gracefully took a sip of his iced tea.

"Charles, I think Kurt is happy with things in his life the way they are."

"Please. This lifestyle he's living. It makes me sick. In my day, if a man was . . . queer, he led a secret life and didn't embarrass his family. In my day these things were kept hidden. A man might feel that way about other men, but he did not act on it," he sermonized.

"Well, things are a little different now, Charles. I don't think Kurt feels he has to hide anything. And, I have to say, I don't think he needs to hide, either."

Ignoring his stepson, Charles bulldozed on. "And if he did act on it, it was in private, out of town, where no one would know. His family wouldn't be hurt. That's the way these things should be handled." He looked at Park expectantly, but Park said nothing. "Anyway, I think I have something that Kurt might like to do. I've recently bought a small publishing house. They do art books, coffee table books, things like that. Kurt's always had that artistic bent. I think he might be good at editing."

"I don't know, Charles. Ask him." Park shrugged.

"No. He'd dismiss it out of hand, coming from me. Nothing I say ever seems to get through to him," he said, a faraway look in his eyes.

You could barely place the two men in the same room without Kurt exploding in a rage over some perceived slight by Charles. Holiday gatherings were always tense, and time had done nothing to ease the situation. Kurt stubbornly refused to listen to his father, and his father was constantly disappointed in his only child. Park, therefore, was often caught in the middle.

"Why is that? I mean, you two used to be so close. It can't just be that he's gay, Charles. What happened between you two?"

"Nothing!" Charles answered a tad too forcefully. He realized this and instantly became unruffled once more. He continued his prepared speech. "What I need is for you to ask him. He idolizes you. You can convince him to do this. It would be the best thing that ever happened to him, David."

"God, I don't know, Charles. I agree he needs to focus his life, but as an editor? I don't know if he'd like that," Park replied, trying to picture Kurt sitting behind a desk, with actual responsibility.

The front door to the restaurant opened, and the movement caught Park's attention. Clay and Travis entered the restaurant and waited to be seated. Clay was still wearing hospital scrubs, obviously his costume for the day.

I can't eat a meal out without running into these two, Park thought.

"Convince him that he would like it," Charles demanded.

"Ha! That'll be the day, when I convince Kurt to do anything," Park laughed.

Clay and Travis were being led toward Park and Charles by the host. Travis spotted Park first and nudged Clay's attention to him. Clay nodded slightly, and they continued to their table, a few past the former detective's. Just as they walked past Park's table Travis happened to glance at the man sitting with him. He turned back to look at his own table but then did a double-take. He stopped dead in his tracks and looked hard again at the older man.

Charles noticed he was being stared at, and looked up at Travis. He looked at him serenely. Travis's mouth opened, then closed. Clay realized that Travis wasn't behind him anymore, and looked back to see his boyfriend staring at some old guy sitting with the hot detective. He walked over to Travis.

"You!" Travis finally snarled.

"I beg your pardon? Can I help you?" asked Charles formally.

"You! It's you! You son of a bitch!" Travis fairly shouted. Other diners began to look up at the emerging scene taking place in the middle of the restaurant.

Park started to rise up out of his chair. "Travis? What in the world . . . ?"

"That's the fucker!" Travis shouted at him, pointing at Charles. "That's the guy that taped me! Him! I'd remember his face as long as I live!"

Charles remained calm, despite the yelling man standing three feet away from him. "I have no idea what you're talking about, young man. Now, if you don't mind . . ."

"I'll kill you, you motherfucker!" Travis screamed, and he lunged at Charles. Clay's quick reaction saved Charles from a hard punch to the face.

Travis had drawn back his cocked fist when Clay grabbed him and wrestled him back. Travis struggled to be let free. Park jumped out of his chair and tried to help subdue Travis.

"You son of bitch!"

"Travis, stop it! Stop it," Clay yelled, trying mightily to hold him in place.

"What the hell is going on? Travis, stop it! Stop!" Park physically got in front of Travis who was now crying and flailing to get free. Charles shakily stood up and started to back away. He was mortified by this scene.

"He's the one I told you about! It was him! He gave me the drugs. . . . He *taped* me!" Travis wailed.

Park looked at Charles and saw from the growing look of guilt on his narrow face that it was true. He turned back to Travis.

"Travis. Travis! Calm down, okay? Calm down . . . Clay? Get him out of here. Now!"

The entire restaurant stared as Clay led his hysterical boyfriend out of the restaurant and into the parking lot, where Travis dropped down to the cement pavement and hugged his knees to his chest. Clay bent down and tried to soothe him.

"Trav, calm down . . . that's it, just calm down. What was that? Who is that man?" he asked.

Travis looked up with hate-filled eyes. "That's the motherfucker who videotaped me getting gang-banged that night at his house. He gave that tape to Jack. It's him. I know it!"

"Oh, my God!" Clay was shocked, and, impetuously, he wanted to go back in the restaurant and beat the crap out of the guy himself.

What Clay didn't know was that Park wanted to do the same thing.

Park had led Charles away from the dining room and back into the hallway leading to the bathrooms. Charles was trying to rearrange his face into something resembling indifference but was failing.

"Who was that man? I want you to arrest him, David! Such a scene, I have *never* in my life—" he started to say.

"Shut up! Is it true? I know about the tape, Chuck. Is it

true? Are you the rich man with the Bentley convertible he told me about?" Park's eyes blazed with barely controlled rage.

Charles, not accustomed to being addressed like this by his wife's son, drew himself up to his full 6-foot-3-inch height. "How dare you even think . . ."

"You son of a bitch! It *is* true, isn't it? You did that! My God!" Park was furious. "You had that man raped, and you taped it, you sick bastard!"

Charles unexpectedly became completely composed. His eyes narrowed, and his facial features turned into a sneer. "So what? I've taped lots of boys getting it, and each and every one of them *wanted* it! I remember him now. He had a blond crewcut then. That piece of trash loved it. He just kept going, taking all comers. In fact, after the other boys were done and gone, I turned the camera off and went a round or two with him myself."

Park recoiled as if hit.

"So what? You think he's got any proof? None! It's my word against his, and each time this happens, I always win. No one questions my word!" Park noticed for the first time how reptilian Charles could look. It made him sick to his stomach.

"Your mother turns a blind eye to my . . . proclivities, if you're thinking of telling her. Once, your brother walked in on me and some piece, and when he tried to tell her, she slapped him. He never mentioned it again."

Now Park understood why Kurt hated the man so much. Why there was always tension between the two. For a brief moment, Park actually thought he was going to throw up.

"I control this family, and don't you ever forget it, *boy.*" Emboldened, Charles took a step forward and poked Park in the chest for emphasis.

For a second, Park was still. Then he drew back his closed fist and threw a punch that landed flat across Charles's right cheek and nose. Park was satisfied not only by the muffled cracking sound he heard, but also by the startled look that briefly flitted across Charles's face before he recoiled backward and hit the back of his head against the door of the ladies' room. He slumped to the floor.

"Don't you *ever* call me 'boy' again, you sorry excuse for a human being." Park leaned down so his face was just inches away from Charles. Blood was pouring out of his broken nose, and he tried to back away, but there was no place to go.

"I'm going to do a little investigating on you, you pathetic old man. And whatever I find, I'm going to scream it from the highest mountaintop." He stood up straight and pivoted to leave. "Mother's going to love *those* headlines."

He left his stepfather lying on the floor, bleeding.

Outside, Clay had gotten Travis up, and they were walking to Travis's car. In a parking space across the lot, Travis noticed a classic Bentley convertible. It was in pristine shape, obviously well cared for and loved, and it was the very same car that he had ridden in with that man so many years before.

There was no doubt in Travis's mind now. The man inside was indeed the man who had caused him so much pain and heartache.

Park ran to catch up with them before they left. He put a comforting hand on Travis's shoulder.

"You okay?" he asked, concerned.

"No. Who is that fucker?" Travis spit out.

"Believe it or not, he's my stepfather."

"Holy fuck!" shuddered Clay.

"Can you arrest him? I know it's him, Parker. I know it!" Travis raged.

"I know he is, too. He admitted it. But he can't be arrested for what he did to you, Travis. What happened to you took place too long ago."

"Fuck! Then he wins!" Travis spat.

"But even if charges were brought against him, it would bring it out in the open. The tape, you, the rape, everything. Would you want that?" Park warned.

Travis exhaled hard. "No."

"And besides, I can't do anything myself now, anyway. I've been suspended."

Clay and Travis looked sharply up at Park.

"What?" Travis was shocked.

"It seems that my helping you out the other night, among other things, didn't go over so well."

"Damn!" Travis swore. "I'm sorry."

"Hey, don't sweat it. It's not your problem."

Clay spoke up. "So, what? Your stepfather gets away with it? How many other guys did he do that to? What about them?"

Park rubbed his forehead with his hand, trying to release some of the tension. "We don't know for sure if there are any others, Clay. But I promise you both this: I will look into it. I would like nothing more than to bring that sick fucker down."

"But I can't do anything, huh? I'm screwed," Travis explosively sighed. "Man. I thought I was over this, but, just seeing him, like, brings everything back. I just want to do *something*." He looked feverishly around, and his eyes constricted when he saw Charles stagger out of the restaurant, heading toward his car, a bloodstained napkin pressed to his nose.

A possessed look overcame Travis's usually handsome face.

He calmly got into his Boxster and shooed away Clay, who attempted to get into the passenger seat. "Get back," he cautioned quietly as he buckled his seat belt.

He gunned the motor and dropped it into reverse. He slammed the gas pedal down as he popped the clutch. The rear wheels spun in a screaming spiral until they grabbed at the pavement, and the car shot backward, gaining speed at a frightening rate.

Clay and Park stood openmouthed as the silver bullet flew backward across the parking lot. When the car was halfway through the lot, Charles looked up and saw the car speeding toward him. Stunned into non-movement, he stood rooted in place.

"Travis! No!" Park yelled, horrified.

Travis clenched his teeth and pressed down harder on the gas pedal. He held on to the steering wheel tightly and braced for impact.

Charles's bladder failed as he watched the car coming toward him, and a dark stain spread across his crotch.

But instead of continuing toward Charles, the Boxster swerved at the last minute and slammed loudly into the pristine Bentley, sending a shower of sparks, broken glass, and bits of taillight up into the air.

The impact drove the Boxster three feet deep into the cabin of the stately car, pushing the driver's door all the way into the front passenger seat. The Boxster's engine compartment compacted forward into the back of the passenger cabin and devoured the back seat. Four airbags blew up instantly, and when the dust cleared, Travis could be heard laughing hysterically.

Charles, who had dropped to the ground and covered his head as the Porsche slammed into his car, looked up. "My car!" he cried out.

The bent and crumpled driver's door of the Boxster opened, and Travis got out, perfectly fine. He was still laughing as he smoothed back his tangled hair.

"Damn! So that's what zero to sixty in six seconds was for!" he howled. He walked confidently over to the prone form of Charles, who looked up at him like he was deranged.

"Don't hurt me!" Charles whimpered.

This caused new peals of laughter from Travis. Clay and Park hiked over to join him.

"Trav! Are you okay?" Clay asked, concerned.

Travis nodded vigorously through his giggles, and Clay, too, began to snicker.

"David! Arrest that man! He tried to kill me! Arrest him!" Charles shrieked.

Park looked at the mangled cars and then at his bleeding, urine-stained stepfather.

"Go fuck yourself," he said simply.

Shocked into silence, Charles struggled to pick himself up off the ground.

"God, that felt good!" Travis crowed, wiping away tears of laughter from his eyes.

"Jesus, Trav! Your car," Clay managed to say.

"Ah, fuck it. I was tired of it, anyway."

Charles regained an upright posture and stumbled to the remains of his car. He'd had this car for over twenty years, and it was his pride and joy. He could tell at once that the Boxster had crushed the side rails and twisted the frame. The car was a total wreck. He wanted to cry.

"Hey, fuck-head," Travis called to him. Charles looked at him, hot tears welling in his eyes. "You got a problem with this? Sue me. If you dare." He then whipped out his cell phone and punched in a few numbers. "Triple A? Hi. I just had an accident. My brakes failed and I just hit another car. Can you send a tow truck to Antonio's on La Cienega? It's the silver Porsche that's sitting in the Bentley. Tow it . . . wherever."

Charles watched as his own stepson walked away from the parking lot and headed toward the UBC studio six blocks down the street, accompanied by the two young men. Charles balled up a fist and slammed it down on the trunk of his car so hard, he heard the snap before he felt it.

He knew at once he had broken his hand.

23

Cissi was waiting impatiently in Clay's dressing room when he and Travis stumbled in, still chuckling. They only had eyes for each other and didn't even see her standing by the bathroom door.

"Did you see the look on his face? I thought he was going to have a stroke!" Travis snorted.

"It was pretty priceless; that's for sure. But Trav, what if he does sue you? You trashed his car. A very expensive car," Clay questioned.

"That's what insurance is for. But I don't think he will. He's not the type. He'll just let it slide. Smarmy bastard. I just wish I had run him over."

"Oh, yeah, that's all you would need. Another crime to add to your ever-growing list of felonies," Clay joked, moving in for a kiss.

"Where were you? I came down to take you to lunch, and you weren't even here!" Cissi broke in. Her hands were on her ample hips, and her fiery hair was already askew. Her ever-present leather bag hung limply off her shoulder.

Clay stopped in midmotion, caught. "Cis! Hi . . . I didn't see you there."

"Obviously."

Travis backed up a pace away from Clay's proximity. "Hey, Cissi," he said, artificially cheerful.

Clay turned to Travis. "It's okay. She knows about us. I told her yesterday," he explained simply.

Shock, concern, and a trace of anger welled up in Travis before he relaxed and smiled. "Well. Guess the cat's out of the bag on us, then, huh? Listen, Clay, I need to get on set. Can we have our talk later? Maybe over dinner?" He took Clay's hand gently in his and squeezed lightly.

"Sure. I'll be down on set myself in a sec," Clay said, giving him a quick peck on the lips before he left the room.

Cissi watched it all in silence.

"So. Sorry I wasn't here, Cis. Trav asked me to lunch. I didn't know you wanted to go with me; we hadn't discussed that," Clay said warmly to his friend.

"I can't believe it! He's bad for you, Clay. And, you know it! You cried to me about what an ass he is all last night! And here you are, back together!" she spat out, her voice filled with venom.

"We're not back together! We went to have lunch to talk about it, but . . . something happened. We never got around to it. Why does this bother you so much?"

"Because I care about you! Don't you know that?" Cissi's hands were clenching into fists, then relaxing. Over and over. "He's bad for you, and you know it!" she repeated more urgently. "You should just take some time away from dating for a while and just figure out what it is that you do want. Maybe what you really want is right under your nose and you don't even see it."

"I don't know what you're talking about. I'm sorry if I'm upsetting you, Cis. I don't want you mad at me. You're the best! I love you, and I know you just have my best interests at heart." He reached for her and took her in a big hug. She squeezed back hard and held on for just a beat too long.

Clay had a brief, glimpsing memory of a picture of her and Jack Benz, also locked in a tight hug. Where had he seen that? Oh, yes, it was in his dreams last night.

"Oh, Clay," Cissi said snuggling up against him. "I do care about you. More than you know. I'd do anything for you, you know that? I've *done* everything for you. Travis is just bad

news, and you'd be better off without him in your life. Don't
you see that?" she said pleadingly.

"I don't know. Maybe you're right. I don't know. I just
need to try and talk to him. Sort it out. I love him, Cis."

The words Clay spoke had an immediate effect on Cissi.
She pulled away from Clay sharply, breaking physical contact. "Then you're an imbecile. He can never give you what
you want." She stormed to the door and yanked it open. "I
just want him completely, totally out of your life. For your
own good!" With that, she whirled around to leave the room.

Her large shoulder bag swung out from her shoulder and
actually smacked up against the door frame, jostling the contents. A lone peanut butter cup popped out and hit the carpeting of the dressing room floor. Cissi stopped, glared at Clay,
then bent over, and scooped it up. She left the room, slamming the door behind her.

Dru sat down hard in her expensive ergonomic office chair.
She had some serious thinking to do.

Lunch with Jake Klein at the Ivy Restaurant had thrown
her a few surprises.

He confided to her that he had suspected for months that
Joan was doctoring the books, but he hadn't been able to
bring himself to investigate. Ashamed, he confessed that Joan
had done such a great job with *Sunset Cove* that he hadn't
wanted to upset the apple cart. Shaking his head sadly, he told
her that Joan had been the best producer he had ever seen.

Dru had sat quietly through his confessional and wondered
where this was headed.

That was when he had offered her Joan's job. Expressing
admiration for her skills in her network position, and for the
quiet way she had handled the Joan issue, he wanted her to
work for him. Loyalty like hers was a rare commodity in
Hollywood, and he was ready to pay exhorbitantly for it. He
mysteriously knew her current salary and bonus plan with
UBC and calmly had offered to double it. She would have
total control over *Sunset Cove,* and she could take over
Klein's other UBC soap, *The Insiders.*

The Insiders was UBC's lowest-rated soap, a dreary show set in a New England city, populated with a boring cast of stock characters. Dru had notified Klein over a month ago that she planned on canceling it in the fall.

Klein offered her forty percent of the show if she would take it on as well. She would have complete creative control. If she turned it around, they would both win. Klein would rather have sixty percent of a show still on the air than one hundred percent of a show off the air. Dru would have financial security. It was a better deal than Joan Thomas could ever have dreamed of.

It was a difficult decision for Dru. While she liked her current position at UBC, she had, of late, grown increasingly tired of the petty politics that network television bred. There would always be another Joan Thomas to deal with, and though she knew she could hold her own with them, she was tired of it.

Working for Klein would give her not only creative freedom but also personal freedom. She was keenly aware that her life had boiled down to two things: working endless hours with almost zero recognition, and going to the gym religiously. A gym, it should be noted, that was full of handsome, built gay men who had absolutely no interest in her, and handsome, built lesbians who did.

Even though it was something she would never admit to anyone, she had dreams of getting married and raising a family one day. She knew that if she continued with the path her life was on, the chances of that happening were remote at best.

Clay was going over his lines when he heard the squawk box buzz to life, paging Travis. At the same time, there was a knock at his door.

"Come in," he called out.

It was Stuart, from Wardrobe. He was carrying a dark-blue Helmut Lang suit, pale-blue Paul Smith shirt, and maroon-striped Canali tie in one hand, and a pair of dress loafers in the other. "Wardrobe change for your next scenes," he said, hanging the suit in the open closet and placing the shoes on the floor. He smiled brightly. "Just change when you can, and leave the scrubs here. I'll pick them up later." He left the dressing room.

Thinking there was no time like the present, Clay stripped out of the scrubs, remembering to remove his wallet from the back pocket. He always kept his wallet close by. It was a habit he had learned the hard way after it was stolen once out of a dressing room on a commercial shoot last year.

He pulled on the pants, buttoned up the shirt, slipped on the shoes, and tied his tie. Checking himself out in the mirror, he noticed that his wallet hit his back hip in a funny place and protruded in an unflattering way. It ruined the line of the beautifully cut suit, and Clay decided he would leave the wallet behind this one time.

He picked up his jeans and started to place the wallet in the hip pocket when it jammed on something and wouldn't go in. Digging in the pocket, he pulled out a folded photograph. Curious, he opened it and stared at the picture of him and Travis.

Like a light switch clicking on, he unexpectedly remembered the extra room in Cissi's apartment. All the pictures of him. The photo albums. The very creepiness of it all. It hadn't been a drunken dream, after all. It had been real. He clearly remembered everything about that room.

Cissi's odd behavior today had been bothering him, but he had been able to put it out of his mind. Now, realizing that Cissi had a deep obsession for him, it was all he could think about.

A dreaded realization began to form in his brain.

Was it possible?

Dru decided to walk down to the *Sunset Cove* stage and watch the taping, something she didn't do that often. She wanted to get out of her office and be in different surroundings. Telling Carole where she was going, she started off down the hallway, when she ran right into Park.

"Hey," she said, surprised.

"Hey," he replied. He looked awkward and uncomfortable.

"Hmm. This doesn't look like a social call," she noted, observing his behavior.

"No, not really. I just got off the phone with a buddy down at the station. Bancroft's coming back here to take Travis in. They found a check of his made out to Jack Benz for fifty thousand dollars. They think he was paying hush money and killed Jack to stop it," he said grimly.

"Oh, no! How bad is this?"

"Look, I like the guy, you know, and my gut tells me he's not the one, and my gut's usually right. But, I've seen him lose control, and who really knows about people? At best, maybe I can talk to him, get him to solidify his story, and actually help him. But I'd need to see him before Bancroft gets here."

"I think he's on set right now. They're taping."

"Then let's go."

In complete silence they walked to the stairs and walked down to the stage floor. At the bottom of the stairs, Park stopped. He took her hand and squeezed it. She gave him a tight, small smile.

Clay desperately wanted to talk to Travis. He needed a sounding board. It was crazy what he was thinking, and Travis was the only one he felt he could trust to listen to it.

The squawk box again called for Travis to report to the stage.

Odd that Travis wasn't already there, thought Clay as he maneuvered down the labyrinthine hallways of UBC. He had been headed for the stage, but he changed course and practically ran to Travis's dressing room, almost running down Cathy Grant in the process.

"Whoa, partner!" she said, stepping back. "Where's the fire? Save your energy for our scene later."

Clay smiled weakly at her and burst into Travis's dressing room. He wasn't there. He must be on the stage by now, Clay reasoned, and he turned to leave. As he was heading out, something glinted on the floor and caught his eye.

Clay allowed himself to take the minute to examine the object. He leaned over and picked up the crumpled foil. It was a peanut butter cup wrapper.

Clay's blood ran cold.

Travis never ate candy.

Cissi had been here.

Sam stepped up to Dru and Park. He gave his attention to Dru.

"Have you seen Travis? We need him for this run-through, and no one can find him." He was exasperated.

"No, I haven't, but we're looking for him, too." Dru looked around the stage, drinking in the bustling activity.

"Popular guy," Sam muttered, walking away. "When you find him, tell him to get his ass down here!"

"Let's try his dressing room," Park offered, leading the way.

They were met en route by an increasingly frantic Clay.

"Have you seen Travis?" he asked them breathlessly.

"Why, no. We were just going to check his dressing room," Park replied.

"He's not there! I have a really bad feeling about this, Detective Parker. I think Cissi is going to kill him!" he blurted out.

"What?" Park and Dru exclaimed together.

"I think she's obsessed with me! I don't have time to go into it now, but Travis and I are dating. . . . I know it sounds crazy, but I think she wants to kill Travis to take him out of my life! We have to find them!"

Park's mind spun into high gear. Cissi's alibi for the morning of Josh's death had simply been that she was at home. There was no one to verify that, but how many people who lived alone could prove they were home alone when they said they were? They had gotten a good tire tread off the skid mark left at the scene, so it wouldn't be hard to match it to her car.

A new thought hit Clay like a hammer. "Oh, my God! I bet she killed Josh so I would get his part! We've got to find them!" Clay urged.

"Let's stay calm here, Clay. I'll check Cissi's office. Dru, you go back to the stage and see if they turn up there. Clay, where else could they be?" Park questioned.

"I don't know. Sometimes Cissi goes up to the roof to eat lunch and stare at the view. I'll look there."

"Good. If any of us finds either one of them, take them to the stage floor. We'll meet up back there."

They split up and went on their separate missions. Clay ran to the stairwell and began the ascent to the roof.

Cathy Grant strolled down the hallway on her way to the stage floor. She could not stop thinking about the amazing woman she had met the night before. Petra. Such an exotic name. Such an exotic woman. She had checked her phone service nine times already today to see if Petra had called, but so far she hadn't. She would, though. Who could turn down a chance to be with America's daytime favorite?

She happened to see a large brown leather bag lying against a wall in the corridor, the thick leather shoulder strap split in two. Its contents had spilled out around it, and she saw several of those fattening peanut butter cups scattered about. How odd that someone would drop that, she thought.

She made no move to pick it up and stepped around it.

She was passing Melina Michele's dressing room when she heard a loud thump. And another one. It sounded like someone was beating an object on the other side of the door. Loud music was blaring in the room as well, but the bumping got Cathy's curiosity up. Melina wasn't on the show today, so Cathy couldn't figure out who would be in her dressing room. She leaned an ear to the door, heard the bump again, and knocked quietly.

"Hello? Melina? Are you there? Is everything okay?" she called out. There was no reply.

She opened the door and walked into the dressing room.

Melina was there after all, her back to the door. She was
dancing suggestively to the loud pop song playing on the CD
player. Wearing a sexy red Marc Jacobs minidress, she was
shaking her head and waving her arms about wildly in time
to the music. Every once in a while she would stomp a foot
down hard, making the thumping noise that Cathy had
heard from the hallway. Melina's dance style seemed oddly
familiar.

Cathy saw that everything was okay, and started to back
up and leave, when Melina suddenly whirled around while
dancing.

It wasn't Melina after all. It was Petra.

Petra?!

"What . . . what are you doing . . . here?!" Cathy asked,
completely astounded.

Peter quit dancing suddenly and stood stone still, but
Melina's wig had moved cockeyed on his head. Shocked and
stunned to see Cathy there, he realized he was caught.

"What the . . . !" Cathy shrieked as she sprang forward
and snatched the crooked wig off his head. Peter raised up his
hands in self-defense, but Cathy just stood there, disbelieving
what she was seeing.

"Peter?!"

"Uh . . . I . . . uh, Cathy . . . I can explain . . ." he stumbled
for the words.

"Oh, my God! It was you?! Oh, my God!" she screamed,
horror-stricken.

"Cathy! Please . . . I'm going to be transgender! I'm going
to become a woman! I . . ."

"Trans*gender?!*"

"I'm going to have an operation . . . to become a woman!"
he rapidly tried to explain.

Cathy's head was swimming. She had let a man, posed as a
woman, finger-fuck her in public! A man!

Her rage grew in direct proportion to her humiliation.

"Well, Peter, or Petra, let me help you get started with that
right now!" she hissed as she drew her left foot back and,
using all her might, kicked him in the crotch.

Peter actually saw stars before he felt the pain. He doubled over, grabbed at his balls through the stretchy fabric of the dress, and fell forward to the floor.

Cathy surveyed his prone figure writhing quietly on the floor.

"That," she said haughtily, "is for not calling me!"

She whipped around and calmly walked out of the room.

24

There was only one door that allowed uncontrolled and unsecured access to the roof. The stairwell closest to the stage floor went up all six levels of the studio, from the sub-basement to the roof. UBC staff had learned long ago that the lock on the door to the roof was broken. It was a well-known secret that was overlooked by the maintenance staff, who also liked to sneak up there and smoke on their breaks.

And not always cigarettes.

The roof was a great place to get some air, read, smoke, make out, and just enjoy unparalleled vistas of Los Angeles. The Hollywood Hills were to the north, with Beverly Hills and West L.A. spreading out to the west. East held a great view of Downtown L.A. (depending on the smog levels) ten miles away, while south revealed the Wilshire corridor, and airplanes coming in for landings at faraway LAX. With its machinery, elevator housings, vents, and skylights, the roof was a somewhat dangerous place, but veteran UBC staffers knew the obstacles and accepted them.

Clay burst through the broken door, causing its rusted hinges to scream in protest. It was incredibly windy up on the roof, and a strong gust of wind slammed the old door back against the stairwell housing. He wildly looked around but didn't see a soul up there. He was about to head back down the stairs when he heard a faint scrunching sound.

He walked around the back of the stairwell housing, the

roof gravel scrunching under his feet in a duplicate of the sound he had just heard.

As he rounded the back wall of the housing, he saw Cissi and Travis arguing. They were standing near the far north ledge, and Cissi was gesturing frantically at him. Travis was holding up his hands in front of himself in a defensive posture. They hadn't observed him.

Relief flooded Clay as he saw that Travis was unhurt. It was only when he saw the gun in Cissi's right hand that he felt true fear.

"Cissi! No!" he yelled.

She and Travis spun their heads in his direction. Clay slowly began to advance on them.

"Clay! She's crazy!" Travis warned, his long dark hair blowing about crazily in the harsh wind.

"Crazy? *Crazy*?! I am not!" She pulled the trigger and shot a round directly at Travis. He spun completely around, 360 degrees, and fell to the roof in a heap.

"Travis! Oh, my God! Travis!" Clay screamed.

"Don't come any closer! Don't!" Cissi yelled back.

Travis stirred, moving slowly, trying to get up. "She shot me! She shot me!"

"Cissi . . . Cissi, please. Don't do this, okay?" Clay said evenly, slowly moving forward. "Please don't do this."

Cissi's face contorted into an anguished play of skin and bone. She was crying heavily, and the large tears fell from her lashes and spotted her voluminous dress, which was whipping about her legs in the fierce Santa Ana wind that was blowing from the east.

"Clay," she wailed. "I love you! Don't you see? He has to go. . . . As long as he's around, you'll never be mine, and I love you!" She kept her right hand steady, pointing the large gun at Travis, who was writhing on the gravel roof, a spreading red stain blooming on his shirt.

"I know that you love me, Cissi. . . . I saw the room at your apartment, with all the pictures . . . "

"You weren't supposed to go in there! It's private! It's private! *Private* means personal!" she screamed at him.

"How long, Cissi? How long have you felt that way about me?"

"Always," she said dreamily. "Since the first time I saw you at that audition. I had to get you close to me. I needed you! I'd been betrayed by another, and I needed you!" She started to cry again.

"You killed Josh, didn't you, Cissi," Clay said smoothly, still advancing. He was about fifty feet away from her now.

"Yes. . . . You should have had that part! I told them! They wouldn't listen." The tears continued to fall. "I had to kill him. . . . It worked! I drove over to his house that morning. . . . He was out in the front yard, leaving for the studio. He waved at me when he recognized me." She giggled through the tears. "Then I shot him. You got what I wanted you to have. . . . It was a present. A gift!"

"Cissi, how could you? Josh was a great guy. . . . He never hurt you." Clay kept walking slowly forward. He didn't know what he planned to do, but he had to do something. Cissi was out of her mind. He wanted to help her.

"Clay, don't piss her off!" Travis warned, moaning. He was clutching his left shoulder with his right hand, and blood was seeping through his fingers. He was staring at the business end of the gun.

"Shut up! You shut up!" Cissi whirled to face him and threateningly moved the gun, weaving the barrel back and forth. "I killed Lance, too!" she revealed proudly.

"Lance? Lance Jackson?" Clay was incredulous.

"I loved Jack! I wanted to help Jack, just like I helped you! I got rid of Lance, and Jack became a big star! All because of me!" she said in a singsong voice.

"How? How did you do that?"

"I followed him home one night and ran him off the road. I hit his car. I hit his car with mine, and I hit it and I hit it and I hit it! Plop! Over the hill! Bye-bye, Lance," she trilled.

"Cissi, you're not well. . . . You need help. . . ."

"No! No! No! I don't! I've had all the help I need!"

"Cissy . . . please. Put down the gun, and let's you and I talk. . . ." Clay held out a hand. Cissi ignored it.

"No! Jack used to say the same thing! He was wrong, and you're wrong. I'm fine. I'm great!"

"Clay! Do something!" Travis pleaded.

"Cissi, did you hurt Jack, too?" Clay asked evenly. Twenty feet to go.

"I did! I did! I loved him. Not like I love you, but I did love him. He was my friend! We hung out. Then he met that fucking Lefty Jannel and stopped being my friend! He stopped calling me. He stopped doing things with me. He made fun of me. I heard him! He had to pay." Her eyes were wild, and her coppery hair kept flying around her face in the high wind, giving her head the look of being on fire.

"Oh, Cissi, I'm so sorry! He shouldn't have done that. . . ." Ten feet to go.

"I snuck onto the stage late that night and unbolted that rig thingy. My daddy taught me all about hydraulics back in the garage in St. Louis. I knew what would happen. It worked perfectly, just liked I planned. He looked so surprised! He shouldn't have! He underestimated me, too!" she rambled.

"Clay . . ." Travis saw Clay getting closer.

"Stop! Stop right there! Don't come any closer! I'll shoot him again! I will! I will!" she screamed, again waving the gun.

"Please don't do that, Cissi. . . . He hasn't hurt you. Let him go," Clay begged softly.

"He has to go away! I want you all to myself! No one loves me! I'm just the fat girl that everyone makes fun of!"

"What are you talking about? Everyone loves you! Cissi; everyone at UBC knows what a special person you are. Everyone," Clay tried to reason with her.

"That's not true! They all make fun of me behind my back! You never did, though," she admitted. "That's why I love you so much!"

"Cissi, I'm telling you the truth. You have more friends than you know. Put down the gun. Don't hurt Travis. We'll go get something to eat; let's leave this place." He crept forward a couple more feet.

"Okay, Clay, that would be great," she said, instantly serene. "But first, I have to shoot your loser boyfriend." She raised the gun up an inch and cocked back the hammer.

"No!" Clay dove at her, reaching for the gun. His fingers barely grazed it, but it was enough to throw off her aim, and the shot missed Travis by millimeters.

Her balance was also thrown off, and she fell back on the small brick lip that held back the loose gravel from the edge of the roof. Dazed, she flailed at Clay, who had fallen on top of her. Travis crawled over and, with his good arm, reached out to help Clay get off Cissi.

Cissi wildly scooted back away from Travis, kicking at the gravel frantically with her legs, trying to get traction. She tried to push Clay off her, but he was tangled in the folds of her diaphanous dress. She didn't see how close to the edge she was. She redoubled her efforts at escaping and placed her left arm back to get stability.

"Cissi! Stop it!" Clay cried out.

She brought her right hand up again and pointed the gun directly at Clay's face. He could actually see down into its blue steel barrel, and he held his breath, waiting for the shot that would kill him.

Travis grabbed a hold of her ankle and pulled hard on it, his blood-soaked fingers slipping as he pulled. The sudden downward movement caused her braced left arm to buckle in, and she dropped to her elbow, smacking it down, hard, on the brick lip.

Screaming out in pain, she kicked at the gravel again and pushed herself back about a foot.

It was six inches too much.

She reached back to put her left hand down but met only empty air. Her hand dropped down, and as her center of gravity shifted, her upper body fell backward. The gun flew out of her right hand as she dropped down, arms now frantically pinwheeling to find a grip on the brick ledge. But her body weight worked against her; she couldn't get her hands back up to get the rail fast enough, and she started to slide over the lip.

Clay pushed himself away from her so he wouldn't fall over with her. Travis held on to her ankle with a death grip, but because of the wetness of the blood, his fingers couldn't get a strong enough hold.

Screaming hysterically, Cissi slid the rest of the way over the edge of the building. Travis finally let go of her ankle, and watched in fascinated horror as her blood-streaked foot disappeared over the side.

The two men could hear her screaming all the way down five stories, until a sickening thud and crashing sound let them know she had hit something. Clay scrambled over to Travis and cradled him in his arms.

"Are you okay? Oh, my God! So much blood! I've got to go get help, Trav . . ."

"Don't leave me," Travis softly whispered, feeling suddenly very drowsy and light-headed. "I don't feel so good. . . ."

Clay noticed the fluttering of Travis's eyelids and became panicked. Travis slipped into unconsciousness.

"Help!" Clay screamed at the top of his lungs. "Help us, somebody!"

Movement by the stairwell housing caused him to look in that direction, and he saw Detective Parker and Dru Gordon running toward him. Detective Parker had pulled out a small handgun and was moving cautiously in a defensive position toward them. Dru had her cell phone out and was busily dialing 911.

"It was Cissi. . . . She tried to kill him," Clay cried. "She fell over the side." He slowly rocked the bleeding form of his lover back and forth.

Park cautiously peered over the edge and looked down.

Cissi had fallen down into the employee parking lot and had crashed through the roof of Peter Dowd's new used Hyundai Sonata, caving it in so far that only the roof pillars remained their original height. Bits of broken glass were scattered all around.

Cissi's eyes were open and unseeing, a look of sheer terror on her now-still face.

25

Six months later

Dru opened her door and welcomed two of her five expected dinner guests. It was her first dinner party in her house with all her new furniture, and she was nervous. She was wearing simple black pants from A Pea in the Pod. A red and green checked Burberry scarf, tucked into the top of her oversized cream Ungaro blouse, added a festive holiday flair.

She leaned forward for the obligatory cheek kiss from Kurt.

"How's my niece or nephew?" he asked, patting her rounded stomach.

"Kicking up a storm! I think there's a soccer match going on in there," she lovingly joked. "I'm thinking of naming it Pele."

Kurt grinned and moved his massive body aside, and Dru got a good look at his date, whom he had been blocking from view. Even though Park had told her Kurt would be bringing someone, she was pleasantly surprised by his choice.

"Well, hi!" She leaned over for a kiss from him as well, and ushered them into the house.

She and Park had just finished putting up the Christmas tree and all the other holiday decorations that afternoon. She was pleased by the soft glow that came from the twinkling lights on the tree. It really warmed up the house.

The dining table was attractively set for six, and she was a tad apprehensive about the chicken that was roasting in the oven. She didn't want to burn it.

Park came upstairs from below and first hugged his brother Kurt, then shook his date's hand warmly. He passed from the two men and came up behind Dru and happily crossed his arms around her, letting his hands rub her ever-growing belly. "It all looks and smells so good," he whispered into her ear.

Kurt and his date wandered about the living room and nodded appreciatively at the furnishings and decor.

"Great place, Dru," Kurt said, opening the sliding doors to the balcony. It was early December, and while not cold by Northern standards, the chilly air flooded into the room, battling against the heat put off by the roaring fire in the fireplace.

"Hey! Close the door! It's freezing!" Park shouted out good-naturedly.

Kurt and his handsome companion walked outside, shut the door, and strolled the balcony, drinking in the lights of the city below. They held hands.

"He looks happy," Dru said to Park, caressing his hands lightly with her own. "How long has this been going on?" she nodded towards the two men outside. "I didn't realize that I was having a another honest-to-God celebrity for dinner tonight."

"A couple of months. He really likes him. Turns out they met at the gym. Kurt says he always had a small crush on him, but the timing was always off. I've never seen him so crazy about another guy. I think this might last a while."

"Well, they seem very well suited for each other. I'm glad." She sniffed the air and again worried about her chicken. "How's Kurt dealing with your mother's divorce?" she asked as she untangled herself from Park and went into the kitchen to check on the meal.

"Better than great," Park replied, following her. "He hated Chuck, and I guess now we all know why. Must have been really difficult to know what was going on all those years and not be able to say anything. Our mother has been bending over backwards to try to make it up to him, because she feels guilty."

As she was seriously studying the chicken, she looked up. "So, your mother never knew? Your stepfather lied when he told you that?"

"Didn't know a thing. She was devastated, of course, by the news that her husband was playing both sides. But I think it just gave her the push she needed to get out of a bad marriage. I think she had wanted out for a long time."

Dru shook her head. "Too bad you couldn't get anything on him. It would have been so satisfying to see a scummy man like that finally pay for his behavior."

"Oh, trust me. He's gonna pay. Where it hurts most. His wallet. Mother is cleaning him out, but good. That's how Kurt got the publishing house." Park grinned.

"Good." Dru reached over to the kitchen counter and brought her glass of spring water up to her lips. She smiled contentedly as she sipped.

Here I am, hosting a dinner party, she thought.

Something she never had time to do before—and probably wouldn't have time to do again, once the baby arrived. Dru was exactly six months pregnant, apparently having conceived on the night that she and Park first made love on the balcony. Which was fine with both of them.

The past few months had been crazy. Her new position at Klein Productions as producer of both *Sunset Cove* and *The Insiders* was better than she had hoped it would be. She got to make real creative decisions that made her proud to be associated with both shows.

The calamitous events caused by the tragically insane Cissi Stanton had caused an immediate spike in ratings as new viewers flocked to see what the fuss had been about. There had been pressure from the network to keep the ratings high over the summer, to provide a strong fall sweeps week.

It was her savvy producing skills that accomplished the job. Her first task had been to revitalize a shell-shocked cast and crew. While not all of the details surrounding the events had been released publicly, it had still taken a few solid weeks before things had returned to an almost normal state.

She had introduced a complete new story line, moving the focus of the show away from the Coltrane family and introducing another prominent family, the Bensons, into the mix. Dealing with the absence of Travis had been especially difficult. She had decided not to recast some of the open roles.

And she had done all this while throwing up at least once every morning.

Lefty Jannel had been busy building new sets and tearing down old ones, and had complained daily about his workload. That stopped when he was offered a supervisory position over both *Sunset Cove* and *The Insiders* and was allowed to hire two other art directors to handle each show separately.

Peter Dowd, or Petra Dowd, as she now preferred to be called, had been promoted to Dru's old position at UBC. There had been some initial fears from New York about having a transgender in such a high-profile position at the network, but Dru had heartily recommended her, stating that not only did she have a man's perspective, but *also* a woman's. Petra was doing a terrific job, and her probation period was over next month. Dru had already been told by Lester Jarvis that Petra was staying on.

The novelty of seeing Petra running around the studio in her ladies' designer clothes had worn off long ago, and now she was just considered one of the girls. Her operation was scheduled for early the next summer, and everyone seemed to have an opinion about how large her implants should be.

Things at UBC had returned to normal.

As a result of everyone's pulling together and working for the common goal, the ratings on *Sunset Cove* were continuing to climb. It had come out number one in the November sweeps, and advertising revenues were higher than ever.

The UBC brass was very pleased.

But it was *The Insiders* that Dru was most proud of. She had taken a dying show, one on the very verge of cancellation, and turned it around. Hard decisions had been made. Long-time cast members were released, and new younger blood had been brought in. A whole new younger, sexier story line had reinvigorated the show, and the ratings were way up. In fact, *The Insiders* was the number four daytime drama on TV now. And climbing.

And she owned forty percent of it.

She glanced over at him. "Say, what are the boys doing?"

"Making out on your balcony." He grinned. "Boys will be boys."

"Hmm. Sounds like fun to me. We should do the same." She winked.

"I'm ready if you are." He moved close to her.

"Darling, I'm *always* ready." She leaned over and they kissed. He placed a hand tenderly on her breast and squeezed softly, causing a low moan to escape Dru's throat. She felt warm all over and again thanked God for allowing her to have this wonderful man in her life.

After the tragic events of last summer, they had stayed together, and when Dru realized she was pregnant, she had allowed him the opportunity to walk away. She was going to have the baby with or without him. Who knew if she would ever have the chance again? Park hadn't needed a second thought.

She knew she was in love with him, and believed wholeheartedly that he felt the same way. He spent almost every night at her house and was excited about the baby, and they had developed an easy routine that they both loved very much. They were talking about his moving in permanently.

"Whoa, partner . . . don't get carried away on me, now," she said, twisting out of his grip. "We have guests!"

The doorbell rang again, and Dru's shoes clacked on the hall tiles as she went to answer the door. "Our last arrivals," she called out.

Clay and Travis stood there in matching red cashmere turtleneck sweaters. Clay was holding a small piece of mistletoe above their heads. She giggled and kissed them both. Travis handed her a bottle of Dom Perignon tied with a bow.

"Our contribution," Travis said, his free arm around Clay's waist.

"Perfect for after dinner!" Dru exclaimed. "Thank you."

"But none for you, Mom." Clay smiled as he patted her stomach. The baby kicked slightly at his touch.

"Oh! The baby moved again!" Dru cried out happily.

The two men quickly placed their hands on her stomach to feel the slight bounces.

"That is so cool!" Travis said.

"Yeah. Just remember that when I call you two up to baby-sit," Dru replied.

"Aww, Uncle Travis and Uncle Clay will be glad to watch the little rugrat," Clay said, leading the small group into the house. "And speaking of the little fella, Merry Christmas! From Travis and me." He pulled in a beautiful navy blue Maclaren pram. The expensive titanium-and-leather eight-wheel baby carriage had all the bells and whistles a parent could want, and Dru was touched by their generosity.

"Oh, you two! Thank you so much!" She gave each of them even bigger kisses. "Park! Come look what the boys gave us!"

Park came in, marveled properly over the pram, and hugged them both thanks.

"Wow," Travis marveled as he looked around the large living room. "I've always wanted to see inside your house. I like it. Thanks for having us up . . . finally," he joshed.

Dru blushed. "Well, it's taken a while to pull together. Thanks for turning me on to your decorator. Go ahead, explore it. Park's in the kitchen, his brother and his date are out on the patio. It's just us six for dinner. Well, six and a half." She patted her abdomen.

She left them to wander the house, and she and Park returned to the kitchen.

Clay and Travis slowly studied the casually elegant room and, seeing the two male forms on the patio, decided to go introduce themselves. Clay pulled open the door for Travis, who was occasionally stiff in his arm—a residual effect from the gunshot wound to his shoulder. They stepped outside.

"Oh, my God. It's the Olsen twins. Which one is Mary Kate, and which one is Ashley?" Kurt joked, nodding towards

Clay and Travis's matching sweaters. He moved forward to shake hands.

"Kurt! No way! You're Park's brother?" Clay asked, astonished.

"Yes. Small world, huh?" He grinned.

"Hi, I'm Travis," Travis said, including himself in the conversation.

"Hi, Travis. I'm a big fan of *Sunset Cove*. I've watched it for years. Though I do tend to lean toward *The Insiders* these days. They've got this hunky new lawyer on now."

"That a boy." Clay winked.

Clay was one of the new lead characters on *The Insiders*, playing a role that had been created especially for him by Dru. He was now Payne Blackwell, Esq. He had a two-year contract and his own parking space, just three over from Travis's.

It was then that Kurt's date revealed himself to Clay and Travis.

"Hi, boys," he said in a slightly embarrassed voice.

Clay and Travis stood in shocked silence for a beat.

Clay recovered first. "Well, Rick Yung. Hello."

They all shook hands.

"You guys all know each other from the studio, right?" Kurt asked.

"Uh, yeah."

"Yes."

"Uh-huh."

There was another moment of awkward silence. Then Travis put his arm around Clay and started to laugh. Clay soon joined in, then finally Rick.

"Okay. What's up? I feel left out," Kurt pouted.

"Oh, honey, I'll tell you all about it later," Rick replied. "Oh. Can I?" he thoughtfully asked Travis.

"Sure. I'm trying to be more open these days. Just don't air it on your newscast tomorrow night."

"I'm so lost," Kurt said as Dru came out to join them.

"Don't be. Weho's just a small town. Very small," Clay said.

"Boys, dinner's ready. Come on in."

Rick and Kurt led the way in. Travis turned to look out at the view. "Hey!" he said excitedly. "You can see my whole house from up here."

Dru looked over and nodded. She had removed the telescope from the balcony earlier that day. Just in case.

She went in, leaving Clay and Travis alone.

"We'll be right in," Clay promised.

She nodded and walked farther into the warm house, glad to be out of the cool night air.

"Trav, I'm so sorry! I had no idea he would be here." Clay hugged his lover.

"It's fine. I've seen him around the studio. We never speak, but it's not a problem."

"You sure?"

Travis smiled warmly. "Of course I'm sure. It happened a long time ago. I'm not threatened by him. I *got* the guy, didn't I?"

"You do say the sweetest things!"

"Oh? How about this: Clay, I am so in love with you, I can't imagine life without you, and I can't thank you enough for giving me the space to work through my bullshit about being gay. I know I'm not as open as you are about it, yet . . ." he said, the emotion of the moment getting to him.

"Oh, Trav," Clay murmured, pulling him close.

"No, let me finish. You have been so good to me the past few months. Helping me heal, nursing me through the recovery, finding my shrink: everything. I just wanted you to know that I really appreciate it."

"I know you do. And don't think that you don't give back, because you do. Every second of every day, you give back to me. That's all I wanted. You see, I feel like I got the guy, too."

Clay had to admit that Travis had been trying hard. While he wasn't going to be marching in any gay pride parades in the near future, that was okay, because Clay wasn't going to, either. Clay just wanted Travis at least to be comfortable enough with who he was now to let their small circle of friends know they were a couple. Dru and Park had been particularly supportive.

And now that Clay's star was on the rise, he had a sense of the pressure that Travis had felt before. The requests for interviews, the constant interruptions by the fans, and the inescapable craving for more: better parts, bigger parts, feature films.

He had tempered his feelings a bit now that he had walked a mile or two in Travis's shoes. It made Travis's strides in accepting who he was, and in allowing himself to be in a committed relationship, so much more meaningful.

Travis still had the fire for success, and now that he was completely healed after a four-month recuperation and back on *Sunset Cove,* his fame was unprecedented. Being the victim of a stalker had placed him in the pages of every tabloid and magazine for months. Barbara Walters had interviewed him, resulting in her highest-rated show ever.

Clay, Dru, Park, and Travis had all sat down and come up with the "official version" of what happened. For Travis's sake, a story was created that left out all references to his love affair with Clay.

It had been decided that Cissi had fixated on Travis. She had been in love with him and killed Jack Benz so his part would beef up more, just as she had killed Lance Jackson years before for her former love, Jack Benz. Since there was no real proof to link her to the murder of Josh Babbitt, that case was still listed as "open."

At Clay's request, his own role in the story was greatly diminished. He still suffered guilt over the death of Josh but had learned to accept the fact that there was nothing he could have done differently to prevent it.

As a result of all the media attention, Travis knew that he was on the cusp of huge things in his career. The movie offers were coming in, and he had just signed on as the costar in the the new Jennifer Lopez film to be shot in the coming spring. It seemed like all his dreams were going to come true. But strangely enough, he was oddly indifferent about it. The extreme tunnel vision he had had with regard to his career had lessened in the face of what he had been through. His love for Clay had taught him what was real and important, and he had reprioritized his life.

Clay came first now.

So, slowly Travis had withdrawn from the whole Hollywood thing, and rarely went to parties or premieres unless Clay had been invited, too. Since they both worked at the UBC studios, on adjoining stages, they saw each other throughout the day. They ate lunch together, hung out in each other's dressing rooms. All Travis really wanted to do after work was spend time with his lover and just be.

The biggest proof of his love for his handsome lover came when Travis asked Clay to move in with him. Citing the fact that Clay practically lived at his house anyway, why not make it official?

So they had.

Clay leased his condo out to Lefty Jannel and moved in with his partner. It was working out surprisingly well. They complemented each other.

Park leaned his head out onto the balcony. "Hey, guys? Dinner?" He smiled.

Startled, both men looked at him.

"Sorry. We're coming in," Clay said hurriedly.

Park walked out to join them, his hands behind his back. "Well, before you do, I have something I want to give you." He stared at Travis.

"What?"

He brought his arms to his front, and there in his hands were two videocassettes.

"What's that?" Clay asked.

Suddenly, Travis stiffened. He knew.

"One is the tape that Jack had of you, Travis. It was locked away in his safe deposit box. I 'accidentally' packed up a few official things from the Jack Benz case when I resigned from the department. I snagged it. I wanted to wait a while for things to settle down before returning it."

Travis, embarrassed, turned his head away and looked down at his house.

"I didn't watch it, though. Just enough to see what it was. Just so you know," Park said gently.

Travis nodded in gratitude.

"What's the other tape?" Clay said after a beat.

"It's the tape of Travis's interrogation. I pulled it the night I interviewed you, Trav. I'm glad I did. It'll never be leaked or seen on *Entertainment Tonight* now." He paused. "I just wanted to give them to you. Do with them what you will." He held them out. Travis straightened his back and took the tapes gratefully.

"Thank you, Park. I'll never forget that you did this," he said, appreciation flooding his voice.

"It's the least I could do, considering my stepfather caused all this to happen."

Travis stood there staring at the tape that had caused him so much pain and anguish. He looked at Clay, who squeezed his arm in support. Then Travis grinned.

"Anyone got a match?"

Park pulled out a classic silver Zippo lighter and handed it to him. Travis walked over to the Weber barbecue grill, lifted the cover, and dropped the tapes on the grate.

"Hey, Park, is this legal? Is this still evidence? Can he do this without getting into trouble later? You're the big-shot lawyer now. Tell me," Clay quizzed.

"Sure. It's his property, to do with whatever he wants. I say torch 'em," Park replied.

After Park resigned from the force, he decided to put his law degree to work. He opened up a small firm specializing in pro bono appeal defenses for people who he felt had gotten a raw deal during their original trials. He was extremely choosy about what cases he took, and he only took those where he truly felt an injustice had been committed. Because of Dru and his new career, he had never been happier in his life.

Clay and Park watched silently as Travis flicked open the lighter and, in seconds, had set the two tapes on fire. The plastic cases and vinyl videotape sizzled and sputtered in the blue-orange flames. The hot, liquified plastic dripped through the grill grate and splattered into the basin.

"I'll buy Dru a new grill," Travis explained, a huge smile of relief on his face.

Park winked at him. "I'm heading in. Let's eat!"

"We'll be right in," Travis said as Park walked back into the house. He turned to Clay.

"Well, I was gonna wait until we got home tonight, but it seems like the right time now." He dug into his front pants pocket and brought out two men's platinum Tiffany wedding bands. "I need to know that you and I are connected all the time. I want to live with you forever, Clay. Go bald together. Get fat. Have our balls drop to the floor with old age. I want us to have a shared life. Will you do me the honor of wearing this?" He held up one of the bands.

Unable to speak, Clay simply nodded as his man slipped the simple silver band on his ring finger. Travis then slid the matching one on his own hand.

"There. Connected at the hip," he joked.

"Not yet. That'll happen after dinner. When we get home." Clay took his partner's beautiful face into his hands and pressed his lips to his.

The deal was sealed with a kiss, you might say.